MIRACLE CREEK

ANGIE KIM

MIRACLE
CREEK

SARAH CRICHTON BOOKS
Farrar, Straus and Giroux
New York

Sarah Crichton Books
Farrar, Straus and Giroux
175 Varick Street, New York 10014

ISBN 9780374156022

Designed by Richard Oriolo

For Jim, always

and

For Um-ma and Ap-bah,
for all your sacrifice and love

MIRACLE CREEK

hyperbaric oxygenation: the administration of oxygen at greater than normal atmospheric pressure. The procedure is performed in specially designed chambers that permit the delivery of 100% oxygen at atmospheric pressure that is three times normal . . . Factors limiting the usefulness of hyperbaric oxygenation include the hazards of fire and explosive decompression . . . Also called *hyperbaric oxygen therapy.*
—*Mosby's Medical Dictionary,* 9th edition (2013)

THE INCIDENT

Miracle Creek, Virginia
Tuesday, August 26, 2008

Y HUSBAND ASKED ME TO LIE. Not a big lie. He probably didn't even consider it a lie, and neither did I, at first. It was such a small thing, what he wanted. The police had just released the protesters, and while he stepped out to make sure they weren't coming back, I was to sit in his chair. Cover for him, the way coworkers do as a matter of course, the way we ourselves used to at the grocery store, while I ate or he smoked. But as I took his seat, I bumped against the desk, and the certificate above it went slightly crooked as if to remind me that this wasn't a regular business, that there was a reason he'd never left me in charge before.

Pak reached over me to straighten the frame, his eyes on the English lettering: *Pak Yoo, Miracle Submarine LLC, Certified Hyperbaric Technician*. He said—eyes still on the certificate, as if talking to *it*, not to me—

"Everything's done. The patients are sealed in, the oxygen's on. You just have to sit here." He looked at me. "That's it."

I looked over the controls, the unfamiliar knobs and switches for the chamber we'd painted baby blue and placed in this barn just last month. "What if the patients buzz me?" I said. "I'll say you'll be right back, but—"

"No, they can't know I'm gone. If anyone asks, I'm here. I've been here the whole time."

"But if something goes wrong and—"

"What could go wrong?" Pak said, his voice forceful like a command. "I'll be right back, and they won't buzz you. Nothing will happen." He walked away, as if that was the end of the matter. But at the doorway, he looked back at me. "Nothing will happen," he said again, softer. It sounded like a plea.

As soon as the barn door banged shut, I wanted to scream that he was crazy to expect nothing to go wrong on this day, of all days, when so much had gone wrong—the protesters, their sabotage plan, the resulting power outage, the police. Did he think so much had already happened that nothing more could? But life doesn't work like that. Tragedies don't inoculate you against further tragedies, and misfortune doesn't get sprinkled out in fair proportions; bad things get hurled at you in clumps and batches, unmanageable and messy. How could he not know that, after everything we'd been through?

From 8:02 to 8:14 p.m., I sat and said nothing, did nothing, like he asked. Sweat dampened my face, and I thought about the six patients sealed inside without air-conditioning (the generator operated the pressurization, oxygen, and intercom systems only) and thanked God for the portable DVD player to keep the kids calm. I reminded myself to trust my husband, and I waited, checking the clock, the door, then the clock again, praying for him to return (he *had* to!) before *Barney* ended and the patients buzzed for another DVD. Just as the show's closing song started, my phone rang. Pak.

"They're here," he whispered. "I need to stand watch, make sure they don't try anything again. You need to turn off the oxygen when the session ends. You see the knob?"

"Yes, but—"

"Turn it counterclockwise, all the way, tight. Set your alarm so you won't forget. 8:20 by the big clock." He hung up.

I touched the knob marked OXYGEN, a discolored brass the color of the squeaky faucet in our old apartment in Seoul. It surprised me how cool it felt. I synchronized my watch to the clock, set my alarm to 8:20, and found the ALARM ON button. Right then, just as I started pressing the tiny nub—that's when the DVD battery died and I dropped my hands, startled.

I think about that moment a lot. The deaths, the paralysis, the trial—might all that have been averted if I'd pressed the button? It's strange, I know, that my mind keeps returning to this particular lapse, given my bigger, more blameworthy mistakes of that night. Perhaps it's precisely its smallness, its seeming insignificance, that gives it power and fuels the what-ifs. What if I hadn't let the DVD distract me? What if I'd moved my finger a microsecond more quickly, managed to turn on the alarm *before* the DVD died, mid-song? *I love you, you love me, we're a hap-py fam-i—*

The blankness of that moment, the categorical absence of sound, dense and oppressive—it pressed in, squeezed me from all sides. When noise finally came—a rap-rap-rap of knuckles against the porthole from inside the chamber—I was almost relieved. But the knocking intensified into fists banging in threes as if chanting *Let me out!* in code, then into full-on pounding, and I realized: it had to be TJ's head banging. TJ, the autistic boy who adores Barney the purple dinosaur, who ran to me the first time we met and hugged me tight. His mother had been amazed, said he never hugs anyone (he hates touching people), and maybe it's my shirt, the exact shade of purple as Barney. I've worn the shirt every day since; I hand-wash it every night and put it on for his sessions, and every day, he hugs me. Everyone thinks I'm being kind, but I'm really doing it for *me*, because I crave the way his arms wrap around and squeeze me—the way my daughter's used to, before she started leaning away from my hugs, her arms limp. I love kissing his head, the fuzz of his red hair tickling my lips. And now, that boy whose hugs I savor was beating his head on a steel wall.

He wasn't crazy. His mother had explained that TJ has chronic pain from intestinal inflammation, but he can't talk, and when it gets too much, he does the only thing he can for relief: he bangs his head, using the new, acute pain to drive out the old one. It's like having an itch you can't stand and scratching so hard it bleeds, how good that pain feels, except multiplied by a hundred. Once, she told me, TJ put his face through a window. It tormented me, the thought of this eight-year-old boy in so much pain that he needed to bash his head against steel.

And the sound of that pain—the pounding, again and again. The persistence, the increasing insistence. Each thud set off vibrations that reverberated and built into something corporeal, with form and mass. It traveled through me. I felt it rumble against my skin, jolting my insides and demanding my heart to match its rhythm, to beat faster, harder.

I had to make it stop. That's my excuse. For running out of the barn and leaving six people trapped in a sealed chamber. I wanted to depressurize and open it, get TJ out of there, but I didn't know how. Besides, when the intercom buzzed, TJ's mother begged me (or, rather, Pak) not to stop the dive, she'd calm him down, but please, for the love of God, put in new batteries and restart the *Barney* DVD *now*! There were batteries somewhere in our house next door, only a twenty-second run away, and I had five minutes to turn off the oxygen. So I left. I covered my mouth to muffle my voice and said in a low, heavily accented voice like Pak's, "We will replace batteries. Wait few minutes," then I ran out.

The door to our house was ajar, and I felt a flash of wild hope that Mary was home, cleaning up like I'd told her to, and finally, something would go right today. But I stepped in, and she wasn't there. I was alone, with no idea where the batteries were and no one to help. It was what I'd expected all along, yet that second of hope had been enough to shoot my expectations high into the sky and send them crashing down. Keep calm, I told myself, and started my search in the gray steel wardrobe we used for storage. Coats. Manuals. Cords. No batteries. When I slammed the door, the wardrobe wobbled, its flimsy metal warbling and booming like an echo of TJ's pounding. I pictured his head hammering steel, cracking open like a ripe watermelon.

I shook my head to expel the thought. "Meh-hee-yah." I yelled out Mary's Korean name, which she hates. No answer. I knew there wouldn't be, but it infuriated me just the same. I yelled "Meh-hee-yah" again, louder, elongating the syllables to let them grate my throat, needing it to hurt and drive out the phantom echoes of TJ's pounding ringing in my ears.

I searched the rest of the house, box by box. With each passing second of not finding the batteries, my frustration grew, and I thought about our fight this morning, my telling her she should do more to help—she was seventeen!—and her walking out without a word. I thought about Pak siding with her, as always. ("We didn't give up everything and come to America so she could cook and clean," he always says. "No, that's my job," I want to say. But I never do.) I thought of Mary's eye-rolls, her headphones on her ears, pretending not to hear me. Anything to keep my anger activated, to occupy my mind and keep out the pounding. My ire at my daughter was familiar and comfortable, like an old blanket. It soothed my panic into a dull anxiety.

When I got to the box in Mary's sleeping corner, I forced the criss-crossed top flaps open and dumped everything out. Teenage junk: torn tickets to movies I'd never seen, pictures of friends I'd never met, a stack of notes, the top one in a hurried scrawl—*I waited for you. Maybe tomorrow?*

I wanted to scream. Where were the batteries? (And in the back of my mind: Who'd written the note? A boy? Waited to do what?) Just then, my phone rang—Pak again—and I saw 8:22 on the screen and remembered. The alarm. The oxygen.

When I answered, I meant to explain how I hadn't turned off the oxygen but would soon, and that was no big deal, he sometimes ran the oxygen over an hour, right? But my words came out differently. Like vomit—outpouring in one stream, uncontrollable. "Mary is nowhere," I said. "We're doing all this for her, and she's never here, and I need her, I need her help to find new DVD batteries before TJ busts his head open."

"You always think the worst of her, but she's here, helping me," he said. "And the batteries are under the house kitchen sink, but don't leave the patients. I'll send Mary to grab them. Mary, go, right now. Take four D batteries to the barn. I'll come in one min—"

I hung up. Sometimes it's better to say nothing.

I ran to the kitchen sink. The batteries were there like he said, in a bag I'd assumed was trash, under work gloves covered in dirt and soot. They were clean just yesterday. What had Pak been doing?

I shook my head. The batteries. I had to hurry back to TJ.

When I ran outside, an unfamiliar scent—like charred wet wood—permeated the air and stung my nose. It was getting dark, harder to see, but I saw Pak in the distance, running toward the barn.

Mary was ahead of him, sprinting. I called out, "Mary, slow down. I found the batteries," but she kept running, not toward the house, but to the barn. "Mary, stop," I said, but she didn't. She ran past the barn door, to the back side. I didn't know why, but it scared me, her being there, and I called again, her Korean name this time, softer. "Meh-hee-yah," I said, and ran to her. She turned. Something about her face stopped me. It seemed to glow somehow. An orange light coated her skin and shimmered as if she were standing directly in front of the setting sun. I wanted to touch her face and tell her, "You are beautiful."

From her direction, I heard a noise. It sounded like crackling, but softer and muffled, the way a flock of geese might sound taking off for flight, hundreds of wings flapping at once to scamper skyward. I thought I saw them, a curtain of gray rippling in the wind and rising higher and higher in the dusky violet sky, but I blinked, and the sky was empty. I ran toward the sound, and I saw it then, what she'd seen but I hadn't, what she'd run toward.

Flames.

Smoke.

The back wall of the barn—on fire.

I don't know why I didn't run or scream, why Mary didn't, either. I wanted to. But I could only walk slowly, carefully, one step at a time, getting closer, my eyes transfixed by the flames in orange and red—fluttering, leaping, and switching places like partners in a step dance.

When the boom sounded, my knees buckled and I fell. But I never took my eyes off my daughter. Every night, when I turn off the light and close my eyes for sleep, I see her, my Meh-hee, in that moment. Her body flings up like a rag doll and arcs through the air. Gracefully. Delicately. Just before she lands on the ground with a soft thud, I see her ponytail, bouncing high. The way it used to when she was a little girl, jumping rope.

A YEAR LATER

THE TRIAL: DAY ONE

Monday, August 17, 2009

YOUNG YOO

SHE FELT LIKE A BRIDE walking into the courtroom. Certainly, her wedding was the last time—the only time—that a roomful of people had fallen silent and turned to stare as she entered. If it weren't for the variety in hair color and the snippets of whispers in English as she walked down the aisle—"Look, the owners," "The daughter was in a coma for months, poor thing," "He's paralyzed, so awful"—she might have thought she was still in Korea.

The small courtroom even looked like an old church, with creaky wooden pews on both sides of the aisle. She kept her head down, just as she had at her wedding twenty years ago; she wasn't usually the focus of attention, and it felt wrong. Modesty, blending in, invisibility: those were the virtues of wives, not notoriety and gaudiness. Wasn't that why brides wore veils—to protect them from stares, to mute the redness of their cheeks? She glanced to the sides. On the right, behind the prosecution, she glimpsed familiar faces, those of their patients' families.

The patients had all gathered together only once: last July, at the orientation outside the barn. Her husband had opened the doors to show the freshly painted blue chamber. "This," Pak said, looking proud, "is Miracle Submarine. Pure oxygen. Deep pressure. Healing. Together." Everyone clapped. Mothers cried. And now, here were the same people, somber, the hope of miracle gone from their faces, replaced by the curiosity of people reaching for tabloids in supermarket lines. That and pity—for her or themselves, she didn't know. She'd expected anger, but they smiled as she walked by, and she had to remind herself that she was a victim here. She was not the defendant, not the one they blamed for the explosion that killed two patients. She told herself what Pak told her every day—their absence from the barn that night didn't cause the fire, and he couldn't have prevented the explosion even if he'd stayed with the patients—and tried to smile back. Their support was a good thing. She knew that. But it felt undeserved, wrong, like a prize won by cheating, and instead of buoying her, it weighed her down with worry that God would see and correct the injustice, make her pay for her lies some other way.

When Young reached the wooden railing, she fought her impulse to hop across and sit at the defense table. She sat with her family behind the prosecutor, next to Matt and Teresa, two of the people trapped in Miracle Submarine that night. She hadn't seen them in a long time, not since the hospital. But no one said hi. They all looked down. They were the victims.

◯

THE COURTHOUSE WAS in Pineburg, the town next to Miracle Creek. It was strange, the names—the opposite of what you'd expect. Miracle Creek didn't look like a place where miracles took place, unless you counted the miracle of people living there for years without going insane from boredom. The "Miracle" name and its marketing possibilities (plus cheap land) had drawn them there despite there being no other Asians—no immigrants at all, probably. It was only an hour from Washington, D.C., an easy drive from dense concentrations of modernity such as Dulles Airport, but it had the isolated feel of a village hours from civilization, an entirely different world. Dirt trails instead of concrete sidewalks. Cows rather than cars. Decrepit wooden barns, not steel-and-glass high-rises. Like stepping into a grainy black-and-white film. It had that feel of being used and discarded; the first time Young saw it, she had an impulse to find every bit of trash in her pockets and throw it as far as she could.

Pineburg, despite its plain name and proximity to Miracle Creek, was charming, its narrow cobblestone streets lined with chalet-style shops, each painted a different bright color. Looking at Main Street's row of shops reminded Young of her favorite market in Seoul, its legendary produce row—spinach green, pepper red, beet purple, persimmon orange. From its description, she would've thought it garish, but it was the opposite—as if putting the brash colors together subdued each one, so the overall feel was elegant and lovely.

The courthouse was at the base of a knoll, flanked by grapevines planted in straight lines up the hill. The geometric precision provided a measured calm, and it seemed fitting that a building of justice would stand amid the ordered rows of vines.

That morning, gazing at the courthouse, its tall white columns, Young had thought how this was the closest she'd been to the America she'd expected. In Korea, after Pak decided she should move to Baltimore with Mary, she'd gone to bookstores and looked through pictures of America— the Capitol, Manhattan skyscrapers, Inner Harbor. In her five years in America, she hadn't seen any of those sights. For the first four years, she'd worked in a grocery store two miles from Inner Harbor, but in a neighborhood people called the "ghetto," houses boarded up and broken bottles everywhere. A tiny vault of bulletproof glass: that had been America for her.

It was funny how desperate she'd been to escape that gritty world, and yet she missed it now. Miracle Creek was insular, with longtime residents (going back generations, they said). She thought they might be slow to warm, so she focused on befriending one family nearby who'd seemed especially nice. But over time, she realized: they weren't nice; they were politely unfriendly. Young knew the type. Her own mother had belonged to this breed of people who used manners to cover up unfriendliness the way people used perfume to cover up body odor—the worse it was, the more they used. Their stiff hyperpoliteness—the wife's perpetual closed-lip smile, the husband's *ma'am* at the beginning or end of *every* sentence—kept Young at a distance and reinforced her status as a stranger. Although her most frequent customers in Baltimore had been cantankerous, cursing and complaining about everything from the prices being too high to the sodas too warm and deli meats too thin, there was an honesty to their rudeness, a comfortable intimacy to their yelling. Like bickering siblings. Nothing to cover up.

After Pak joined them in America last year, they'd looked for housing in Annandale, the D.C. area's Koreatown—a manageable drive from Miracle Creek. The fire had stopped all that, and they were still in their "temporary" housing. A crumbling shack in a crumbling town far from anything pictured in the books. To this day, the fanciest place Young had been in America was the hospital where Pak and Mary had lain for months after the explosion.

THE COURTROOM WAS LOUD. Not the people—the victims, lawyers, journalists, and who knew who else—but the two old-fashioned window-unit air conditioners on opposite sides behind the judge. They sputtered like lawn mowers when they switched on and off, which, because they weren't synchronized, happened at different times—one, then the other, then back again, like some strange mechanical beasts' mating calls. When the units ran, they rattled and hummed, each at a slightly different pitch, making Young's eardrums itch. She wanted to stick her pinkie deep inside her ear into her brain and scratch.

The lobby plaque said the courthouse was a 250-year-old historical landmark and asked for donations to the Pineburg Courthouse Preservation Society. Young had shaken her head at the thought of this society, an entire group whose sole purpose was to prevent this building from becoming modern. Americans were so proud of things being a few hundred years old, as if things being old were a value in and of itself. (Of course, this philosophy did not extend to people.) They didn't seem to realize that the world valued America precisely because it was not old, but modern and new. Koreans were the opposite. In Seoul, there would be a Modernization Society dedicated to replacing this courthouse's "antique" hardwood floors and pine tables with marble and sleek steel.

"All rise. Skyline County Criminal Court now in session, the Honorable Frederick Carleton III presiding," the bailiff said, and everyone stood. Except Pak. His hands clenched his wheelchair's armrests, the green veins on his hands and wrists popping up as if willing his arms to support his body's weight. Young started to help, but she stopped herself, knowing that needing help for something basic like standing would be worse for him than not standing at all. Pak cared so much about appearances, conforming to rules and expectations—the quintessentially Korean things she'd strangely never cared about (because her family's wealth afforded her the luxury of being immune to them, Pak would say). Still, she understood his frustration, being the lone sitting figure in this towering crowd. It made him vulnerable, like a child, and she had to fight the urge to cloak his body with her arms and hide his shame.

"The court will now come to order. Docket number 49621, Commonwealth of Virginia versus Elizabeth Ward," the judge said, and banged the gavel. As if by plan, both air conditioners were off, and the sound of wood striking wood reverberated off the slanted ceilings and lingered in the silence.

It was official: Elizabeth was the defendant. Young felt a tingle inside her chest, like some dormant cell of relief and hope had burst and was spreading sparks of electricity throughout her body, zapping away the fear that had hijacked her life. Even though almost a year had passed since Pak was cleared and Elizabeth arrested, Young hadn't quite believed it, had wondered if this was a trick, and if today, as the trial started, they'd announce her and Pak as the real targets. But now the waiting was over, and after several days of evidence—"overwhelming evidence," the prosecutor said—Elizabeth would be found guilty, and they'd get their insurance money and rebuild their lives. No more living in stasis.

The jurors filed in. Young gazed at them, these people—all twelve, seven men and five women—who believed in capital punishment and swore they were willing to vote for death by lethal injection. Young had learned this last week. The prosecutor had been in a particularly good mood, and when she asked why, he'd explained that the potential jurors most likely to be sympathetic to Elizabeth had been dismissed because they were anti-death-penalty.

"Death penalty? Like hanging?" she'd said.

Her alarm and revulsion must have shown, because Abe stopped smiling. "No, by injection, drugs in an IV. It's painless."

He'd explained that Elizabeth wouldn't necessarily get death, it was just a possibility, but still, she'd dreaded seeing Elizabeth here, the terror that would surely be on her face, confronting the people with the power to end her life.

Now, Young forced herself to look at Elizabeth, at the defense table. She looked like a lawyer herself, her blond hair twisted into a bun, dark green suit, pearls, pumps. Young had almost looked past her, she looked so different from before—messy ponytail, wrinkled sweats, unmatched socks.

It was ironic—of all the parents of their patients, Elizabeth had been the most disheveled, and yet she'd had by far the most manageable child. Henry, her only child, had been a well-mannered boy who, unlike many other patients, could walk, talk, was toilet-trained, and didn't have tantrums. During orientation, when the mother of twins with autism and epilepsy asked Elizabeth, "Sorry, but what's Henry here for? He seems so normal," she'd frowned as if offended. She recited a list—OCD, ADHD, sensory and autism spectrum disorders, anxiety—then said how hard it was, spending all her days researching experimental treatments. She seemed to have no clue how she sounded complaining while surrounded by kids with wheelchairs and feeding tubes.

Judge Carleton asked Elizabeth to stand. She expected Elizabeth to cry as he read the charges, or at least blush, her eyes down. But Elizabeth looked straight at the jury, her cheeks unflushed, eyes unblinking. She studied Elizabeth's face, so empty of expression, wondering if she was numb, in shock. But instead of looking vacant, Elizabeth looked serene.

Almost happy. Perhaps it was because she was so used to Elizabeth's worried frowns that their absence made Elizabeth look contented.

Or perhaps the newspapers were right. Perhaps Elizabeth had been desperate to get rid of her son, and now that he was dead, she finally had a measure of peace. Perhaps she had been a monster all along.

MATT THOMPSON

H E WOULD'VE GIVEN ANYTHING not to be here today. Maybe not his entire right arm, but certainly one of its three remaining fingers. He was already a freak with missing fingers—what was one more? He did not want to see reporters, cameras flashing when he made the mistake of covering his face with his hands—he cringed, picturing how the flash would reflect off the glossy scar tissue covering the doughy clump that remained of his right hand. He did not want to hear whispers of "Look, the infertile doctor," or face Abe, the prosecutor, who'd once looked at him, head tilted as if studying a puzzle, and asked, "Have you and Janine considered adoption? I hear Korea has lots of half-white babies." He did not want to chat with his in-laws, the Chos, who tsked and lowered their eyes in unison at the sight of his injuries, or hear Janine rail at them for their shame over any perceived defect, which she'd diagnose as yet another of their "typically Korean" prejudices and intolerances. Most of all, he did not want to see anyone from Miracle Submarine, not the other patients, not Elizabeth, and definitely, most certainly, not Mary Yoo.

Abe stood and, walking by, put his hand on Young's, draped across the railing. He patted gently, and she smiled. Pak clenched his teeth, and when Abe smiled at him, Pak stretched his lips as if trying to smile but not quite managing it. Matt guessed that Pak, like his own Korean father-in-law, did not approve of African-Americans and thought it one of America's great flaws that it had an African-American president.

He'd been surprised when he met Abe. Miracle Creek and Pineburg seemed so provincial and white. The jury was all white. The judge was white. Police, firemen—white. This wasn't the kind of place he'd expect to have a black prosecutor. Then again, it wasn't the kind of place anyone would expect to have a Korean immigrant running a mini-submarine as a so-called medical device, but there it was.

"Ladies and gentlemen of the jury, my name is Abraham Patterley. I am the prosecutor. I represent the Commonwealth of Virginia against the defendant, Elizabeth Ward." Abe pointed his right index finger at Elizabeth, and she startled, as if she hadn't known that she was the accused. Matt stared at Abe's index finger, wondered what Abe would do if he, like Matt, lost it. Right before the amputation, the surgeon had said, "Thank God your career's not too affected by it. Imagine being a pianist or surgeon." Matt had thought about that a lot. What job could one have and not be too affected by amputation of the right index and middle fingers? He would've put lawyers in the category of "not too affected," but now, looking at Elizabeth withering under Abe's simple gesture of pointing at her, the power that finger gave Abe, he wasn't sure.

"Why is Elizabeth Ward here today? You've already heard the charges. Arson, battery, attempted murder." Abe stared at Elizabeth before turning his body square to the jury box. "Murder."

"The victims sit here, ready and eager to tell you what happened to them"—Abe motioned to the front row—"and to the defendant's two ultimate victims: Kitt Kozlowski, the defendant's longtime friend, and Henry

Ward, the defendant's own eight-year-old son, who can't tell you themselves, because they are dead.

"Miracle Submarine's oxygen tank exploded at about 8:25 p.m. on August 26, 2008, starting an uncontrollable fire. Six people were inside, three in the immediate area. Two died. Four, severely injured—hospitalized for months, paralyzed, limbs amputated.

"The defendant was supposed to be inside with her son. But she wasn't. She told everyone she was sick. Headache, congestion, the works. She asked Kitt, the mother of another patient, to watch Henry while she rested. She took wine she'd packed to the creek nearby. She smoked a cigarette of the same type and brand that started the fire, using the same type and brand of matches that started the fire."

Abe looked at the jurors. "All of what I just told you is undisputed."

Abe closed his mouth and paused for emphasis. "Un-dis-pu-ted," he said, enunciating it like four separate words. "The defendant here"—he pointed that index finger again at her—"*admits* all this, that she intentionally stayed outside, faking an illness, and when her son and friend were being incinerated inside, she was sipping wine, smoking using the same match and cigarette used to set the blast, and listening to Beyoncé on her iPod."

○

MATT KNEW WHY he was the first witness. Abe had explained the need for an overview. "Hyperbarics, oxygen this and that, it's complicated. You're a doctor, you can help everyone understand. Plus, you were there. You're perfect." Perfect or not, Matt resented the hell out of having to speak first, to set the scene. He knew what Abe thought, that this submarine healing business was kooky and he wanted to say, Look, here's a normal American, a real M.D. from a real medical school, and he did this, so it can't be that crazy.

"Place your left hand on the Bible and raise your right hand," the bailiff said. Matt placed his right hand on the Bible, raised his left hand, and looked square into the bailiff's eyes. Let him think he was a dumbfuck who didn't know right from left. Better that than showcasing his freaky hand, see everyone flinch and flit their eyes around like birds above a dump site, unsure where to land.

Abe started easy. Where Matt was from (Bethesda, Maryland), college (Tufts), medical school (Georgetown), residency (same), fellowships (same), board certification (radiology), hospital credentials (Fairfax). "Now, I have to ask the first question I had when I heard about the explosion. What is Miracle Submarine, and why do you need a submarine in the middle of Virginia, nowhere near the ocean?" Several jurors smiled, as if in relief that others also wondered this.

Matt stretched his lips into a smile. "It's not a real submarine. Just designed like one, with portholes and a sealed hatch and steel walls. It's actually a medical device, a chamber for hyperbaric oxygen therapy. H-B-O-T, pronounced 'aitch-bot' for short."

"Tell us how it works, Dr. Thompson."

"You're sealed in, the air pressurizes 1.5 to 3 times normal atmospheric pressure, and you breathe in one hundred percent oxygen. The high pressure causes the oxygen to be dissolved at greater levels in your blood, fluids, and tissue. Damaged cells need oxygen to heal, so this deep penetration of extra oxygen can result in faster healing and regrowth. Many hospitals offer HBOT."

"Miracle Submarine isn't a hospital chamber. Is that different?"

Matt thought of sterile hospital chambers attended by technicians in scrubs, then the Yoos' rusted chamber lying crooked in an old barn. "Not really. Hospitals usually use clear tubes for one person to lie in. Miracle Submarine is bigger, so four patients plus their caregivers can go in together, making it much less expensive. Also, private centers are open to treating off-label conditions that hospitals wouldn't."

"What kind of conditions?"

"A big variety. Autism, cerebral palsy, infertility, Crohn's, neuropathies." Matt thought he heard tittering from the back at the condition he'd tried to hide in the middle of the list—infertility. Or perhaps it was the memory of his own laughter the first time Janine suggested HBOT after the sperm analysis.

"Thank you, Dr. Thompson. Now, you became Miracle Submarine's first patient. Can you tell us about that?"

Boy, could he. He could go on at length about it, how Janine staged it perfectly, inviting him to dinner at her parents' house without one word about the Yoos or HBOT or, worst of all, Matt's expected "contribution." A fucking ambush.

"I met Pak at my in-laws' house last year," Matt said to Abe. "They're family friends; my father-in-law and Pak's father are from the same Korean village. Anyway, I learned that Pak was starting an HBOT business, and my father-in-law was investing in that." They'd all been sitting around the dinner table, and the Yoos had hurried to stand when Matt walked in, as if he were royalty. Pak looked nervous, the sharp angles of his face accentuated by his tight smile, and when he gripped Matt's hand for a handshake, his knuckles bulged into jagged peaks. Young, his wife, had bowed slightly, eyes downcast. Mary, their sixteen-year-old, was a copy of her mother, with eyes that looked too big for her delicate face, but she'd smiled easily, mischievously, as if she knew a secret and couldn't wait to see his reaction when he found out, which, of course, was exactly what was about to happen.

As soon as Matt sat down, Pak said, "Do you know HBOT?" Those words were like the cue for a well-rehearsed performance. Everyone converged around Matt, leaning in conspiratorially, and spoke in turns without pause. Matt's father-in-law said how popular this was with his Asian acupuncture clients; Japan and Korea had wellness centers with infrared saunas and HBOT. Matt's mother-in-law said Pak had years of HBOT experience in Seoul. Janine said recent research showed HBOT to be a promising treatment for numerous chronic diseases, did he know?

"What was your reaction to this business?" Abe asked.

Matt saw Janine put her thumb in her mouth and gnash at the flesh around her nails. Something she did when she was nervous, the same thing she did at that dinner, no doubt because she knew exactly what he'd think. What all their hospital friends would think. Total crap. Another of her father's alternative, holistic therapies that desperate, stupid, and crazy patients got duped into. Matt never said this, of course. Mr. Cho had disapproved of Matt enough, merely for not being Korean. If he found out that Matt regarded his whole profession—all of Eastern "medicine," really—as bullshit? No. That would not be good. Which was why

Janine had been brilliant to announce the whole thing in front of her parents and their friends.

"Everyone was excited," Matt said to Abe. "My father-in-law, an acupuncturist for thirty years, was standing behind this, and my wife, who's an internist, verified its potential. That was all I needed to know." Janine stopped biting her cuticle. "You have to realize," Matt added, "she got much better grades in med school than me." Janine laughed along with the jurors.

"And you signed up for treatment. Tell us about that."

Matt bit his lip and looked away. He'd known to expect the question, had practiced how he'd answer: matter-of-factly. The same way Pak had said that night that Matt's father-in-law was investing, that Janine had been "appointed"—as if it were a presidential commission or something—a medical advisor, and they all agreed: "You, Dr. Thompson, must become our first patient." Matt thought he'd misheard. Pak spoke English well, but he had an accent and syntax errors. Perhaps he'd mistranslated "director" or "chairman." But then Pak added, "Most patients will be children, but it is good to have one adult patient."

Matt sipped wine, not saying anything, wondering what in God's name could've made Pak think that a healthy man like Matt might need HBOT, when a possibility occurred to him. Could Janine have said something about their—*his*—"issue"? He tried to ignore the thought, focus on dinner, but his hands shook, and he couldn't pick up the galbi, the slippery morsels of marinated rib meat sliding through the thin silver chopsticks. Mary noticed and came to his rescue. "I can't use steel chopsticks, either," she said, and offered him wooden ones, the kind from Chinese takeouts. "This is easier. Try it. My mom says that's why we had to leave Korea. No one will marry a girl who can't use chopsticks. Right, Mom?" Everyone else seemed annoyed and remained silent, but Matt laughed. She joined him, the two of them laughing amid frowning faces like kids misbehaving in a room full of adults.

It had been at this moment, as Matt and Mary were laughing, that Pak said, "HBOT has high rate of curing infertility, especially for people like you—low sperm motility." Right then, at this confirmation that his wife had shared details—medical details, personal details—not only with her parents but also with these people he'd never met before, Matt felt something hot in his chest, as if a balloon filled with lava had stretched and burst in his lungs, displacing the oxygen. Matt stared into Pak's eyes and tried to breathe normally. Strangely, it wasn't Janine's gaze he needed to avoid, but Mary's. He hadn't wanted to know how those words—*infertility*, *low sperm motility*—would change the way she looked at him. If her previously curious (possibly interested?) look would now be tinged with disgust or, worse, pity.

Matt said to Abe, "My wife and I had problems conceiving, and HBOT was an experimental treatment for men involved in these situations, so it made sense to take advantage of this new business." He left out that he hadn't agreed at first, had refused to even address it for the rest of dinner. Janine said what she'd clearly practiced, how Matt's volunteering as a patient would help launch the business, how the presence of a "regular doctor" (Janine's words) would reassure potential clients of HBOT's safety and effectiveness. She didn't seem to notice that he wasn't answering, that he was keeping his eyes focused strictly on his plate. But Mary did. She noticed and came to his rescue again and again, laughing at his chopsticks technique and interjecting jokes about kimchi-garlic flavors mixing with wine.

For days afterward, Janine had been a pain in the ass, going on about HBOT's safety, its many uses, blah blah. When he didn't budge, she tried to guilt him, said his refusal would cement her father's suspicion that Matt didn't believe in his business. "I *don't* believe in it. I don't think what he does is medicine, and you've known that from day one," he'd said, which led to her most hurtful comment. "The fact is, you're against anything Asian. You dismiss it."

Before he could rail against her for accusing him of racism, point out that he'd married *her*, for Christ's sake (and besides, wasn't she always going on about how racist old-time Koreans like her parents were?), Janine sighed and said in a pleading voice, "One month. If it works, no IVF. No jerking off into a cup. Isn't that worth a try?"

He never said yes. She just pretended his silence was acquiescence, and he let her. What she said was right, or at least not wrong. Plus, maybe it would get his father-in-law to start forgiving him for not being Korean.

"When did you start HBOT?" Abe asked.

"The first day it opened, August fourth. I wanted to get the forty sessions done in August—better traffic—so I signed up for two dives each day, the first at 9:00 a.m. and the last at 6:45 p.m. There were six sessions each day, and those times were reserved for us 'double-dive' patients."

"Who else was in the double-dive group?" Abe asked.

"Three other patients: Henry, TJ, and Rosa. Plus their mothers. Aside from a few times when someone was sick or stuck in traffic or whatnot, we were all there, every day, twice a day."

"Tell us about them."

"Sure. Rosa is the oldest. Sixteen, I believe. She has cerebral palsy. She has a wheelchair and feeding tube. Her mother is Teresa Santiago." He pointed to her. "We call her Mother Teresa because she's extremely kind and patient." Teresa blushed, as always when called that.

"There's TJ, who's eight. He has autism. Nonverbal. And his mother, Kitt—"

"That's Kitt Kozlowski, who was killed last summer?"

"Yes."

"Do you recognize this picture?" Abe placed a portrait on an easel. A posed shot with Kitt's face in the center, like one of those Geddes baby flowers, except framed by her family's faces instead of petals. Kitt's husband above (standing behind her), TJ below (on her lap), two girls on the right, two on the left, all five kids with the same frizzy red curls as hers. A tableau of happiness. And now the mom was gone, leaving a sunflower with no center disk to hold up the petals.

Matt swallowed and cleared his throat. "That's Kitt, with her family, with TJ."

Abe placed another picture next to Kitt's. Henry. Not one of those fake studio shots, but a slightly blurred picture of him laughing on a sunny day, blue sky and green leaves behind him. His blond hair mussed up a little, his head back and his blue eyes almost slits from laughing so hard. A missing tooth smack in the middle, as if he'd been showing it off.

Matt swallowed again. "That's Henry. Henry Ward. Elizabeth's son."

Abe said, "Did the defendant accompany Henry for the dives, like the other mothers?"

"Yes," Matt said. "She always came in with Henry, except for the last dive."

"Every single dive, and the only time she sat out just happened to be when everyone inside was hurt or killed?"

"Yes. The only time." Matt looked at Abe, tried hard not to look at Elizabeth, but he could see her in the periphery. She was staring at the pictures, sucking her lips into her mouth to gnaw on them, the pink lipstick gone. It looked wrong, her face with makeup lining her blue eyes, color on her cheeks, shadow accentuating her nose, then nothing under the nose—just white. Like a clown who's forgotten to draw in lips.

Abe placed a poster on a second easel. "Dr. Thompson, would this be helpful in explaining Miracle Submarine's physical setup?"

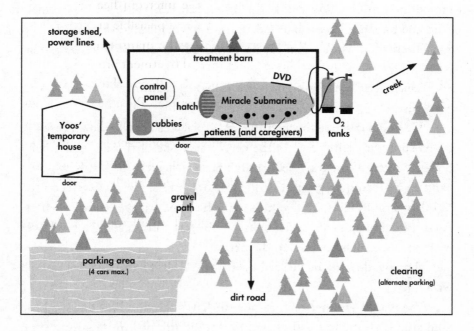

"Yes, very," Matt said. "This is my crude drawing of the lot. It's in the town of Miracle Creek, ten miles west of here. Miracle Creek is an actual creek—it runs through the town; thus the name. Anyway, the creek runs through the woods next to the treatment barn."

"Sorry, did you say 'treatment barn'?" Abe looked puzzled, as if he hadn't seen the barn four thousand times.

"Yes. There's a wooden barn in the middle of the lot, and the HBOT chamber is inside. When you walk in, to the left is the control panel where Pak sat. Plus cubbies for us to leave anything not allowed in the chamber, like jewelry, electronics, paper, synthetic clothing, anything that could set off a spark—Pak had very strict safety rules."

"And what's outside the barn?"

"In the front, there's a gravelly parking spot big enough for four cars. To the right, the woods and the creek. To the left, a little house where Pak's family lives, and to the back, a storage shed and the power lines."

"Thank you," Abe said. "Now take us through a typical dive. What happened?"

"We'd crawl into the chamber through the hatch. I usually went last and sat closest to the exit. That's where the intercom headset was, for communicating with Pak." That sounded like a plausible enough reason, but the truth was, Matt preferred being on the margins of the group. The moms liked to talk, trading experimental treatment protocols, telling life stories. That was fine for them, but he was different. He was a doctor, for one, who didn't believe in alternative therapies. Plus, he wasn't a parent at all, much less the parent of a special-needs kid. He wished he could've brought in a magazine or paperwork, some shield against their constant questions. It was ironic, how he was in there to try to have kids, but everywhere he turned, he felt like, God, do I really want kids? So much can go wrong.

"So then," Matt said, "the pressurization. It simulates how a real dive feels."

"What's that like? For those of us who haven't experienced submarine rides," Abe said, eliciting appreciative smiles from several jurors.

"It's like a plane landing. Your ears feel heavy, and they can pop. Pak pressurized slowly to minimize the discomfort, so it took about five minutes. Once we were at 1.5 ATA—that's like seventeen feet below sea level—we put on oxygen helmets."

One of Abe's minions handed Abe a clear plastic helmet. "Like this?"

Matt took the helmet. "Yes."

"How does this work?"

Matt turned toward the jury and pointed to the blue latex ring at the bottom. "This here fits around your neck, and your whole head goes inside." He stretched the opening like a turtleneck and put it on, the clear bubble encasing his head.

"Next, the tubing," Matt said, and Abe handed him a clear plastic coil. It slithered out and seemed to go on forever, like one of those tiny snakes that become ten feet when they unfurl.

"What does that do, Doctor?"

Matt inserted the tube into an opening in the helmet by his jaw. "It connects the helmet to the oxygen spigot inside the chamber. There are oxygen tanks behind the barn, and tubing connects them to the spigots. When Pak turned on the oxygen, it would travel through the tubes into our helmets. The oxygen would expand and make the helmet puffy, like inflating a ball."

Abe smiled. "Then you look like you're wearing a fishbowl on your head." The jurors laughed. Matt could tell they liked Abe, this plain-spoken guy who told it like it was, didn't act like he was too smart for them. "Then what?"

"Pretty simple. The four of us would breathe normally, and be breathing in one hundred percent oxygen, for sixty minutes. At the end of the hour, Pak would turn off the oxygen, we'd remove the helmets, then depressurization, and exit," Matt said, and removed the helmet.

"Thank you, Dr. Thompson. It's helpful to get this overview. Now, I'd like to get to why we're here, what happened on August 26 last year. Do you remember that day?"

Matt nodded.

"I'm sorry. You have to answer verbally. For the court reporter."

"Yes." Matt cleared his throat. "Yes."

Abe's eyes squinted a bit, then widened, as if he was unsure whether he should be apologetic or excited about what was to come. "Tell us, in your words, what happened that day."

The courtroom shifted then, almost imperceptibly, all the bodies in the jury box and gallery moving forward a tenth of an inch. This was what the people had come for. Not just the gore, though there was that— the blow-up photos and the charred remains of the equipment—but the drama of tragedy. Matt saw it every day in the hospital: broken bones, car accidents, cancer scares. People cried about it, sure—the pain, the unfairness, the inconvenience of it all—but there were always one or two in every family who got energized by being at the periphery of suffering, every cell in their bodies vibrating at a slightly higher frequency, woken from the mundane dormancy of their everyday lives.

Matt looked down at his ruined hand, thumb, fourth finger, and pinkie sticking out of a red blob. He cleared his throat again. He'd told this story many times. To the police, to the doctors, to the insurance investigators, to Abe. One last time, he told himself. Just once more through the explosion, the scorch of the fire, the obliteration of little Henry's head. Then he'd never have to talk about it again.

TERESA SANTIAGO

IT HAD BEEN A HOT DAY. The kind that made you sweat at 7:00 a.m. Full sun after a three-day downpour—the air dense and heavy, like being in a dryer full of wet clothes. She'd actually looked forward to that morning's dive; it'd be a relief to be sealed up in an air-conditioned chamber.

Teresa nearly hit someone pulling into the lot. A group of six women were holding signs and walking in an oval, like a picket line. Teresa was slowing down, trying to read the signs, when someone walked into her path. She braked hard, barely missing the woman. "My God!" Teresa said, stepping out of her van. The woman kept walking. No yell, no finger, no glance. "Excuse me, but what's happening here? We need to get inside," Teresa said to them. All women. Holding signs saying I'M A CHILD, NOT A LAB RAT!; LOVE ME, ACCEPT ME, DON'T POISON ME; and

QUACK MEDICINE = CHILD ABUSE—all scrawled in block letters in primary colors.

A tall woman with a silver bob came over. "This strip here's public property. We have a right to be here, to stop you. HBOT is dangerous, it doesn't work, and you're just teaching your kids you don't love them the way they are."

A car honked behind her. Kitt. "We're down here. Ignore the crazy bitches," she said, and motioned down the road. Teresa shut her van door and followed. Kitt didn't go far. Just to the next pull-off area, a clearing in the woods. Through the thick foliage, she glimpsed the post-storm Miracle Creek, brown and swollen and lazy.

Matt and Elizabeth were already there. "Who the hell are those people?" Matt said.

Kitt said to Elizabeth, "I know they've been saying awful things about you and making crazy threats, but I never thought they'd actually *act* on them."

"You know them?" Teresa said.

"Only from online stuff," Elizabeth said. "They're fanatics. Their kids all have autism, and they go around saying how it's the way they're meant to be, and all treatments are evil and sham and kill kids."

"But HBOT's nothing like that," Teresa said. "Matt, you can tell them."

Elizabeth shook her head. "There's no reasoning with them. We can't let them affect us. Come on, we're going to be late."

They went through the woods to avoid the protesters, but it didn't matter. The protesters spotted them and ran over, blocking them. The silver-bob-haired woman held up a flyer of an HBOT chamber surrounded by flames and *43!* on top. "Fact: there have been forty-three HBOT fires, even some explosions," the woman said. "Why would you put your children in something so dangerous? For what? So they'll make more eye contact? Flap their hands less? Accept them the way they are. It's the way God made them, the way they were *born*, and—"

"Rosa wasn't," Teresa said, stepping forward. "She wasn't born with cerebral palsy. She was healthy. She walked, she talked, she loved the monkey bars. But she got sick, and we didn't take her to the hospital quickly enough." She felt a hand squeeze her shoulder—Kitt. "She's not *supposed* to be in a wheelchair. And you're criticizing me, *condemning* me, for trying to heal her?"

The silver-bobbed woman said, "I'm sorry for that. But our goal is to reach parents with autistic children, which is different—"

"Why's it different?" Teresa said. "Because they're born with it? What about kids born with tumors, cleft palates? God clearly *meant* for that, but does that mean their parents shouldn't pursue surgery, radiation, whatever it takes to get them healthy and whole?"

"Our kids are already healthy and whole," the woman said. "Autism isn't a defect, just a different way of being, and any so-called treatment for it is quack nonsense."

"Are you sure about that?" Kitt said, stepping up next to Teresa. "I used to think that, then I read that many autistic kids have digestive issues, and that's why they walk on tiptoes—the muscle-stretching helps with the pain. TJ's always toe-walked, so I got him tested. It turned out he had severe inflammation, and he couldn't tell us."

"The same with her." Teresa pointed to Elizabeth. "She's been trying tons of treatments, and her son's improved so much that the doctors say he's not autistic anymore."

"Yeah, we know all about her *treatments*. Her son's very lucky that he's survived them all. Not all kids do." The woman held the flyer on HBOT fires right up to Elizabeth's face.

Elizabeth scoffed and shook her head at the woman, pulling Henry close to her and walking away. The woman grabbed Elizabeth's arm and yanked, hard. Elizabeth yelped, tried to get away, but the woman tightened her grip, wouldn't let go. "I'm done letting you ignore me," the woman said. "If you don't stop, something terrible *will* happen. I guarantee it."

"Hey, back off," Teresa said, stepping between them and slapping the woman's hand away. The woman turned her way, her hands closing into a fist as if to punch her, and Teresa felt a cold tingle in her shoulders crawl down her back. She told herself not to be silly, this was just a mom with strong opinions, nothing to be scared of, and said, "Let us through. Now."

After a moment, the protesters backed away. Then they raised their signs and quietly resumed walking in a crooked oval.

○

IT WAS STRANGE. sitting in court and listening to Matt recount those same events from the morning of the explosion. Teresa hadn't expected an exact match between his memories and hers—she watched *Law & Order*; she wasn't *that* naïve—but still, the extent of the difference was unnerving. Matt reduced the encounter with the protesters to one phrase—"a debate about the efficacy and safety of experimental autism treatments"—with no mention of Teresa's points about other diseases, the substance of the argument lost on him, or maybe just irrelevant. The hierarchy of disabilities—to Teresa, that was central, something she agonized over, and to Matt, it was nothing. If he had a disabled child, it'd be different, of course. Having a special-needs child didn't just change you; it transmuted you, transported you to a parallel world with an altered gravitational axis.

"During all this," Abe was saying, "what was the defendant doing?"

"Elizabeth didn't get involved at all," Matt said, "which struck me as odd, because she's usually very vocal about autism treatments. She just kept staring at the flyer. There was text on the bottom, and she kept squinting, like she was trying to make out what it said."

Abe handed Matt a document. "Is this the flyer?"

"Yes."

"Please read the bottom text."

"'Avoiding sparks in the chamber is not enough. In one case, a fire started outside the chamber under the oxygen tubing led to an explosion with fatalities.'"

"'Fire started outside the chamber under the oxygen tubing,'" Abe repeated. "Isn't that exactly what happened to Miracle Submarine later that very day?"

Matt looked over to Elizabeth, his jaws tensing as if gritting his molars. "Yes," he said, "and I know she was focused on that because she went straight up to Pak afterward and told him about their flyer. Pak said that couldn't happen to us, he wouldn't let any of them near the barn, but Elizabeth kept saying how dangerous they were, and she made him promise to call the police and report that they're threatening us, to get that on the record."

"What about during the dive? Did she say any of this then?"

"No, she was silent. She seemed distracted. Like she was thinking intensely about something."

"Like she was planning something, perhaps?" Abe said.

"Objection," Elizabeth's attorney said.

"Sustained. The jury will disregard the question," the judge said, but in a lazy tone. A judicial version of "Yeah, yeah, yeah." Not that it mattered. Everyone was already thinking it—the flyer had given Elizabeth the idea to set the fire and blame the protesters for it.

"Dr. Thompson, after Miracle Submarine exploded in precisely the same way as highlighted by the defendant, did she try to lay suspicion on the protesters again?"

"Yes," Matt said. "That night. I heard her tell the detective she was sure the protesters did it, they must've started the fire under the oxygen tubes outside." Teresa had heard that, too. She'd been convinced, as had everyone, at first—the protesters had been the primary suspects for almost a week—and even after Elizabeth's arrest, she'd still been suspicious. Just this morning, when Elizabeth's lawyer reserved her opening statement until after the prosecution's case, she'd been disappointed, sure that the defense would've painted the protesters as the real killers.

"Dr. Thompson," Abe said, "what else happened that morning, after the protesters?"

"After the dive, Elizabeth and Kitt left first, and I helped Teresa get Rosa's wheelchair through the woods. When we got to the pull-off area, Henry and TJ were already in their cars, and Elizabeth and Kitt were by the woods, on the other side from us. They were fighting." Teresa remembered—they'd been yelling, but in the whispered shouts of people carrying on a private argument in public.

"What were they saying?"

"It was hard to hear, but I heard Elizabeth calling Kitt a 'jealous bitch' and something like, 'I'd love to lie around and eat bonbons all day instead of taking care of Henry.'" Teresa had heard "bonbons," but not the rest. Matt had been closer, though; as soon as they got there, he'd noticed something on his windshield and run to get it.

"I'm sorry," Abe said. "The defendant called Kitt a 'jealous bitch' and said she'd love to eat bonbons instead of taking care of her son, Henry— this just hours before Kitt and Henry were killed in the explosion. Do I have that right?"

"Yes."

Abe looked over to the pictures of Kitt and Henry and shook his head. He closed his eyes briefly, as if to compose himself, then said, "Did the defendant have other fights with Kitt that you know of?"

"Yes," Matt said, looking straight at Elizabeth. "Once, she yelled at Kitt in front of us and pushed her."

"*Pushed?* Physically?" Abe let his mouth hang in an open O. "Tell us about that."

Teresa knew which story Matt was going to tell. Elizabeth and Kitt were friends, but there was an undercurrent of tension that occasionally burst into tiffs. Just bickering, nothing major, except once. It happened after a dive. As everyone was leaving, Kitt handed TJ what looked like a toothpaste tube decorated with Barney.

"Oh my God, is that that new yogurt?" Elizabeth said.

Kitt sighed. "Yes, it's YoFun. And yes, I know it's not GFCF." Kitt said to Teresa and Matt, "GFCF is gluten-free, casein-free. It's an autism diet."

Elizabeth said, "Is TJ off it?"

"No. He's GFCF for everything else. But this is his favorite, and it's the only way he'll take supplements. It's only once a day."

"Once a *day*? But it's made with *milk*," Elizabeth said, making "milk" sound like "feces." "The primary ingredient is *casein*. How can you claim to be casein-free if he's eating casein every day? Not to mention, there's *food coloring* in that. And it's not even *organic*."

Kitt looked like she might cry. "What am I supposed to do? He spits out his pills unless he swallows with YoFun. This makes him happy. Besides, I don't think the diet really works. It never made a difference for TJ."

Elizabeth pressed her lips tightly together. "Maybe the diet didn't work because you never did it properly. *Free* means *none*. I use different plates for Henry's food; I even have a different sponge for cleaning his dishes."

Kitt stood up. "Well, I can't do that. I have four other kids I have to cook and clean for. It's hard enough just trying. Everyone says, do the best you can, and cutting out most of it's better than nothing. I'm sorry I can't be a hundred percent perfect like you."

Elizabeth shrugged her eyebrows. "It's not me you should say sorry to. It's TJ. Gluten and casein are neurotoxins for our kids. Even a tiny bit interferes with brain function. It's no wonder TJ's still not talking." She stood up, said, "Come on, Henry," and started to walk out.

Kitt stepped in front of her. "Wait, you can't just—"

Elizabeth pushed her away. Not hard, nowhere near hard enough to hurt Kitt, but it shocked her. It shocked all of them. Elizabeth kept walking out, then turned back. "Oh, and by the way, can you please stop telling people you haven't seen any improvements on the diet? You're not doing the diet, and you're discouraging people for no reason." She slammed the door.

After Matt finished telling the story, Abe said, "Dr. Thompson, has the defendant lost her temper like that any other time?"

Matt nodded. "The day of the explosion, during her fight with Kitt."

"The one where the defendant called Kitt a 'jealous bitch' and said she'd love to eat bonbons all day instead of taking care of her son?"

"Exactly. She didn't do anything physical this time, but she ran off in a huff and slammed her car door, really hard, and she revved and backed out so fast, she almost hit my car. Kitt yelled for her to calm down and wait, but . . ." Matt shook his head. "I remember being worried for Henry because Elizabeth drove off so fast. The tires were squealing."

"What happened next?" Abe said.

"I asked Kitt what happened, if she was okay."

"And?"

"She looked really upset, like she was about to cry, and she said no, she wasn't okay, that Elizabeth was really mad at her. Then she said she had done something and she needed to figure out how to fix it before Elizabeth found out, because if she found out . . ." Matt looked to Elizabeth.

"Yes?"

"She said, 'If Elizabeth finds out what I did, she's gonna kill me.'"

PAK YOO

THE JUDGE CALLED FOR RECESS AT NOON. Lunch, which Pak dreaded, knowing that Dr. Cho—not Janine, but her father, who went by "Dr. Cho" even though he was an acupuncturist, not a doctor—would insist on treating them. Forced charity. Not that he wasn't tempted—they'd eaten nothing but ramen, rice, and kimchi since the hospital bills started arriving—but Dr. Cho had already given them too much: monthly loans for necessities, assumption of Pak's mortgage, a generous sum in exchange for Mary's car, power bill payments. Pak had no choice but to accept it all, even Dr. Cho's latest brainstorm, a fund-raising website in English *and* Korean. An international proclamation of Pak Yoo as a destitute invalid begging for handouts. No. No more. Pak told Dr. Cho they had other plans and hoped he wouldn't see them eating in their car.

On their way to the car, he saw a dozen geese waddling around, directly in their path. Pak expected Young or Mary to shoo them away, but they kept walking, rolling Pak closer and closer, like a bowling ball toward the pins. And the geese—they were equally oblivious, or maybe just lazy. It wasn't until his wheelchair was centimeters from knocking one over and he was about to yell that one honked and the whole gaggle took off for flight. Young and Mary kept walking, paces steady as if nothing had happened, and he wanted to scream at their insensitivity.

Pak closed his eyes and breathed. In, out. He told himself he was being ridiculous—he was actually angry at his wife and daughter for not noticing geese! It would be comical if it weren't so pathetic, this oversensitivity to geese from his four years alone.

Ghee-ruh-ghee ap-bah. *Wild-goose father.* What Koreans called a man who remained in Korea to work while his wife and children moved abroad for better education, and flew (or "migrated") annually to see them. (Last year, when alcoholism and suicide reached alarming levels among Seoul's 100,000 goose fathers, people started calling men like Pak—men who couldn't afford any visits, so never flew—*penguin fathers*, but by then, his identification with geese was fixed, and penguins never bothered him the way geese did.) Pak hadn't set out to become a goose father; they'd planned to move to America together. But while waiting for a family visa, Pak heard about a host family in Baltimore willing to sponsor a child and one parent to live with them for free, arranging for the child to attend a nearby school, in exchange for the parent working at their grocery store. Pak sent Young and Mary off to Baltimore, promising he'd join them soon.

In the end, it had taken four more years for the family visa. Four years of being a father without a family. Four years of living alone in a closet-studio in a sad, disheveled "villa" full of sad, disheveled goose fathers. Four years of working two jobs, seven days a week, of skimping and saving. All that sacrifice for Mary's education, for her future, and now, here she was, scarred and unanchored, no college on the horizon, attending murder trials and therapies instead of seminars and parties.

"Mary," Young was saying in Korean, "you have to eat." Mary shook her head and looked out the car window, but Young put the bowl of rice on Mary's lap. "A few bites."

Mary bit her lip and picked up the chopsticks—tentatively, as if scared to try some exotic food. She picked up one grain of rice and put it just inside her lips. Pak remembered Young showing Mary this way of eating back in Korea. "When I was your age," Young had said, "your grandmother made me practice eating rice grain by grain. She said, 'This way, food is always in your mouth, so you are not expected to talk, but without appearing to be a pig. No man wants a wife who eats or talks too much.'" Mary, laughing, had said to Pak, "Ap-bah, did Um-ma eat like that when you were dating?" Pak had said, "Definitely not. Good thing I like pigs," and they'd all laughed and eaten the rest of the dinner as sloppily and noisily as possible, taking turns making pig grunts. Had that really been so long ago?

Pak looked at his daughter, chewing one grain of rice after another, and his wife, studying their child, worry lines framing her eyes. He picked up kimchi to force himself to eat, but the stink of fermented garlic swirling in the sweltering heat formed a mask over his face, overpowering him. He cranked the window open and stuck his head out. In the sky, the geese were flying away, the majestic symmetry of their V-formation visible in the distance, and he thought how unfair it was, calling men like him "goose fathers." Real male geese mated for life; real goose families stayed together, foraged, nested, and migrated together.

Suddenly, a vision: a cartoon of male geese in a courtroom, suing Korean newspapers for defamation and demanding retractions of all goose-father references. Pak chuckled, and Young and Mary looked at him with confusion and concern. He thought about explaining, but what could he say? *So these geese file a class-action lawsuit* . . . "I thought of something funny," he said. They didn't ask what. Mary went back to eating rice, Young back to looking at Mary, and Pak back to looking out the window, watching the wedge of geese fly farther and farther away.

○

AFTER LUNCH, entering the courtroom, Pak recognized a silver-haired woman in the back. A protester, the one who'd threatened him that morning, saying she wouldn't rest until he was exposed as a fraud and his business shut down for good. "If you don't stop right now," she'd said, "you *will* regret it. I promise you." And now that her promise had come to fruition, here she was, surveying the room like a proud director on opening night. He imagined facing her, threatening to expose her lies about that night, to tell the police everything he saw. How satisfying it would be, watching the smugness drain from her eyes, replaced by fear. But no. No one could know he was outside that night. He had to maintain his silence, no matter the cost.

Abe stood up and something fell to the floor: the flyer, with *43!* in a red, fiery font. Pak stared at it, this piece of paper that had started everything. If only Elizabeth hadn't seen it and gotten fixated on the idea of sabotage, of fire being set under the oxygen tube, he'd be driving Mary to college right now. A surge of heat coursed through him, sending his muscles quivering, and he wanted to grab that flyer, tear and ball it up, and hurl it at Elizabeth and the protester, these women who'd wrecked his life.

"Dr. Thompson," Abe said, "let's pick up where we left off. Tell us about the last dive, during which the explosion occurred."

"We started late," Matt said. "The dive before us is usually done by 6:15, but they were running late. I didn't know, so I got there on time, and the front lot was full. All us double-divers had to park in the alternate spot down the street, like that morning. We didn't start until 7:10."

"Why the delay? Were the protesters still there?"

"No. The police took them away earlier. They apparently tried to stop the dives by releasing Mylar balloons into utility lines, which caused a power outage," Matt said. Pak almost laughed at the succinctness, the efficiency, of Matt's description. Six hours of chaos—the protesters upsetting the patients; the police saying they were powerless to stop "peaceful protests"; the AC and lights going dead during an afternoon dive, scaring the patients; the police finally arriving; the protesters' shrieks of "What power lines?" and "What on earth do balloons have to do with outages?" All that, reduced to a ten-second summary.

"How could the dives continue with an outage?" Abe said.

"There's a generator, a safety requirement. Pressurization, oxygen, communications—all that still worked. Just secondary things like AC, lights, and the DVD didn't work."

"DVD? Air-conditioning, I understand, but why DVD?"

"For the kids, to help them sit still. Pak attached a screen outside a porthole and put in a speaker system. The kids loved it, and I can tell you the adults appreciated it as well."

Abe chuckled. "Yes, in my house, anyway, kids tend to be significantly quieter in front of a TV."

"Exactly." Matt smiled. "Anyway, Pak managed to hook up a portable DVD player outside the rear porthole. He said dealing with all this caused delays. Not to mention, some of the earlier patients got scared by the protesters and canceled their dives, which took more time."

"What about the lights? You said they were out?"

"Yes, in the barn. We started after 7:00, so it was starting to get dark, but it being summer, there was still enough sunlight to see."

"So the power's out, and the dive's delayed. Anything else odd about that evening?"

Matt nodded. "Yes. Elizabeth."

Abe raised his eyebrows. "What about her?"

"You have to remember," Matt said, "earlier that day, I saw her stomp off after a fight with Kitt, so I expected her to still be mad. But when she came in, she was in a really good mood. Unusually friendly, even to Kitt."

Abe said, "Perhaps they'd talked and worked it out?"

Matt shook his head. "No. Before Elizabeth arrived, Kitt said she tried to talk to her, but she was still mad. In any case, the really strange part was that Elizabeth said she felt sick. I remember thinking it was odd, how upbeat she was when she was supposedly coming down with something." Matt swallowed. "Anyway, she said she wanted to sit out, just stay in her car and rest during the dive. And then . . ." Matt's eyes darted to Elizabeth, his face scrunched up like he was hurt, betrayed, and disappointed all at once, the way a kid looks at his mother when he finds out there's no Santa.

"And then?" Abe touched Matt's arm as if comforting him.

"She asked Kitt to sit next to Henry and watch over him during the dive, and maybe I could sit on the other side and help, too."

"So the defendant arranged for Henry to sit between Kitt and you?"

"Yes."

"Any other seating-related suggestions from the defendant?" Abe said, emphasizing the word *suggestions* so it sounded ominous.

"Yes." Matt peered at Elizabeth with that hurt-disappointed-betrayed-kid look again. "Teresa started going in first, like always. But Elizabeth stopped her. She said since the DVD screen was in the back and Rosa didn't watch shows, TJ and Henry should sit back there."

"That seems reasonable, no?" Abe said.

"No, not at all," Matt said. "Elizabeth was very particular about the DVDs Henry watched." Matt's face tightened, and Pak knew he was thinking about the DVD-selection fight. Elizabeth had wanted something educational, a history or science documentary. Kitt had wanted *Barney*, TJ's favorite. Elizabeth gave in, but after a few days, Elizabeth said, "TJ is eight. Don't you think you should introduce something more appropriate for his age?"

"TJ needs this to be calm. You know that," Kitt said. "Henry's fine; an hour of Barney won't kill him."

"An hour without Barney won't kill TJ, either."

Kitt stared into Elizabeth's eyes for a long time. She seemed to smile. "Fine. We'll do it your way." She threw the *Barney* DVD into her cubby.

That session had been a disaster. TJ screamed when the documentary started. "Look, TJ, it's about dinosaurs, just like Barney," Elizabeth tried to say over TJ's howls, but all hell broke loose when TJ yanked off his helmet and started banging his head against the wall. Henry cried that his ears hurt, and Matt screamed for Pak to put in the *Barney* DVD, ASAP.

After summarizing the incident, Matt said, "After that day, Pak always put in *Barney*, and Elizabeth always sat Henry away from the DVD screen. She said *Barney* was junk, and she didn't want him near it. So for her to suddenly change her mind and have Henry sit by the DVD—that was beyond strange. Kitt even asked if she was sure, and Elizabeth said it was a special treat for Henry."

"Dr. Thompson," Abe said, "did the defendant's seating change affect anything else?"

"Yes. It changed which oxygen tank everyone was connected to."

"Sorry, I don't quite understand," Abe said.

Matt looked to the jurors. "Before, I explained that you connect your helmet to an oxygen spigot inside the chamber. There are two spigots, one front and one back, each connected to a separate oxygen tank outside. Two people hook up to one spigot and share an oxygen tank." The jurors nodded. "Because of the way Elizabeth changed the seating, Henry connected his oxygen tube to the *back* spigot instead of the front one like always."

"So the defendant made sure Henry would be connected to the back oxygen tank?"

"Yes. And she told me to make sure to hook up mine to the front and Henry's to the back. I said, okay, but what difference does it make?"

"And?"

"She said I'm closer to the front and Henry to the back, and if we got our tubes crossed, Henry's OCD—obsessive-compulsive disorder—might flare up."

"Had Henry exhibited signs of this OCD 'flare-up'"—Abe drew quotes in the air—"in any of the thirty-plus dives you'd done together?"

"No."

"And then?"

"I said okay, I'll make sure we don't cross our tubes, but she wasn't satisfied. She crawled in and hooked up Henry's tube to the back spigot herself."

Abe walked over, directly in front of Matt. "Dr. Thompson," he said, and as if on cue, the air conditioner near Matt sputtered. "Which oxygen tank exploded?"

Matt fixed his eyes on Elizabeth's and spoke without blinking. Slowly. Deliberately. Each syllable punctuated, coated with venom, and targeted to hit her and make her bleed. "The back tank blew up. The one connected to the back spigot. The one which *that woman*"—Matt paused, and Pak was sure he'd raise his arm and point his finger at her, but instead he blinked and looked away—"made sure was connected to her son's head."

"And after the defendant set everything up the way she wanted, what then?" Abe said.

"She said to Henry, 'I love you so, so much, sweetie.'"

"I love you so, so much, sweetie," Abe repeated as he turned to Henry's picture, and Pak saw the jurors frown at Elizabeth, some shaking their heads. "And then?"

"She left," Matt said, his voice quiet. "She smiled and waved, like we were going on a roller-coaster ride, and she walked away."

MATT

S O THE DEFENDANT LEAVES and the evening dive starts. What happened next, Dr. Thompson?" Abe said.

He'd known the dive was seriously fucked up the moment the hatch closed. The air had been unnaturally still, which, combined with the baked stench of body odor and Lysol that permeated the chamber, made it a bitch to breathe. Kitt asked Pak to take the pressurization extra slow for TJ, who was recovering from an ear infection, so that took ten minutes instead of the usual five. With the pressurization, the air got denser and hotter, if that was possible. The portable DVD wasn't hooked up to the sound system, and the filtered sound of Barney singing *What'll we see at the zoo-zee-zoo?* through the thick glass porthole made the dive feel surreal, like really being underwater.

"It was hot with no AC, but otherwise, things were normal," Matt said, which wasn't really true. He'd expected the women to spend the dive deconstructing Elizabeth's unexpected chumminess and obviously faked illness, but they'd both remained silent. Maybe it was the awkwardness of talking with Matt between them, or maybe the heat. In any case, he was glad for the chance to sit and think; he needed to figure out what to say to Mary.

"What was the first sign of trouble?" Abe said.

"The DVD went dead, right in the middle of a song." The silence of that moment was absolute. No hum of the AC, no *Barney*, no chattering. After a second, TJ knocked on the porthole, as if the DVD player were a sleeping animal he could wake up. "It's okay, TJ; I bet it's just the batteries," Kitt said with the kind of forced evenness you used when you happened upon a sleeping bear.

The next part he remembered in jags, like one of those old-fashioned films that go tat-tat-tat when they turn, the scenes spliced crudely, jumping from one image to the next. TJ pounding his fists on the porthole. TJ taking off and throwing his oxygen helmet aside, then hammering his head on the wall. Kitt trying to get TJ away from the wall.

"Did you ask Pak to stop the dive?"

Matt shook his head. Now, in the light of day, that seemed the obvious thing to do. But back then, everything had been fuzzy. "Teresa said maybe we should stop, but Kitt said no, we just needed to restart the DVD."

"What did Pak say?"

Matt glanced Pak's way. "It was chaos in the chamber, very noisy, so I couldn't really hear, but he said something about getting batteries, it taking a few minutes."

"So Pak's working to fix the DVD. Then what?"

"Kitt calmed down TJ and got the helmet back on him. She sang songs to keep him calm." It had been one song, actually: the *Barney* song that cut off when the DVD died. Over and over, soft and slow, like a lullaby. Sometimes, drifting off to sleep, Matt would hear it: *I love you, you love me, we're a hap-py fam-i-ly.* He'd jolt awake, heart thumping his chest, and he'd picture himself ripping Barney's fat purple head off and stomping on it, its purple hands stopping mid-clap and decapitated purple body toppling.

"What happened next?" Abe said.

Everyone had been still and quiet, Kitt half murmuring, half singing, and TJ leaning against her chest, eyes closed. Suddenly, Henry said, "I need the pee jar," and reached to grab the urine-collection container in the back for bathroom emergencies. Henry's chest smashed against TJ's legs, and TJ startled, jolting his arms and legs like he'd been defibrillated, and started kicking, out of control. Matt pulled Henry back, but TJ yanked off his helmet, threw it in Kitt's lap, and started banging his head again.

It was hard to believe that a child's head could repeatedly strike a steel wall, producing such heavy thuds, and not crumple into pieces. Listening to the pounding, being sure that TJ's head would crack with the next blow, made Matt want to pull off his own helmet, slap his palms over his ears, and shut his eyes tight. Henry seemed to feel the same, turning to Matt with eyes so wide they bulged into circles with pinpoint pupils. Bull's-eye.

Matt took Henry's small hands into his own. He brought his face closer to Henry's, smiled eye to eye, their helmets between them, and said everything was okay. "Just breathe," he said, and puffed in a deep breath, keeping a steady gaze on Henry's eyes.

Henry breathed with Matt. In, out. In, out. The panic in Henry's face began to dissipate. His eyelids relaxed, his pupils dilated, and the edges of his lips curled into the beginnings of a smile. In the gap in Henry's top front teeth, Matt noticed the tip of a budding tooth. Hey, you're getting a new tooth, Matt was opening his mouth to say, when the boom sounded. Matt thought of TJ's head cracking open, but it was louder than that, the sound of a hundred heads banging steel, a thousand. Like a bomb going off, outside.

Matt blinked—how long did that take? A tenth of a second? A hundredth?—then, where Henry's face had been, there was fire. Face, then blink, then fire. No, faster than that. Face, blink, fire. Face-blink-fire. Facefire.

· · ·

ABE DIDN'T SPEAK for a long time. Matt didn't, either. Just sat there, listening to the sobs and sniffles from the gallery, jury box, everywhere except the defense table.

"Counsel, would you like a recess?" the judge asked Abe.

Abe looked at Matt with raised eyebrows, the lines around his eyes and mouth saying that he was tired, too, that it was okay to stop.

Matt turned to Elizabeth. She'd been remarkably composed, to the point of appearing disinterested, all day. But he'd expected the façade to break by now, for her to wail that she loved her son, that she could never hurt him. Something, anything, to show the devastation that any decent human being would feel, being accused of murdering her own child and hearing the gruesome details of his death. To hell with decorum, to hell with rules. But she'd said nothing, done nothing. Just listened to it all gazing at Matt with a casual curiosity, as if she were watching a show on Antarctica's climate pattern.

Matt wanted to run up and grab her shoulders and shake her. He wanted to shove his face into hers and scream that he still had nightmares about Henry in that moment, looking like some alien in a kid's drawing—a bubblehead of flames, the rest of his body perfectly intact, his clothes untouched, but his legs thrashing in a silent scream. He wanted to zap that image into her head, transfer it or mind-meld it or whatever it took to pop that fucking composure off her and heave it way the hell away where she could never find it again.

"No," Matt said to Abe, no longer tired, no longer in need of the break he'd prayed for. The sooner he got this sociopath hauled off to death row, the better. "I'd like to continue."

Abe nodded. "Tell us what happened to Kitt after the explosion outside."

"The fire was isolated to the back oxygen spigot. TJ's helmet was also connected to that, but TJ had taken it off and Kitt was holding it. The flames shot out of the opening, onto Kitt's lap, and she caught on fire."

"What then?"

"I tried to get Henry's helmet off, but . . ." Matt looked down at his hands. The scar tissue over the amputated stumps looked glossy and new, like melted plastic.

"Dr. Thompson? Were you able to?" Abe said.

Matt looked up. "I'm sorry. No." Matt forced his voice to be louder, his words to come faster. "The plastic started to melt, and it was too hot; I couldn't keep my hands on it." It had been like grabbing a red-hot poker and trying to hold on. His hands refused what his mind willed them to do. Or maybe that was a lie; maybe he'd wanted to do just enough to tell himself he'd tried his best. That he hadn't let a boy die because he didn't want to damage his precious hands. "I took off my shirt, wrapped it around my hands to try again, but Henry's helmet started disintegrating and my hands caught fire."

"What about the others?"

"Kitt was screaming, smoke was everywhere. Teresa was trying to get TJ to crawl up, away from the flames. We were all screaming for Pak to open up."

"Did he?"

"Yes. Pak opened the hatch and pulled us out. Rosa and Teresa first, then he crawled in and pushed TJ and me out."

"And then?"

"The barn was on fire. The smoke so thick, we couldn't breathe. I don't remember how . . . somehow, Pak got Teresa, Rosa, TJ, and me out of the barn, then he ran back in. He was gone awhile. Eventually, he came out carrying Henry and laid him down on the ground. Pak was hurt—coughing, burns all over—and I told him to wait for help, but he wouldn't listen. He went back in for Kitt."

"What about Henry? What was his condition?"

Matt had walked toward Henry quickly, had fought off the way every cell in his body screamed at him to run the fuck away. He slumped down and held Henry's hand—unblemished, not a scratch, like the rest of his body from the neck down. His clothes unburned, socks still white.

Matt tried not to look at Henry's head. Even so, he could see that his helmet was gone. Pak must've managed to finally get it off, he thought, but he saw the blue latex around Henry's neck and realized: the helmet's clear plastic had melted away, leaving behind the sealed ring. The fire-retardant piece that protected everything below Henry's neck and kept it pristine.

He forced himself to look at Henry's head. It was smoldering, the hair singed away, every inch of his skin charred and blistered and bloody. The damage was the worst near his right jaw, the point at which the oxygen—the fire—blew into the helmet. His skin had burned off completely there, and his bone and teeth flashed through. He saw Henry's new tooth, the gums previously hiding it now gone. Perfect and tiny, set above the others, which you could tell were baby teeth because the grown-up teeth yet to grow in were above them, in plain sight. A gentle wind blew, and Matt got a whiff of charred flesh, of singed hair, cooked meat.

"By the time I got to him," Matt said to Abe, "Henry was dead."

YOUNG

HER HOUSE WAS NOT EXACTLY A HOUSE. More of a shack. It could look quaint, if you looked at it a certain way. Shaped like a tiny log cabin or tree house, the kind a teenager might build with his not-so-handy father, and to which a kind mother might comment, "Very good effort. And you've never even had a class on woodworking!"

The first time she saw it, Young said to Mary, "It doesn't matter what it looks like. It'll keep us dry and safe. That's what's important." It was hard to feel safe, though, in a creaky shack that drooped to one side, as if the whole structure was slowly sinking into the ground. (The lot was soft and muddy, so this seemed possible.) The door, the single "window"— clear plastic duct-taped to a hole in the wall: both were lopsided, and the plywood lay on the floor unevenly. Whoever built this hut had not been familiar with levels or the concept of right angles.

But now, opening the crooked door and stepping onto the wobbly floor, safe was exactly how Young felt. Safe to do what she'd wanted since the judge banged the gavel to end the first day of trial: laugh out loud, both rows of teeth showing, and shout that she loved American trials, loved Abe, loved the judge, and, most of all, loved the jurors. She loved how they ignored the judge's instructions not to discuss this case with *anyone*, even one another, and, as soon as he stood to leave—Young loved that most, their not even waiting until he was gone—started talking about Elizabeth, how creepy she was, and what nerve, showing her face here in front of people whose lives she'd ruined. She loved how they stood to leave and glared down at Elizabeth in unison, like a gang, the same expression of disgust on their faces—the beautiful uniformity of it, as if it had been choreographed.

Young knew she shouldn't feel this way, not after Matt's horrifying testimony recalling Henry's and Kitt's deaths, his burns, the amputation of his fingers, the difficulty of learning to do everything with his left hand. But she'd lived the last year in perpetual sadness, remembering Pak's screams in the hospital burn unit and imagining a future without functioning limbs, and hearing about it no longer affected her. Like those frogs that get so used to hot water, they stay in the boiling pot. She'd gotten used to tragedy, become numb to it.

But joy and relief—those were relics, buried and forgotten, and now that they were unearthed, there was no containing them. When Matt testified about the minutes before the explosion and there was no question, not a hint, of Pak's absence from the barn: it was as if sludge had been in her veins, cutting off her organs, and right then, a dam broke and it all rushed out. The story Pak had invented to protect them had, with time and repetition, become the truth, and the only person who could challenge it had cemented it instead.

Young turned to help Pak inside. As she approached him, he said, "Today was a good day," and grinned at her. He looked like a boy, his mouth crooked, one corner higher than the other, a dimple only on one cheek. "I waited until we were alone to tell you the good news," he continued, his grin getting wider and more crooked, and Young felt a delicious conspiratorial togetherness with her husband. "The insurance investigator was in court. We talked when you were in the bathroom. He's filing his report as soon as the verdict's announced. He said it'll take only a few weeks for us to get all the money."

Young tilted her head back, clapped her hands, and closed her eyes to the sky, the way her mother always did to praise God for good news. Pak laughed, and she did, too. "Does Mary know?" she said.

"No. Would you like to tell her?" he said. It surprised her, his asking her preference rather than ordering it done a particular way.

Young nodded and smiled, feeling unsure but happy like a bride on her wedding's eve. "You rest. I'll go tell her." Passing him, she put her hand on his shoulder. Instead of rolling away, Pak placed his hand on hers and smiled. Their hands together—a team, a unit.

Young savored the giddiness that frothed through her like helium-infused bubbles, and even Mary's sadness—apparent in the way she stood before the barn, slumped, gazing at the ruins and crying softly—couldn't mar it. If anything, Mary's tears buoyed Young more. Since the explosion, Mary's personality had flipped from a hot-tempered, talkative girl to a detached, mute facsimile of her daughter. Mary's doctors had diagnosed her with post-traumatic stress disorder (PTSD, they called it—Americans had such a penchant for reducing phrases to acronyms; saving seconds was so important to them), and said her refusal to discuss that day was "classic PTSD." She hadn't wanted to attend the trial, but her doctors said others' accounts might trigger her memory. And Young had to agree, today had definitely loosened something. The way Mary had focused on Matt's testimony, intent on learning every detail about that day—the protesters, delays, power outage, all the things she'd missed because she'd been in SAT classes all day. And now, crying. An actual emotion—her first nonblank reaction since the explosion.

Getting closer to Mary, Young realized Mary's lips were moving, emitting barely audible murmurs. "So quiet . . . so quiet . . . ," Mary was saying, but ethereally, hypnotically, like a meditative chant. When Mary first awoke from her coma, she said this a lot, variations in English and Korean on the quietness before the explosion. The doctor explained that trauma victims often focus intently on one sensory element of the event, reliving and turning that single detail over and over in their minds.

"Victims of explosions often become haunted by the explosion's sound," he'd said. "It's natural that she'd fixate on the auditory juxtaposition of that moment—the silence before the blast."

Young stepped next to Mary. Mary didn't move, kept her eyes focused on the charred submarine, tears still trickling. Young said in Korean, "I know today was hard, but I'm glad you're able to cry about this, finally," and reached to rest her hand on Mary's shoulder.

Mary snatched her shoulder away. "You know nothing," she said in English, choked in sobs, and ran into their house. The rejection stung, but that was momentary, soothed by Young's realization that what had just happened—sobbing, yelling, running away, all of it—was typical of the real, pre-explosion Mary. It was funny, how she'd hated the teenage-girl melodrama and scolded Mary to stop that nonsense, and yet had missed it once it was gone and now was relieved at its return.

She followed Mary in and opened the black shower curtain demarcating Mary's sleeping corner. It was too flimsy to afford her (or Pak and Young on the other side) much privacy and served mostly as a symbol, a visual declaration of a teenager's demand to be left alone.

Mary was lying on her sleeping mat, face sunken into her pillow. Young sat and smoothed Mary's long black hair. "I have good news," Young said, making her words gentle. "Our insurance is coming through, as soon as the trial ends. We can move soon. You've always wanted to see California. You can apply to college there, and we can forget all this."

Mary raised her head a bit, like a baby struggling with the weight of her head, and turned to Young. Crease marks from the wrinkled pillow-case lined Mary's face, and her eyes were puffy slits. "How can you think about that? How can you talk about college and California when Kitt and Henry are dead?" Mary's words were accusatory, but her eyes were wide, as if impressed by Young's ability to focus on nontragic things and searching for clues on how to do the same.

"I know it's terrible, everything that's happened. But we need to move on. Focus on our family, your future." Young smoothed Mary's forehead lightly, as if ironing silk.

Mary put her head down. "I didn't know that's how Henry died. His face . . ." Mary closed her eyes, and tears dropped and stained her pillowcase.

Young lay down next to her daughter. "Shhh, it's okay." She brushed Mary's hair away from her eyes and combed it with her fingers the way she had every night in Korea. How much she'd missed this. Young hated many things about their American life: being a splintered goose family for four years; discovering (*after* settling in Baltimore) that their host family expected her to work from six a.m. to midnight, seven days a week; becoming a prisoner, locked away in bulletproofed isolation. But the thing she regretted most was the loss of closeness with her daughter. For four years, she never saw her. Mary was asleep when Young got home and still asleep when she left. Mary visited the store the first few weekends, but she spent the whole time crying about how much she hated school, how mean the kids were, how she couldn't understand anyone and she missed her father and missed her friends and on and on. Then came anger, Mary's shouts accusing Young of abandoning her, leaving her an orphan in a strange country. Then finally, worst of all, silent avoidance. No yells, no pleas, no glares.

The thing Young never understood was why Mary directed her anger solely at her. Pak staying in Korea, the Baltimore host-family arrangement—everything had been his plan. Mary knew this, had witnessed him issuing commands and silencing Young's objections, and yet Mary somehow blamed *her*. It was as if Mary associated all the transition pains of immigration—separation, loneliness, bullies—with Young (because Young was in America), whereas Pak, by virtue of his location, she grouped with her warm memories of Korea—family, togetherness, fitting in. Their host family said to wait, that Mary would follow the typical pattern of immigrant kids hyperassimilating, too fast and too much, driving parents crazy with their preferences of English to Korean, McDonald's to kimchi. But Mary never thawed, to Young or to America, even after she started making friends and speaking exclusively in English on the rare occasions she deigned to speak to Young, until eventually those early associations became a mathematical truth, forever constant:

(Pak = Korea = happiness) > (Young = America = misery)

But was that over? For here was her daughter now, letting Young rake her fingers through her hair while she cried, being comforted by this intimate act. After five minutes, maybe ten, Mary's breathing slowed to an even rhythm, and Young looked at her sleeping face. Awake, Mary's face was all sharp angles—thin nose, high cheekbones, deep frowns that lined her forehead like train tracks. But asleep, everything softened like melting wax, the angles giving way to gentle curves. Even the scar on Mary's cheek looked delicate, like she could brush it off.

Young closed her eyes and matched her breathing to her daughter's, and she felt a pinch of dizziness, of unfamiliarity. How many times had she lain next to Mary and held her? Hundreds of times? Thousands? But all years ago. In the last decade, the only time she'd allowed Young to touch her for sustained periods was in the hospital. People talked so much about the loss of intimacy between married couples as the years progress, so many studies about the number of times a couple has sex in the first year of marriage versus the remaining years, but no one measured the number of hours spent holding your baby in the first year of life versus the remaining years, the dramatic dissipation of intimacy—the sensual familiarity of nursing, holding, comforting—as children pass from infancy and toddlerhood to the teens. You lived in the same house, but the intimacy was gone, replaced by aloofness, with splashes of annoyance. Like an addiction, you could go for years without it, but you never forgot it, never stopped missing it, and when you got a dab of it, like now, you craved it more and wanted to gorge on it.

Young opened her eyes. She brought her face close and touched her nose to Mary's, the way she used to long ago. Her daughter's warm breaths blew on her lips, like gentle kisses.

●

FOR DINNER, Young made the dish that Pak pretended was his favorite: tofu-and-onion soup in a thick soybean paste. His *actual* favorite food was galbi, marinated short ribs—had been since they'd met in college. But ribs, even poor-quality scraps, were over four dollars per pound. Tofu cost two dollars per box, which they could manage if they stuck to rice, kimchi, and the dollar-per-dozen ramen the rest of the week. On his first day home from the hospital, she'd served this soup, and he'd breathed in deeply, filling his lungs with the pungent zest of soybean curd and sweet onions. He closed his eyes after the first bite, said that four months of bland hospital food had left him craving strong flavors, and declared Young's soup his new favorite. She knew he was just saving his honor— Pak was ashamed of their finances and refused to even discuss them—but regardless, his obvious delight with every bite had pleased her, and she'd made it as often as she could.

Standing over the simmering pot, stirring in the curd paste and watching the water turn a rich brown, Young had to laugh at how contented she felt, at the fact that this was the happiest she could remember feeling in America. Objectively, this was the lowest point of her American—no, *entire*—life: her husband paralyzed; her daughter a catatonic mess, her face scarred and psyche shattered; their finances nonexistent. Young should've been in despair, so weighed down by the bleakness of her situation, by others' pity, that she could barely stand.

And yet, here she was. Enjoying the feel of the wooden spoon in her hand, the simple motion of stirring sliced onion into the current of the liquid, breathing in the tangy vapors wafting up and warming her face. She replayed Pak's words about the incoming insurance money and, even more, the way his hand had nestled hers, the warmth of his smile. She and Pak had laughed together today—when was the last time they'd done that? It was as if being deprived of joy for so long had made her oversensitive to it, so that even a sliver of pleasure—the everyday kind she expected and therefore didn't notice when life was normal—now left her in the kind of celebratory state she associated with milestones such as engagements and graduations.

"Happiness is relative," Teresa had told her once, a few days before the explosion. Teresa had arrived early for the morning dive, so Young invited her to wait in the house while Pak got the barn ready. Mary stopped on her way out to SAT class. "Ms. Santiago, nice to see you again. Hi, Rosa," Mary said, bending down to put her face level with Rosa's. It amazed Young how friendly Mary could be, to everyone except her mother. Even Rosa responded to the cheerful lilt in Mary's voice; she smiled and seemed to strain to say something, a half grunt, half gurgle coming from her throat.

"Listen to that," Teresa said. "She's trying to talk. This whole week, she's been making so many sounds. HBOT's really working for her." Teresa put her forehead to Rosa's, mussed up her hair, and laughed. Rosa closed her lips and hummed, then opened her lips, making a "muh" sound.

Teresa gasped. "Did you hear that? She said *Ma.*"

"She did! She said *Ma,*" Mary said, and Young felt a tingle rush through her.

Teresa crouched down, looking up at Rosa's face. "Can you say it again, my sweet girl? *Ma. Mama.*"

Rosa hummed again, then said, "Ma," then again, "Ma!"

"Oh my God!" Teresa kissed Rosa all around her face, feathery pecks that made Rosa laugh. Young and Mary laughed, too, feeling the wonder of the moment ripple across them, binding them in shared amazement. Teresa put her head back, as if in a silent prayer of thanks to God, and Young saw it then: tears streaming down her face, her eyes closed in bliss so complete that she couldn't contain it, couldn't keep her lips from stretching so wide, her molars showed. Teresa kissed Rosa's forehead. Not a peck this time, but a lingering savoring of Rosa's skin against her lips.

Young felt a jolt of envy. It was ridiculous to feel jealous of a woman with a daughter who couldn't walk or talk, with no college, husband, or children in her future. She should feel sorry for Teresa, not envious, she told herself. And yet, when had *she* felt pure joy like that radiating from Teresa's face? Certainly not anytime recently, when everything she said caused Mary to frown and yell or, worse, ignore her and pretend she didn't know her.

To Teresa, Rosa saying "Mama" was a miraculous achievement, something that gave her more happiness than . . . than what? What had Mary done, what could she do, to make Young feel that much wonder? Get into Harvard or Yale?

As if to underscore this point, Mary said a warm good-bye to Teresa and Rosa, then turned to leave without saying anything to Young.

Young felt her cheeks flush and wondered if Teresa noticed. "Drive safely, Mary." Young put a false brightness into her voice. "Dinner is 8:30," she said in English, not wanting to be rude to Teresa by using Korean, even though she felt self-conscious speaking English in front of Mary, knowing that her accent, like everything else, embarrassed Mary.

Young turned to Teresa and forced out a chuckle. "She is so busy. SAT classes, tennis, violin. Can you believe she is already researching colleges? I guess that is what sixteen-year-old girls do." Even before she said it, she'd wanted to stop her words. But it was as if she were watching a movie already made, unable to stop what was coming. The fact was, for a moment—the briefest moment, but long enough to do damage—she'd wanted to hurt Teresa. She'd wanted to inject a dose of dark reality into her bliss and snap her out of it. She'd wanted to remind her of all the things that Rosa should be doing but was not and never would.

Teresa's face went saggy, the corners of her eyes and lips drooping dramatically, as if some invisible line holding them up had been cut. It was exactly the reaction she'd sought, but as soon as she saw it, Young hated herself.

"I am sorry. I do not know why I said that." Young reached out to touch Teresa's hand. "I was very insensitive."

Teresa looked up. "It's all right," she said. Young's doubt must have showed, because Teresa smiled and clasped her hand. "Really, Young, it's fine. When Rosa first got sick, it was hard. Every time I saw a girl her age, I'd think, 'That should be Rosa. She should be playing soccer and having slumber parties.' But, at some point"—she stroked Rosa's hair—"I accepted it. I learned not to expect her to be like other kids, and now I'm like any mom. I have good days and bad, and sometimes I'm frustrated, but sometimes she does something that makes me laugh or something new she's never done, like now, and then life is pretty good, you know?"

Young had nodded, but she hadn't really grasped how Teresa could look happy, *be* happy, when her life was, by any objective measure, so hard and tragic. But now, kissing Pak's cheek to wake him for dinner, seeing him smile as he said, "You made my favorite. That smells wonderful"— she understood. It was why all the studies showed that rich, successful people who should be the happiest—CEOs, lottery winners, Olympic champions—weren't, in fact, the happiest, and why the poor and disabled weren't necessarily the most depressed: you got used to your life, whatever accomplishments and troubles it happened to hold, and adjusted your expectations accordingly.

After waking Pak, Young walked to Mary's corner and stomped on the floor twice—the faux knock they used to enhance the illusion of privacy—and opened the shower curtain. Mary was still asleep, her hair wild and mouth agape like a baby rooting for milk. How vulnerable she looked, just the way she'd looked after the explosion, body crumpled and blood streaming from her cheeks. Young blinked to dislodge that image and knelt next to her daughter. She placed her lips on Mary's temple. She closed her eyes and let her kiss linger, savoring the feel of Mary's skin against her lips, the rhythm of her blood pulsing underneath, and wondered how long she could stay like this, joined to her daughter, skin to skin.

MARY YOO

SHE AWOKE TO THE SOUND of her mother's voice. "Meh-hee-yah, wake up. Dinnertime," she said, but in a whisper—as if, contrary to her words, she were trying not to wake her. Mary kept her eyes closed and tried to quell the surge of disorientation she felt, hearing her mother say "Meh-hee" in a gentle tone. For the last five years, her mother had used her Korean name only when she was annoyed with her, during fights. In fact, her mother hadn't said "Meh-hee" at all in a year; since the explosion, her mother was being extra nice and used "Mary" exclusively.

The funny thing was, Mary hated her American name. Not always. When her mother (who'd studied English in college and still read American books) suggested "Mary" as the closest approximation of "Meh-hee," she'd been excited to find a name with the same starting syllable as her own. On the fourteen-hour flight from Seoul to New York—her last hours as Yoo Meh-hee—she'd practiced writing her new name, filling an entire sheet with M-A-R-Ys and thinking how pretty the letters looked. After they landed, when the American immigration officer labeled her "Mary Yoo," rolling the r in that exotic way her Korean tongue couldn't replicate, she felt slightly glamorous and dizzy, like a butterfly newly emerged from a cocoon.

But two weeks into her new middle school in Baltimore—during roll call, when she was secretly reading letters from friends back home and she didn't recognize her new name and didn't answer and the kids started tittering—the newborn-butterfly feeling gave way to a sense of deep dissonance, like forcing a square into a round hole. Later, when two girls reenacted the scene for the cafeteria, the ramen-haired girl's crescendoing repetition of her new name—"Mary Yoo? Ma-ry Yoooo? MA-REEEEE? YOOOOO?"—felt like hammer blows, her square corners shattering.

She knew, of course, that the name wasn't to blame, that the actual problem was not knowing the language, customs, people, anything. But it was hard not to associate her new name with the new her. In Korea, as Meh-hee, she'd been a talker. She got in trouble constantly for chatting with friends and argued her way out of most punishments. The new her, Mary, was a mute math geek. A core of quiet, obedient and alone, wrapped by a carapace of low expectations. It was as if discarding her Korean name had weakened her, like cutting Samson's hair, and the replacement came with a meek persona she didn't recognize or like.

The first time her mother called her "Mary" was the weekend after the roll-call/cafeteria incident, during Mary's first visit to their host family's grocery store. The Kangs had spent two weeks training her mother, and they'd deemed her ready to take over the store's management. Prior to the visit, Mary had envisioned a sleek supermarket—everything in America was supposed to be impressive; that was why they'd moved here—but walking from the car, Mary had to sidestep broken bottles, cigarette butts, and someone sleeping on the sidewalk under torn newspaper.

The store vestibule was like a freight elevator, in both size and looks. Thick glass separated the customers from the vault-like room containing the products, and signs lined the lazy Susan transaction window:

PROTECTED BY BULLETPROOF GLASS, CUSTOMER IS KING, and OPEN 6 A.M. TO 12 A.M. 7 DAYS A WEEK. As soon as her mother unlocked the bullet- and apparently odor-proof door, Mary got a whiff of deli meat.

"Six to midnight? Every day?" Mary said before she even stepped in. Her mother gave an embarrassed smile to the Kangs and led Mary down a narrow corridor past the ice-cream cooler and deli slicer. As soon as they reached the back, Mary faced her mother. "How long have you known about this?" she said.

Her mother's face crinkled in pain. "Meh-hee-yah, all this time, I thought they wanted me to help them, as an assistant. I only realized last night—they're considering this their retirement. I asked if they'd hire someone to help, maybe once a week, but they said they can't afford that, not with what they're paying for your school." She stepped back and opened a door to reveal a cupboard. A mattress was stuffed in, almost fully covering the concrete floor. "They set up a place for me to sleep. Not every night, just if I'm too tired to drive home."

"So why don't I stay here with you? I can go to school here, or maybe I can come after school and help you," Mary said.

"No, the schools in this neighborhood are terrible. And you can't be here at nighttime at all. It's so dangerous, so many gangs, and . . ." Her mother shut her mouth and shook her head. "The Kangs can bring you for short visits on weekends, but it's so far from their house . . . We can't impose on them too much."

"*Us* impose on *them*?" Mary said. "They're treating you like a slave, and you're letting them. I don't even know why we came here. What's so great about American schools? They're doing math I did in fourth grade!"

"I know it's hard now," her mother said, "but it's all for your future. We need to accept that, try our best."

Mary wanted to rail against her mother for giving in, refusing to fight. She'd done the same thing in Korea, when her father first told them of his plans. Mary knew her mother hated the idea—she'd overheard their fights—but in the end, her mother had given in, the way she always did, the way she was doing now.

Mary said nothing. She stepped back and squinted to see her mother more clearly, this woman with tears pooling in the creases between her fingers, clasped together as if in prayer. She turned her back and walked away.

Mary stayed the rest of the day, while the Kangs went out to celebrate their retirement. As upset as she was with her mother, she couldn't help but be impressed by the finesse and energy with which she ran the store. She'd been training for only two weeks, but she knew most of the customers, greeting them by name and asking after their families in English—halting and with an accent, but still, better than Mary herself could do. In many ways, she was maternal with her customers: anticipating their needs; lifting their mood with her affectionate, almost coquettish laughter; but being firm when needed, as when she reminded several customers that food stamps could not buy cigarettes. Watching her mother, it occurred to Mary: the possibility that her mother actually liked it here. Was that why they were staying? Because running a store was more fulfilling than being a mere mother to her?

Late afternoon, two girls walked in, the younger around five and the older Mary's age. Her mother immediately unlocked the door. "Anisha, Tosha. You both look so pretty today," she said, and hugged them. "Meet my daughter, Mary."

Mary. It sounded foreign in her mother's familiar, lilting tone, like a word she'd never heard before. Unnatural. Wrong. She stood there, silent, as the five-year-old smiled and said, "I like your mommy. She gives me Tootsie Rolls." Her mother laughed, handed the girl a Tootsie Roll, and kissed her forehead. "So *that's* why you come in every day."

The older girl told her mother, "Guess what? I got an A on my math test!" As her mother said, "Wow! I told you, you can do it," the girl said to Mary, "Your mom's been helping me with long division this whole week."

After they left, her mother said, "Aren't they sweet girls? I feel so bad for them; their father died last year."

Mary tried to feel sad for them. She tried to feel proud that this beloved, generous woman was her mother. But all she could think was that these girls would see her, hug her every day, and she would not. "It's dangerous opening the door like that," Mary said. "Why have the bulletproof door if you're just going to open it and let people inside?"

Her mother gazed at her for a long moment. She said, "Meh-hee-yah," and tried to put her arms around her. Mary stepped back to avoid her touch. "My name is Mary now," she said.

●

THAT WAS THE DAY Mary started calling her "Mom" instead of "Um-ma." Um-ma was the mother who knitted her soft sweaters, who greeted her every day after school with barley tea and played jacks with her while listening to stories about what happened that day. And those lunches—who at school hadn't envied Um-ma's special lunches? The standard lunch-box fare in Korea was rice and kimchi in a stainless-steel container. But Um-ma always put in extras—fluffy bits of fish with the bones plucked out, a fried egg nested perfectly in the rice mound like a snowy volcano erupting yellow yolk, ghim-bop seaweed rolls with daikon radish and carrots, and yoo-boo-bop, sweet sticky rice tucked inside doll-sized pil-lowcases of fried tofu.

But that Um-ma was gone, replaced by Mom, a woman who left her alone in someone else's house, who didn't know about the boys who called her "stupid chink" and the girls who giggled about her in front of her, who didn't know that her daughter was struggling to know who Mary was and where Meh-hee had gone.

So as she left the store that day, Mary said "Farewell" in Korean—she deliberately chose the formal phrase that implied distance, meant for strangers—then, looking straight into her eyes, said "Mom" instead of "Um-ma." Seeing the jolt of hurt on her mother's face—her cheeks blanch-ing and mouth opening, as if to protest, but closing after a second, in resignation—Mary expected to feel better, but she didn't. The room seemed to tilt. She wanted to cry.

The next day, her mother started managing the store by herself and sleeping there more often than not. Mary had understood, at least in-tellectually: the drive home was thirty minutes, time better spent on sleep instead, especially since Mary wouldn't be awake. But that first night, lying in bed, Mary thought how she hadn't seen or talked to her mother all day for the first time in her life, and she hated her. For being her mother. For bringing her to a place that made her hate her own mother.

That was her summer of silence. The Kangs went on a two-month trip to California to visit their son's family, leaving Mary alone, with no school, no camp, no friends, no family. Mary tried to relish the freedom, told herself she was living a twelve-year-old girl's fantasy—never bothered by parents or siblings, left alone all day to do, eat, and watch whatever she wanted. Besides, it wasn't as if she'd seen much of the Kangs even before the trip—they were quiet and unobtrusive, doing their own activities and never bothering her. So she didn't see how being on her own would be too different.

There's something, though, about the sounds that other people make. Not talking, necessarily. Just their sounds of living—creaking upstairs, humming a tune, watching TV, clanging dishes—that blot away your loneliness. You miss them when they're gone. Their absence—the total silence—becomes palpable.

And so it was with her. Mary went days without seeing another human being. Her mother made sure to come home every night, but not until one a.m., and she was gone before dawn. She never saw her.

She did hear her, though. Her mother always came into her room when she returned home, stepping over Mary's piles of dirty clothes to pull the blanket up, kiss her good night, and, some nights, just to sit on her bed, combing Mary's hair with her fingers over and over, the way she used to in Korea. Mary was usually still awake, consumed by images of her mother caught in gunfire stepping out of the bulletproof vault in the middle of the night—a real possibility, the main reason for her mother's refusal to bring Mary to the store. When she heard her mother tiptoeing in the hallway, a mix of relief and anger coursed through her. She thought it best not to speak, so she pretended to be asleep. Kept her eyes shut and her body still, willing her heartbeat to slow and calm, wanting the moment to continue, wanting to relish the reliving of her mother as Um-ma and savor the old affection.

That was five years ago, before the Kangs returned and her mother started sleeping at the store again, before Mary became fluent in English and the bullies moved on, before her father came to America and moved them to a place where, once again, she felt like a foreigner, where people asked where she was from, and when she said Baltimore, said, "No, I mean, where are you *really* from?" Before cigarettes and Matt. Before the explosion.

But here they were again. Her mother, combing her fingers through Mary's hair, and Mary, pretending to be asleep. Lying here in the haze of half sleep, Mary felt transported back to Baltimore and wondered if her mother knew she'd been awake all those nights, how she'd waited for Um-ma's return.

"Yuh-bo, dinner's getting cold," Mary's father's voice sounded, breaking the moment. Her mother said, "Okay, coming," shook her gently, and said, "Mary, dinner's ready. Come out soon, okay?"

Mary blinked and mumbled, as if just starting to rouse. She waited for her mother to leave and close the curtain before slowly sitting up, reorienting herself, forcing her mind to take in her surroundings. Miracle Creek, not Baltimore, not Seoul. Matt. The fire. The trial. Henry and Kitt, dead.

At once, images of Henry's charred head and Kitt's chest on fire rushed back to her thoughts, and hot tears stung her eyes again. All year, Mary had tried hard not to think about them, about that night, but today, hearing about their last moments, imagining their pain—it was as if the images were needles surgically implanted throughout her brain, and every time she moved the tiniest bit, they poked her, sending white-hot flashes bursting behind her eyeballs and making her want to relieve the pressure, just open her mouth and scream.

Next to her mat, she saw a newspaper she'd picked up in the courthouse. This morning's, with the headline *"Mommy Dearest" Murder Trial Begins Today.* A picture showed Elizabeth gazing at Henry with a dazed smile, her head tilted, as if she couldn't believe how much she adored her son, the same way she'd looked at HBOT: always pulling Henry close, smoothing his hair, reading with him. It had reminded Mary of Um-ma in Korea, and she'd felt a pang, seeing this mother's singular devotion to her child.

It had all been a ruse, of course. It had to be. The way Elizabeth had sat through Matt's testimony about Henry being burned alive—without flinching, without crying, without screaming and running out. No mother with an ounce of love for her child could've done that.

Mary looked at the picture again, this woman who'd spent last summer pretending to love her child while secretly planning his murder, this sociopath who'd placed a cigarette inches from an oxygen tube, knowing that the oxygen was on and her son inside. Her poor son, Henry, this beautiful boy, his wispy hair, baby teeth, all engulfed in . . .

No. She shut her eyes tight and shook her head, side to side—hard, harder—until her neck hurt and the room spun and the world zigzagged sideways and upside down. When nothing remained in her head and she could no longer sit, she fell on the mat and buried her face in her pillow. She let the cotton soak up all her tears.

ELIZABETH WARD

THE FIRST TIME SHE HURT HER SON on purpose was six years ago, when Henry was three. They'd just moved into their new house outside D.C. A cookie-cutter McMansion—nice enough in isolation, but downright silly when clumped, as it was, with identical McMansions built too close on tiny lots separated by strips of grass. Elizabeth was not a fan of suburbia, but her then-husband, Victor, vetoed urban ("Too noisy!") and rural ("Too far!") choices and declared this house (close to two airports *and* three "feeder" preschools) a no-brainer.

Their first week, their neighbor Sheryl threw a cul-de-sac party. When Elizabeth walked in with Henry, the kids—pretend-riding horse brooms, Thomas trains, and Cars cars—were ricocheting around the cavernous basement and squealing (in joy, fear, or pain, she couldn't tell). The parents were cramped into a corner bar separated from the kids by childproof gates, looking like caged animals in a zoo exhibit, all gripping wineglasses and leaning in to talk over the racket.

A few steps in, Henry held his palms to his ears and screamed, a high-pitched yell that sliced through the pandemonium. All eyes turned, converging at first on Henry, then rushing to her, the mom.

Elizabeth turned to hug him tight, burying his face in her chest and muffling his scream. "Shhhh," she said, over and over, patting his hair, until he stopped. She turned to the others. "I'm sorry. He's very sensitive to noise. And moving and unpacking—he's really overwhelmed."

The adults smiled and muttered platitudes: "Of course" and "No worries" and "We've all been there." One man said to Henry, "I've been wanting to scream like that for an hour, so thanks for doing it for me, bud," and chuckled so good-naturedly, so cheerfully, that Elizabeth wanted to hug him for defusing the tension. Sheryl opened the childproof gate to let the adults out and said in singsong, "Hey, kids, we have a new friend. Let's all introduce ourselves."

One by one, the kids—all toddlers and preschoolers—answered Sheryl's prompts for their names and ages, even the youngest, Beth, who pronounced her name as "Best" and held up her tiny index finger for her age. Sheryl turned to Henry. "And *you*, handsome knight," she said, making the kids giggle, "what's *your* name?"

Elizabeth willed Henry to say, "Henry. I'm three," or at least hide his face in her skirt so she could credibly say, "Henry's shy around strangers," which would prompt choruses of "Oh, how sweet!" from the moms. But that didn't happen. Henry's face remained blank. He stared off into space, eyes rolled up and mouth ajar, looking like a shell of a boy—no personality, no intelligence, no emotion.

Elizabeth cleared her throat and said, "His name is Henry. He's three," managing to sound casual, with none of the thickness of embarrassment that was threatening to gag her. When little Beth toddled up and said, "Hi, Hen-wee," the adults said some variant of "Awwww, isn't that adorable?" and went back to their corner, chatting and offering drinks to Elizabeth, leaving her to wonder if she alone had registered the intense awkwardness. Was that possible?

For the next five minutes, while Elizabeth mingled, Henry stood quietly in one spot. He didn't play with the kids, didn't look to be having fun, but at least he wasn't calling attention to himself, which was the important thing. Elizabeth gulped her wine, its cool acidity soothing her throat and warming her stomach. An invisible dome seemed to veil her, making the kids look distant and unreal, like a movie, and muting their cacophony into a pleasant buzz.

The moment broke when Sheryl said, "Poor Henry. He's not playing with anyone." Later that night, waiting for Victor's call (conference in L.A.—the third that month), she'd imagine the different ways of handling that moment. She could've said, "He's tired. He needs a nap," and left, or she could've given Henry one of those music baby toys he fixated on so that he'd appear to be playing *near*, if not exactly *with*, the other kids. For sure, when Sheryl started a game to include Henry, she should've stepped in.

In the days to come, Elizabeth would blame her inaction on the fog of wine, the way it tricked her into a fizzy state of numbness. She kept drinking as Sheryl and her husband sat five feet apart and held up their arms to form a gate. No one explained the rules, but it seemed simple enough: whenever they said *bee-beep* and raised their arms, kids ran, trying to make it through before their arms came down. She wasn't sure why this was funny, but everyone guffawed, even the parents.

After a few gate-opening-closing cycles, Sheryl said, "Henry, you want to play? It's really fu-un." One of the boys—a three-year-old, like Henry—held out his hand. "Come on, let's run together."

Henry stood, not reacting, as if he were blind to the boy's hand and deaf to his voice, nothing registering in his senses. Henry looked up at the ceiling, so intently that half the others looked up to see what was so interesting, then he turned his back to everyone, sat down, and started rocking.

Everyone stopped and stared. Not for long—three seconds, five at most—but something about the moment, the absolute silence and stillness apart from Henry's rocking, stretched time. She'd never understood the concept of time freezing during accidents, the preposterous notion of your whole life flashing before your eyes in one second, but that was exactly what happened: as Elizabeth stared at Henry's rocking, snippets of her life played like a spliced movie in her mind. Newborn Henry refusing her breast, rock hard with milk. Three-month-old Henry crying for four hours nonstop; Victor coming home from a late-night client dinner to find her lying on the kitchen floor, sobbing. Fifteen-month-old Henry, the only one not crawling or walking at their playgroup, the mom of the girl who was already running and speaking in short sentences saying, "It doesn't matter. Babies develop at their own pace." (Funny, how it was always the moms of precocious kids who extolled the virtues of not worrying about developmental milestones, all the while flashing those smug smiles of parents congratulating themselves for having "advanced" children.) Two-year-old Henry still not talking, Victor's mom running around his birthday party saying, "Einstein didn't talk until he was five!" Henry just last week at his three-year checkup, not making eye contact, his pediatrician saying the dreaded a-word ("Now, I'm not saying it's autism, but testing can't hurt"). Yesterday, the Georgetown scheduler saying the autism-test wait list is eight months, Elizabeth furious at herself for not calling a year ago—hell, *two* years ago—when, let's face it, she knew there was something wrong, of course she did, but she wasted all that time just hoping and denying and talking about effing Einstein. And now, here he was, rocking—rocking!—in front of their new neighbors.

Sheryl broke the silence. "I don't think Henry feels like playing right now. Come on, who's next?" There was a noticeably forced casualness to her voice, a fake joviality, and Elizabeth realized: Sheryl was embarrassed for Henry.

Everyone turned back and resumed their game-playing and wine-sipping and small-talk-making, but cautiously, anxiously, at half the volume and energy level as before. The adults were trying hard to avoid looking Henry's way, and when little Beth said, "What's Hen-wee doing?" her mother whispered, "Shhh, not now," and turned and said to Elizabeth, "Isn't this dip great? It's from Costco!" Elizabeth knew that everyone's let's-pretend-nothing's-wrong act was for her sake. Maybe she should've been grateful. But somehow, it made it worse, as if Henry's behavior were so deviant that they had to cover it up. If Henry had cancer or hearing loss, everyone would've felt pity, sure, but not shame. They would've gathered around, asking questions and expressing sympathies. Autism was different. There was a stigma to it. And she'd stupidly thought she could protect her son (or was it herself?) by saying nothing and desperately hoping no one would notice.

"Excuse me," Elizabeth said, and walked across the room toward Henry. Her legs felt heavy, as if chains were tethering her to a cage, and it took all her strength to move. The moms pretended not to notice, but she could see their eyes darting at her, could see in their faces intense gratitude that they weren't her, and she felt fury surge up her throat. She grudged and envied and coveted and downright hated them, these women with their exquisitely normal kids. Walking through the kids laughing and talking, her arms ached to pick up one, any of them, and claim that child as her own. How different her life would be, full of mirth and trivialities ("I'm at my wit's end—Joey won't drink juice!" or "Fannie dyed her hair fuchsia!").

When she reached Henry, she crouched behind him. Although she couldn't see them, she could feel the adults' stares, coming from all directions and converging on her back like sunlight through a magnifying glass, the heat rising up to her cheeks and ears, making her eyes water. She steadied her hands, placed them on Henry's shoulder. "It's okay, Henry," she said as gently as she could manage. "Let's stop."

He seemed not to hear her, not to feel her hand. He kept rocking. Back and forth. Same rhythm. Same pace. Like a malfunctioning machine stuck in one mode.

She wanted to scream in his ear, to grab and shake him hard and fast and break him out of the world he was trapped in, make him look at her. Her face felt hot. Her fingers tingled.

"Henry, you need to stop. Right. Now," she said in a whispered yell, then moved to shield her hand from everyone's view and squeezed his shoulders. Hard. He paused, but only for a micro-beat, and when he resumed rocking, she squeezed harder, forcing the soft flesh between his neck and shoulder into a thin strip and pinching, harder and harder, wanting, needing it to *hurt*, for him to scream or hit her or run away, something to indicate that he was alive, in the same world as hers.

The shame and fear would come later, over and over in waves that choked her. When she saw the moms whispering as they left, making her wonder if they'd seen. At bathtime, when she took off Henry's shirt and saw the crescent-shaped break in his skin, the splotch of red under the surface. When she tucked him in and kissed his head, praying she hadn't harmed his psyche irreparably.

But before all that, in that moment, as Elizabeth pressed her fingers together, all she felt was a release. Not the sudden release of slamming a door or hurling a plate, but a slow, gradual dissipation of her fury, giving way to pleasure, the sensuous delight of squeezing something soft, like kneading dough. When Henry finally stopped rocking and twisted away, his mouth scrunched in pain, his eyes looking directly into hers—the first deep, sustained eye contact he'd made with her in weeks, maybe months—she felt power coursing through her and exploding into elation, her pain and hatred shattered into tiny shards she could no longer feel.

THE COURTHOUSE PARKING LOT was almost empty, which wasn't surprising given that court had adjourned hours ago. Since then, her lawyer had kept her waiting in a side room, citing "urgent business" (probably hiding away her murderess-client until everyone was gone). Not that it mattered; it wasn't like she had places to be or things to do. The terms of her house arrest allowed her to go only to the courthouse or Shannon's offices, to be driven only by Shannon.

Shannon's car, a black Mercedes, had been sitting in the sun all day, and when Shannon started the car, the fan blasted out on maximum and struck Elizabeth's right jawline. The air was torch hot, the AC not having had time to cool. Elizabeth touched her jaw and remembered Matt's testimony, the eruption of fire hitting Henry in that exact spot. The pictures, the skin and muscle from Henry's right jaw scorched away. She opened her mouth and threw up onto her lap.

"Oh, shit." Elizabeth opened the car door and stumbled out, getting vomit all over the leather seat, door, floor, everything. "Oh God, I'm making a mess. I'm sorry, I'm so sorry," she said, half sitting, half falling down onto the concrete. She tried to say she was fine, just needed water, but Shannon fussed over her, doing mother-y/doctor-y things—pulse-checking, forehead-feeling—before leaving, saying she'd be right back. After a while—two minutes? ten?—Elizabeth saw security cameras pointed her way, and she pictured herself, sprawled on the ground in her suit and heels, covered in vomit, and she started laughing. Violently. Hysterically. By the time Shannon returned with paper towels, Elizabeth realized she was crying, which was surprising; she didn't remember transitioning from one to the other. Shannon, bless her, said nothing, just cleaned up methodically while Elizabeth sat, laughing and crying alternately, sometimes together.

On the drive back, as Elizabeth sat in the empty state of hypercalmness that follows a violent purge, Shannon said, "Where was all that emotion earlier today?"

Elizabeth didn't answer. Just shrugged slightly and looked out at the cows—must've been twenty—crowding around a skinny lone tree in a field.

"You do realize the entire jury thinks you don't give a damn what happened to your son, right? They'd love to send you to death row right now. Is that what you were going for there?"

Elizabeth wondered if the mostly white cows with black spots—Jersey cows? Holsteins?—were cooler than the dark brown ones. "I was just doing what you wanted," Elizabeth said. "Don't let them get to you, you said. Calm and collected."

"I meant, don't act crazy. Don't yell or throw shit. I didn't mean become a robot. I've never seen anyone so stoic, and definitely not through evidence about their own child's death. It was downright creepy. It's okay to show people you're hurting."

"Why? What difference would that make? You've seen the evidence. I don't stand a chance."

Shannon looked at Elizabeth, bit her lip, and swerved off the road and slammed on the brakes. "If you think that, why are we doing this? I mean, why hire me and plead not guilty and put on a defense at all?"

Elizabeth looked down. The truth was, it all stemmed from the research she'd started the day after Henry's funeral. There were so many methods—hanging, drowning, carbon-monoxide inhaling, wrist-slitting, and on and on. She'd made a pro/con list and was wavering between sleeping pills (pro: painless; con: death uncertain—discovery/resuscitation risk) and gun (pro: death certain; con: waiting period to buy?) when the police cleared the protesters and arrested her. When the prosecutor announced he'd be seeking the death penalty, that's when she realized: going through the trial would be the best atonement for her sin—the irrevocable, unforgivable action she took that day during one moment of anger and hatred, the moment that played over and over in her mind, morning and night, awake and asleep, and tore away at her sanity. To publicly and officially be blamed for Henry's death, to be forced to sit through the details of his suffering, then to be killed by poisons injected directly into her blood. The exquisite torture of it all—wouldn't that be better than some easy, blink-and-it's-over death?

But Elizabeth couldn't say that. She couldn't tell Shannon how it felt today, forcing herself to look everyone in the eye, listen to every word, take in every exhibit, all the while keeping her face still, afraid the slightest movement might set off a domino reaction of emotion. The cauterizing shame of a hundred people pelting their stares of judgment at her like poison darts. Accept and absorb the blame. Gulp it down, more and more, until every cell in her body was bursting. She hadn't just been ready for it; she'd craved it, relished it, couldn't wait for more of it.

Elizabeth said nothing, and Shannon, apparently interpreting this as silent surrender, resumed driving. After a minute, Shannon said, "Oh, good news. Victor's not testifying. He's not coming at all."

Elizabeth nodded. She knew why this was good, why Shannon had worried about a grief-stricken father affecting the jury, but his absence wasn't something she could celebrate. He hadn't contacted her at all since her arrest, which she'd expected, and, yes, she knew he had a busy life in California with his new house and new wife and new kids, but she'd assumed he'd at least show up at the trial for his son's murder. She felt bile rise and snake around her chest, choking her heart. Poor Henry. Born to two such pathetic parents. One responsible for hurting and killing him, the other too worthless to give a shit.

Shannon's phone rang. An obviously expected call—she answered with "You got it? Read it to me." Elizabeth breathed in deep. The stench of vomit stung her nose, and she opened the window, which made it worse, the mix of sweet manure from outside and sour vomit smelling like rotting Chinese food. She closed the window just as the call ended, and said to Shannon, "You should get the car cleaned. Put it on my bill. Although, can you imagine your billing partner going, 'Why are there car-vomit-cleaning charges under murder-trial expenses?'" Elizabeth laughed. Shannon didn't.

"Listen. One of the Yoos' neighbors was in court." A hint of a smile tugged at the corners of Shannon's lips. "He came forward with something he didn't think was important until today. So I put the team on it all day, and we found something. I didn't want to tell you until we confirmed it."

Somewhere outside, cows were mooing in unison. Elizabeth swallowed. Her ears clicked. "The protesters? You finally got something? I told you to focus on them, I knew they—"

Shannon shook her head no. "Not them. Matt. He's lying. I can prove it. Elizabeth, I have evidence that someone else deliberately set the fire."

THE TRIAL: DAY TWO

○

Tuesday, August 18, 2009

MATT

H E THOUGHT TODAY WOULD BE EASIER than yesterday. Once the story was told, he'd feel purged, like puking after overdrinking.

But walking up, taking the stand again, it had been harder to raise his head. How many people were wondering why he, a healthy young man, a fucking doctor, for Christ's sake, had allowed a little boy to be burned alive in front of him?

"Good morning, Dr. Thompson, I'm Shannon Haug, Elizabeth Ward's attorney."

Matt nodded.

Shannon said, "I want you to know how sorry I am for the horrible things you've experienced. And I have to apologize in advance for making you recall all that again, sometimes in great detail. My goal is not to upset you, but simply to find the truth. If you need to stop at any time, just let me know. Okay?"

Matt felt his jaw relax and, despite himself, he smiled. Abe rolled his eyes. Abe did not like Shannon. He'd described her as a "bigwig from a fancy litigation factory," and Matt had expected a TV-show-lawyer type: hair in one of those French buns, suit with pencil-thin skirt, stilettos, mysterious smile, gorgeous as hell. Instead, Shannon Haug looked and sounded like a kind aunt, totally benign, her suit wrinkled and loose, her shoulder-length graying hair a matted blob. Nurturing, with a generous bust—less femme-fatale vixen, more wet nurse. "She's the enemy," Abe had warned, but Matt craved this, a woman's gentle pampering, and he clung to it.

"Now," Shannon said, "let's start with some basics. Easy yes-no stuff. Did you ever see Elizabeth set fire anywhere around Miracle Submarine?"

"No."

"Ever see her smoking, or even just holding a cigarette?"

"No."

"Ever see anyone else affiliated with HBOT smoking?"

Matt felt his face flush. He had to tread lightly here. "Pak didn't allow smoking at HBOT. We were all clear on that."

Shannon smiled, stepped closer. "Is that a no to my question? Have you seen anyone on Miracle Submarine's premises with cigarettes, matches, anything like that?"

"Yes. I mean, my answer is no," Matt said. He wasn't lying, not technically—the creek was outside "the premises"—but still, his heart beat faster.

"To your knowledge, does anyone affiliated with Miracle Submarine smoke?"

Mary had once said that Camels were Pak's favorite. But, he reminded himself, he wasn't supposed to know that. "I couldn't say. I've only seen them at HBOT, where smoking's prohibited."

"Fair enough." Shannon shrugged and walked to her table, like this was a perfunctory checklist of questions she hadn't expected anything from. Halfway there, she turned mid-step and said in a throwaway tone, "By the way, do *you* smoke?"

Matt felt a tingling in his missing fingers, could almost feel the thin roll of a Camel suspended between them. "Me?" He hoped his chuckle didn't sound as fake as it felt in his mouth. "The number of smoker-lung X-rays I see, I'd need a death wish to smoke."

She smiled. Thankfully, she was trying to butter him up and didn't call him on his nonanswer. She picked up something from her table and sauntered back to him. "Back to Elizabeth. Ever see her hit Henry? Harm him in any way?"

"No."

"Ever see her yell at him?"

"No."

"How about neglect? Tattered clothes, junk food—anything?"

Matt pictured Henry in socks with holes, eating Skittles, and almost laughed; Elizabeth would never let him near anything not organic, dye-free, *and* sugar-free. "Definitely not."

"To the contrary, she put a great deal of effort into Henry's care, isn't that fair to say?"

Matt raised his eyebrows in a half shrug. "I suppose."

"She checked his eardrums with an otoscope before and after every dive, right?"

"Yes."

"No other parents did that, correct?"

"No. I mean, correct."

"She read books with him before the dives?"

"Yes."

"She gave him all homemade snacks?"

"Yes. Well, that's what she said, anyway."

Shannon looked at him, tilting her head. "Elizabeth made everything from scratch because Henry had severe food allergies, isn't that right?"

"Again, that's what she said."

Shannon stepped closer and tilted her head the other way, as if studying an abstract painting whose proper orientation she could not determine. "Dr. Thompson, are you accusing Elizabeth of lying about Henry's allergies?"

Matt felt his cheeks redden. "Not necessarily. I just don't know for a fact."

"Well, let me correct that." Shannon handed him a document. "Tell us what that is."

Matt skimmed. "It's a lab report confirming Henry's severe allergies to peanuts, fish, shellfish, dairy, and eggs." Abe looked at him and shook his head.

"Let's try this again. Elizabeth gave Henry homemade snacks she made sure were allergen-free, correct?"

"That appears to be correct."

"Do you recall an incident involving peanuts, Henry's most severe allergy?"

"Yes."

"What happened?"

"TJ had peanut butter on his hands, from a sandwich. He got some on the hatch handle, going in. Henry grabbed the same spot, and luckily, Elizabeth noticed."

"How did she react?"

She'd freaked out, screaming, "Henry could *die*!" and acting like the brown glob was a fucking cobra. But wouldn't that play into the devoted-mother routine Elizabeth's lawyer was putting on? "Elizabeth asked the boys to wash up, and Pak cleaned the chamber." He made it sound like nothing, but it had been an *ordeal*, Elizabeth demanding that TJ brush his teeth, wash his face, and even change his clothes.

"If Elizabeth hadn't noticed the peanut butter, what would've happened?"

Before Shannon even finished the question, Abe stood, the screech of his chair scraping the floor announcing his objection like a trumpet call. "Objection. If that doesn't call for speculation, I don't know what does."

Shannon said, "Your Honor, a little leeway? I'm getting somewhere, I promise."

The judge said, "Get there fast. Overruled."

Abe sat and moved his chair, the slamming sound of the chair legs the equivalent of a petulant teenager's door slam. Shannon smiled at Abe the way an amused mother might, then turned to Matt. "Again, Doctor, what would've happened if Elizabeth hadn't noticed Henry touching the peanut butter?"

Matt shrugged. "It's hard to know."

"Let's think it through together. Henry bit his nails. You'd seen that, right?"

"Yes."

"So it's fair to say peanut butter probably would've gotten in his mouth during the dive?"

"I suppose so, yes."

"Doctor, given the severity of Henry's peanut allergy, what would've happened?"

"The airway swells and shuts off, and you can't breathe. But Henry had an EpiPen, epinephrine, which counteracts that."

"Was there an EpiPen in the chamber?"

"No. Since food's not allowed, Pak had Elizabeth leave it outside."

"How long does it take to depressurize and open the hatch?"

"Pak usually depressurized slowly, for comfort, but he could do it quickly if necessary, in a minute or so."

"One full minute with no air. If you wait more than a minute to inject epinephrine, can it fail?"

"It's not likely, but yes, that *could* happen."

"So Henry could've died?"

Matt sighed. "I doubt that. I could've done a tracheotomy." He turned to the jurors. "You can make a small incision in the larynx to relieve an obstruction in the airway. You can even do it with a ballpoint pen, in an emergency."

"Was there a ballpoint pen inside?"

Matt felt his cheeks redden again. "No."

"And you didn't happen to have a scalpel, either, I'm guessing?"

"No."

"So again, Henry could've died? Is that a possibility, Doctor?"

"A *very* small possibility."

"And Elizabeth prevented that. Made sure that couldn't come close to happening, isn't that right?"

Matt sighed. "Yes," he had to say. He waited for the logical next question, *If Elizabeth wanted Henry dead, wouldn't it have been easier to say nothing about the peanut butter?* No, he'd say, and point out again that there was no real risk of Henry dying from that, and certainly no guarantee, like when a freaking fireball exploded in your face. But Shannon didn't ask the question; she looked from the jury to Elizabeth with her gentle-auntie face, waiting for them to arrive at that conclusion on their own, and Matt could see the jurors' faces softening. He could see them looking at Elizabeth, her still-stoic face, wondering if maybe it wasn't that she was cold and uncaring, but just tired. Too tired to move a muscle.

As if to accentuate this theme, Shannon said, "Doctor, you've told Elizabeth she's the most devoted mother you've ever met, right?"

True; he'd said that. But he'd meant it as criticism, telling her to ease up, for God's sake. To tell her she'd gone beyond helicoptering to direct controlling. Puppeteer-parenting. But what could he say? Yes, I said that, but I was being sarcastic because I hate devoted mothers? "Yes," he finally said. "I thought she spent a lot of effort *acting* like she was devoted to Henry."

Shannon gazed at him, the corners of her mouth turning upward slowly as if she'd just figured something out. "Doctor, I'm curious. Do you like Elizabeth? I mean, before the accident. Did you ever like her?"

Matt marveled at that, Shannon's brilliance at that moment, asking a question with no good answer. *Yes, I liked her* would continue Elizabeth's humanization, and *No, I never did* would make him looked biased. "I didn't really know her too well," he finally said.

Shannon smiled, the forgiving smile of a mother who's decided to let slide a toddler's obvious lie. "What about . . ." She scanned the gallery, the way stand-up comics scan the audience for victims ". . . Pak Yoo? Do you think *he* liked Elizabeth?"

Something about this question made Matt flinch. Maybe it was Shannon's tone—too casual, deliberately so, as if the question were a throwaway. As if she couldn't care less about the answer, only that she got to bring up Pak at an unexpected moment, in an unexpected way.

Matt matched Shannon's this-doesn't-matter-too-much tone and said, "I'm not great at reading other people's minds. You'd have to ask *Pak*."

"Fair enough. Let me rephrase. Did he ever say anything negative about Elizabeth?"

Matt shook his head. "I've never heard him say anything negative about Elizabeth." And that was true: he'd heard about Pak's annoyance with her from Mary frequently enough, but never directly from Pak. He blinked and continued. "Pak is professional. He wouldn't gossip with patients, especially about another patient."

"But you weren't just another patient, right? You're family friends."

They may have been "family friends," but Pak wasn't particularly friendly. Matt suspected that, like many Korean men he knew, Pak disapproved of white guys being with Korean women. He said, "No. I was a client. That's it."

"So he never discussed, say, fire insurance with you?"

"What?" Where the fuck had that come from? "No. Fire insurance? Why would we discuss fire insurance?"

Shannon ignored his questions. Just stepped toward him, looked straight into his eyes, and said, "Has *anyone* affiliated with Miracle Submarine, including your family, ever discussed fire insurance with you?"

"Absolutely not."

"Ever hear anyone discuss or even mention it?"

"No." Matt was getting pissed now. And a little scared, though he couldn't say why.

"Do you know which company insures Miracle Submarine?"

"No."

"Ever place a call to Miracle Submarine's insurer?"

"What? Why would I . . . ?" Matt felt something itch in his missing knuckles. He wanted to punch something. Maybe Shannon's face. "I just told you, I don't even know what company it is."

"So it's your sworn testimony that you never called Potomac Mutual Insurance Company the week before the explosion, is that correct?"

"What? No, of course I didn't."

"You're positive?"

"One hundred percent."

Shannon's whole face seemed to lift—her eyes, mouth, even ears—and she walked—no, she *strutted*—to the defense table, picked up a document, strutted back to him, and thrust it at him. "Do you recognize this?"

A list of phone numbers, dates, and times. His own number at the top. "It's my phone bill. My cell."

"Please read the highlighted item."

"August 21, 2008. 8:58 a.m. Four minutes. Outgoing. 800-555-0199. Potomac Mutual Insurance." Matt looked up. "I don't understand. You're saying *I* made this call?"

"Not so much me as that document." Shannon looked amused, almost triumphant.

Matt read again. 8:58 a.m. Maybe he'd misdialed. But four minutes? "Maybe I heard an ad for an insurance deal and I called for a quote?" He didn't remember doing that, but it was a year ago. Who knew how many random, boneheaded things he did on a whim on a daily basis that were so insignificant he couldn't remember them a week later, much less a year?

"So you did make this call, but in response to an ad?"

Matt looked to Janine. She had both hands to her mouth. "No. I mean, maybe. I don't remember this call, and I'm trying to figure out . . . I mean, I've never even heard of this company. Why would I call them?"

Shannon smiled. "It just so happens that Potomac Mutual logs all incoming calls." She handed documents to Abe and the judge. "Your Honor, I apologize for the lack of notice, but we found out about this call yesterday and only got the log last night."

Matt stared at Abe, willing him to see the *What-the-fuck-do-I-do* question on his face, rescue him somehow, but Abe kept reading and frowning. "Any objections, Mr. Patterley?" the judge said. Abe mumbled, "No," still reading.

Finally, Shannon held out the document to Matt. He wanted to snatch it from her hand, but he waited, managing not to even look at it until she asked him to read it out loud. Under the heading with the date, time, wait length (<1 minute), and total call length (4 minutes), it read:

NAME: Declined to give.

SUBJECT: Fire insurance—Arson

SUMMARY: Caller interested in whether all our fire policies pay out
             in cases of arson. Caller happy when told that arson
             coverage included in all policies, with exception only
             if policyholder involved in planning/committing arson.

Matt read calmly, with the clinical tone of someone *not* about to be accused of conspiracy to commit arson, and looked up when done. Shannon said nothing—just looked at him, as if waiting for him to break the silence. *I had nothing to do with this*, he reminded himself, then said, "I guess it wasn't for a quote, after all." No one laughed.

"Let me ask again, Doctor," Shannon said. "You made an anonymous call to Miracle Submarine's insurer the week before the explosion asking if they'll pay out if someone deliberately burns it down, didn't you?"

"Absolutely not," Matt said.

"Then how do you explain that document in your hand?"

A good question, one with no good answer. The air felt dense with anticipation, too dense to breathe in, and he couldn't think. "Maybe it's a mistake. They got my number crossed with someone else's."

Shannon moved her head in an exaggerated nod. "Sure, that makes sense. Some random person calls, and by some incredible coincidence, both the phone *and* insurance companies get the number wrong, and by another incredible coincidence, you end up being the star witness in a murder trial where, lo and behold, the deaths are caused by arson. Do I have that right?" Some of the jurors tittered.

Matt sighed. "All I know is I didn't make that call. Someone must've used my phone."

Matt expected Shannon to mock him again, but she looked satisfied. Interested. She said, "Let's explore that. This was last August, on a Thursday morning, at 8:58. Was your phone lost or stolen around then?"

"No."

"Anyone use it? Borrow it because they forgot theirs, that type of thing?"

"No."

"So who had access to your phone around 8:58 a.m.?"

"I was definitely at HBOT. I never missed a morning dive. The official dive time is 9:00, but we'd start earlier if everyone's there, and later if someone's late. It's been a year, so I don't remember when we started that particular morning."

"So let's say you started late that day, say at 9:10. Could someone have used your phone without you knowing?"

Matt shook his head. "I don't see how. I either left my phone in the car, which is locked, or I kept it with me and put it in the cubby right before the dive started."

"And what if it started early—say, 8:55? By 8:58, you're in the chamber, along with the others, including Elizabeth. Who could've used your phone?"

Matt looked at Shannon, the excitement plain in the way her eyebrows lifted in anticipation, a smile curling her lips, and he realized: this entire line of questioning had been for show. She'd never thought for a moment he'd made that call. She'd just made him think it so he'd become rattled, desperate to think up an alternative suspect to hand to her on a platter. The obvious alternative. The only one, really.

"For the morning dives, the only person in the barn," Matt said, "was Pak." This was hardly a secret. But still, saying it out loud felt like betrayal. He couldn't look at Pak.

"So Pak Yoo had access to your phone during your morning dives, which sometimes started before 8:58, the time of the call in question, is that correct?"

"Yes," Matt said.

"Dr. Thompson, is it a fair reading of your testimony that Pak Yoo must've called his insurance company anonymously, using your cell phone, to ask whether his fire insurance policy will pay out if someone else sets fire to his business, something which is alleged to have happened a few days after? Is that a fair summary?"

Put it like that, and Matt wanted desperately to say, No, Pak didn't do this, Elizabeth did, and now you're taking some fucking call to say . . . what, that Pak blew up his own business? Killed his patients for money? It was ridiculous. He saw Pak during the fire, saw his desperation to save his patients, never mind the risk of injuries and even death to himself. But the relief of knowing that Pak was the target, not him—it was overwhelming, the relief. Matt's respect for Pak, his firm belief in Pak's innocence, his need to see Elizabeth punished—his relief engulfed all these things, submerged and smothered them away. Besides, answering yes was nothing more than a logical extension of everything else he'd already admitted. He wasn't saying Pak set the fire. There were four thousand steps between this phone call and the explosion.

So Matt told himself it was no big deal and said, "Yes." He heard buzzing, the sound of horseflies feasting on a carcass. Or maybe it was the whispered murmurings of the spectators in the back.

Pak's face was red—with shame or anger, Matt couldn't tell. Shannon said, "Doctor, are you aware that, on the night of the explosion, Elizabeth found a note by the creek, written on paper with the H-Mart logo on it, saying, 'This needs to end. We need to meet tonight, 8:15'?"

It was automatic, the reaction. His eyes zoomed to Mary like metal to a magnet. He blinked, hoped no one caught his mistake. He moved his gaze around, like he was scanning the whole Korean clan. "No, I never heard that. I know that paper, though." Matt turned to the jury. "H-Mart is a Korean supermarket. We shop there sometimes."

"Isn't it true that Pak Yoo always used that notepad?"

Matt had to force himself not to sigh in relief. Shannon thought the note was from Pak. It hadn't even crossed her mind that Matt had written it. And Mary—she wasn't a factor at all. "Yes, Pak used it," Matt said.

Shannon slowly turned her gaze to Pak, then back to Matt. "What is your understanding of where he was at 8:15 that night, until the explosion ten minutes later?"

Something about the way she said "your understanding" unnerved Matt. "Um, Pak was in the barn." Was there any question about that?

"How do you know that?"

He had to think. How *did* he know, other than just assuming it to be true because that's what everyone said? All the Yoos were in the barn, they said. When the DVD died, Pak sent Young to their house to find batteries. She took too long, so Mary went to help, but she noticed something behind the barn, walked there, and *boom*. But if Pak did this . . .

could the Yoos have been lying? Covering for him? Then again, if he'd set the fire, Pak wouldn't have risked his life in the rescue, and he undoubtedly would've made sure Mary was nowhere nearby. No. Matt said, "I know because he supervised the dive. He sealed us in, he talked to me, and after the explosion, he opened the hatch and got us out."

"Ah, the hatch opening. You said earlier, it takes as little as one minute to depressurize and open the hatch. Correct?"

"Yes."

"So if he'd been present, the hatch should've opened one minute after the explosion?"

"Yes."

"Doctor, let's try something. Here's a stopwatch. I'd like you to close your eyes and go through in your mind everything that happened from the explosion until the hatch opening. Then stop the timer. Could you do that?"

Matt nodded and took the stopwatch, a digital one that counted in tenths of seconds. He laughed at the ridiculousness, trying to remember a year later whether the incineration of a boy's head took 48.8 seconds or 48.9 seconds. He clicked START, closed his eyes, and went through it. The face-blink-fire, the thrashing, the flames whooshing from the shirt around his hands. When he reached the screech of the hatch opening, he clicked STOP. 2:36.8. "Two and a half minutes. But this hardly seems reliable," he said.

Shannon held up a folded piece of paper. "This is a report from the prosecution's own accident-reconstruction expert, including an estimate of the time between the explosion and the hatch opening. Would you read it, Doctor?"

He took the paper and unfolded it. Highlighted in fluorescent yellow, buried in the middle of the report, were five words. "Minimum two, maximum three minutes."

"So you and the report agree," Shannon said. "The hatch opened more than two minutes after the explosion, more than a full minute after it should have if Pak Yoo had been present."

"Again," Matt said. "This doesn't seem very scientific."

Shannon looked at him with amused pity, the way teens look at kids who still believe in the tooth fairy. "Now, the other reason you thought Pak Yoo was in the barn: you talked through the intercom. Yesterday, you testified, quote, 'It was chaos in the chamber, very noisy, so I couldn't really hear.' Do you remember that?"

Matt swallowed. "Yes."

"And since you couldn't really hear, you assumed it was Pak Yoo, but you can't know for sure, isn't that right?"

"No, I couldn't hear all the words, but I heard the voice. I know it was Pak," Matt said, but even saying it, he wondered if that was true. Was he just being stubborn?

Shannon looked at him like she was sad for him. "Doctor," she said, her voice softer, "are you aware that Robert Spinum, who lives by the Yoos, has signed an affidavit that he was outside on a call from 8:11 until 8:20 that night, and that for the entirety of that call, he saw Pak Yoo a quarter mile *outside* the barn?"

Abe stood immediately, objecting—something about lack of foundation—but Matt focused on the gasp from behind Abe. From Young, with her hands over her mouth. She looked terrified. But not surprised.

Shannon said, "Your Honor, I was merely asking if the witness happened to be aware of this development, but I'm happy to withdraw my question. Mr. Spinum is standing by, ready to testify, and we will definitely be calling him at our earliest opportunity." She narrowed her eyes at Matt as she said this last part, as if in a threat, and said, "Doctor, let me ask again. You can't be *sure* that the voice you heard over the intercom was Pak Yoo's voice, isn't that right?"

Matt rubbed the stump of his missing index finger. It stung and throbbed, which, strangely, felt nice. "I thought it was, but I guess I can't be a hundred percent sure."

"Given this, plus your testimony regarding the hatch opening, isn't it possible that Pak Yoo was not inside for at least ten minutes prior to the explosion? That, in fact, no one was supervising the dive?"

Matt glanced over at Pak and Young, both looking down, their bodies slumped. He licked his lips. He tasted salt. "Yes," he said. "Yes, it's possible."

YOUNG

I T SURPRISED HER HOW QUIET IT GOT when Shannon finished her questions. No one whispered or coughed. The air conditioners didn't sputter or hum. As if someone had pressed PAUSE and everyone froze in place, their heads turned to Pak. Frowning at him with revulsion, the way they had at Elizabeth earlier. From hero to murderer in an hour. How had that happened? Like a magic show, but without the *zap* to mark the moment of mutation.

There should've been a bang, or maybe thunder. Life-changing disasters came with loud noises, didn't they? Sirens, alarms, *something* to signal the break in reality: normal one minute, crazy-altered remnant the next. Young wanted to run up to grab the gavel and bang it down—crack open the silence, right in half. *All rise. Commonwealth of Virginia versus Young Yoo.* For actually believing that her family's troubles were over. For being that stupid, after seeing again and again how quickly things can fall apart, like a tower of matchsticks.

When Abe stood, Young had a moment of residual hope, of expecting him to ask Matt how dare he lie, how dare he implicate an innocent man. But Abe spoke in a defeated voice, asking perfunctory questions about who else uses the H-Mart paper and how Matt couldn't be sure of his explosion-to-hatch-opening estimate, and Young felt her body deflate, air rushing out of her like a punctured ball.

Young wanted to stand up and scream. Scream at the jurors that Pak was honorable, a man who literally threw himself into fire for his patients. Scream at Elizabeth's lawyer that he wouldn't risk killing himself and his daughter for money. Scream at Abe to fix this, that she'd believed him that every scrap of evidence pointed to Elizabeth.

The judge announced lunch recess, and the courtroom doors creaked open. Young heard it then. The sound of hammering in the distance. Thunk-clang, thunk-clang, matching the tha-dunk of her heartbeat pulsating in her temples, sending blood whooshing through her eardrums—resonant and magnified, as if underwater. Probably workers in vineyards. She'd seen them earlier, piling wooden posts by the hill. Stakes for new vines. There must've been loud bangs all morning. She just hadn't heard them.

○

THEY WALKED FROM COURT to Abe's office in single file—Abe in front, then Young pushing Pak's wheelchair, Mary in back. The line they formed, led by a hulking man, and the crowds unzipping as they approached, as if repelled—Young felt like a criminal being paraded by an executioner through town, its people gawking and judging.

Abe marched them into a yellow building, down a dark hall, and into a conference room, and said to wait while he met with his staff. When the door closed, Young stepped closer to Pak. For twenty years, he'd towered above her, and it felt strange being above him now, seeing the hair whorl on top of his head. She felt braver. As if the act of tilting her face down opened some dam that usually blocked her words. "I knew this would happen," she said. "We should've told the truth from the beginning. I told you we shouldn't lie."

Pak frowned and gestured with his chin toward Mary, who was looking out the window.

Young ignored him. What did it matter what Mary heard? She already knew they'd lied. They'd had to tell her—she'd been part of the story he concocted. "Mr. Spinum saw you," Young said. "Everyone knows we were lying."

"No one knows anything," Pak said in a whisper, even though no one nearby could understand their rapid Korean. "It's our word against his. You, me, and Mary against an old, racist man with thick glasses."

Young wanted to grab his shoulders, to yell and shake him so hard that her words would penetrate his skull and rattle around his brain like a pinball. Instead, she dug her nails into her palms and forced her words to be quiet, having learned long ago that calm words penetrated her husband's attention better than loud ones. "We can't keep lying," she said. "We didn't do anything wrong. You just went out to check on the protesters, to protect us, and you left me in charge. Abe will understand that."

"And what about the part where no one was there, leaving everyone sealed up in a burning chamber, unattended. You think he'll understand *that*?"

Young slumped into the chair next to Pak. How many times had she wished she could go back and redo that moment? "That's my fault, not yours, and I can't live with you taking the blame to protect me. I feel like a criminal, lying to everyone. I can't do this anymore."

Pak put his hand on top of hers. Green veins meandered through the back of his hand and seemed to continue on hers. "We're not the guilty ones here. We didn't set the fire. It doesn't matter where we were—we couldn't have done anything to stop the explosion. Henry and Kitt would've died even if we were both there."

"But if I'd turned off the oxygen in time—"

Pak shook his head. "I keep telling you, there's residual oxygen in the tubes."

"But the flames wouldn't have been as intense, so if you'd opened the door right away, maybe we could have saved them."

"You don't know that," Pak said, his voice gentle and calm. He reached under her chin and raised her face to meet his gaze. "The fact is, if I'd been there, I wouldn't have turned off the oxygen at 8:20, either. You have to remember—TJ took off his helmet. Whenever he did that, I added extra time, to make up for the lost oxygen—"

"But—"

"—which means," Pak continued, "that the oxygen would have been on, and the fire and explosion exactly the same, if I'd been there."

Young closed her eyes and sighed. How many times had they gone around this same issue? How many hypotheticals and justifications could they throw at each other? "If we did nothing wrong, why not tell the truth?"

Pak clutched her hand, hard. It hurt. "We need to stick to our story. I left the barn. You're not licensed. The policy is clear—breaking regulations like that is automatically considered negligence. And negligence means no payout."

"Insurance!" Young said, forgetting to keep her voice down. "Who cares about that?"

"We need that money. Without it, we have nothing. Everything we've sacrificed, Mary's future—all gone."

"Listen." Young knelt in front of him. Perhaps the act of looking down would help him take in her words. "They think you lied to cover up murder. That lawyer's trying to send you to prison in Elizabeth's place. Don't you see how much worse this is? You could be executed!"

Mary gasped. Young had thought Mary was off in her own world, as she often was, but she was facing them. Pak glared at Young. "You've got to stop being melodramatic. Now you've got her scared for no reason."

Young reached to squeeze her arms around Mary. She waited for Mary to shake her off, but Mary stayed still. "We're worried about you," Young said to Pak. "I'm being realistic, and you're not taking this seriously enough."

"I'm taking it seriously. I'm just being calm. You getting hysterical, gasping in the courtroom—did you see how everyone turned to look? *That's* the kind of thing that makes me look guilty. Changing our story now is the worst thing we could do."

The door opened. Pak glanced at Abe and continued in Korean, saying, "No one say anything. I'll do the talking," but in a relaxed tone, like he was talking about the weather.

Abe looked feverish. His face, normally the color of oiled mahogany, was a blotched russet, and a film of half-dried sweat matted his skin. When his eyes met Young's, instead of his usual toothy smile, he looked away quickly as if in embarrassment. "Young and Mary, I need to talk to Pak alone. You can wait down the hall. There's lunch there."

"I want to stay. With my husband," Young said, and put her hand on Pak's shoulder, expecting a hint of gratitude for her support—a smile or nod, or maybe his hand on hers, like the night before. Instead, Pak frowned and said in Korean, "Just do what you're told." His words were quiet, almost whispers, but they had the sound of a command.

Young dropped her hand. She'd been foolish to think that just because of one moment of tenderness last night, Pak was no longer what he'd always been: a traditional Korean man who expected nothing but meek obedience from his wife in public. She left with Mary.

They were halfway down the hall when the door shut behind them. Mary stopped, looked around, and tiptoed back to the conference room.

"What are you doing?" Young said in a whispered yell.

Mary put her finger to her lips in a silent *shhhhh* and put her ear to the door.

Young looked down the hallway. No one else was around. She ran on tiptoes to join Mary and listen in.

There was no sound, which surprised Young. Abe was one of those people who didn't like silence. She couldn't remember a meeting that didn't overflow with Abe's words strung into one continuous sound with no pauses. So what did this mean, this silence? Was Abe being guarded and slow, carefully considering every word, because Pak was now a murder suspect?

Abe finally said, "Many things came out today. Troubling things." His words had the heft and forced evenness of a requiem.

Pak spoke immediately, as if he'd been waiting to speak. "I am suspect now?"

Young expected Abe to protest, *No! Of course not!* But there was nothing. Just the soft crunch-crunch of Mary gnawing on a thick strand of her hair, a bad habit that started their first year in America.

After a moment, Abe said, "You're no more a suspect than anyone else."

What did that mean? Abe said things like this a lot, things that were meant to be reassuring but, really, when you thought about it, left wiggle room the size of a cathedral. Like after the police investigated Pak for negligence and Abe said, "You're as good as cleared." You were either cleared or not—how could anything other than actually cleared be as good as cleared?

Abe continued. "There are some . . . inconsistencies. The insurance call, for one. Did you make it?"

"No," Pak said. Young wanted to shout at Pak to elaborate, to say he had no reason to call because he already knew the answer. Before signing, she'd helped him translate the policy, and they'd laughed over the idiocy of American contracts taking multiple paragraphs to say obvious things even children know. She'd specifically pointed out the arson section. ("Two pages saying they won't pay if you burn down your own property or get someone else to!")

"You should know," Abe said, "the company's retrieving the recording of the call."

"Good. That will prove I am not caller." Pak sounded indignant.

Abe said, "Did anyone else have access to Matt's phone during the morning dive?"

"No. Mary left house at 8:30 for SAT class. Young cleaned up breakfast. I was always alone for first dive, every day. But . . ." Pak's voice trailed off.

"But what?"

"One day, Matt said he had Janine's telephone, and Janine had his telephone. They exchanged, by mistake." Young remembered. Matt had been upset; he'd almost skipped the dive to get his phone back right away.

"Was this the day of the call? The week before the explosion?"

"I am not sure."

There was a long silence, then Abe said, "Did Janine know who your policy was with?"

"Yes," Pak said. "She recommended the company. Same one her office use."

"Interesting." Something about this last exchange seemed to break Abe's caution; his normal fast, up-and-down cadence—the vocal equivalent of merry-go-round horses—returned. "Now, this other business of your neighbor. Did you leave the barn that last dive?"

"No," Pak said. His unequivocal denial made Young flinch, wonder who she'd married, this man who could lie so effectively, absolutely, with no hesitation.

"Your neighbor says he saw you outside for ten minutes before the explosion."

"He is lying or his memory is wrong. I check electric lines that day, many times, check if power company is there to fix. But always during breaks. Never during dives." Pak sounded confident, almost arrogant.

Abe, his stiffness fully broken, said, "Listen, Pak. If there's anything you're not telling me, now's the time. You suffered a major trauma. It's enough to make anyone fuzzy. It's natural to get a few things wrong. You wouldn't believe how many witnesses swear they remember perfectly and tell me X, then I tell them something somebody else said, and *bam*, they remember something they'd completely forgotten. The important thing is to come clean now, before you've testified. You just tell the jury everything the first time, it'll be fine. You wait until later, though, that won't fly. Suddenly, the jury wonders, *What's he hiding? Why'd he change his story?* Then *bam*, Shannon screams there's their reasonable doubt, and everything falls apart."

"That will not happen. I am telling the truth." Pak's voice rose, got louder.

"You have to realize," Abe said, "your neighbor's very convincing. He was on the phone, telling his son about you fooling with the balloons in the power lines and whatnot. The son verified it. The phone records match up. Your story and theirs can't both be true."

"They are wrong," Pak said.

"Now, what I can't figure out," Abe continued as if Pak hadn't spoken, "is why you'd fight this. That's a golden alibi right there, a neutral party verifying you were nowhere near where the fire started. Shannon can yell and scream all day long about you not opening the hatch, but none of that changes the fact that Elizabeth set the fire. So for my purposes, getting that woman in prison, I'm fine with what Spinum says. What I'm not fine with is you lying about it. Because you lying about *anything* makes me wonder what you're covering up, you know?"

Mary started chewing her hair again, the sound of her teeth gnawing on her hair growing louder in the silence, more insistent, matching the rhythm of Young's crescendoing heartbeat in her ears.

"I was in the barn," Pak said.

Mary shook her head. Her face was one big frown, scrunched in agitation, and the scar across her cheek popped out, puffy and white. "We need to do something. He needs help," Mary said in English.

"Your father told us to do nothing. We must do what he says," Young said in Korean.

Mary looked at her, her mouth open as if to say something but unable to produce a sound. Young recognized the look. Right after Pak came to America, when he told them he'd decided to move them to Miracle Creek, Mary had fought with him, cried and yelled that she didn't want to move to the middle of nowhere where she knew no one. When Pak scolded her for disrespecting her parents' authority, she'd turned to Young. "Tell him," she'd said. "I know you agree with me. You have a voice. Why can't you use it?"

Young had wanted to. She'd wanted to shout that they were in America now, where she'd spent four years parenting, running a store, and handling finances all on her own, and Pak barely knew them anymore and certainly didn't know America half as well as she did, so who was he to order her what to do? But the way he'd looked—bewildered anxiety blooming on his face, like a boy at a new school, wondering where he fit in—she'd seen how much the years of separation had stripped from him, his desperation to reestablish his role as head of the family. She'd ached for him. "I trust you to decide what's best for our family," she'd told Pak and seen on Mary's face the same look as now: a mix of disappointment, contempt, and, worst of all, pity for her powerlessness. She'd felt small, as if she were the child and Mary the adult.

Young wanted to explain all this to her daughter now. She reached out for Mary's hand, to guide her away, where they could talk. But before she could do anything, say anything, Mary turned, opened the door, and said in a loud, clear voice, "It was me."

○

THE ANGER THAT Mary had acted like a child—without thinking first, with no regard for consequences—would come later. In the moment, though, what bubbled to the surface was envy. Envy that her daughter, a *teenager*, had the courage to act.

"What was you?" Abe said.

"Who Mr. Spinum saw, that was me," Mary said. "I was out there before the explosion. My hair was up in a baseball cap like my dad wears, and I guess, from a distance, he thought I was my dad."

"But you were in the barn," Abe said, his frown deepening. "That's what you've said all along, that you stayed with your dad until right before the explosion."

Mary's face blanched. Clearly, she hadn't thought through how to reconcile their story with her new one. Mary looked to Young and Pak, her eyes darting in a panicked plea for help.

Pak came to her rescue and said in English, "Mary, the doctors say your memory will return slowly. Do you remember new something? You went outside to help Mom find batteries, maybe something else happened?"

Mary bit her lip, like she was trying not to cry, and slowly nodded. When she finally spoke, her words were halting and unsure. "I had a fight with my mom earlier—helping out more, cooking, cleaning . . . I figured . . . if we were alone, she'd just yell at me more, so I . . . didn't go in the house. I remembered . . ." Mary's brow furrowed in focused concentration, as if trying to recall a fuzzy memory. "I knew about the power lines, so . . . I went there instead. I thought maybe . . . I could free the balloons, but . . . I couldn't reach the strings. So I came back." She looked at Abe. "That's when I saw smoke. So I went there, behind the barn, and then . . ." Mary's voice broke off and she closed her eyes. A tear glided down her cheek, as if on command, accentuating the bumps and crevices of her scar.

Young knew that she should act the part of the mother aching for her daughter who, until now, had never talked about that night. That she should hug her, smooth her hair, do all the things mothers do to comfort their children. But she could only stand still, nauseated, worry coursing through her, sure that Abe must see right through Mary's story.

But he didn't. He bought it all—acted like it, anyway—and said this explained a lot, and of course it was understandable for memories to slowly rise to the surface, in dribs and drabs, like the doctors said. He seemed intensely relieved at hearing a plausible explanation for Mr. Spinum's story, and if Abe had doubts about Mary's story—how someone could, even from a distance, mistake a girl for a middle-aged man, or how to reconcile Mary's few-minutes-by-the-power-lines timing with Mr. Spinum's ten-plus minutes—he glossed over them with mutterings about failing eyesight, old white men thinking all Asians look the same, and teenagers losing track of time.

Abe said to Pak, "I don't know why Shannon's decided to pick on you. There's no motive. Even if you wanted insurance money, why wouldn't you wait until the chamber was empty? Why risk killing kids? It makes no sense. If it weren't for this mix-up about you being outside, she'd have nothing on you."

Mary let out a half chortle, half sob. "It's my fault. If only I'd re-membered before . . ." She looked at Abe, her face crinkled in pain. "I'm so sorry. This won't hurt my dad, right? He didn't do anything wrong. He can't go to jail."

Mary knelt next to Pak and rested her head on his shoulder. Pak patted her head, as if to say it was okay, all was forgiven, and Mary held out her hand to Young, inviting her to join her and Pak. Even after she went to them, one hand in Mary's, the other in Pak's, forming a circle, Young felt a sense of being an outsider, of being excluded from the bond between her husband and daughter. Pak had forgiven Mary for dis-obeying his plan; would he have been so understanding of Young? And Mary—she'd broken through her months-long silence for Pak; would she have done that for Young?

Abe said, "Don't worry, we'll work it out. Pak, I'll have you explain tomorrow during your testimony. Mary, I may have to put you on the stand." Abe stood up. "But I can't help unless you're straight with me, and I don't want another day like today. So let me ask you: Is there anything, *anything*, you haven't told me?"

Pak said, "No."

Mary said, "No, nothing."

Abe looked at Young. Young opened her mouth but no words came out. She realized that she'd said nothing this entire time, since Mary opened the door.

"Young? Is there something else?" Abe said.

Young thought of Mary on that night, helping Pak to keep watch over the protesters while she was alone, ransacking the house for batteries. She thought of her call with Pak, her complaining about and his defending their daughter, as always.

"Anything at all? Now's the time," Abe said. Pak's and Mary's hands squeezed hers tight, urging her to join them.

Young looked down at the faces of her husband and daughter, turned to Abe, and said, "You know everything." Then she stood, united with her family, as Abe told them that after the next witness's testimony, no one, absolutely *no one*, would have the slightest doubt that Elizabeth wanted her son dead.

TERESA

SHE COULDN'T STOP THINKING ABOUT SEX. All through lunch
recess, munching her food, strolling through the shops, gazing at
the vineyards: sex, sex, sex.

It started at one of the oh-so-cute cafés that peppered Main Street.
The walls were lilac with hand-painted grape drawings, clearly a ladies-
who-lunch place. The guy at the register, though, had been a *man*, right
out of central casting for Hot Young Dude, his chiseled muscularity accentuated by its juxtaposition to the dainty background. Approaching
him to pay for her salad, Teresa caught a whiff of something familiar,
deep from her past. Something spicy—maybe Polo, her high school boy-
friend's cologne—mixed with drying sweat. The musky, pungent scent of
orgasm—not the kind she was used to, by herself under the covers with
only her index finger moving in small circles, but the kind she hadn't had

in eleven years, held down by the weight of a man's body on hers, their bodies slippery with sweat.

"It's hot out there. You sure you want this to go?" the guy said.

She said, in what she thought was a vaguely sexual tone, "I like it hot." She gave him a half smile of the suggestive variety and sauntered out, savoring the swivel of her skirt, the graze of silk against her skin. A block later, she saw Matt, who called her Mother Teresa, and she had to fight not to laugh out loud at the combined deliciousness and ridiculousness of the moment.

It may have been the skirt. She hadn't worn one in years. With all the bending necessary to manage Rosa's wheelchair and tubes, skirts were not an option. Or maybe it was being alone. Remarkably, wonderfully, dizzyingly *alone*, with no one to take care of. Liberated from the roles of 24/7 Mom-Nurse to Rosa and Spare-Time Mom to Carlos (a.k.a "The Other Kid," as he called himself) for the first time in eleven years.

Not that she never had free time; a few hours every week, church volunteers took turns babysitting. But those outings were rushed, filled with errands. Yesterday was the first time in a decade she'd spent an entire day away from Rosa—the first time she didn't handle all her feedings and diaper changes, didn't drive her to therapies in their handicap-modified van, didn't greet her out of sleep and kiss her good night. It had been nerve-racking, and the volunteers had had to push her out the door, saying not to worry, just focus on the trial. She'd called home as soon as she got to court and twice during the first break.

During lunch recess yesterday, Teresa called home, ate the sandwich she'd packed, and looked at her watch. Fifty minutes left, with nothing she *had* to get done. So she walked. Aimlessly. There were no Targets or Costcos. Only jewel-toned shops designed for frivolity, flaunting their deliberate rejection of the practical. She walked into a used bookstore with a whole section on ancient maps but not one book on special-needs parenting, a clothing store with fifteen varieties of slap-on bracelets but no underwear or socks. With each passing minute of just browsing, of not being a caregiver, Teresa felt herself shedding that role, cell by cell, like a snake with its skin, unearthing what had been covered. Not Teresa the Mother or Teresa the Nurse, but simply Teresa, a woman. The world of Rosa, Carlos, wheelchairs, and tubes becoming surreal and distant. The intensity of her love and worry for them growing fainter like stars at dawn—still there, but not as visible.

After the first day of the trial, Teresa drove home in the borrowed coupe, singing to rock songs. When she got home ten minutes before Rosa's bedtime, she drove past her house, parked in a hidden wooded spot, and, for fifteen minutes, read a book she'd bought during recess, a 99-cent Mary Higgins Clark mystery, savoring the extra stolen minutes.

It was like those Method actors, who get more into character the longer they pretend to be someone else. Today, Teresa left the house earlier than necessary. She acted the part of a single woman—put on makeup in the car, wore her hair long, stared at vineyard workers. And for the briefest moment with the cashier guy, she actually *felt* like a free woman, a woman without the male-repellent combination of a disabled daughter and a surly son.

She waited until the last minute to return to court. At the door, two women she'd met a few times—Miracle Submarine patients from the morning dive after hers—greeted her. One woman said, "I was just saying how hard this is, me being here. My husband's not used to taking care of the kids," and the other said, "Same here. I hope the trial ends soon."

Teresa nodded and tried to shape her lips into an I-feel-the-same-way smile. She wondered if it made her a bad person, her self-indulgent delight at this hiatus from her life. Was she a bad mother if she didn't miss Rosa's curled lips, opening to say "Mama"? A bad friend to the volunteers if she prayed the trial would last a month? She opened her mouth to say, "I know, I feel so guilty," when she saw their faces—not guilty, but excited, their eyes darting everywhere, caught up in the drama of the courtroom. It occurred to her then: the possibility that these women, like Teresa, were playing the part of Good Mother, trying to pretend they weren't relishing this quasi-vacation that forced their husbands into the chaotic mundanity of their day-to-day lives. Teresa looked at them, smiled, and said, "I know exactly how you feel."

IT WAS MUGGY in the courtroom. She'd expected relief from the heat—over a hundred, someone said—but the air was just as dense inside.

Maybe from everyone who'd walked in the hot sun, soaking up the humidity like a sponge, now stepping in and releasing the dank heat. The air conditioners were on, but they sounded feeble, sputtering once in a while as if exhausted. The air dribbling out, not cooling the room so much as ushering sweat particles around it.

Abe announced his next witness: Steve Pierson, an arson specialist and lead investigator. As he walked up, his bald head slimy and pink with sweat, Teresa could almost see steam rise from it. Teresa was barely five feet tall, so most people seemed big to her, but Detective Pierson was a giant, even taller than Abe. The witness stand squeaked as he stepped up, and the wooden chair looked like a toy next to his bulk. When he sat, the streaming sun hit his hairless head-bulb like a spotlight, casting a halo around his face. It reminded Teresa of the first time she saw him, the night of the explosion: him standing against the backdrop of the fire, with twitching flames reflecting off the gloss of his scalp.

It had been a nightmare scene. Sirens in varying pitches from fire trucks, ambulances, and police cars blaring above the steady crackle of the fire eating through the barn. The emergency vehicles' flashing lights against the darkening sky creating a psychedelic nightclub vibe, with foam-water lines from hoses crisscrossing in midair like streamers. And stretchers. Stretchers with their bright white sheets, everywhere.

Both Teresa and Rosa were fine, miraculously, just smoke inhalation for which they were given—an irony—pure oxygen. As she breathed in, she saw Matt fighting off EMTs holding him down. "Let me go! She doesn't know yet. I need to tell her."

Teresa stopped breathing. Elizabeth. She didn't know her son was dead.

That's when Steve Pierson had come into view, with his freakishly wide shoulders and hairless head like a caricature of a movie villain. "Sir, we'll find the deceased boy's mother," he said in a high, nasal squeak, all the more alien because it contrasted with the booming bass she expected from such a big body. It seemed wrong, as if his real voice had been dubbed by a recording from a prepubescent boy. "We'll deliver the news."

Deliver the news. *Ma'am, I have news*, Teresa imagined this man saying, as if Henry's death were an interesting CNN foreign-correspondence report. *Your son is deceased.*

No. She would not let some stranger who looked like a Scandinavian sumo wrestler and spoke like Alvin the Chipmunk tell Elizabeth, would not let him infect that moment she'd relive again and again. Teresa herself had lived that, an oh-so-busy-and-important doctor telling her, "I'm calling to inform you that your daughter is in a coma," then cutting off her shocked "What? Is this a joke?" with "I'd suggest getting here as soon as possible. She likely won't survive much longer." Teresa wanted a friend to tell Elizabeth gently, to cry with and hug her the way she wished her ex-husband had instead of delegating to a stranger.

Teresa left Rosa with the EMTs and went to find Elizabeth. It was 8:45, so the dive was supposed to have ended a while ago. Where was she? Not in her car. Maybe she'd gone for a walk? Matt had said once that there was a nice trail by the creek.

It took her five minutes to find her, lying on a blanket by the creek. "Elizabeth?" Teresa said, but she didn't answer. Walking closer, she saw white buds in her ears. Tinny echoes of blaring music leaked out of them, mixing with the gurgling creek and chirping crickets.

The darkening sky cast a purplish shadow on Elizabeth's face. Her eyes were closed, a slight smile on her face. Serene. A pack of cigarettes and matches lay on the blanket, next to a cigarette butt, crumpled paper, and a thermos bottle.

"Elizabeth," Teresa said again. Nothing. Teresa bent down and snatched the earbuds away. Elizabeth startled, her body jerking awake. The thermos fell over and a pale straw liquid gurgled out. Wine?

"Oh my God, I can't believe I fell asleep. What time is it?" Elizabeth said.

"Elizabeth," Teresa said, and cupped her hands. Flashing lights from the ambulance brightened the sky in spurts, like distant fireworks. "Something awful has happened. There was a fire, an explosion. It happened so quickly." She gripped Elizabeth's hands. "I'm afraid that Henry was . . . involved, and he . . . he's . . ."

Elizabeth didn't say anything. Didn't ask *He's what?*, didn't gasp, didn't scream. She just blinked at Teresa in even beats, as if counting down the seconds until Teresa could utter the last word in her sentence. *Five, four, three, two, one.* Hurt, Teresa yearned to say. Near death, even. Anything with just a shard of hope.

"Henry died," Teresa finally said. "I'm so sorry, I can't tell you—"

Elizabeth squeezed her eyes shut and held up her hand as if to say, Stop. She swayed slightly, back and forth, like a shirt on a hanger in the summer breeze, and as Teresa leaned in to steady her, she opened her mouth in a silent howl. She snapped her head back, and Teresa realized: Elizabeth was laughing. Out loud, in a high-pitched, maniacal cackle, as she repeated like a mantra, "He's dead, he's dead, he's *dead*!"

○

TERESA LISTENED to Detective Pierson's testimony about the rest of that night. How Elizabeth had scanned the scene with an eerie calmness. How he'd led her to Henry's stretcher and, before he could stop her, she'd pulled back the white sheet covering his face. How she hadn't screamed or cried or clung to the body like other grieving parents, and he told himself it must be numbness from shock, but boy, it sure was creepy.

All through the recitation of these facts she'd known, lived through, Teresa looked down, smoothing the wrinkles on her hands, and thought about Elizabeth shouting "He's dead!" Her guffaw in that moment—that was what told her Elizabeth didn't kill Henry, or if she did, it wasn't on purpose, wasn't murder. When she was eight, Teresa had fallen through ice, on a pond. The water had been so cold, it felt boiling hot. Elizabeth's laugh had felt like that, like she'd been in so much pain that she'd bypassed crying, straight past it to something beyond: a grief-stricken cackle that transmitted more pain than any sob or scream. But how could she put that into words, explain that Elizabeth's laugh had not been a laugh? Her drinking and smoking—unmotherly things—were bad enough. Laughing when told of her son's death would make her seem at best crazy, and at worst psychopathic. So she'd never told anyone.

Abe was putting something on the easel. A blowup of notepad paper, phrases scrawled everywhere. Mostly to-do lists: phone numbers, URLs, grocery items. Five phrases, scattered around the page, were highlighted in yellow: *I can't do this anymore*; *I need my life back*; *It needs to end TODAY!!*; *Henry = victim? How?*; and *NO MORE HBOT*, this last phrase circled a dozen times in one stroke, like a child's drawing of a tornado. Uneven lines crisscrossed the paper; it had been torn and put back together like a puzzle.

Abe said, "Detective Pierson, tell us what this is."

"It's an enlarged and highlighted copy of a note found in the defendant's kitchen. It had been torn into nine pieces and discarded in the trash can. Handwriting analysis confirmed the writing as the defendant's."

"So the defendant wrote, tore, and threw this away. Why's it significant?"

"It seems to be a planning document of sorts. The defendant had enough of caring for her special-needs child. She planned to 'end' it all that night." He drew air quotes. "'No more HBOT,' she wrote. By matching the URLs and numbers here with the defendant's Internet history and phone records, we determined that she wrote this on the day of the explosion. So hours after she writes this, the HBOT blows up, killing her son. And as that's happening, she's celebrating by drinking wine and smoking, which one might view as the ultimate symbol of freedom from parental responsibilities." Pierson frowned at Elizabeth as if he'd bitten down on spoiled food, and Teresa wondered if he'd give her the same look if he'd seen her last night, hiding out in her car for a few more minutes of freedom from her disabled child.

"Perhaps the defendant was writing about being tired and planning to quit HBOT. Isn't that possible, Detective?"

Pierson shook his head. "She sent e-mails that very day canceling Henry's therapy—speech, OT, physical, social—all except HBOT. Why not quit HBOT, too, if 'No more HBOT' meant she wanted to quit, unless of course there's no need because she knew it'd be destroyed?"

"Hmmm, very peculiar." Abe put on his I-can't-figure-this-out look.

"Yes, quite a coincidence, the defendant deciding to quit HBOT on the very day that it happens to explode and everything she wrote down comes true, *and* conveniently, Henry no longer needs the services she just canceled."

"But coincidences do happen," Abe said, voice animated, clearly putting on a good cop, bad cop show for the jurors.

"True, but if she decided to quit, why go to the next dive? Why make the long drive then lie that she's sick? Why do that *after* spending the afternoon researching HBOT fires, as confirmed by our forensic analysis of her computer?"

Abe said, "Detective Pierson, as an expert in arson investigations, what conclusion did you draw from the defendant's computer searches and notes?"

"Her searches focused on the mechanics of HBOT fires—where they start, how they spread—which indicate a person planning arson, figuring out how best to set fire to ensure the death of people inside an HBOT chamber. Her note, 'Henry=victim? How?' demonstrates her focus on how to ensure that Henry is, in fact, the victim, the one who's killed. Her later orchestrating Henry's seating to ensure his placement in the most dangerous spot confirms that."

"Objection." Elizabeth's lawyer asked for a sidebar. While the lawyers conferred with the judge, Teresa looked at the poster. Every scrawl was something Teresa herself might have written. How many times had she thought, *I can't do this anymore. I need my life back*? Hell, it was part of her nightly prayers: "Dear God, please help Rosa, please bring us a new cure or drug or *something*, God, because I need my life back. Carlos needs his life back. Rosa, most of all, needs her life back. Please, God." And last summer, making the long drive twice a day, hadn't she counted down the days, said to Rosa, "Nine more days, my girl, then NO MORE HBOT!"?

And the *Henry=victim? How?* note. Pierson's explanation made sense logically, intellectually, but something about that phrase triggered something. *Henry equals victim, how. Henry is a victim, Henry as a victim? How?* she repeated, losing herself in the rhythm that felt so familiar, like a long-ago lullaby.

It came to her suddenly. The protesters that morning. "You're harming them," the silver-bob-haired woman had said. "You've turned them into victims of your warped desire to have textbook-perfect children." This had gotten to Elizabeth—her face had blanched even though it had been sauna-hot—and Teresa had said, "Come on, Henry a victim? That's ridiculous. You buy Henry organic underwear, for God's sake." But later, she'd thought, *Is Rosa a victim of my inability to accept her? But I just want her healthy. How is that wrong?* If she'd had paper, she might have doodled *Rosa = victim? How?*

The lawyers returned to their tables and Abe put up another poster.

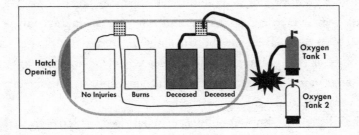

"Detective," Abe said. "Tell us what this is."

"It's an illustration from the last website the defendant saw before the explosion. She searched for 'HBOT fire start outside chamber,' presumably to find the case listed on the protesters' flyer, and found this: a chamber similar to Miracle Submarine, where the fire started outside. The fire cracked the oxygen tubing, allowing oxygen to escape and to come in contact with flames. Tank One exploded and killed the two patients connected to it."

"So the defendant saw this image a few hours before putting her son in the third spot, marked *Deceased*. Is that what you're telling us?"

"Exactly. Now remember"—Pierson looked at the jury—"Miracle Submarine exploded in the exact same way. The fire started in the same spot, under the U-shaped drop of oxygen tubing. The fatalities were also the same, in the two rear positions where she *insisted* her son be seated."

Teresa looked at the left box marked *No injuries* where Rosa had sat. In every other dive, she'd sat in the red box marked *Deceased*. If Elizabeth hadn't insisted on changing things, Rosa's head would've been the one engulfed in flames, charred to the bones. Teresa shivered and shook her head to expel the thought, fling it away. She felt relief so intense that her knees buckled, then a rush of shame that she was, let's face it, thanking God for someone else's child dying an excruciating death. It occurred to Teresa then—was it possible that she was rooting for Elizabeth not because she thought her innocent, but out of gratitude to Elizabeth, for planning the explosion in a way that left Rosa safe? Was her selfishness coloring her interpretation of Elizabeth's laugh, her notes?

Abe said, "Did you discuss the fire's point of origin with the defendant?"

"Yes, right after the defendant identified her son's body. I told her we'd find whoever was responsible and how this happened. She said, 'It was the protesters. They set the fire outside, under the oxygen tubing.' Remember, at this point, we didn't know where or how the fire started. Later, when our analysis confirmed that very spot as the fire's point of origin, we were surprised, to say the least."

"Could she have known because of what she claimed—the protesters set the fire and their flyer made it clear how they did it?" Abe said, sounding like an innocent schoolboy asking if the Easter bunny was real.

"No." Pierson shook his head. "We investigated them thoroughly and ruled them out for several reasons. First, all six protesters were released from questioning at 8:00 p.m. They said they all drove back to D.C. immediately without stopping anywhere, and cell tower pings corroborate that. Second, all six have impeccable backgrounds as peaceful, law-abiding citizens, with the primary goal of protecting children from harm."

Teresa shook her head at this, hard, wishing that she could tell the jury not to be fooled by their supposed "peacefulness." They hadn't seen those women that morning, jaws clenched, contempt in their eyes. They'd looked ready to do *anything* necessary to stop HBOT, like those fanatics who gun down abortion doctors in the name of saving lives.

Teresa took deep breaths to calm herself. On the stand, Pierson was saying, "Even if you believe they'd do something as drastic as commit arson to scare people into stopping HBOT, it makes no sense that they'd do it when the oxygen was on full blast and children were inside."

When the oxygen was on full blast. This phrase triggered a thought that sent chills through her body: What if they didn't know the oxygen was on? That morning, as she was rushing past them after the first dive, the silver-bobbed woman had yelled, "We're not going anywhere. See you tonight at 6:45." She hadn't thought much of it, she'd just been annoyed, but now, Teresa realized: the protesters had known their exact schedule. Which meant they'd expected the oxygen to be off by 8:05. According to Pierson, whoever started the fire had lit the cigarette between 8:10 and 8:15. That was the perfect timing: the protesters expected the dive to be ending but the oxygen turned off, which meant the fire would burn slowly, allowing the patients to see it on their way out, at which point they'd be terrified, quit, and report Pak. No more HBOT. It made perfect sense.

Abe said, "I can see why you ruled out the protesters as suspects. But if they weren't involved, how could the defendant know the fire's exact origin?" Again, that tone of confused curiosity, as if he genuinely had no clue.

"Two possibilities," Pierson said. "One, she set the fire herself at that spot to implicate the protesters. Frame someone else for murder: a classic plan. A clever one, which might've worked if not for the strong evidence we found against her."

"And the second possibility?"

"An unbelievably lucky guess."

Several jurors chuckled, and Teresa felt pressure squeezing her lungs. Elizabeth hated the protesters; that had been obvious. Had that hatred been enough for her to risk setting fire to the barn? Not to kill anyone, but to get the protesters in trouble? That last dive, TJ's ears had hurt, so Pak took twice as long as usual to pressurize and start the oxygen. Not knowing that, Elizabeth would've expected the oxygen to be off by 8:15. She could've set the fire then, expecting everyone to be out shortly and discover the fire before it grew. That would explain why she'd clearly been devastated but not surprised when told about the fire and Henry's death. The realization that she'd caused her own son's death—the irony, the unbearable knowledge that he'd paid for her hubris, her hatred, her sin—would no doubt cause her breakdown, that cackle of agony Teresa couldn't forget.

Abe said, "Detective, how exactly did the fire start?"

Pierson nodded. "Our forensic arson team determined that a burning cigarette and matchbook placed in the middle of a pile of sticks under an oxygen tube started the fire. The tubing cracked, putting the oxygen in contact with the fire. And even though oxygen itself isn't flammable, it mixing with the contaminants in and around the equipment resulted in an explosion, and the force of that blast blew away the cigarette and matchbook before they were completely incinerated. We recovered several pieces of each item intact, and conducted lab testing on the chemical contents and color patterns. We identified the brand of the cigarette as Camel, and the matchbook as one that 7-Eleven stores in this area distribute."

Abe's lips wiggled, like he was trying to suppress a smirk. "What brands were the cigarettes and matches found at the defendant's *picnic* area?" he said, making *picnic* sound like a dirty word.

"Camel cigarettes, and a 7-Eleven matchbook."

The whole courtroom seemed to rise and vibrate, everyone sitting taller in their chairs, leaning forward and sideways to catch a glimpse of Elizabeth's reaction.

Abe waited for the whispers and creaks of chairs to quiet. "Detective, did the defendant ever try to explain away this correlation?"

"Yes. After her arrest, the defendant said she found an open pack of cigarettes and matches that night in the woods." Pierson's voice took on a singsong quality, the tone of a babysitter reading fairy tales to kids. "She said it looked discarded, so she took it and smoked it. She said there was also a note with an H-Mart logo on it saying, 'This needs to end. We need to meet tonight, 8:15.' She said she didn't realize it at the time, but those must've been discarded by the arsonists."

"How did you respond to this explanation?"

"I didn't find it credible. Teenagers smoking discarded cigarettes, I buy. But a forty-year-old upper-class woman? But be that as it may, we took her 'explanation' seriously." He drew air quotes. "We dusted the cigarette pack and matchbook for fingerprints."

"What did you find?"

"Curiously, we found only the defendant's fingerprints, no one else's. She explained *that* by saying she used"—Pierson's face twitched, as if trying not to laugh—"antibacterial wipes to clean them before she used them. Because, you know, they'd been on the ground."

Soft giggles swept the room. Someone laughed out loud. Abe frowned, deliberately crinkling his face. "I'm sorry, did you say antibacterial *wipes*?"

The jurors smiled, seemingly amused, but Teresa found herself hating the transparent theatrics, his pretense at surprise. "So she was willing to smoke these random cigarettes belonging to God knows who, as long as she used her *antibacterial wipes*?" Abe's repetition of "antibacterial wipes" seemed juvenile, a form of bullying, and Teresa wanted to shout at him to shut up, that Elizabeth really did have a habit of wiping everything with those wipes she carried everywhere, and so fricking what?

"Yes," Pierson said, "and in the process, conveniently 'wiped away' any evidence that could have corroborated *or* contradicted her story." Teresa wanted to jump up and smack this man's fat, bunny-drawing fingers.

"What about fingerprints on the H-Mart note? Surely, the defendant didn't use *antibacterial wipes* on paper."

"We didn't find any note."

"Could it have gotten overlooked?"

"The night of the explosion, we set up a wide perimeter around the picnic site and combed through it the next morning. There was no H-Mart note in that vicinity."

A tingle jolted Teresa's scalp and spread down her shoulders, warm and thick, like a shawl. There had been a note that night. Close her eyes, and she could see it—a crumpled ball of paper on the blanket. She couldn't make out the words, but she could see bright red and black splashes, the way H-Mart's logo might look scrunched up.

Teresa imagined telling Abe. Would he believe her? He'd ask why she didn't tell him before. The truth was, to avoid talking about Elizabeth laughing when told of Henry's death, she'd said she couldn't remember much about that conversation, including what items she saw nearby. "I was so focused on telling her Henry was dead, I guess I blocked everything out," she'd said. She could say Pierson's testimony triggered her memory, but Abe wouldn't buy it; he'd peck at it like a vulture until her story fell apart. Which meant she might be forced to come clean, explain about Elizabeth laughing. And that might hurt Elizabeth far more than Teresa saying she saw something that vaguely maybe could be an H-Mart note.

So going to Abe in private was a no-go. But staying quiet was not an option, either; the jury had to know that Elizabeth wasn't lying about the note.

When Teresa opened her eyes, Pierson was saying there was nothing to corroborate Elizabeth's version of events. Teresa stood up. She cleared her throat. She said, "That's not true. I saw it. I saw the H-Mart note."

The judge banged the gavel and called for order and Abe said to sit back down, but Teresa remained standing and looked to Elizabeth. Shannon was saying something to Elizabeth, but Elizabeth looked past her and met Teresa's gaze. Elizabeth's bottom lip quivered and stretched into a half smile. Elizabeth blinked, and the tears pooling in her eyes rolled down her cheeks. Fast, like they'd burst from a dam.

ELIZABETH

THE WEEK BEFORE THE TRIAL STARTED. Shannon told Elizabeth they needed as many people as possible to sit behind her in court. Hand her tissues, glare at Abe's witnesses, that type of thing. Family was out—Elizabeth was an only child and her parents died in the 1989 San Francisco earthquake—so that left friends. The problem: she had none. "We're not talking womb-to-tomb bosom buddies here. Just anyone willing to sit by you. Sit—that's it. Hairdresser, dental hygienist, the Whole Foods checkout girl. Anyone," Shannon said. Elizabeth said, "Why don't we hire some actors?"

It wasn't that she'd never had friends. True, she'd always been on the shy side, but she'd had close friends in college and at the accounting firm; she'd had three bridesmaids and been one twice. But since Henry's autism diagnosis six years ago, she'd been too busy for anything not

Henry-centric. During the day, she drove Henry to seven types of therapy—speech, occupational, physical, auditory processing (Tomatis), social skills (RDI), vision processing, neurofeedback—and, between those, roamed holistic/organic stores for peanut/gluten/casein/dairy/fish/egg-free foods. At night, she prepared Henry's food and supplements and went on autism-treatment boards such as HBOTKids and Autism-DoctorMoms. After a few years of no contact, her friends stopped reaching out. What could she do now? Call and say, Hi! Long time no talk! I was wondering if you'd be interested in coming to my murder trial, hang out a bit before I get executed. Oh, by the way, sorry for not returning your calls for six years, but I was busy with my son—you know, the one I was indicted for murdering?

So yes, Elizabeth knew no one would be coming to support her (other than Shannon, who didn't count, since she had to pay her $600 per hour). But when she walked in yesterday and saw the empty row behind her—the only empty seats in the entire courtroom—she felt a punching gut pain, as if an invisible boxer were pummeling her. For two days, the row behind Elizabeth remained empty, broadcasting to the world the total lack of support for her, flaunting her aloneness.

When Teresa blurted out that she saw the H-Mart note, the judge tried to undo it. He banged the gavel and told Teresa she couldn't shout stuff out and instructed the jury to disregard it. Teresa apologized, but when he told her to sit—this was the part Elizabeth would replay again and again, lying in bed—Teresa stepped over the Yoos, crossed the aisle, walked into the empty row, and sat directly behind Elizabeth. Some in the jury gasped. They seemed to regard Elizabeth like a leper—not contagious, maybe, but something you stay away from all the same.

Elizabeth turned to look at Teresa. Having someone stand up for her, declare herself on her side, sit by her without shame—those were things she'd written off, things she'd told herself she didn't care about now that nothing seemed worth living for. But it had hurt, the double divers she'd spent hours with every day, not bothering to come see her or ask for themselves if she did it. The automatic assumption of her guilt.

But now, here was one of them, willing to be a friend. Gratefulness expanded inside her like water in a balloon, threatening to burst and gush out in torrents of thank-yous she couldn't voice. She gazed at Teresa, tried to convey her gratitude with her eyes.

Just then, she glimpsed a shock of silver in the crowd. The leader of the protesters, the woman with the sanctimonious username Proud-AutismMom. She'd expected Shannon to expose that woman's so-called alibi as a sham at trial and bring her down, but the arson call changed Shannon's focus to Pak, enabling that woman to sit comfortably, spectating the trial as if she were an innocent bystander. Elizabeth felt bile worm up her throat, the familiar punch of fury and hatred and blame. If it weren't for that woman, her son would be alive right now. He'd be nine, about to start fourth grade. Ruth Weiss, with her menacing threats and attempts to destroy Elizabeth's life, all of which she discovered during that fateful call with Kitt she wished to God she'd never had. That call had sent Elizabeth reeling, stripping away her rationality and leading her to the moment she'd regret for as long as she lived. The series of idiotic, incomprehensible acts that had come to define her life—and Henry's, too, as it turned out.

Elizabeth turned back to Teresa and thought of her trapped in the horror of the fire while she was drinking wine, toasting the end of HBOT, and marveling at the cigarette between her fingers. She wondered what Teresa would think if she knew everything about that day, if she knew that Elizabeth—her hatred for Ruth Weiss—was to blame for Henry's death.

◯

SHANNON HATED DETECTIVE PIERSON. "What a condescending, smug son of a bitch," she'd said after their first meeting and again after his direct testimony. "I can't stand that squeaky voice of his. I literally have hives."

Elizabeth thought it'd be painful to see him—the man who'd led her to Henry's corpse, her son as an inanimate object. But she didn't remember him. Not his face, not even his hideously incongruous voice. She didn't remember any of the things he was saying, and instead of pinpointing inaccuracies like Shannon wanted, she took it in like a passive TV viewer.

When the judge told Shannon to begin her cross-examination, Shannon said to Elizabeth, "You sit back and enjoy; I'm going to rip him apart." But when she stood up, Shannon looked at Pierson out of the corners of her eyes (could it be? Was Shannon pretending to be seductive?) and smiled, both dimples showing. She said, "Good afternoon, Detective," in an artificially low voice (trying to be sexy or to accentuate his high voice, she couldn't tell), and walked to him in small steps, her hips moving back and forth in what she guessed was supposed to be a sashay.

"Detective," Shannon continued in the guttural voice that made Elizabeth want to clear her throat, "let's talk about *you* a bit. As we heard, you're an *expert* in criminal investigation, with twenty years of experience, and the *lead* investigator here. In fact, I heard a rumor that you teach a seminar on evidence gathering." She turned to the jurors and said, like a proud mother bragging about her son, "A required class for all incoming detectives, apparently." She turned to him. "Is that right?"

"Um, yes." This was clearly not what he'd expected.

"Is it true the seminar's called Criminal Investigation for Dummies?" Shannon said and—could it be true?—giggled. Shannon, the serious, professional, slightly overweight lawyer who wore unfitted plaid suits and opaque pantyhose, *giggling* like a four-year-old.

"That's not the official name, but yes, that's what some call it."

"And I hear you created such a good chart, that's all you use to teach the class. Just one page, is that right?"

Pierson looked bewildered. He looked over to Abe like a schoolboy asking a friend for the answer. Abe shrugged slightly. "Yes, I have a one-page chart to teach the seminar."

"I'm sure you tried to ensure that the chart reflects your experience, not just the textbook stuff but your real-world knowledge about what evidence is the most reliable, most relevant. Is that fair?"

"Yes."

"Wonderful." Shannon put a poster on the easel.

CRIMINAL INVESTIGATION FOR DUMMIES

DIRECT EVIDENCE	CIRCUMSTANTIAL EVIDENCE
**BETTER, RELIABLE!!!!	(Not as reliable, need more than 1 category)

DIRECT EVIDENCE
BETTER, RELIABLE!!!!
- Eyewitness
- Audio/video recordings of commission of crime
- Photos of suspect committing crime
- Documentation of crime by suspect, witness, or accomplice
- Holy grail: confession (need to verify!!!!!)

CIRCUMSTANTIAL EVIDENCE
(Not as reliable, need more than 1 category)
- Smoking gun: proof of suspect's usage of weapon (fingerprint, DNA)
- Suspect ownership/possession
- Opportunity to commit crime—alibi?
- Motive to commit crime—threats, prior incidents
- Special knowledge and interest (bomb expertise or research example)

"Detective, is this your chart?" Shannon asked. The sweetness in her voice seemed saccharine, with a touch of mockery sprinkled in.

Simultaneously, Pierson said, "How the hell did you get this?" and Abe said, "Objection. That's misleading. Ms. Haug knows very well that Virginia law doesn't differentiate direct and circumstantial evidence."

Shannon said, "Your Honor, we can fight about legal technicalities when we're hashing out jury instructions. Right now, I'm questioning the lead investigator about his investigation methods. This document is not confidential, and it's his own words, not mine."

"Overruled," the judge said.

Abe opened his mouth in disbelief. He shook his head as he took his seat.

"Detective, I'll ask again," Shannon said, her voice back to her serious tone now, the saccharine layer stripped away like a banana peel. "This *is* your chart, the one you use to instruct other investigators, including those on this case?"

Detective Pierson glared at Shannon before muttering, "Yes."

"So this chart tells us that in your experience, direct evidence is better and more reliable than circumstantial evidence. Correct?"

Pierson looked at Abe, who frowned and raised his eyebrows as if to say, I know, but what the hell can I do about this crazy judge? "Yes," Pierson said.

"What's the difference between those types of evidence? You use the runner example in your seminar, correct?"

A jumble of surprised awe and annoyance distorted Pierson's face. For sure, he was working out who'd squealed, imagining what he'd do to the traitor. He shook his head as if to clear his thoughts and said, "Direct evidence of a person running is someone seeing him actually running. Circumstantial evidence is someone seeing him in a running suit and shoes near a track, his face red and sweaty."

"So the circumstantial evidence could be wrong. The sweaty person could've been planning to run later, and could've simply been in a hot car, for example. Correct?"

"Yes."

"Let's turn to our case. The all-important direct evidence first, per your expert instruction. The first type of direct evidence you list is 'eyewitness.' Did anyone witness Elizabeth setting a fire?"

"No."

"Anyone witness her smoking or lighting a match near the barn?"

"No."

Shannon took a fat marker and crossed out the first bullet-point item under DIRECT EVIDENCE, *Eyewitness*. "Next, any recordings or pictures of Elizabeth setting the fire?"

"No." She crossed out *Audio/video recordings of commission of crime* and *Photos of suspect committing crime*.

"Next, we have 'Documentation of crime by suspect, witness, or accomplice.' Anything?"

"No." Another slash.

"So that leaves us with your 'holy grail'—a confession. Elizabeth has never confessed to setting the fire, correct?"

His lips clenched into a pink line. "Correct." Slash.

"So there's no direct proof that Elizabeth committed a crime here, none of what you regard as the, quote, 'better, reliable' type of evidence against her, correct?"

Pierson took in a sharp breath, his nostrils flaring like a horse. "Yes, but—"

"Thank you, Detective. No direct evidence at all." Shannon slashed a thick line through the words DIRECT EVIDENCE on the chart.

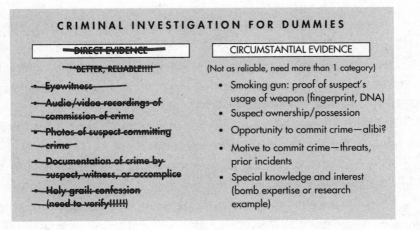

Shannon stepped back and smiled. It was an unbridled smile, the triumph of winning reflected in every facet of her face—eyes, cheeks, lips, jaws, even her ears upturned. It was funny how invested she was even though the trial's outcome wouldn't affect her life, not really. Win or lose, she'd still have the same billable earnings, same house, same family, whereas for Elizabeth, the trial's outcome meant the difference between suburbia and death row. So why was she feeling none of Shannon's excitement?

Shannon continued. "So we're left with circumstantial evidence, which, in your own words, is quote, 'not as reliable.' The first of these is the 'smoking gun,' or the smoking cigarette, as the case may be here." Several jurors chuckled. "Did you find Elizabeth's DNA, fingerprints, or any other forensic evidence on the cigarette or match at the explosion site?"

"The fire caused too much damage for us to retrieve such identifying information," Pierson said.

"That would be a no, Detective?"

His lips tightened. "Correct."

Shannon crossed out *Smoking gun* under CIRCUMSTANTIAL EVIDENCE.

"Next, let's skip down to 'Opportunity to commit crime.' The fire was set outside, behind the barn, correct?"

"Yes."

"Anyone could've walked right up there and set the fire, right? There's no lock or fence?"

"Sure, but we're not talking *theoretical* opportunity. We're looking for a *realistic* opportunity to commit the crime, someone in the vicinity and with no alibi, like the defendant."

"Vicinity and no alibi. I see. Well, how about Pak Yoo? He was in the vicinity. In fact, he was much closer than Elizabeth, isn't that so?"

"Yes, but he has an alibi. He was inside the barn, as verified by his wife, daughter, and patients."

"Ah, yes, the alibi. Detective, you are aware that a neighbor has come forward to say that Pak Yoo was outside the barn before the explosion?"

"I am," Pierson said, sounding confident, smiling the delicious smile of someone who knows something no one else knows. "And are *you* aware, Ms. Haug, that Mary Yoo has since clarified that *she* was outside that night, and that the neighbor, upon hearing this, admitted that the person he saw from a distance could well have been Mary?" Pierson shook his head and chuckled. "Apparently, Mary was wearing a baseball cap with her hair bunched up, so he thought she was a man. An innocent mistake."

Shannon said, "Objection. Please order the response stricken—"

Abe stood. "Ms. Haug opened the door, Your Honor."

"Overruled," the judge said.

Shannon turned her back to the jury and looked down, as if reading her notes, but Elizabeth could see her eyes scrunched shut, deep frown lines dividing her brows. After a moment, her eyes popped open. "So let's get this straight." She turned to Pierson. "The Yoos are all inside, then Young Yoo leaves to get batteries, then Mary Yoo goes outside where her neighbor sees her. Right?"

Pierson blinked repeatedly, rapidly, like one of those futuristic androids processing information. "That's my understanding," he said, his voice tentative.

"Which means Pak Yoo was alone in the barn before the explosion—

in the vicinity *and* had no alibi, meeting your criteria for 'opportunity to commit crime,' isn't that right?"

He stopped blinking. He seemed to be holding his breath; there was no movement in his face or body. After a moment, he swallowed, his Adam's apple bobbing up. "Yes."

A grin overtook Shannon's face, and she wrote *P. YOO* in red letters next to *Opportunity to commit crime.* "Next, motive. Tell me, Detective: What's the most typical motive for arson you see?"

"This isn't a typical arson case," he said.

"Detective, I didn't ask if this was a typical arson case. Please answer my question: What's the most typical motive for arson that you've seen?"

He clamped his lips, like a boy refusing to answer his mother, then spat out, "Money. Insurance fraud."

"Here, Pak Yoo stood to gain 1.3 million dollars from fire insurance, correct?"

He shrugged. "Maybe, sounds right. But again, this isn't a typical case. In most insurance-fraud cases, fires are set when the building is unoccupied, and no one's injured."

"Really? That's funny, because I have here your notes from your most recent arson case"—Shannon looked at a document in her hand—"let's see, in Winchester last November. You wrote, 'Perpetrator set fire and remained inside, believing insurer might suspect fraud if building empty. Perpetrator believed if he was injured, insurer more likely to believe it was accidental and pay out.'" She handed the document to Pierson. "This *is* your report, correct?"

Pierson clamped his jaws and narrowed his eyes, barely looking down at the paper, before saying, "Correct."

"So, based on your experience, would you say that a 1.3-million-dollar policy *can* provide motive for an owner such as Pak Yoo to set fire to his own building, even when the building is occupied?"

Detective Pierson looked at Pak, looked away, then finally said, "Yes."

Shannon wrote *P. YOO* in big red letters next to *Motive to commit crime.* She pointed to the next bullet point. "Detective, for 'Special knowledge and interest,' you have 'bomb expertise or research example' in parentheses. What does that mean?"

"It's for specialized crimes. For instance, in a bombing, if the suspect knew how to make that particular type of bomb or researched it, I'd consider that strong evidence. Much like the evidence found on the defendant's computer here."

"Detective, isn't it true that Pak Yoo had specialized knowledge of HBOT fires? That, in fact, he'd studied previous fires just like the one here?"

"I don't know what he knows. You'd have to ask *him* that."

"Actually, I don't, because your assistants did it for me." Shannon held up another document. "An office memo to you, recommending that Pak Yoo be cleared of criminal negligence in the fire." She handed it to him. "Please read the highlighted part."

He cleared his throat and read, " 'Pak Yoo was well aware of the risks of fire. He studied previous fires, including the case in which fire started under oxygen tubes outside the chamber.' "

"So, let me ask again, isn't it true that Pak Yoo had specialized knowledge and interest in hyperbaric fires similar to what happened here?"

"Yes, but—"

"Thank you, Detective." Shannon wrote *P. YOO* next to *Special knowledge and interest* and stepped back. "So here we have Pak Yoo, Miracle Submarine's owner, who had the motive, opportunity, and special knowledge to commit the crime. Let's talk about the last remaining item on your chart: ownership of the weapon. Now, you're assuming that the weapon here—the cigarette and matches used to set the fire—belonged to Elizabeth, correct?"

"I'm not *assuming* it, Ms. Haug. The facts are, a Camel cigarette and 7-Eleven matches started the fire, and the defendant was a short distance away with Camel cigarettes and 7-Eleven matches."

"But she told you they weren't hers, that she found them in the woods. Someone very well could've used them to set the fire, then thrown them away to get rid of the evidence. Did you even investigate the possibility that someone other than Elizabeth bought those items?"

"Yes, we investigated it. My team went to every 7-Eleven near Miracle Creek and in the defendant's neighborhood and searched for receipts and the like."

"Well, that's a relief. So you must've asked those stores' clerks if they recognized any of the others, including Pak Yoo, who we know had the motive, opportunity, and specialized knowledge to set this fire." Shannon pointed to the three bright red *P. YOO*s.

Pierson glared at Shannon. He kept his mouth clenched shut.

"Detective, did you ask a single 7-Eleven clerk if Pak Yoo ever bought Camels?"

"No." The word had a touch of defiance in it.

"Did you check his credit card bills for 7-Eleven charges?"

"No."

"Go through his trash for 7-Eleven receipts?"

"No."

"I see. So the extensive search you did, you did only for my client. Well, let's hear it. How many 7-Eleven store clerks recognized Elizabeth?"

"None."

"None? Well, how about receipts? You must have gone through her trash, car, purse, pockets, looking for 7-Eleven receipts, correct?"

"Yes. And no, we didn't find anything."

"Elizabeth's credit card statements?"

"No. But the fingerprints conclusively—"

"Ah, the fingerprints. Let's talk about them. You don't believe that Elizabeth found the cigarettes and matches. According to you, they were hers, despite the fact that there's zero evidence she bought them. And that's why no other prints were on them—because she's the only one who touched them, correct?"

"Exactly."

"Detective, this is the part that confuses me. If the cigarettes and matches were hers, she must've bought them somewhere. So shouldn't the store clerk's fingerprints be on them?"

"Not if she bought a carton of cigarettes."

"A carton, ten packs. Two hundred cigarettes. Did you find an open carton of Camels or any other cigarettes anywhere in her house or trash?"

"No."

"In her purse?"

"No."

"Her car?"

"No."

"Any cigarette butts in her car or in trash bins in her house? Anything indicating that she smoked regularly such that she'd buy a whole carton of cigarettes?"

Pierson blinked a few times. "No."

"And the matches, even when someone buys a whole carton, they still hand you individual matchbooks, right?"

"Yes, but over time, with a lot of handling, the defendant's fingerprints would displace the clerk's, on both the matches and the cigarette pack. So it doesn't surprise me that the clerk's prints wouldn't be on those items."

"Detective, on an item used frequently enough to displace older fingerprints, you'd expect to find multiple overlapping fingerprints of the owner, correct?"

"I suppose."

Shannon walked to her table, flipped through a file, and picked out a document, a triumphant smile on her face. She strutted back and handed it to him. "Tell us what this is."

"It's the fingerprint analysis of the items found in the picnic area."

"Please read for us the highlighted passages."

As he scanned the document, his face started to droop like a wax figurine on a hot day. "Matchbook, exterior: one full and four partial fingerprint marks. Cigarettes, exterior: four full and six partial print marks. Ten-point analysis identification: Elizabeth Ward."

"Detective, in your office, is it customary practice to report the presence of overlapping fingerprints if there are, in fact, any?"

"Yes."

"How many overlapping fingerprint marks did your office find on either item?"

His nostrils flared. He swallowed and stretched his lips as if pretending to smile. "None."

"Only five prints on the matches and ten on the cigarettes, all belonging to Elizabeth, no overlapping prints, and not a smudge from anyone else. Pretty clean, wouldn't you say?"

He looked to the side. After a moment, he licked his lips and said, "I suppose so."

"And since at least one other person, a store clerk, must've handled these items, the lack of other prints must mean they've been wiped off at some point, isn't that right?"

"I suppose, but—"

"And any number of people, including Pak Yoo, could've handled the items prior to them being wiped off, and there's no way to know, isn't that right?"

"No, there's no way to know," he said, narrowing his eyes into slits. As Shannon wrote *Any number of people (incl. P. YOO)* on the chart next to *Suspect ownership/possession*, he said, "Don't forget, though, it's the *defendant* who wiped them off in the first place."

"Why, Detective," Shannon said, her eyes widening, "I thought you didn't believe she wiped them. I'm glad you finally changed your mind." She smiled—no, beamed—at him like a mother proud of her toddler for finally learning to color inside the lines, and stepped back to reveal the finished chart.

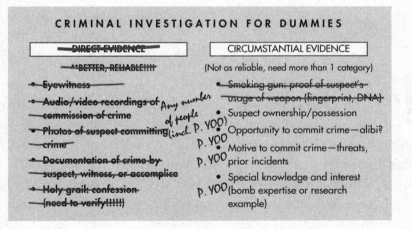

CRIMINAL INVESTIGATION FOR DUMMIES

~~DIRECT EVIDENCE~~	CIRCUMSTANTIAL EVIDENCE
~~**BETTER, RELIABLE!!!!**~~	(Not as reliable, need more than 1 category)
• ~~Eyewitness~~	• ~~Smoking gun: proof of suspect's usage of weapon (fingerprint, DNA)~~
• ~~Audio/video recordings of commission of crime~~ *Any number of people (incl. P. YOO)*	• Suspect ownership/possession
• ~~Photos of suspect committing crime~~	*P. YOO* • Opportunity to commit crime—alibi?
• ~~Documentation of crime by suspect, witness, or accomplice~~	*P. YOO* • Motive to commit crime—threats, prior incidents
• ~~Holy grail: confession (need to verify!!!!!)~~	*P. YOO* • Special knowledge and interest (bomb expertise or research example)

"Thank you for your illuminating testimony, Detective," Shannon said. "I have nothing further."

MATT

HE DROVE TO THE 7-ELEVEN thinking about fingerprints—the arches, loops, and whorls bifurcated by lines and wrinkles, sweat and oil soaked in the curved grooves leaving near-invisible traces on cups, spoons, flush handles, and steering wheels, smudging and covering up other prints left seconds or days or years before, the prints of each person different, each *finger* of each person different, the dizzyingly high number—billions? trillions?—of unique fingerprints in existence, each one unchanging even as a person grows from a six-month fetus to a full-sized adult and then shrinks back into old age.

He'd had ten, like everyone else. The same ten patterns for thirty-three years, from the time he'd been the size of a foot-long sub in his mother's womb and his finger pads were the size of peas. And now they were all gone. Burned and sliced away. His right index and middle fingers amputated under the OR's bright lights, then discarded, prints and all, the medical waste incinerator finishing the flesh-to-dust job the fire started. And the pads of his eight remaining fingers melted into ridgeless, glossy pink scars. Almost as if the slick-smooth plastic of Henry's helmet were still clinging to his fingers, refusing to let go.

As far as he could remember, he'd never been fingerprinted, unless you counted the kindergarten Thanksgiving project with his handprint decorated like a turkey. Which meant there was no record of his fingerprints. Gone, with no way to know which of the gazillions of latent prints on walls, doorknobs, and X-ray films in the world belonged to him.

Right after the amputation, when he'd been glum with self-pity, his favorite burn-ward nurse had said, "Look on the bright side. Some people actually *want* their fingerprints taken off." "Yeah, mobsters and drug lords," he said, and she laughed and said, "I'm just saying, you managed to do what some people dream of, *and* you got insurance to pay for it!" He laughed with her—not out loud, more of a smile, really, but still, the first time he'd done anything but grimace since the amputation—and said, "Yup, now I never have to worry about some cop using my prints to tie me to some murder somewhere."

Matt thought about this often. The transformation of his statement—the random joke he'd cracked for a tired nurse's benefit—from idiotic to downright *prescient* a week later, when Detective Pierson said they found out a cigarette started the fire and were combing the woods for discarded butts and packs. Matt thought of the hollow tree stump by the creek he'd used for trash and panicked—not that he thought for a second he'd be implicated in the fire, but still, there'd be hell to pay with Janine, not to mention public humiliation, if the whole business with Mary came out—but when Pierson said not to worry, they'd find the culprit, fingerprints never lied, Matt remembered his joke and had to cough to cover his relief. There could be a lab-ready set of his prints on every cigarette in the woods, and no one would know. No problem.

But 7-Eleven: *that* could be a problem, one he hadn't seen coming. This morning in court was the first he'd heard that both the fire-starting *and* Elizabeth-picnic cigarettes were Camels from 7-Eleven—the same brand and store Matt used all last summer. It hadn't occurred to him before, but was it possible that those were his? Had he dropped them somewhere, and had Elizabeth or Pak or God knows who else found and used them to set the fire, rendering Matt the unwitting provider of the murder weapon? And now, after the way Shannon had badgered Pierson about his lame-ass "investigation," wouldn't the cops go to every 7-Eleven in the area flashing pictures of Pak and, for good measure, the others, maybe even Matt?

And the note—what did it mean that Elizabeth claimed she'd found what was undoubtedly his note next to the cigarettes? He'd written *This needs to end. We need to meet, 8:15 tonight. By the creek* on H-Mart paper and left it for Mary on her windshield the morning of the explosion. Mary had added *Yes*, then left it on *his* windshield. Matt got it after the morning dive, and he'd crumpled it up and put it in his pocket, but had he dropped it and it blew away and, in a huge coincidence, ended up near the cigarettes?

Matt turned into the 7-Eleven, parked far from the entrance, and looked at its image in the rearview mirror. The store hadn't changed since his last time here, almost a year ago. An aura of neglect permeated this place—the 7-Eleven sign still cracked and listing to one side as if from old age, the handicapped-parking sign missing from the rusted pole, the white parking-space lines faded into ghostly dashes and dots. Across the street stood a gleaming Exxon, bustling with cars and trucks in line, people in and out, the door flapping open and shut in constant motion. The day he first bought cigarettes last summer, he'd almost gone there. He'd gotten in the left-turn lane for the Exxon behind two semis waiting to turn, and after a few minutes, Matt gave up and went to the 7-Eleven down the road. A little run-down, sure, but at least it'd be quick.

Now, sitting here squinting, trying to make out the cashier through the grimy glass, it occurred to Matt: What if he'd been patient for thirty more seconds for the trucks to turn, then gone to the Exxon? For sure, he wouldn't be worried about the clerk identifying him now; the clerks across the street were busy, had to be, wouldn't remember him from Adam. Not like the 7-Eleven clerk, the Santa look-alike who'd teased Matt for worrying about his hacking cough while buying *cigarettes* of all things, who started calling him "the Smoking Doc." Hell, he wouldn't have gotten cigarettes in the first place if he'd just stuck to Exxon. He'd only wanted a quick bite—a doughnut and coffee, maybe, or a corn dog and Coke. Some combination from Janine's bad-for-fertility banned-foods list. It wasn't until he passed the smokers outside 7-Eleven that he decided that cigarettes—probably even worse for sperm motility than junk food—were exactly what he needed. If not for that, he wouldn't have hiked to the creek to smoke, wouldn't have run into Mary, bought another pack and the next and God knows how many more, one of which may have ended up in a murderer's hands. Could it be that by turning right rather than left one day a year ago—an *impulse*, no more a "decision" than picking which tie to wear—he'd changed everything? If he'd turned left, would Henry still be alive, head intact, and Matt at home right now, hands unmangled, taking pictures of a sleeping newborn instead of at this decrepit lot, spying to figure out if the man who could tie him to a murder weapon still worked here?

Matt shook his head to evict these thoughts. He needed to stop this mental masochism, the asking of unanswerable if-only questions that hurt his brain, and focus on his task. It took five minutes: one to see that the cashier was a girl, and four to call from the pay phone outside and tell the girl cashier he was looking for an employee, an older guy with white hair. The second she said no, no guy like that worked there, hadn't for the ten months she'd been there, Matt hung up and breathed in deeply. He expected relief from the muck of dread he'd felt all day—for the pressure squeezing his lungs to lift, for the act of breathing to refresh rather than exhaust him. But none of that happened; if anything, his unease intensified, as if his worry about the 7-Eleven clerk had been covering up something else, like a bandage, and now that it was ripped away, he was having to face the bigger worry, the real worry, the thing he'd been dreading ever since he whispered, "6:30, same place, tonight," passing by her in the courthouse: his meeting with Mary.

○

MATT'S FIRST MEETING with Mary last summer had been on Ovulation Day, a.k.a. As Much Sex as Possible Day. Another manifestation of

Janine's hyper-anal-retentivity, which (like snoring, burning food, and the mole below her butt) he'd found charming at first but irritating as hell now. How had that happened? He couldn't remember making the switch; was it like falling off a cliff, and one day, he'd still loved these quirks and the next, he woke up hating them? Or did the charm wear off bit by bit, like a new car's scent, declining linearly with each hour of the marriage's aging until he'd crossed the line without ever noticing? One hour, the tiniest bit likable, neutral the next, the tiniest bit annoying the following, and in ten years, it'd sink to the level of repulsive, and in thirty, I'll-take-an-ax-to-your-head-if-you-don't-shut-the-fuck-up detestable?

It was hard to believe now, but Janine's all-encompassing focus on future goals was one of the reasons he fell for her when they first met. Not that it was unusual. Pretty much every med-school student had a pathetic need to achieve, which peaked even higher into warp-drive levels among the Asians he knew. What was unusual about Janine was *why*. Unlike his Asian-American friends who told sob stories about their parents forcing them to study 24/7 and harping about Ivy League schools, Janine's achievement orientation was born out of rebellion, because her parents *hadn't* pushed her. She'd told him on their first date how she'd loved her freedom, relative to her younger brother—her parents forcing him (but not her) to go to school even when he was sick, for example, or punishing him (but not her) for getting A-minuses—until she realized: they expected more because he was a *boy*, their all-important firstborn male. She became determined to achieve what they expected from him (go to Harvard, become a doctor) just to spite them.

It was an interesting story, for sure, but what drew Matt in was the way Janine told it. She'd railed against the blatant, unapologetic sexism inherent in Korean culture and confided that because of it, sometimes she hated Koreans, hated *being* Korean, and then she'd laughed at how ironic it was that by trying to escape Asian *gender* stereotyping, she'd fallen into white America's *racial* stereotyping and become a cliché: the overachieving Asian geek. She was fierce and funny, but also vulnerable, a little lost and sad, and it made him want to hail and protect her simultaneously. He wanted to join in her crusade to prove her parents wrong, especially after her mother said to him at their first meeting, "We prefer she marry a

Korean man. But at least you are a doctor." (And yes, it occurred to him that dating him might be part of Janine's rebellion (but no, he didn't let that bother him (too much.)))

Which was why, all throughout school, Matt supported Janine's total focus on grades and fellowships, the way she set each goal and checked it off with methodical ease. It was impressive to watch. Sexy, even. Sure, it required sacrifices in the present—canceled dinners, no movies—but he hadn't minded. It wasn't as if he'd expected any different from med school; after all, what was grad school but the institutionalization of a future-oriented mind-set? For the present, pull all-nighters, eat shitty food, and go into debt, but it'll all be worth it when you *arrive*—when you graduate, get a job, and start living for real. The thing was, though, there was no arriving with Janine. Only delaying. Any goal reached meant setting a new one, bigger, harder. Matt thought she'd stop and declare victory when her brother dropped out of college to become an actor, but maybe the endless goal-setting had become so much a habit by then that she couldn't stop. She kept at it, but stripped of that previous freshness of rebellion, everything she did seemed futile, like Sisyphus rolling a boulder up a hill every day, except instead of the boulder rolling back down every night like in the myth, the hill got twice as tall every night.

Sex was the one thing in their life immune from this future orientation. Even the decision to start trying for kids, unlike every other marital decision—from her taking his name (no) to type of lightbulb (LED)—hadn't been the product of hours of discussion. Just a moment of spontaneity during foreplay one night when he reached for a condom and she said, "Do we need that?" and rolled on top, positioning her vulva just above the tip of his penis. As he shook his head no, she lowered her pelvis slowly, the delicious novelty of her impulsivity, her being in the moment, intertwining with the exquisiteness of her slippery warmth directly on his skin, engulfing him millimeter by millimeter. The next morning, the next night, and for the rest of the month, they continued with the condomless sex. Neither of them mentioned cycles or babies.

When Janine's period came, there was no announcement, just an oh-by-the-way mention. But it was too casual, intentionally so, with a tinge of anxiety. The next month, her delivery was anxious with a tinge of desperation, and the following, desperate with a tinge of hysteria. Books on how to conceive appeared on their nightstand.

When Janine announced Ovulation Week—she'd track her cycle, and around her ovulation, they'd have as much sex as possible—Matt realized: her goal-setting, the exhausting tethering of every act to future milestones, had now infected sex. She'd said nothing about *not* having sex the other three weeks, but that was how it played out. And just like that, sex became something they did for no reason except conception. Clinical and schedule-based. Somewhere around the sperm viability and motility tests, Ovulation Week became Ovulation Day, a twenty-four-hour period for having sex as many times as possible, followed by twenty-seven days of "resting up."

And then came the special-needs kids from HBOT—not only Rosa, TJ, and Henry, but also the kids he sometimes ran into from the other sessions—and even more upsetting, the mothers' stories he was forced to hear for two hours every day. As a radiologist, he saw sick and hurt kids all the time, but witnessing the day-to-day challenges of actually raising these kids—it scared the shit out of him, and it was hard not to think that between his infertility and the HBOT patients, some higher power must be telling him (no, screaming at him) to stop, or at least wait and think things through first.

About a week into HBOT, after a morning dive when Kitt told them about TJ's new "behavior," fecal smearing ("*Fecal*, as in shit?" he'd said, and she'd said, "Yup, and *smearing*, as in rubbing all over walls, curtains, books, everything!"), Matt got a voice mail from Janine that according to her urine test, today was Ovulation Day and could he come home immediately? He ignored it, went to the hospital, and turned off his phone; ignored her increasingly frequent pages. He thought he'd gotten away with it when his mother-in-law barged into his office. "Janine want you home right now. She say it is day for . . . what is the word?" she said. Matt hurried to close the door before she could say "ovulation," but before he could, she said in a clear, loud voice, "Orgasm. It is day for orgasm."

When Matt got home, Janine was already naked, in bed—probably had been since her voice mail six hours ago. He started to say sorry, his phone had died, but she said, "Whatever. Just get over here. We're running out of time. Hurry!"

He undressed, unbuttoning his shirt and unbuckling his belt methodically, slowly. He got in bed, put his lips to hers, and tried to focus on her nipples, on her fingers touching his penis, but nothing happened. "Come on," she said, and pumped his penis, a little too hard. He saw the ovulation stick on a tissue on the nightstand, just sitting there—it seemed to be silently commanding him, Get on with it! Fuck your wife right now!— and he had to laugh at the absurdity, at the way this 99-cent pink stick from CVS had come to control and hijack what remained of his sex life.

"What is going on with you?" Janine said.

Matt lay back. What could he say? "I'm sorry, honey, but discussing orgasms with your mother has put me a bit out of the mood, and besides, I think God doesn't want us to have kids, and also, have you heard of 'fecal smearing'?" He said, "Maybe it's HBOT. I haven't been sleeping. Let's skip this month."

She didn't say anything. They lay there side by side, their bodies close but not touching, naked, looking at the ceiling. After a minute, she sat up. "You're right—let's forget it. You need a break," she said, and moved down. She stopped at his penis—the flaccid dough of flesh retreating into folds of skin—and took him in her mouth. The thought that this was not geared toward a child, toward the future, zapped something, switched on some previously dormant neuron. He held her head, not wanting her to take him out of the warm cavity of her mouth and throat. He came in her mouth.

Afterward, he'd wonder how the hell he didn't see it coming, how he could've deluded himself into thinking she could so easily give up on the day—the whole month! But in the drowsy sweetness of the post-orgasm fog, it didn't occur to him to wonder why Janine sprang up and positively *bounded* to the bathroom. He just lay there like an idiot, warm and happy, half wondering but not really caring what in God's name she could be doing, making such a racket—cabinet doors squeaking, plastic ripping, liquid pouring and shaking, and finally, spitting. When Janine slipped into bed, Matt rolled toward her, ready to drape his arm across and pull her close.

"I need help here. Will you get those pillows and put them under my butt?" Janine spread her legs wide open and raised her hips. She held a needle-free syringe in her hand. Inside, mucous globules lay suspended in clear liquid. Of course—his sperm. The turkey-baster method, which she'd made fun of ("I'm telling you, some women actually use real turkey basters. Seriously!"). She inserted the syringe into her vagina, raised her hips, and slowly pushed the liquid into her body. "I really need the pillows *now*."

Matt placed the pillows against her thighs where, just moments before, he'd thought his tongue would be about now. As he got up and slowly put his clothes back on, he thought how Janine had managed to futurize an orgasm from oral sex, the most present-based thing Matt could think of, how she'd repurposed this act of pure pleasure ("You need a break," she'd said!) into an act of contrived conception.

Matt left early for the evening dive, muttering about traffic. As he closed their bedroom door, he caught a glimpse of Janine, lying naked with her legs straight up in the air, like some soft-porn version of a Cirque du Soleil ad. For the rest of the afternoon—driving to Miracle Creek, stopping at 7-Eleven, buying cigarettes (Camels, on sale), walking to the creek, throughout it all—he thought of his sperm, sliding down Janine's vaginal wall toward her cervix, pulled into her uterus not by the force of their own motility but by gravity. And as he lit the cigarette and breathed in, he imagined his sperm, their whiplike tails propelling them toward the egg, but too slowly, too weakly, to penetrate its shell.

Matt was on his third cigarette when Mary came up. They'd met only once, at the dinner at Matt's in-laws, but she plopped down next to him, none of the awkward oh-hello-what-are-you-doing-heres of near strangers. Just a "Hey," said with the casual familiarity of kids meeting up after school.

"Hey," he said, and eyed the tome in her hand. "SAT words. Want me to quiz you?"

Later, whenever he puzzled over what on God's green earth could've made him so fucking stupid as to start this—what was it?—whatever this *thing* was with Mary, it always came back to this: the way she flung away that *Barron's* like a Frisbee, while giving him that look—a dart of the eyes, almost an eye-roll but not quite, combined with a head shake and frown of disgust. It was Janine's look, her patented no-fucking-way-we're-even-discussing-this look first seen in school when he suggested taking a study break for a movie, and last seen just today when he said that maybe, just a thought, not saying they're giving up or anything, but maybe they should get on some adoption waiting lists. Something about Mary looking like a young Janine while casting away her studies—it made him remember their first date, Janine saying how the real her didn't care about school, how she sometimes wanted to dump her textbooks out her dorm window.

"Camels. My favorite. You mind?" Mary held up his cigarettes.

Matt opened his mouth to say yes, of course I mind, you're a kid and I won't supply a minor, but that strange déjà-vu-like sensation of being with the carefree, "real" Janine, his desperate longing for the pre-real-life, pre-infertility her—those formed a dam in his throat, stopping the words. Mary took his nonresponse as permission and took one.

She lit and held it between her fingers, looking at it lovingly, almost reverently (the look—yes, he knew she was a teenager and he tried not to think it but *not* thinking it made him think it that much more—he imagined Janine giving his penis before sliding it in her mouth) before placing it between her lips. She sucked in (he was actively *not* thinking it), blew out through the O of her lips, and lay back, her long black hair fanning out over the gravel. This reminded him of Janine, too, the way Janine's hair—also long and black, an intense black that looked almost blue—fanned out over her pillow.

Matt looked away. "You shouldn't smoke. How old are you, anyway?" he said.

"Seventeen soon." Mary took another puff. "How old are *you*? What, like thirty?"

"You do this a lot? Smoking?"

She shrugged as if to say, No big deal. "I stashed away some of my dad's cigarettes. Tons of Camels. I'll bring some next time."

"Pak smokes?"

"He says he quit, but . . ." She shrugged again and closed her eyes, a crooked grin on her mouth. She pulled the cigarette to her mouth and breathed slowly, her chest rising before falling again. In, through her body, out. In, out. Matt matched his breath with hers, and something about the synchrony of their breath and the silence between them—a comfortable silence, the kind that wraps the moment in intimacy—made him want to kiss her. Or maybe it was her face, so smooth it seemed to reflect the blue of the sky. He bent down toward her face.

"So, how's the tr—" Mary opened her eyes when Matt's head was above hers. She stopped talking, and her brows lifted in surprise then scrunched into a frown with a dash of annoyance (at his perversion, for trying to kiss her, or at his cowardice, for stopping?).

Matt wanted to tell her. But how could he make her understand? That she'd looked so peaceful—no, it zoomed beyond peace to pure bliss—that he wanted, needed, to partake in it, imbibe the beautiful translucence of her skin and make it his own? "Sorry, I saw a bug, a mosquito, I mean, on your cheek and I wanted to, um, get it," Matt said, willing the capillaries in his face *not* to dilate and send blood gushing to his cheeks.

Mary raised herself up into a half-reclined position, supported by bent elbows.

Matt took a drag. "What were you saying? How's the what?" He tried to sound casual.

It could've been the look he glimpsed as she lay back down: the secret smugness of a woman pleased by a man's interest. Or it could've been what she said next: "I was saying, how's the treatment? You know, HBOT. Is your sperm fixed now?" said matter-of-factly, lightly, with no mocking or pity, as if his infertility were not the Serious Matter of Tragedy that Janine, their doctors, and her goddamned parents treated it like it was, had convinced *him* it was. Whichever it was, in that moment, the failure of his sperm to do what it was supposed to do, what it was *planned* to do, was no longer the cause of grief and penitence, but of relief and hope. Of worry-free, future-free, goddamned fucking freedom.

○

THE MOSQUITOES were a bitch. Funny, how they'd never bothered him last summer, sitting right here with Mary, but now, without the smoke repelling them, they were swarming him, droning their feverish excitement at the arrival of warm flesh, brined in sweat all day, hot blood surging through the veins puffed up by the heat. Matt slapped at the black bodies feasting on his wrists and neck. He wished he had a cigarette.

He stopped when he saw Mary approaching. Fuck it with the mosquitoes—it was more important to appear, to actually be, composed, and besides, his slapping wasn't helping any. "Thanks for coming. I wasn't sure you would," Matt said when she stopped walking, pretty far away, just close enough to hear each other.

"What do you want?" she said. Her voice was a monotone, lower than before the explosion, as if she'd aged twenty years.

"I heard you might be testifying tomorrow," he said.

She didn't respond. Just gave him that look—the no-fucking-way-we're-even-discussing-this look she and Janine shared—then turned and walked away.

"Mary, wait." He thought he saw a pause mid-step, but he blinked and she was still walking. He ran to her. "Mary," he said again, softer this time, and touched her arm. It was strange, seeing his fingers contacting her skin, but unable to feel its smoothness through his nerveless scars, his brain paralyzed over this sensory tug-of-war between sight and touch.

She stopped and looked at his hand, a wince of something—disgust? pity?—flashing across her face before she pulled her arm away. Slowly, cautiously, as if his hand were a bomb about to go off.

He wanted to reach out, touch his scar to hers, but he stepped back. "I'm sorry."

"For what?"

He opened his mouth, but it was as if everything he'd wanted to apologize for—the notes, his wife, his testimony, and most of all, her birthday last summer—was racing to his vocal cords, causing a verbal traffic jam. He cleared his throat. "I need to know if you've told anyone."

Mary twirled her ponytail around her index finger. She let go, then did it again.

Matt sucked the dense, musty air into his lungs. It almost felt like smoking. "Your parents. Do they know?"

"Know what?"

"You know," he said. He was getting a cramp in his missing finger, which was unfortunate, since he couldn't rub it.

Mary narrowed her eyes, as if trying to read small writing on his face. "No. I haven't told anyone."

He realized he'd been holding his breath. He felt dizzy, heard mosquitoes buzzing, the pitch of their drone getting higher, then lower, like sirens passing by.

"And Janine?" Mary said. "She's on the witness list. Is she going to say anything?"

Matt shook his head. "She doesn't know."

Mary frowned. "What do you mean she doesn't know? What are we talking about here?"

"Us," Matt said. "Our notes, smoking, she doesn't know any of that. I never told her."

Mary's face contorted with bitter disbelief before she stepped forward and shoved him, hard. "You fucking liar!" Her voice rose to its preexplosion high pitch. "You think I forgot because of my coma? I remember everything. It was the most humiliating moment of my life, having her treat me like I'm some crazy stalker who won't leave her poor husband alone. You know, I get it if you could never face me again. But why would you send your *wife*?"

Matt stumbled. It was as if Mary's shove had set off a hundred pinballs in his chest, colliding into one another, his ribs, his spine, making it hard to stand straight. "She . . . she what?"

Mary stepped back, her face still overflowing with distrust but softening at Matt's obvious confusion. "You didn't know? But . . ." She clenched her eyes shut and rubbed her face. Her scar turned bright red against her paled skin, like lava oozing crookedly down a mountain. "She said she knew. She said you told her everything the day before the explosion."

Blink, and he could see it: in their bedroom the night before the explosion, Janine's arm reaching from behind, holding Mary's latest note. *I don't know why we need to discuss it. Can't we just forget it ever happened?* Janine's disembodied voice from behind him—"This was in the closet. What's this about? Who's it from?" The lie he'd told, how he'd been sure she'd bought it. Had he been wrong?

"Well? Did you tell her or not?" Mary said.

Matt focused on Mary's face. "She found one of your notes, but I told her it was from an intern who made a pass at me and got embarrassed. Janine believed me, I know she did. She never mentioned it again. When did she talk to you? Where?"

Mary took her ponytail to her lips then let go, letting it fall away. "The night of the explosion, around eight. Right around here."

"Eight? Here? But I talked to her. I called to tell her the dive was delayed and I'd be late. She didn't say anything about driving here or you or—"

"She knew about the delay? But she said . . ." Mary's voice trailed off, her mouth still open but no words coming out.

"What? What did she say?"

Mary shook her head as if to refocus her thoughts. "I was waiting for you, here. She came up, said you told her everything. I said I didn't know what she was talking about, and she said you were too nice to say, but I was stalking you and I'd better stop. She said you weren't coming to meet me, that you couldn't be bothered, and you'd already left and asked her to take care of getting me to leave you alone."

Matt closed his eyes. "Oh my God," he said. Or maybe he just thought it. It was hard to tell. His head was spinning.

"I kept saying I had no idea what she was talking about, but she had this bag, and she . . ." Mary's voice faltered. "She took out a cigarette pack and threw it at me. And matches and a note, too, yelling that it was all mine."

Matt wondered if this was a dream, and he'd wake up and everything would make sense again. But no, dreams felt logical when you were in them. The surreal feeling that was drowning him now came after, not during. "And then?"

"I just said they weren't mine and walked away."

Matt pictured his wife standing here, enraged, cigarettes and matches by her feet and him inside an oxygen chamber mere minutes away. Blood swooshed in his ears.

"Do you think the cigarettes she threw are the ones Elizabeth found?"

Matt nodded. Of course they were. The only unknown was what, if anything, Janine did with them before Elizabeth found them.

After a minute, Mary said, "Were you planning to meet me that night?"

Matt opened his eyes and nodded again. His head felt hollow, and the motion seemed to knock his brain against his skull. "Yeah," he forced himself to say out loud, his voice hoarse as if he hadn't used it in days. "I figured we'd meet later, after the dive."

Mary looked at him, didn't say anything, and he tried to figure out what he saw on her face. Was it longing? Regret?

Mary shook her head. "I have to go. It's getting late." She walked away. After a few steps, she stopped and turned to him. "Do you ever feel guilty? Like maybe we should tell everything we know, and let whatever might happen just happen?"

Matt felt his arteries constrict, sending his organs into panic mode, his heart forced to pump harder, blood to rush faster, lungs to inflate bigger. Yes, he'd worried about his shenanigans with a teenager coming out. But that was laughable, child's play, compared with what the jury would think—and let's be honest, what he himself was thinking—if they found out that Janine was here before the explosion and lied about it.

"I've thought about it." Matt forced his words to sound slow and calm, as if he were considering an interesting side point in a lecture. "But I don't think we have anything relevant to offer. What you, Janine, and I were doing has nothing to do with the fire. The note, the cigarettes— sure, it's interesting to speculate where they came from, but at the end of the day, that has nothing to do with who actually set the fire. I'm worried we'll just confuse the issue. You've seen how these lawyers twist everyone's words."

"Yeah," she said. "You're right. Good night."

"Mary." He stepped toward her. "If you say anything, I mean *any-thing*, our families, all our futures—"

Mary put up her palm like a stop sign and looked into his eyes for a long moment. Slowly, she put her hand back down, turned, and walked away.

When she went around a bend and he could no longer see her, Matt breathed slowly. His arteries seemed to dilate, sending blood rushing to his organs, which were tingling as they unclenched one by one. Matt felt something itch. He looked down. A mosquito sat on the crook of his arm, leisurely sucking on his blood. He slapped at it, fast and hard, and removed his hand. The mosquito lay crushed in his palm, a black smudge stuck in the splatter of the crimson blood it had sucked up in the moments before its death.

MARY

SHE WALKED TO HER FAVORITE SPOT in the woods. A secluded hideaway where Miracle Creek meandered through a dense grove of weeping willows. This was where she came to think whenever she was upset, where she'd come last year after that horrifying birthday night with Matt and again right before the explosion, after Janine threw cigarettes at her. Sitting here on the flat, smooth rock, the gurgling water nearby and green curtain of willows separating her from the world—she felt safe and serene, at one with the woods, as if her skin were molting into the air and the air burrowing into her skin, the cell-by-cell exchange of skin and air making her blurry at the edges like an impressionist painting, her insides seeping out through her pores and dissipating into the sky, leaving her lighter, less substantial.

Mary crouched and put her hands in the water. The current was strong here, the rushing water swirling pebbles, tickling her fingers. She scooped up a handful and scrubbed her arm where Matt touched her. Her stomach calmed, but her brain was still stuck in that bizarre state of hyperspeed paralysis, the thoughts coming so fast, she couldn't think. She stood and breathed, matching the sway of the willow branches nearby, the veil of green undulating side to side in the wind like the grass skirt of a hula dancer. She needed to untangle her thoughts, think things through rationally, one strand at a time.

The cigarette and matches that started the fire were the same ones Janine threw at her. That seemed certain. The only question was the matter of who: Who took them from the woods to the barn, built a mound of sticks, lit the cigarette, placed it on top, and walked away? Janine or Elizabeth? Maybe even the protesters?

Janine had been Mary's original suspect. After waking from the coma, lying in the hospital while doctors prodded and jabbed her, she'd remembered Janine's fury and guessed that she'd done it in an uncontrollable burst of anger, to destroy anything having to do with Mary.

But as she'd been agonizing about what to tell the police—did she have enough courage to tell them everything? Would she have to reveal the humiliating details of her birthday night with Matt?—her mother had told her about Elizabeth, about her smoking, child abuse, computer searches, and on and on, and Mary had been convinced. Everything fit: Elizabeth must have found the cigarettes where Janine threw them, and used them to set up the fire in the way most likely to kill her son *and* incriminate the protesters. The horrifying efficiency of it all. That, plus Abe's "beyond one hundred percent" certainty of Elizabeth's guilt—those were what Mary clung to when her conscience struck, when she longed to break her silence about that night.

But today had changed all that. Not only the cross-examinations (Abe's case against Elizabeth was far from the slam dunk he'd promised), but also the revelations from Matt just now. According to Matt, he'd never talked to Janine about Mary or asked her to confront Mary for him. But what did that mean? Had Janine's lies and secrets been part of some arson-murder plot? Had she been even more furious than Mary had guessed—had she somehow found out about the birthday night?—and had she placed the cigarette by the barn, knowing her husband was inside, to try to kill him?

No. That wasn't possible. Only a monster would put a lit cigarette by flowing oxygen, knowing that helpless children and their mothers were inside. And Janine—a doctor, who was dedicated to saving people's lives, who'd worked hard to help build Miracle Submarine—was not a monster. Was she?

On top of all that, something strange had come out today about the protesters. Detective Pierson said he'd ruled them out because they'd gone straight to D.C. after leaving the police station that night. But that wasn't true; her father had seen them driving around their property only ten minutes before the explosion. So why were the protesters lying? What had they done that needed covering up?

Mary walked to the nearest willow tree and touched the branches that draped almost to the ground. She ran her fingers through, separating them, the way her mother combed her fingers through her hair. She stepped into the veil of willows, feeling the feathery strands gently stroke her face, making the area around her scar feel tingly and tickly.

Her scar. Her father's useless legs, in a wheelchair. Death of a woman and a boy. The boy's mother on trial for murder, which, if she had nothing to do with the fire, was putting her unjustly through hell. And now, Mary's father being accused of murder. So much pain and destruction, her silence enabling it all. Given everything she now knew, given her suspicions about Janine and the protesters, her rising doubts about Elizabeth's role in the fire, didn't Mary have a duty to come forward, no matter what the consequences?

Abe said she might testify soon. Maybe that was exactly what she needed. A chance—no, a mandate—to tell the truth. She'd wait one more day. Abe said he'd be presenting the most shocking, incontrovertible proof of Elizabeth's guilt tomorrow. She'd wait to see what that was. And if any doubt remained, if there was the slightest chance that Elizabeth wasn't to blame, she'd stand up in court and tell everything that happened last summer.

JANINE CHO

SHE WENT STRAIGHT TO THE KITCHEN CABINET where she kept the wok. It had been a bridal-shower present from one of Matt's cousins, who'd said, "I know this isn't on your registry, but it seemed so appropriate . . ." She hadn't explained how it seemed "appropriate," but Janine knew it was because she was Asian. Woks are a Chinese thing, not a Korean thing, she'd wanted to say, but she'd bitten that back and thanked her for such a thoughtful gift. She'd meant to donate or regift it, but she'd kept it, stored away behind all the other junk they never used.

She opened the box with the wok—only the second time ever—and grabbed the instructions/recipes booklet. She flipped through until she found it: the infamous H-Mart note, which she'd hidden away and tried to forget about for the last year.

Today in court was the first time she'd realized that anyone other than Matt, Mary, and she herself even knew about it, much less that its existence was a point of contention. And to think, she'd almost missed when it came up in court today. After Pierson said the protesters were innocent, she'd been preoccupied with thoughts of that night—how she'd seen the protesters driving by Miracle Submarine, what time that was (8:10? 8:15?) and how reliable these "cell tower pings" could be if they corroborated their lies, and, oh God, was there a record of her own cell tower pings somewhere?—when Teresa stood and yelled out, "I saw the H-Mart note." Janine's heart had pounded her rib cage and she'd had to rearrange her hair to hide her burning cheeks.

Why had she kept it? She could think of no purpose, no reason other than her supreme idiocy. In the hospital after the explosion, when she overheard detectives talking about finding cigarettes and needing to comb through the woods in the morning, she'd panicked and driven to Miracle Creek in the middle of the night to retrieve the things she'd stupidly left behind. She couldn't find the cigarettes or matches; the note was the only thing she found, behind a bush near a square area cordoned off with yellow tape (Elizabeth's picnic spot, she later learned). She grabbed the note and, for some bizarre reason she couldn't explain, chose to keep it.

Of course, everything she did back then seemed inexplicable now, a year later. But on that day, with the insanity-inducing mix of shame and rage coursing through her, all her actions had made perfect sense. Even the note-in-wok placement—it had seemed strangely appropriate to keep the proof of her husband's relationship with a Korean girl inside a present from the woman who'd first accused him of having an "Oriental fetish."

It had happened the Thanksgiving after their engagement, at Matt's grandparents' house. After introductions, Janine was returning from the bathroom when she overheard a group of female voices—Matt's cousins, all perky blondes with Southern accents in varying degrees of thickness—saying in whispers, as if sharing shameful secrets, "I didn't know she was Oriental!" "What is this now, the third?" "I think one was Pakistani—does that count?" "I've been telling you, he has an Oriental fetish, some men are just like that."

At this last utterance (made by the soon-to-be wok-gifter), Janine padded back. She locked the bathroom door, turned on the faucet, and looked at herself in the mirror. Oriental fetish. Was that what she was? An exotic plaything to quench some deep-seated psychosexual aberration? *Fetish* implied something wrong. Obscene, even. And the word *Oriental*—it conjured up alien images of third-world, backward villages from long ago. Geisha and child brides. Submission and perversion. She felt hot shame sweeping through her, head to toe, side to side, each sweep flooding her in torrents. And anger, a piercing sense of unfairness: she'd had white boyfriends, but no one accused her of harboring a Caucasian fetish. And she had friends who'd dated only blondes or Jewish women or Republican men (by coincidence or intent, no one knew or cared), but they didn't get accused of having a blonde fetish or Jew fetish or Republican fetish. But take any non-Asian guy who's dated at least two Asian women—well, that was a fetish, he must have wanted them to fulfill some kinky, psychologically aberrant need he had for exotic Orientalness. But why? Who decided it was normal to be attracted to blondes and Jews and Republicans, but not to Asian women? Why was "fetish," with its connotation of sexual deviance, reserved for Asian women and feet? It was offensive, it was bullshit, and she wanted to scream out, *I am not "Oriental," and I am not a foot!*

At dinner, Janine sat next to Matt (but not too close), feeling wrong and dirty, wondering who else thought *Oriental fetish* looking at them. Her acute awareness of her foreignness churned in her stomach anytime anyone remarked about Asians, even the benignly stereotypical or intended-to-be-flattering comments she normally laughed off: Matt's kind grandmother saying, "Imagine what gorgeous kids you'll have. I saw this special on the Vietnam War half-breed kids, and I'm not kidding, they're just *beautiful*," for instance, or Matt's solicitous uncle saying, "Matt says you're first in your class. I'm not surprised. I knew some Asian kids in college—Japanese, I think—and boy, were they wicked smart." (Followed by his wife's "Half of Berkeley's Asian now," then to Janine, "Not that there's anything wrong with that.")

Afterward, Janine tried to forget it, reminded herself it was an ignorant comment uttered by an ignorant person, and in any event, Matt had plenty of non-Asian ex-girlfriends (specifically, six whites, versus two

Asian-Americans—she'd checked the next day). But from time to time—when she saw Matt joking with an Asian nurse in the café, for instance, or when a woman she'd never liked said, "You guys should double-date with the new podiatrist and his wife, she's Asian, too"—she thought of the wok cousin and felt heat sear her eyes and cheeks.

But those times, she knew he'd done nothing wrong and she was being irrationally reactionary. The notes were different. The first one she found—the night before the explosion, while doing laundry, in Matt's pants pocket—she'd shown to Matt, who said it was from a hospital intern whose passes he'd rebuffed. She'd tried to believe him, had wanted to, but she couldn't help looking the next morning—through his clothes, car, even the trash—and found more with the same handwriting. Most were short, variations on *See you tonight?* or *Missed you last night*, but she came across one reading *Hate SAT words! NEED smokes tonight!*, and she knew: Matt had lied.

When she found the final note—the now-infamous H-Mart note that she'd stored with the wok for a year and was now holding in her hand—and read her husband's scribbled handwriting, *This needs to end. We need to meet, 8:15 tonight. By the creek*, and the *Yes* in girlish writing on the bottom, that was when she realized: the proposed time (right after a dive) and location (he'd mentioned only one "creek") had to mean that the girl he was meeting, the girl he'd smoked with and God only knew what else, was Mary Yoo.

It made her crazy. She could see that now. Finding this note, realizing that Matt was involved with a Korean girl, not knowing which humiliated her more—the teenage part, or the Korean part?—and wondering if the wok cousin had been right. A blast of heat blew through her, so hot and fast she felt feverish and weak, and she wanted to slap Matt and scream, ask what the hell was it with him and this fetish, and yet, at the same time, she hated herself for buying into this fetish bullshit, and she wanted to never say it out loud to him, it was too shameful.

Now, standing in her kitchen, Janine held the note, this piece of paper that had been the beginning and ending of everything she wished she could undo that night: from driving out to Miracle Creek to confront Mary with it, to retrieving it in the middle of the night, plus all the awful things between. She took it to the sink and ran it under the water. She tore it into pieces, again and again, and released the bits into the stream, letting them fall in. She switched on the disposal, focusing on the grating sound of the metal blade turning around and around, obliterating the note into particles of pulp. Once she was calm, once she could no longer hear the rushing of blood in her eardrums, she shut off the disposal and the water, put the wok booklet back in the box, and closed it up. She put the box back in the cabinet, behind all the things she'd never use, and shut it tight.

THE TRIAL: DAY THREE

Wednesday, August 19, 2009

PAK

PAK YOO WAS A DIFFERENT PERSON in English than in Korean. In a way, he supposed, it was inevitable for immigrants to become child versions of themselves, stripped of their verbal fluency and, with it, a layer of their competence and maturity. Before moving to America, he'd prepared himself for the difficulties he knew he'd experience: the logistical awkwardness of translating his thoughts before speaking, the intellectual taxation of figuring out words from context, the physical challenge of shaping his tongue into unfamiliar positions to make sounds that didn't exist in Korean. But what he hadn't known, hadn't expected, was that this linguistic uncertainty would extend beyond speech and, like a virus, infect other parts: his thinking, demeanor, his very personality itself. In Korean, he was an authoritative man, educated and worthy of respect. In English, he was a deaf, mute idiot, unsure, nervous, and inept. A bah-bo.

Pak accepted this long ago, on the first day he joined Young at the Baltimore grocery store. The preteen hoodlums saying "Ah-so" in fake accents, pretending they couldn't understand his "May I help you?" and sniggering as they repeated in bastardized singsong, "Meh-yee ah-ee hair-puh yoooooh?"—that, he could dismiss as the antics of children trying on cruelty like a shirt in a store. But the woman who'd ordered a bologna sandwich: her struggle to understand his "Would you like a soda also?"—a phrase he'd memorized that morning—had been genuine. She said, "I couldn't hear; could you repeat that?" After his louder, slower repetition, she said, "Say that one more time," then, "I'm sorry; something's wrong with my ears today," and finally, just an embarrassed smile—the embarrassment for *him*, Pak realized—and shake of her head. With each of the four repetitions, he felt heat radiating through his cheeks and forehead, as if his head were bowed over burning coal and being pushed down centimeter by centimeter. He ended up pointing to a Coke and miming drinking it. She laughed in relief, saying, "Yes, I'd love one," and taking her money, he thought of the beggars outside, taking change from people like this woman, with kind but repugnant pity in her eyes.

Pak became quiet. He found relief in the relative dignity of silence and retreated into invisibility. The problem was, Americans didn't like silence. It made them uneasy. To Koreans, being sparing with words signaled gravitas, but to Americans, verbiage was an inherent good, akin to kindness or courage. They loved words—the more, the longer, and more quickly said, the smarter and more impressive. Quietness, Americans seemed to equate with an empty mind—nothing to say, no thoughts worth hearing—or perhaps sullenness. Deceit, even. Which was why Abe was worried about Pak testifying. "The jury has to think you *want* to give them information," he'd said, preparing Pak. "You take those long pauses, they'll wonder, 'What's he hiding? Is he figuring out how best to lie?'"

Sitting here now, with the jury seated and all whispered conversations on pause, Pak closed his eyes and savored this last moment of silence before the slinging and pummeling of words would begin. Perhaps he could drink in the silence and keep it in reserve, like a camel in the desert, use it to refresh himself bit by bit on the stand.

○

BEING A WITNESS was like acting. On a raised stage, all eyes on him, trying to recall someone else's scripted words. At least Abe started with basic questions with easy-to-memorize answers: "I am forty-one years old," "I was born and raised in South Korea," "I moved to America last year," "At first, I worked in a grocery store." The kind of question-answer sets listed in Pak's old English textbooks, which he'd used to teach Mary back in Korea. He'd drilled her, making her recite her answers again and again until they became automatic, the same way she'd drilled him last night, correcting his pronunciation, forcing him to practice just once more. And now, Mary was at the edge of her seat, staring at him with an unblinking intensity as if to telegraph her thoughts to his, the way he used to during her monthly math competitions in Korea.

This was the thing he regretted most about their move to America: the shame of becoming less proficient, less adult, than his own child. He'd expected this to happen eventually, had seen how children and parents switch places as the parents age, their minds and bodies reverting to childhood, then infancy, then nonbeing. But not for many years, and certainly not yet, when Mary still had a foot in childhood. In Korea, *he* had been the teacher. But after his move, when he visited Mary's school, her principal had said, "Welcome! Tell me, how are you liking Baltimore?" Pak smiled, nodded, and was deciding how to answer—perhaps the smile-nod had been enough?—when Mary said, "He loves it here, running the store right by Inner Harbor. Right, Dad?" The rest of the meeting, Mary continued speaking for him, answering questions directed his way, like a mother with her two-year-old son.

The irony was, this was precisely why they'd immigrated to America: so that Mary might have a better life, a brighter future, than theirs. (Wasn't that what parents were supposed to hope for, that their children would become taller/smarter/richer than they?) Pak was proud of his daughter for the speed with which she achieved fluency in this foreign language that eluded him, for her sprint down the path of Americanization. And his inability to keep up—that was *supposed* to happen. Not only because she'd been here four years longer but because children were better at languages, the younger, the better; everyone knew that. At puberty, one's tongue set, lost its ability to replicate new sounds without an accent. But it was one thing to know this, and another thing entirely to have your child witness you struggle, to transform in their eyes from a demigod to someone small.

"Pak, why did you start Miracle Submarine? Korean-run groceries, I've seen. But HBOT seems unusual," Abe said, the first of challenging questions requiring longer narratives.

Pak looked at the jurors and tried to imagine them as new friends he was getting to know, as Abe had advised. He said, "I worked . . . at a wellness center . . . in Seoul . . . It was my dream to . . . start same facility . . . to help people." The words he'd memorized didn't feel right in his mouth, stuck like glue. He'd have to do better.

"Tell us why you got fire insurance."

"Fire insurance is recommended by hyperbaric regulators." Pak had practiced this over a hundred times last night, the seven *r*'s in a row straining his tongue, making him stutter. Thankfully, the jury seemed to understand him.

"Why 1.3 million?"

"The company determined the policy amount." At the time, he'd been outraged, having to pay so much—and every month!—for something that might never materialize. But he'd had no choice. Janine had insisted on the policy, had made it a condition of their deal. Just behind Abe, Janine was looking down, her face pale, and Pak wondered if she lay awake at night, regretting their secret arrangement, the cash payments, wondering how their excited plans had ended here.

"Yesterday, Ms. Haug accused you of calling the company regarding arson, using Matt Thompson's phone. Pak"—Abe stepped closer—"did you make that call?"

"No. I never use Matt's telephone. I never call my company. There is no need. I already know answer. It is written in the policy."

Abe held up a document, as if to show off its thickness—two centimeters at least—then handed it to Pak. "Is this the policy you're referring to?"

"Yes. I read before I signed."

Abe put on a look of surprise. "Really? It's a mighty long document. Most people don't read the fine print. I don't, and I'm a lawyer."

The jurors nodded. Pak guessed they were in the category of people—most Americans were, Abe said—who just signed things, which seemed to be incredibly trusting or just lazy. Maybe both. "I am not familiar with American business. So I must read. I translated to Korean using dictionary." Pak flipped to the arson page and held it up. The jurors were too far to make out the words, but they could surely see his scribbles in the margins.

"And the answer to the arson question is in that document?"

"Yes." Pak read the provision, a model of American verbal excess, an eighteen-line sentence full of semicolons and long words. He pointed to his Korean scribble. "This is my translation. *You get money if someone sets fire, but not if you are involved.*"

Abe nodded. "Now, another thing the defense tried to pin on you is the H-Mart note the defendant *claims* to have found." Abe clenched his jaw, and Pak guessed he was still upset about Teresa's "defection," as he'd called it. "Pak, did you write or receive any such note?"

"No. Never," Pak said.

"Know anything about it?"

"No."

"But you *do* own an H-Mart notepad?"

"Yes. I had in the barn. Many people use it. Elizabeth used it. She liked the size. I gave her one pad. For her purse."

"Wait, so the defendant kept an entire H-Mart notepad in her purse?" Abe looked shocked, as if he hadn't known, hadn't scripted Pak's answer.

"Yes." Pak resisted the urge to smile at Abe's theatrics.

"So she could've easily crumpled up H-Mart paper and left it for others to see?"

"Objection, calls for speculation." Shannon stood.

"Withdrawn." A smile passed through Abe's face like a fast-moving cloud as he put a poster on the easel. "This is a copy of the marked-up chart Ms. Haug introduced yesterday."

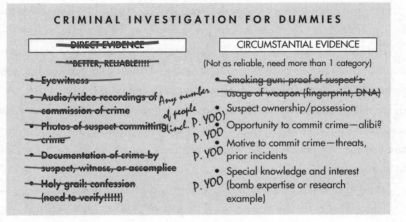

Pak looked at the red letters blaming him for the destruction of his patients' lives, his daughter's face, his own legs.

"Pak, your name is all over this chart. Let's explore that. First, ownership or possession of the weapon—in this case, Camel cigarettes. Did you have any last summer?"

"No. I have no-smoking rule. It is too dangerous with oxygen."

"How about before last summer? Have you ever smoked?"

Pak had asked Abe not to ask this, but Abe said Shannon was sure to have evidence of his past smoking, and admitting it first would deflate her planned attack. "Yes, in Baltimore. But never in Virginia."

"Have you bought cigarettes or anything else from any 7-Eleven, anywhere?"

"No. I saw 7-Eleven in Baltimore, but I never go inside. I never saw 7-Eleven near Miracle Creek."

Abe stepped closer. "Did you buy or even touch any cigarettes last summer?"

Pak swallowed. There was no shame in white lies, answers that were technically untrue but ultimately served the greater good. "No."

Abe took out a red marker, marched to the easel, and crossed out *P. YOO* next to *Suspect ownership/possession*. Abe closed the marker, the cap's click an auditory exclamation point to the slashing of Pak's name. "Next, *Opportunity to commit crime*. There's been a lot of confusion here, with your neighbor, your voice, all that. So tell us, once and for all: Where were you during the last dive, before the explosion?"

Pak spoke slowly, deliberately, elongating each syllable. "I was inside the barn. The entire time." This wasn't a lie. Not really. Not when it had no impact on the ultimate question of who set the fire.

"Did you immediately open the hatch?"

"No." And it was true, he wouldn't have done that. Pak explained what he would've done if he'd been there: turn off oxygen at the emergency valves in case the controls were damaged, then extra-slow depressurization to make sure the pressure changes wouldn't cause another detonation, resulting in the delay of the hatch opening by more than a minute.

"That makes sense. Thank you," Abe said. "Now, Pak, do you have any other proof that you never went outside by the oxygen tanks before the explosion?"

"Yes, my cell telephone record," Pak said, as Abe handed out copies. "8:05 to 8:22 p.m., I was on the telephone. I called the power company to ask when they will fix, and also my wife, to ask her when she will return with batteries. Seventeen minutes, continuous telephone calls."

"Okay, I see that, but so what? You could've been on the phone while you were outside, setting fire under the oxygen tube."

Pak couldn't help a little smile as he shook his head. "No. That is impossible."

Abe frowned, pretending to be mystified. "Why?"

"There is no cell reception near oxygen tank. Yes, in front of the barn.

Not in back. Inside or outside. All my patients know this. If they wish to call, they must walk to front."

"I see. So you couldn't be anywhere near the fire's starting point from 8:05 until the explosion. No vicinity, no opportunity." Abe popped the marker open and crossed out his name next to *Opportunity to commit crime*. "Let's turn to 'Special knowledge and interest,' next to which Ms. Haug has written 'P. YOO.'"

Pak heard tittering, and he thought of Abe's explanation of the juvenile humor of this abbreviation. "Intentional, I'm sure. I hate that woman," Abe had said.

"Pak, as a licensed HBOT operator, you *did* research HBOT fires, correct?"

"Yes. I researched to learn how to avoid fires. Improve safety."

"Thank you." Under the *P. YOO* next to *Special knowledge and interest*, Abe wrote *(for good reason—safety)* and said, "We come to the last remaining item. Motive. Let me ask straight-out: Did you set fire to your own business with your patients inside and your family nearby to get 1.3 million dollars?"

Pak didn't have to fake laughing in incredulity at this notion. "No." He looked at the jurors, focusing in on the older faces. "If you have any children, you know. I never, *never* risk my child for money. We came to America for our daughter. Her future. Everything is for my family." The jurors nodded. "I was excited about my business. Miracle Submarine! Many parents of disabled children call, we have waiting list for patients. We are happy. There is no reason to destroy this. Why?"

"I suppose some would answer, 1.3 million dollars. That's a lot of money."

Pak looked down at his useless legs in the wheelchair, touched the steel—even in this hot courtroom, it remained cold. "The hospital bills. They are one-half-million dollars. My daughter was in a coma. Doctors say maybe I never walk again." Pak looked at Mary, her cheeks wet from tears. "No. 1.3 million dollars is not a lot of money."

Abe looked at the jurors, all twelve now looking at Pak with sympathy in their eyes, leaning forward in their seats toward him as if they wanted to reach across the railings and touch him, comfort him. Abe touched the tip of the red marker to the *P* in *P. YOO* next to *Motive to commit crime*. He stared and shook his head. Slowly, definitively, he put a red gash through Pak's name.

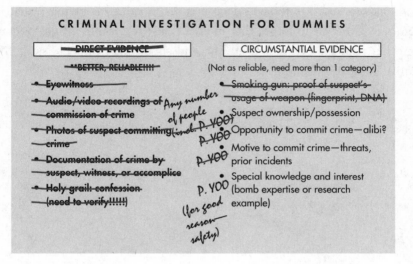

"Pak," Abe said, "Matt Thompson told us that you ran into the fire, into the burning chamber, multiple times, even after you were severely injured. Why?"

This was not on the script, but strangely, Pak did not feel panic at having to give an unrehearsed answer. He looked to the gallery, to Matt and Teresa, the other patients behind them. He thought of the children, Rosa in the wheelchair, TJ flapping his arms like a bird, but most of all, Henry. Shy Henry, with eyes that always floated up, as if tethered to the sky. "This is my duty. My patients. I must protect them. *My* harm, it does not matter." Pak turned to Elizabeth. "I tried to save Henry, but the fire . . ."

Elizabeth looked down, as if in shame, and reached for her water glass. Abe said, "Thank you, Pak. I know this is difficult. One final question. Once and for all, did you have anything whatsoever to do with the cigarette, the matches, *anything* even remotely related to setting the fire that killed two of your patients and nearly killed you and your daughter?"

He was opening his mouth to answer when he saw Elizabeth's hand shake slightly bringing the water to her mouth. It came to him then, the familiar image that too often wormed its way out of the recesses of his mind to invade his dreams: a cigarette between gloved fingers, shaking slightly, moving toward a matchbook beneath the oxygen tube.

Pak blinked. He took in deep breaths to calm his racing heart. He reminded himself to forget that moment, just roll it into a tight ball and smother it away. He looked at Abe and shook his head. He said, "No, nothing. Nothing at all."

YOUNG

WHEN ELIZABETH'S LAWYER SAID, "Good afternoon, Mr. Yoo," the memory that rushed to Young was, strangely, of Mary's birth. It must have been the look on Pak's face: every muscle in his face clenched still into the emotionless mask of a man bracing himself to hide his fear. It was the same look he'd had nearly eighteen years ago (no, exactly eighteen years ago—Mary's birthday was tomorrow, but it was already tomorrow in Seoul, where she'd been born) when the doctor came in with a grave look and walked the length of Young's recovery room without a word. They'd had to do an emergency hysterectomy, the doctor said. At least the baby's fine, he said. The baby was a girl. They were sorry. (Or was it, The baby was a girl—they were sorry?)

Like most Korean men, Pak had wanted a son, expected one. He'd tried to hide his disappointment; when his family bemoaned his misfortune in his only child being a girl, he said, "She's as good as ten sons." But a little too firmly, as if trying to convince them of something he didn't quite believe. Young heard the strain in his voice, the false brightness he'd tried to inject, making his voice higher-pitched than usual.

Which was exactly how he sounded now, saying, "Good afternoon."

Elizabeth's lawyer didn't spend any time buttering him up, like she had with the others. "You said you've never been to a 7-Eleven around here, is that correct?"

"Yes. I never saw. I do not know the locations," Pak said, and Young smiled. Abe had told him not to simply say "yes," that that's what she needed to trap him. Elaborate, explain, he'd said, and Pak was doing just that.

Shannon lowered her chin, smiled, and stepped toward Pak like a hunter with prey. "Do you have an ATM card?"

"Yes." Pak frowned, probably mystified by the sudden change in topic.

"Does your wife use that card?"

Pak's frown deepened. "No. My wife has separate card."

Shannon handed him a document. "Recognize this?"

Pak flipped through. "It is my bank account statement."

"Please read for us the highlighted lines under 'ATM cash withdrawals.'"

"June 22, 2008—ten dollars. July 6, 2008—ten dollars. July 24, 2008—ten dollars. August 10, 2008—ten dollars."

"What's the location for those four entries?"

"It is 108 Prince Street, Pine Edge, Virginia."

"Mr. Yoo, do you remember what's at that location, 108 Prince Street in Pine Edge?"

Pak looked up, his face scrunched in concentration, and shook his head. "No."

"Let's see if we can refresh your recollection." Shannon placed a poster on the easel: a picture of a 7-Eleven with an ATM under its orange-green-red-striped awning. Clearly visible on the glass door was the address—108 Prince Street, Pine Edge, VA. Young felt something drop in her stomach and grind against her bowels.

Pak held still, but his face paled into the weathered gray of a gravestone.

"Mr. Yoo, what is next to the ATM at this location?"

"7-Eleven is there."

"You testified that you've never been to or even seen a 7-Eleven nearby, and yet there's one at the ATM you used four times last summer. Do I have that right?"

"I do not remember this ATM. I never go there," Pak said. His face looked resolute, but there was doubt in his voice. Could the jury hear it, too?

"Is there any reason to think your bank statement might be wrong? Was your card lost or stolen at all last summer?"

Something came to Pak then. A thought that excited him and caused him to open his mouth. But just as suddenly, he closed his mouth and lowered his eyes. "No. No stolen."

"So you admit that your bank records *prove* you went to this 7-Eleven multiple times, but you claim you don't remember being there, is that right?"

Pak said, still looking down, "I do not remember."

"Much like you can't *remember* buying cigarettes last summer?"

"Objection, badgering the witness," Abe said.

"Withdrawn," Shannon said, and continued. "Didn't you go to 7-Eleven on August 26, mere hours before the explosion?"

"No!" Outrage powered Pak's voice and brought color back to his face. "I never go to 7-Eleven. Never, and not day of explosion. I never leave my business all day."

Shannon raised her brows. "So you didn't leave your property at all that day?"

Pak opened his mouth eagerly, and Young expected him to say "Yes!" but instead, his mouth closed and his body slumped like a punctured blow-up toy, losing air fast. Shannon said, "Mr. Yoo?" and Pak looked up. "I remember now, I went shopping. We needed baby powder." He looked at the jurors. "We use it on oxygen helmet seal. For sweat. To keep dry."

Young remembered Pak saying they needed more powder but he couldn't leave with the protesters on-site. And later, before the last dive, he'd grabbed cornstarch from the kitchen as an alternative to powder. So why was he lying?

"Where did you go?" Shannon said.

"Walgreen to get baby powder. Then ATM near there."

"Mr. Yoo, please read the line dated August 26, 2008, on your bank statement."

Pak nodded. "'ATM cash. One hundred dollars. 12:48 p.m. Creek-side Plaza, Miracle Creek, Virginia.'"

"That's the ATM you went to, after Walgreens?"

"Yes." Young thought back. 12:48, during lunch break. He'd asked her to prepare lunch while he went to reason with the protesters once more. He'd returned twenty minutes later, saying he'd tried and they wouldn't listen. Had he gone out to town instead? But why? Shannon put another picture on the easel. "Is this the Creekside Plaza ATM?"

"Yes." The picture showed the entire "plaza," which sounded grand but was actually just three stores and four empty storefronts with "For Lease" signs. The ATM was in the center, next to Party Central.

"What I find interesting is this 7-Eleven, right behind this plaza. You see it, right?" Shannon pointed at the unmistakable stripes in the corner.

Pak didn't look at the picture, just said, "Yes."

"I also find it interesting that you went to *this* ATM, miles away from Walgreens, even though there's an ATM inside Walgreens, which you seem to use regularly, based on your bank statement. Do I have that right?"

"I did not remember I need cash until after Walgreen."

"It's strange how you didn't remember you needed cash while paying for powder, with your wallet out, at Walgreens," Shannon said, then smiled and started walking back to her table.

Pak looked up and said, "Walgreen sell cigarettes."

Shannon turned. "I'm sorry?"

"You think I use Plaza ATM because I go to 7-Eleven for cigarettes. But if I want cigarettes, why I would not buy at Walgreen?" Of course. Shannon's argument didn't hold up. Young felt a thrill of triumph at Pak's logic, at his look of pride, at the jurors' nods at him.

Shannon said, "Because I don't think you went to Walgreens that day. I think you went to 7-Eleven to get Camels and went to the ATM nearby, and Walgreens is something you came up with today to explain why you left your business." If Shannon had shouted this or said it in a *gotcha!* way, Young could've dismissed it as the rantings of a biased enemy. But Shannon said it gently, with the regretful tone of a teacher telling a kindergartner his answer was wrong—not wanting to, but forced to by duty—and Young found herself agreeing, *knowing* that Shannon was right. Pak hadn't gone to Walgreens. Of course he hadn't. But where had he gone, to do what, that he'd hidden from her, his wife?

Abe objected, and the judge told the jury to disregard the last exchange. Shannon said, "Mr. Yoo, isn't it true that you smoked daily for about twenty years before last summer?"

Young could almost hear the whirs inside his brain trying to figure out how to avoid the resigned "Yes" he eventually muttered.

"How did you quit?" Shannon said.

Pak frowned, seemed puzzled. "I just . . . not smoke."

"Really? You must have used gum or patches, surely." There was an incredulity in Shannon's voice, but it wasn't hostile. It was gentle—admiring, even—and again, Young found herself sympathizing with Shannon, questioning, how *did* he manage to cut off a twenty-year habit so easily? She could see the same question in the jurors' faces.

"No. I just stop."

"You just stopped."

"Yes."

Shannon looked at Pak for a long moment, both their eyes unblinking like in a staring contest. Shannon broke the stare, blinked, and said, "Okay. You just stopped." The way she smiled, she may as well have been a mother, patting her three-year-old's head, saying, *You saw a purple elephant dancing in your room? Okay. Of course you did, sweetheart.* "Now, before you"—she paused—"*quit* smoking, was Camel your favorite?"

Pak shook his head. "In Korea, I smoke Esse, but they do not sell here. In Baltimore, I smoke many brands."

Shannon smiled. "If I were to ask the delivery guys you took smoking breaks with—say, a Mr. Frank Fishel—would they say you had no favorite American brand?" Frank Fishel, the name they hadn't recognized on the defense witness list Abe showed them. They'd known the delivery guy as Frankie, had never known his full name.

Abe stood. "Objection. If Ms. Haug wants to know about other people, she should ask *them*, not Pak."

"Oh, I plan to. Frank Fishel is ready to drive down from Baltimore. But you're right, I withdraw my question." Shannon turned to Pak. "Mr. Yoo, what brand did you tell others was your favorite American cigarette?"

Pak shut his mouth and glared, looking like a recalcitrant boy refusing to accept responsibility for some naughty deed despite obvious proof.

"Your Honor," Shannon said, "please direct the witness to answer—"

"Camel," Pak spat out.

"Camels." Shannon looked satisfied. "Thank you."

Young looked at the jurors. They were frowning at Pak, shaking their heads. If Pak had admitted it right away, they might have believed it was a coincidence, but Pak's near refusal had transformed it into something of significance in their eyes and hers as well. Could the cigarette under the oxygen tube be Pak's, one he'd bought earlier that day? But why?

As if in answer, Shannon said, "You were angry with the protesters, weren't you?"

"Maybe not *angry*. I did not like them bothering my patients," Pak said.

Shannon picked up a file from her desk. "According to a police report, the day after the explosion, you accused the protesters of setting the fire and you stated, quote, 'They threatened to do whatever it took to shut down HBOT.'" Shannon looked up. "Is the report correct?"

Pak looked away for a moment. "Yes."

"And you believed their threats, right? After all, they caused the power outage, disrupting your business, and even as the police were taking them away, they promised to return and keep at it until they shut you down for good, right?"

Pak shrugged. "It does not matter. My patients believe in HBOT."

"Mr. Yoo, isn't your patients' belief in you based on your experience working at an HBOT facility in Seoul for over *four years*?"

Pak shook his head. "My patients see results. The children improve."

"Isn't it true," Shannon continued, "that the protesters threatened to dig up anything they could on you, and said they'd contact the center in Seoul where you worked?"

Pak didn't say anything. His jaw clenched.

"Mr. Yoo, if the explosion hadn't happened and they had, in fact, contacted the center's owner, what would Mr. Byeong-ryoon Kim have told them?"

Abe objected and the judge sustained. Pak didn't move, didn't blink.

"The fact is," Shannon said, "you were *fired* for *incompetence* less than a year into your job, more than three years prior to coming to America, isn't that right? And if the protesters discovered that and exposed your lies to your patients, your business could go down the tubes, leaving you with nothing. And you couldn't let that happen, isn't that so?"

No, that couldn't be. But Young saw Pak's face, deep purple with fury—no, shame, the way his eyes were cast downward, unable to meet Young's gaze—and remembered Pak telling her not to use his work e-mail anymore, that there was a new rule forbidding personal e-mails. As Abe objected and Pak shouted that he never harmed his patients and the judge pounded the gavel, Young had to look away. Her eyes whirled around the courtroom and stopped on the picture on the easel, the glare of sunlight gleaming off something shiny in the Party Central window. She'd passed it on their way to court yesterday, and if she closed her eyes, she could almost pretend it was still yesterday, back when she knew nothing of her husband's secrets and lies and she'd been wondering how much it would cost to get streamers and balloons for Mary's birthday.

Balloons. Young's eyes snapped open at the thought, zoomed to the easel. In the picture, you couldn't make out what in the display was giving off the glare. But yesterday, driving by, Young had seen them, floating lazily inside, next to the ATM: shiny, metallic Mylar balloons with stars and rainbows. Just like the ones that blew out the power lines on the day of the explosion.

○

WHEN MARY (then Meh-hee) was a year old, after Young told him of their baby's glee at seeing balloons for the first time, Pak brought some home from a work event, carrying them on the crowded subway and bus. This made him late getting home—he said he'd had to wait more than thirty minutes for the trains to clear so they wouldn't pop—but when he got home, Meh-hee squealed with delight, toddled on her fat legs across the room, and wrapped her tiny arms around the balloons, as if to hug them. Pak guffawed and acted like a clown, bopping the balloons against his head while making goofy noises, as Young stood by, wondering who this man was, not at all who she'd assumed him to be until that moment (and who he continued to be except around their daughter): a practical, serious man who tried to exude an air of quiet dignity, who rarely told jokes or lost himself in laughter.

It was the same feeling she had now, looking at Pak and telling herself that this man—glaring at Shannon with veins popping in his forehead and sweat dampening his hair into a droopy flop—was the same man who'd brought home balloons bigger than their baby's head. Except back then, the he's-a-different-man-than-I-thought realization had been figurative—the welcome discovery of a previously unseen side of her husband—whereas now it was literal: Pak had not, in fact, been what she thought he was, the wellness-center manager and HBOT expert he pretended to be.

As Pak wheeled down from the stand for recess, Young tried to catch his eyes, but he avoided her. He looked almost relieved when Abe stepped in, saying they needed to prepare for his redirect, and wheeled him away without a glance her way.

Redirect. More questions to Pak, more lies explaining away the lies he'd already told. Young felt her stomach churn, acid lurching up her esophagus to the back of her throat. She bent forward, trying to hold down the contents of her stomach, and swallowed hard. She needed to get out of here; she couldn't breathe.

Young grabbed her purse and told Mary she didn't feel well. Must be something she ate, she said, and hurried out, trying not to stumble. She knew she should tell Mary where she was going, but she didn't know herself. She only knew she needed to get away. Right now.

SHE WAS DRIVING too fast. The road out of Pineburg was an unpaved country road that, on rainy days like today, turned muddy and slippery.

But it felt calming to take the hairpin curves at top speed, having to turn the steering wheel with both hands while pumping the brake, the out-of-control exhilaration of her body sliding into the door. If Pak were here, he'd yell at her to slow down, drive like a proper *mother*, but he was far away and Young was alone. Alone to focus on the feel of the tires crunching the gravel beneath, the rain pattering on the car's rooftop, the thick trees forming a tunnel high overhead. Her nausea abated and she could breathe again.

When the creek alongside the road was bloated, like today, it reminded her of Pak's home village outside Busan. She'd said this once, but Pak said not to be ridiculous, it was nothing like his village, and he accused her of being a city person to whom anything remotely rural all looks the same. And it was true that there were vineyards here instead of rice paddies; deer, not goats. But the water covering the rice paddies—that was the exact shade Miracle Creek turned during storms: the light brown of old chocolate gone crumbly. That was the thing about being nowhere like this; there was nothing to orient you to place and time, and you could be transported to the other side of the globe, to a time long past.

It had been in Pak's village where they'd had their first fight. They'd gone right after their engagement, to pay respects to his parents. Pak was nervous; he was convinced that she, who'd always lived in high-rises with indoor plumbing and central heating, would hate his home. What Pak didn't understand was that she actually *liked* his village, the tranquility of escaping the chemical-scented smog and construction noises from every corner of Seoul as it remade itself for the Olympics. Stepping outside the car in the village, she smelled the sweet stench of compost—like kimchi when you first opened the sealed jar after days of fermentation. She scanned the hills, the kids running around the creek beds where their moms were washing clothes on wooden boards, and said, "It's hard to believe you come from a place like this." Pak took it as belittling, as confirmation of his long-simmering belief that Young's family (and, by extension, Young herself) regarded him as "beneath" her, when in fact Young meant it as a compliment, a tribute to his raising himself from squalor to the university. The fight had ended with Pak saying he was going to refuse her father's offer of a dowry as well as the sales job at her uncle's electronics company. "I don't need charity," he'd said.

Remembering this now, Young gripped the steering wheel. Something ran across the road—a raccoon?—and she veered, sending a tire thumping off the road and the car skidding toward a giant oak. She braked hard and turned, but the car kept sliding, slipping, slowing too slowly. She pulled on the parking brake. The car lurched to a stop, and her head jerked back.

The tree trunk was directly in front of the car, centimeters away from the bumper, and—yes, she knew it was inappropriate, but she couldn't help it—she guffawed. It must have been the panic and relief, mixing into a bizarre sense of triumph. Invincibility. She breathed to calm herself down, watching the rainwater meander around the tree's knots and gnarls, and she thought of Pak, her proud husband, fired less than a year after his family left for another country. They'd talked infrequently in those four years of separation—international calls were expensive and their work schedules incompatible—and she herself had avoided bad news in those calls. Was she surprised that he hadn't wanted to expose his shame over the phone or in an e-mail? Sitting here, away from the immediacy of her shock at his deceit, Young's anger began to crumble away at the edges, displaced by sympathy. Yes, she could see how easy it would have been to justify keeping silent about something happening literally a world away, something she could have done nothing about. Maybe she could even forgive it.

But beyond all that, there was still the matter of the balloons. The thing was, Pak knew Mylar balloons could short power circuits. Probably every Korean parent did. Household items causing electrical accidents were popular science-fair entries in Korea—a boy had won Mary's fifth-grade competition with an exhibit featuring Mylar balloons, hair dryers falling in tubs, and worn power cords starting fires—and she'd been surprised that most Americans seemed to have no idea. (Then again, America was low on international science-education rankings.) And Pak *had* been at a balloon store within hours of the outage. But did that mean he caused it? It made no sense. And what of Pak's smoking? A few times last summer, she thought she smelled smoking, but it had been so faint, she'd thought it must be from neighbors walking their dogs and smoking nearby. And if he really *had* lost his job in Korea, how had he managed to save up so much money before coming to America?

She shut her eyes and shook her head hard, hoping to clear these thoughts, but the questions seemed to bounce off her skull into one another, multiplying with each impact and tearing into her brain, leaving her dizzy. A squirrel jumped onto her car hood and peered through the windshield, its head tilted sideways like a child examining fish in a bowl and asking, What in the world are you doing?

She needed answers. She released the brakes, backed away from the tree, and faced the road. If she turned left, she could get back to the courthouse before recess was over, back to her husband's side. But there would be no answers there. Only more lies, leading to more questions. And now, when Mary and Pak were both away, was the perfect opportunity, the only opportunity, to do what she needed. No more waiting to be fed someone else's vague, nonsensical answers. No more watching and trusting.

She turned right. She needed to search for the answers. On her own.

THE STORAGE SHED was on the edge of their property, within spitting distance of the utility pole where the balloons got stuck that day. When Young stepped inside, smells she couldn't begin to identify assaulted her, pungent, dank, and sour. The rain pelted the aluminum roof in fast micro-beats like snare drumming, and water dripped through cracks onto the rotting floorboards in bass-drum beats. Tools and dead leaves littered the ground, camouflaged by a shroud of dust, rust, and mold, which had congealed into green-black slime in the corners.

She wondered how long she'd have to stand still before spiders started crawling on her. One year of neglect—a drizzly autumn followed by one hurricane, four snowstorms, and a summer of record-shattering humidity levels. That was all it had taken to transform their years in Seoul and Baltimore into this pile of forgotten items in varying states of decay. There was no attic or closet in their shack. If Pak was hiding anything, it had to be here.

She walked to the corner pile of three moving boxes and pulled off the trash bag on top, its former transparency veiled by dried cobwebs.

Chalky dust rose like mist before the air's dampness weighed it down into a free fall, and Young smelled something dank, like earth buried deep getting dug up and hitting air for the first time.

It was in the third box—the bottom one, the least accessible—that she found it. The top two boxes were nearly empty, but the third was full of old philosophy textbooks she'd forgotten she'd kept. If she'd just riffled through, she'd have missed the item, wrapped neatly inside a paper bag and nestled between similarly sized books: the tin case from the grocery store where they stored loose cigarettes from damaged packs, which she'd had the idea to sell for fifty cents apiece. After she informed the welfare customers that food stamps couldn't buy cigarettes but that she couldn't prevent their using *change* from food-stamp purchases to buy singles, sales went way up and she started having to open perfectly fine packs to keep up with demand.

The last time she'd seen this case was during their move here. It had been on top of sweaters waiting to be packed, and she'd opened it to see it full of loose cigarettes. She asked Pak why he was bringing it—hadn't he said he was quitting?—and he said he didn't want to throw away perfectly good cigarettes, there must be a hundred in there. "What, you're saving *cigarettes* to pass down to our grandkids?" She laughed. He smiled, his eyes not meeting hers, and she told him that actually, it was part of the store inventory, which belonged to the owners. She asked him to put it with the things they needed to return. That was the last time she'd seen the case—in Baltimore, in Pak's hands, as he took it to deliver to the Kangs. And now here it was, in another state, deliberately hidden from view.

Young took the tin case out of the paper bag and yanked open the lid. Like the last time she saw it, slim rolls of cigarettes neatly lined the box like soldiers, but on top were two packs of Doublemint gum (Pak's favorite) and a travel-size can of Febreze ("ELIMINATES ODORS").

Young slapped the lid shut and looked at the moving box. What else was hiding in there?

She picked up the whole box. It was heavy, its bottom grimy with mold, but she gripped tighter, lifted, and turned it upside down. Everything fell out, sending a plume of dust up and dried cobwebs scattering all around. She hurled the empty box at the wall—it felt good, hearing it smack, though not as satisfying as the deep thuds of the heavy books pummeling the ground, one after the other—and scanned the items looking for . . . what? Receipts for balloons? Matches from 7-Eleven? H-Mart notes? *Something.* But there was nothing. Just Korean books, all around her, some torn from the impact of the fall, and one trio of books that had somehow fallen together, as if glued, and ended up in a neat stack.

Young stepped over to the three books. Once closer, she could see: the middle book wasn't lying flat. Something was inside it, making it bulge. She touched the top book with her sandal's tip—cautiously, as if the books were poisonous snakes that looked dead but might simply be sleeping—and kicked with just enough force to knock it off the tower. She bent down and reached for the second book, now on top. John Rawls's *A Theory of Justice*, her favorite book in college. Which meant the thing making it bulge must be—yes, opening the book, she could see the familiar paper folded inside—her notes for her master's thesis comparing Rawls, Kant, and Locke as applied to Raskolnikov in *Crime and Punishment*. She'd never finished it; she'd stopped at her mother's insistence ("No husband wants a wife more educated than him; it would humiliate him!"), and she'd forgotten she'd kept it. She flung it to the side and flipped through the bottom book. Nothing.

It wasn't until Young checked all the books that she realized she'd been holding her breath. She closed her eyes and breathed out, relieved by the expulsion of stale air from her lungs, the tingling of her fingers that meant oxygen was resaturating her body. She'd expected to find something else, been sure of it to the point of dread. But really, what had she found? Evidence that Pak hadn't quit smoking and had pilfered (if you could call it that) fifty dollars' worth of cigarettes? So what? Yes, he kept secrets from time to time. What husband didn't? He smoked, and after the explosion, he decided to hide his smoking out of fear of being unfairly judged. Was that so wrong?

She checked her watch. 2:19. Time to return to court. She'd take the tin case and find a quiet time to confront Pak about it. No, not confront—that was too harsh a word. Ask. Discuss. Yes, she'd show it to him and see what he'd say.

Reaching for the tin case, her hands shook slightly, and she had to chuckle at herself, the level of panic she'd worked herself up to, so sure she'd uncover incontrovertible evidence of her husband as a liar. No, it was more than that. Now that the moment was over, she could admit it; she'd actually expected to find proof that her husband, the gentle man who loved her and their daughter, the man who jumped into *fire* for his patients, was a murderer. "Sahr-een. Bang-hwa," Young said, out loud. *Murder. Arson.* She felt small for having thought it, having allowed it to enter even her unconscious. A bad wife.

She grabbed the case and picked up the paper bag it came in. She opened the bag to put the case back inside it when she noticed something. She reached in. It was a pamphlet in Korean, *Requirements for Reentry to South Korea*, paper-clipped to the business card of a Realtor in Annandale and a handwritten note in Korean: *How exciting that you're moving back. I hope the pamphlet is helpful. Enclosed are some listings meeting your requirements. Please call anytime.*

A stapled document was behind the pamphlet. Listings of apartments in Seoul, all for units with immediate availability. She turned back to the first page. Next to *Search date* was *08/08/19*. The Korean date format for August 19, 2008.

Exactly a week before the explosion, Pak had been planning to move them back to Korea.

TERESA

TWO DAYS AFTER THE EXPLOSION, she overheard people discussing "The Tragedy," as they called it in those initial days. She'd been in the hospital cafeteria, drinking coffee—or rather, stirring and pretending to drink it.

"It's a miracle two of those kids survived," said a woman's voice—low-pitched and raspy, which Teresa was sure was deliberate, a woman trying to sound either sexy or like a man.

"Yup, sure is," a man's voice responded.

"Makes you think, though—God sure has a strange sense of humor."

"What do you mean?"

"Well, the kid who's pretty much normal is the one who ends up dead, while the autistic kid's injured but lives, and the kid with severe brain damage is totally fine. It's ironic."

Teresa focused on her stirring, circling the spoon faster and faster, the white bits of congealed cream swept up in its torrents. She could almost hear the liquid rush down the spiral; a buzzing whirl filled her ears, overtaking the cafeteria noise. She stirred faster, harder, ignoring the coffee splashing over the rim and wetting her hands, willing the coffee cyclone to reach the bottom of the mug.

Something knocked the spoon out of her grip. She blinked and, somehow, the mug was on its side, the coffee everywhere. The buzzing ended, and in the silence she heard an echo of a clang, like an auditory afterimage. She looked up. Everyone was looking at her, no one and nothing moving except for the spilled coffee creeping outward toward the table's edge.

"Here, ma'am. You okay?" the low-pitched woman said, slapping down napkins to form a dam between the coffee and the edge. The woman handed her one, and Teresa said, "Sorry. I mean, thanks." The woman said, "It's nothing." She put her hand on Teresa's and said again, "It was nothing, really," her eyes sliding downward and a flush blooming on her cheeks, and Teresa knew she recognized her as the mom of the ironically fine girl.

The low-pitched woman turned out to be Detective Morgan Heights, and Teresa saw her now, walking to court after lunch. For some reason she couldn't understand, Teresa felt a hot flush of shame every time she remembered the detective's words in the cafeteria, what everyone probably thought: that Rosa, by virtue of being the most disabled, should've been the one who died. How fair that would've been. How logical. Clean. Get rid of the defective kid with the ravaged brain, the one who can't talk or walk, the one who might as well be dead anyway.

Teresa positioned her umbrella to hide herself from Detective Heights. Standing in line to enter the courthouse, she heard someone say, "They might institutionalize him. He says the fecal smearing's gotten worse. And the school's having to use a straitjacket, his head banging's gotten so bad." Another voice said, "Poor thing. He's lost his mother. No wonder he's acting out, but—" Three teenagers got in line, drowning out the voices with their loud chatter.

TJ. Fecal smearing. Kitt had talked about it once, during a dive.

Elizabeth had been discussing Henry's "new autism behavior," perseverating about rocks, when Kitt said, "You know what I did for four hours yesterday? I cleaned up shit. Literally. TJ's new thing is fecal smearing. He takes off his diaper and smears shit—walls, curtains, rug, everything. You have no clue what it's like. You saying TJ and Henry both have autism, they're the same—it's offensive to me. You complain that Henry can't sustain eye contact, can't read faces, doesn't have enough friends? You think that's heartbreaking, and yeah, maybe it is. There's heartbreak in parenting every day. Kids get teased, break bones, don't get invited to parties, and when that happens to my girls, of course I feel heartbreak and cry with them. But that normal stuff, that's nowhere near what I have to go through with TJ, not even in the same frigging galaxy."

They did this often, spat about the comparative difficulties of their kids' symptoms—the special-needs version of parental bragging wars—and Teresa always threw in one of *her* worries, like the possibility of Rosa dying from choking on saliva or sepsis from bedsores, which usually shut them up pretty quick. But listening to Kitt's story, imagining the stench, filth, and misery of cleanup, Teresa was stumped. Fecal smearing might be the one thing for which there was no counterstory to make Kitt think, *At least my life isn't that bad.*

And now Kitt was dead, her burden shifted to her husband, and he was sending TJ away. Teresa thought of Rosa in an institution, in a sterile room lined with steel beds, and she wanted to run home and kiss her dimples. She looked at her watch. 2:24. There was just enough time to call home. To tell Rosa she loved her and listen to her say "Ma," again and again.

◯

TERESA TRIED TO pay attention. Pak's redirect was important; Shannon had raised disturbing questions that, based on the snippets she heard during recess, had people wavering for the first time since the trial began. But when it started, everyone turned to the empty seat next to Mary and whispered about where Young was and what her absence meant. ("Meeting with a divorce lawyer's my bet," a man behind her said.) Throughout

Pak's redirect—more emphatic denials about 7-Eleven and cigarettes, as well as his explanation that he got fired for moonlighting, not incompetence, and got another HBOT-center job right away—Teresa looked at Mary, sitting between the empty spaces usually occupied by her parents, alone. Seventeen, like Rosa, but her face so crinkled with worried concentration that her scar appeared to be its only smooth portion.

The first time Teresa saw Mary's scar was right after the cafeteria coffee-spilling incident. She'd told herself she should visit to lend support to Young, but the fact was, she'd wanted to see Mary in a coma. Watching Mary through the window-blind slats, bandages on her face and tubes sticking out of her body, Teresa thought how the low-pitched woman had been wrong: there were four kids involved, not three. What would the woman say with Mary in the equation? Yes, Henry was "pretty much normal" compared with Rosa and TJ, but Mary was as perfect as you could get: pretty, good grades, bound for college. Which would be the bigger irony, the bigger tragedy, to the woman: an almost-pass-for-normal boy being burned alive, or an actually normal girl winding up in a coma, her above-average face scarred and above-average brain possibly damaged?

Teresa went in and hugged Young—tightly, for a long time, the way people do at funerals, in shared grief. Young said, "I think again and again, she was healthy just last week."

Teresa nodded. She hated when people commiserated by telling their own stories, so she kept quiet, but she understood. When five-year-old Rosa got sick, she'd sat by her hospital bed, stroking her arm like Young was with Mary, thinking in an endless loop, *But she was fine just two days ago.* She'd been on a business trip when Rosa got sick. The night before the trip, when Rosa came downstairs to say good night, she'd been holding the then-squirmy toddler Carlos on her lap, clipping his fingernails, so she'd said, "Good night, sweetie. Love you," not looking up—that was the part that killed her, that she didn't look at her daughter during this, their last normal moment together—and tilted her head for Rosa's kiss. The click of Carlos's nails being cut, the bubble-gum smell of Rosa's toothpaste, the sticky smack of lips against her cheeks, then a quick, "Night, Mommy. Night, Carlos"—this was Teresa's last memory of preillness Rosa. The next time she saw her, the girl who could sing and jump and say "Night, Mommy" was gone.

So yes, Teresa could understand the utter incomprehension Young was surely feeling. And when Young said, "The doctor says there may be brain damage, she may never wake up," Teresa gripped her hands and cried with her. But under the jolt of her pain and empathy (and she *did* ache for Young, she truly did), there was a part of her—the tiniest, most minute part, just one-tenth of one cell deep within her brain—that was glad, actually happy, that Mary was in a coma and might end up like Rosa.

It was undeniable: Teresa was a bad person. She didn't understand people saying, "I wouldn't wish that on my worst enemy"; no matter how much she told herself she wouldn't, shouldn't, wish her life on anyone, there were moments when she wanted every parent alive to go through what she did. Disgusted by her thoughts, she tried to justify it; if Rosa's brain-robbing virus became an epidemic, surely billions of dollars would be spent on a cure, and all children would be restored in short order. But she knew—it wasn't for *Rosa's* benefit that she wished for contagion of her tragedy. It was envy, pure and simple. She resented being targeted for misery alone, begrudged her friends who came by with casseroles to cry with her for an hour before rushing their kids to soccer and ballet, and if she couldn't return to her normal life, then by God, she wanted to slap everyone off their pedestal of normalcy, so they could share her burden and make her feel less alone.

She tried not to think this with Young. For the two months of Mary's coma, she visited every week. Sometimes she brought Rosa to sit with Mary while she talked to Young. It was strange, seeing the two girls together— Mary bandaged, lying with her eyes closed, and Rosa in a wheelchair, above her—for the first time as equals, almost like friends.

The day Mary came out of the coma, Teresa had been alone. When she opened Mary's door, she saw doctors surrounding her bed and, through the bodies, Mary, sitting up, eyes open. Young tackled her, the force of her hug pushing Teresa against the wall, and said, "She woke up! She is fine. Her brain is okay." Teresa tried to return her hug, to tell Young how wonderful this was, a miracle, but it was as if invisible ropes were binding her arms, forming a noose around her neck, choking her and sending tingles up her throat to her sinuses, bringing tears to her eyes.

Young didn't notice. Before rushing back to Mary, she said, "Thank you, Teresa. You are here for me all of the time. You are a good friend." Teresa nodded and slowly backed out of the room. She went into the bathroom, walked into a stall, and locked it. She thought of Young's words—"good friend," she'd called her. She put her hand on her stomach, tried to swallow back the envy and fury and hatred she felt for the woman who'd hugged her so tightly it had hurt. She tried to remember that this was what she'd prayed for. Then she took off her jacket, balled it up, and screamed and cried into it, flushing over and over again so that no one could hear.

○

YOUNG ENTERED the courtroom just as Detective Morgan Heights started testifying. Young looked sick. Her normally peach skin looked coated in a dull film of ash, like a longtime hospital patient's, and as Young shuffled down the aisle, her eyes so tired her lids drooped, Teresa felt a pang of guilt. She never went back to visit after Mary woke up from her coma. This had coincided with the start of Rosa's cord-blood therapy, so Teresa had an excuse, but still, she knew the sudden drop-off had bewildered Young, and she felt a deep shame at having abandoned a friend because her child got healthy. Was that why she'd turned her support to Elizabeth, when Young needed her most—to punish her for Mary's return to health?

A buzz of whispers erupted in the gallery. Shannon was standing, saying, "I renew my objection to this entire line of questioning, Your Honor. It's hearsay, irrelevant, and highly prejudicial." The judge said, "Noted and overruled. Detective, you may answer."

Detective Heights said, "The week before the explosion, a woman called the Child Protective Services hotline on August 20, 2008, at 9:33 p.m., to report that a woman named Elizabeth was subjecting her son, Henry, to illegal, dangerous medical treatments, including one called IV chelation, which had recently killed several children. The caller stated that Elizabeth was starting a treatment involving drinking bleach, which worried her greatly. She did not know their last name, nor their address. I'm a licensed psychologist and our office's investigative liaison to CPS, so I was assigned to investigate."

"Who was the caller?" Abe said.

"The call was anonymous, but we've since learned that the caller was Ruth Weiss, one of the protesters." Ruth. The one with the silver bob. Teresa looked at her, sitting in the back with her face flushed, and wanted to slap her. What a coward. Anonymous accusations, with no repercussions, no responsibility. Again, she thought of them lurking behind the barn, waiting until the perfect time to set the fire when they expected the oxygen to be off. She needed to tell Shannon her theory, how they knew the exact HBOT schedule.

Abe said, "How did you find Elizabeth and Henry?"

"The caller knew where Henry went to summer camp from online chats. I went there at dismissal the next day, but Elizabeth wasn't there. A friend was picking up Henry. I explained why I was there, and asked if she knew about these medical treatments."

"What did this friend say?"

"She wouldn't say anything at first, but I pressed, and she admitted to being concerned that Elizabeth seemed obsessed—that was her word, *obsessed*—with treatments Henry didn't need. She said Henry was a 'quirky kid'—again, her words—and he had issues before but he was fine now, and yet Elizabeth kept trying every autism treatment that popped up. The friend said she had majored in psychology, and she wondered if Elizabeth had Munchausen by proxy."

"What's Munchausen by proxy?"

"It's a psychological disorder sometimes referred to as 'medical abuse.' It involves a caretaker exaggerating, fabricating, or even causing medical symptoms in a child to get attention."

"Was that the extent of this friend's worries?"

"No. When I pressed for more, she said—again, very reluctantly— that the camp teacher said the cat scratches on Henry's arms were hurting him, so they applied ointment and bandages. The friend was confused because Henry doesn't have cats, but she didn't say anything."

Teresa remembered seeing scratches, too. On Henry's upper left arm, dotted lines of red where the blood vessels had burst in spots. Elizabeth had noticed Teresa noticing and said Henry got some sort of bug bite and couldn't stop scratching. There was nothing about cats.

"The friend was also worried about Henry's self-esteem," Heights continued. "She said she complimented him once, and he said, 'But I'm annoying. Everybody hates me.' She asked why he thought that, and he said, 'My mommy told me.'"

Teresa swallowed. *I'm annoying. Everybody hates me.* She remembered Elizabeth telling him to stop talking nonstop about rocks. She'd crouched so her face was next to his, nose to nose, and whispered, "I know you're excited, but you're talking and talking, out loud to yourself. That's extremely annoying to most people, and if you keep doing that, I'm worried that everyone will hate you. So you need to try really hard to stop. Okay?"

Abe said, "What happened at this point?"

"The friend declined to give her own name, but she did provide Henry's last name and address. That was on Thursday, August 21. The following Monday, we interviewed Henry at camp. The Code of Virginia allows us to interview a child without parental notification or consent, outside their presence. We chose to do that here, to minimize parental coaching."

"Did the defendant ever find out about the child abuse investigation?"

"Yes, on the evening of Monday, August 25, the day before the explosion. I went to their residence and informed her of the allegations." Teresa thought of the police knocking on her door, barging in with abuse charges. No wonder Elizabeth had been so distant the day of the explosion. What would that feel like, to be told that someone—someone you know, maybe even a friend—had accused you of child abuse?

Abe said, "Did the defendant deny the allegations?"

"No. She only said she wanted to know who filed the complaint, and I informed her it was anonymous. I didn't know myself. But the next morning, I got a call from the friend, the one picking up from camp."

"Really? What did she say?"

"She was upset because she'd just had a big fight with the defendant."

Abe stepped closer. "This is the morning of the explosion?"

"Yes. She said Elizabeth accused her of filing the CPS complaint and was furious with her. She asked me to please tell Elizabeth who *did* file it, so she'd know it wasn't her."

"How did you respond?"

"I told her I couldn't, it was anonymous," Heights said. "She became more upset and said she was sure it was the protesters. She said again how angry Elizabeth was, and she should never have talked to me. She said, quote, 'She's so mad, she's ready to kill me.'"

"Detective Heights," Abe said, "have you since then discovered the identity of this friend, the one who called on the morning of the explosion and said the defendant was, quote, 'so mad, she's ready to kill me'?"

"Yes. I recognized her from the morgue pictures."

"Who was it?"

Detective Heights looked at Elizabeth and said, "Kitt Kozlowski."

ELIZABETH

K ITT AND ELIZABETH WERE more like sisters than friends. Not
in the we're-closer-than-friends-could-ever-be! way, but in the I-
wouldn't-have-chosen-you-as-a-friend-but-we're-stuck-together-
so-let's-try-to-get-along way. They met because their sons were diagnosed
with autism on the same day at the same place, six years ago at Georgetown Hospital. Elizabeth had been waiting for Henry's evaluation results
when a woman said, "This is like waiting for the guillotine, isn't it?" Elizabeth didn't answer, but the woman went on, saying, "I don't understand
how men can focus on work at a time like this," looking at Victor and
another man—her husband, presumably—both working on laptops.
Elizabeth gave the tersest smile she could and grabbed a magazine. The
woman, though, kept blathering on about her son—almost four, his
birthday was coming up, she was making a Barney cake, he adored

Barney, was positively obsessed—and how he didn't talk (could it be because he couldn't get an effing word in edgewise?) but it was probably because he was the youngest, she had four other kids, all girls who talked nonstop (apparently a genetic trait), you know how girls can be, et cetera, et cetera. The woman—Kitt, like Kit-Kat, with two *t*'s, she introduced herself mid-monologue—was not making conversation so much as spitting out words in one long strand, oblivious to Elizabeth's nonresponse. She didn't stop until the nurse called for Henry Ward's parents.

The doctor said, "Let's see . . . Ah, yes, Henry. I know you're anxious, so let's cut to the chase. Henry was found to be autistic." He said this casually, between sips of coffee, as if it were a normal thing, an everyday thing, to announce to parents that their child was autistic. Of course, for him, a neurologist at an autism clinic, it *was* an everyday thing, probably an every-hour thing. But for her, the parent, this was a moment—*the* moment—that would divide her world into Before and After, the life-defining scene she'd replay over and over, so was the oh-so-nonchalant drinking of the venti Frappuccino really effing necessary? And his choice of words: "Henry was found to be," as if he didn't do the finding himself but discovered Henry lying somewhere, stamped AUTISTIC by some mysterious force of nature; and *autistic*—was that even a word? It offended her, him turning a disorder into an adjective, the net effect of which was to declare autism to be Henry's defining characteristic, the sum total of his identity.

These semantic issues—why people were "diabetic" but not "canceristic," for instance, and the difference between "moderately severe" (Henry's autism-spectrum placement) and "severely moderate"—were occupying her when she passed Kitt. Elizabeth wasn't crying, hadn't cried at all, in fact, but her face must have screamed out her devastation, because Kitt stopped and hugged her, a tight, never-ending hug reserved for the most intimate of friends. She had no idea why this inappropriate hug from this inappropriate stranger should feel anything other than awkward, but it felt comforting, like family, and she hugged her back and cried.

Elizabeth never expected to see her again, didn't exchange numbers, e-mails or even last names. A week later, though, they ran into each other, first at the county autism preschool orientation, then at a speech therapist's, and again at an applied behavior analysis info session—not surprising given that Georgetown had recommended them all, but still, it had a kismet feel, a little too coincidental to be coincidence. They started doing everything together when Henry and TJ ended up in the same class at the same school. "Autism boot camp," they'd called it. They carpooled to school and therapies, attended lectures on coping with the grief of an autism diagnosis, and joined the local autism moms' group. In that way, they fell into closeness, as if by accident. Not because they particularly enjoyed each other's company, but out of habit, because they were thrust together daily, like it or not. The repeated proximity grew into intimacy; once, after Victor dropped the bombshell about his newfound love in California, they even went on a drunken girls' night out.

Elizabeth was an only child, so she'd never experienced this, but the thing about being together and sharing so much—everything from their sons' quarterly autism-severity scores to their teachers' daily counts of "perseverative behaviors" (rocking for Henry, head banging for TJ)—was that it bred an intense rivalry. It infected everything they did, crept into the nooks and crannies of their relationship and turned it slightly sour. Elizabeth knew competition was rampant in the "typical" kids' moms' world, had heard women comparing their kids' all-star and gifted-program-admission statuses in line at Trader Joe's. But like everything else, the jealousy shot into overdrive in the world of autism moms, which was at once the most cooperative and the most competitive she'd seen, with stakes that *mattered*—not which college your kids got into, but their very survival in society: whether they'd learn to talk, if they'd ever move out of your house, and how they'd live when you died. Unlike in the "typical" world, when someone else's child's success meant your own was falling short, the sharing, helping, and celebrating of others' successes was far more intense and complex because another child improving meant hope for your own, but also put more pressure on you to come through for your own. In the case of Henry and TJ, all these factors were magnified because they were the same age, in the same class, impossible not to compare and contrast.

When the biomedical treatments started and Henry improved and TJ didn't, that was when Elizabeth and Kitt's relationship warped into something that resembled friendship on the outside—still carpooling and having coffee every Thursday—but felt like something else on the inside. The funny thing was, it was Kitt who'd first told her about Defeat Autism Now!, a group of doctors (most with kids with autism) who advocated treatments for "recovery" from autism—something Elizabeth hadn't known was possible. To be sure, the concept was a strange one, no less because the world at large didn't believe autism was something you could "recover" from. Broken bones, yes. Pneumonia, sure. Maybe even cancer, if you were lucky. But autism? That was a lifelong thing. Besides, "recovery" implied a baseline of normalcy that had been lost, whereas autism was supposed to be an inborn trait, which meant, of course, there was nothing lost to recover. She'd been skeptical, but trying the treatments was the same as baptizing Henry despite her atheism: if she was right, they were just pouring water on Henry's head (no harm), but if Victor was, they were saving him from eternal damnation in hell (big upside). Similarly, special diets and vitamins wouldn't harm him, but if there was the slightest possibility of "recovery," the potential upside was life-changing. Risk, nil. Reward, probably nil, but possibly huge. Simple math.

So she did it. Cut out dyes, additives, gluten, and casein from Henry's diet, enduring teachers' oh-you-crazy-neurotic-mother looks when she asked them to substitute her organic grapes for their rainbow Goldfish snacks. Cajoled Henry's pediatrician to run tests despite his resistance ("I won't inflict unnecessary blood draws on a little boy, not to mention the waste for the insurance company") and, when they came back abnormal in the way predicted by the DAN! doctors (high copper, low zinc, high viral titers), got the ever so slightly humbled pediatrician to agree that yes, he supposed it wouldn't be *harmful*, exactly, to give Henry B_{12}, zinc, probiotics, and such.

None of this made her different; a dozen others in her autism moms' group were on the "biomed track," had been for years. The difference had been Henry. He was the Holy Grail of biomed treatments, the so-called Super Responder. One week (one!) after Elizabeth removed food dyes, Henry's rocking went from an average of twenty-five to six episodes per day. Two weeks after starting zinc, he started making eye contact—fleeting and sporadic, but compared with none and never, a breakthrough. And the month after she added B_{12} shots, his MLU (mean length of utterance) doubled, from 1.6 to 3.3 words.

Talking with Kitt, Elizabeth was careful to avoid gloating, to be sensitive to the fact that TJ exhibited no changes. The problem was, they had opposite approaches to the therapies—Elizabeth anal, Kitt loosey-goosey—and it was hard not to think that her own type-A fastidiousness—buying a separate toaster and cookware for Henry's food to ensure absolute compliance with the diet, for example—must've played *some* part in Henry's dramatic response. Kitt, by contrast, let TJ "cheat" on his diet for special occasions, which, because he had four sisters, four grandparents, nine cousins, and thirty-two classmates, occurred once a week, and she regularly forgot his supplements. Elizabeth told herself that TJ wasn't her child and everyone had their own way of doing things, but she ached for TJ, hated seeing him stagnate while Henry soared, and she yearned to take control and restore the parity between them, and with it—yes, she could admit it, she wanted this back most of all—her closeness with Kitt. Elizabeth offered to help—she volunteered to organize TJ's supplements into weekly pill dispensers and bring diet-compliant cupcakes for classroom birthdays—but Kitt said, "And have the Autism Nazi take over my life? No, thanks." She said it jokingly, with a wink and a laugh, but there was venom there, under the surface.

The day the principal announced Henry's move from the autism class to one for "milder" issues such as articulation and ADHD—the oxymoronically named "general special education" class—Kitt hugged her and said, "It's amazing news. I'm thrilled for you," but she blinked a little too fast for a little too long, smiled a little too wide, and ten minutes later, passing by Kitt's car in the lot, Elizabeth saw her slumped over the steering wheel, her whole body heaving in sobs.

Remembering this now, Elizabeth wished she could return to that moment and open the door and tell Kitt not to cry, that none of it mattered. For what difference did it make how much "higher functioning" Henry was, how many more words he could speak, when he was now in a coffin and TJ was not? When TJ would eat and run and laugh, while Henry could never do those things again? What would Kitt have said if she'd known that in a few years, Elizabeth would give anything to change places with her, to be the dead mother to the alive child rather than the alive mother to the dead child, to have died protecting her son, never to feel the torture of imagining her son's pain and the guilt of knowing she'd caused it herself?

But neither of them knew what was to come, of course. Driving past Kitt that day in the parking lot, she thought of their first meeting, Kitt stopping and hugging her tight, and she wanted to stop the car, run over, and hug and cry with her. She wanted to say she was sorry for her judging and tacit criticisms disguised as "help," that she'd quit and just listen and support her. But how would Kitt feel, having Elizabeth—the mom of the kid who'd caused her pain—comfort her and pretend to understand? Was she really thinking of Kitt, or was she being selfish, not wanting to feel like she was losing her only friend?

Elizabeth kept driving, all the way home. Later that day, Kitt e-mailed to say carpooling didn't make sense anymore, since Henry's new class was in a school five miles away, and oh, by the way, she couldn't make coffee this Thursday, she had a field trip for one of the girls. Elizabeth said that was fine, she'd see her soon. There was no e-mail the next week, but Elizabeth went to their usual Starbucks on Thursday and waited. Kitt never came. Elizabeth didn't call or e-mail. She just kept going to Starbucks every Thursday, sitting by the window, and waiting for her friend to walk in.

○

SITTING IN COURT, Elizabeth remembered back to the Thursday before the explosion, the day Detective Heights went to Henry's camp and met Kitt. As usual, she'd been sitting at Starbucks, thinking about Kitt. She hadn't seen her much after Henry moved schools, just monthly autism moms' meetings, but she'd expected their closeness to return with HBOT. And, in a way, it did; they talked for hours every day in the sealed chamber and caught up on all they'd missed. But there was an awkwardness, a sense of them (or rather, her) trying too hard to revive an old intimacy gone stale. And then, of course, came the YoFun fight, after a particularly awkward dive when she tried telling Kitt about new therapies and camps, and Kitt kept nodding politely without engaging. Elizabeth's frustration built and built, and at some point, it boiled over and she became—it hurt to admit it—an abrasive, overbearing, sanctimonious bitch. She knew it and wanted to stop, but it was as if all the balled-up hurt had erupted, spewing out in chunks she couldn't contain.

She put down her coffee and decided: she needed to apologize to Kitt, properly, in person. Not at HBOT (they were never alone), and she couldn't just show up at her house (too desperate, stalkerish), but she could call Kitt, say she was running late and ask her to get Henry from camp (one block from TJ's camp). Then, when Elizabeth went to Kitt's house for Henry, she could talk to her. She could say she was sorry, she missed her, and maybe with the bitterness poured out, a true closeness without rancor could emerge. So that's what she did, which meant—God, the irony of this!—Elizabeth herself was responsible for Kitt meeting Detective Heights and verifying the child abuse complaint. And she'd never even gotten to apologize; when she went to get Henry, Kitt seemed upset and mentioned cat scratches, panicking Elizabeth into leaving and turning the soul-baring session she'd imagined into a one-minute doorway conversation.

And now, Kitt was dead and a psychologist-detective was on the stand, telling the world exactly what she'd thought and said about Elizabeth, her crazy ex-friend. Abe said, "When Kitt called the day of the explosion and said the defendant was, quote, 'so mad, she's ready to kill me,' did she say anything else?"

Heights said, "Yes. She said she found out Henry was about to undergo IV chelation." She looked to the jury. "Chelation is the intravenous administration of powerful drugs used to rid the body of toxic metals. It's FDA-approved for heavy-metal poisoning."

"Henry had poisoning?" Abe said, the familiar look of feigned surprise on his face.

"No, but some believe that metals and pesticides in our air and water cause autism, and that by cleansing the body, you can cure it."

"That sounds unorthodox, certainly, but isn't this a matter of medical judgment?"

"No. Children have *died* from it, which the defendant knew. She posted about it online, but didn't tell Henry's own pediatrician. She used an out-of-state naturopath, an alternative practice not recognized by

Virginia, and ordered the drugs online. In my opinion, this is endangerment, subjecting your child to a potentially fatal and *secret* experimental treatment."

"Did Kitt say which aspect of this treatment worried her?"

"Yes. She said Elizabeth was planning to combine this with an even more extreme treatment called MMS."

Abe held up a ziplock bag containing a book and two plastic bottles. "Do you recognize this, Detective?"

"Yes, it's what I found under the defendant's kitchen sink. The book is *MMS: The Miracle Mineral Solution*, a how-to guide for the latest autism fad where you mix sodium chlorite and citric acid, these two bottles here, which forms chlorine dioxide." She looked to the jury. "That's bleach. You're supposed to administer this solution orally—make him drink bleach, in other words—eight times a day."

Abe put on an outraged expression. "The defendant did this to her son?"

"Yes, a week before his death. She recorded in a chart in the book that he cried, had stomach pain and a 103-degree fever, and vomited four times."

"The defendant recorded these details, like she was conducting experiments on a rat?" Shannon objected, and the judge sustained, telling Abe to keep to the facts, but she saw it in the jurors' faces: disgust and horror, the image of sadistic Nazi doctors torturing prisoners in their minds, nothing at all like her memory: holding Henry tight, telling him he'd be okay, how hard it was to read the thermometer with her hands shaking and eyes blurred with tears.

Heights said, "This dovetailed with Kitt's account. Apparently, Elizabeth said she needed to stop MMS because it was making Henry too sick and she didn't want him missing camp, but she'd resume it, combined with chelation, when camp was over. That way, he could get really sick, and it wouldn't matter."

"'Really sick, and it wouldn't matter,'" Abe repeated, his eyes glazed and fixed as if picturing Henry's suffering, then shaking his head. Kitt had done the same thing—repeated Elizabeth's phrase and shaken her head, except in a tone of outrage. "Really sick, and it won't matter? Listen to yourself. He's doing great. Why do you keep doing this shit?" Kitt said before making her usual bonbons comment—the words that made Elizabeth crazy and led to the huge fight ten hours before Kitt's death.

The first time Kitt said it was at the autism moms' meeting after Georgetown's neurologist retested Henry and pronounced him as "no longer falling within the autism spectrum." There was champagne in party cups with rainbow-lettered *Wow!*s, and the moms were toasting, some even crying—though not necessarily from happiness; based on her own uncontrollable crying whenever she read those "my kid miraculously recovered from autism" memoirs, she knew the tears came from an oscillation between despair ("Someone else's kid got better, while mine didn't") and hope ("Someone else's kid got better, so mine could, too").

Someone said something about good-bye, how they'd miss her at meetings. When Elizabeth said no, she planned to continue everything—meetings, biomed treatments, speech therapy, et cetera—that's when Kitt did it. Shook her head at Elizabeth like she was crazy and said with a chuckle, "If I had a kid like yours, I'd lie around on my couch and eat bonbons all day."

Elizabeth felt a jolt, like a prick, but she tried to smile. Tried to overlook the forced lightness in Kitt's voice and the contemptuousness in her chuckle, the tonal equivalent of a teenager's eye-roll at an overbearing mother. She told herself that Kitt was brash and sarcastic, a no-filters type, and the bonbons comment was her way—trying to be funny, with no idea how acidic her words were—of congratulating Elizabeth for finishing the marathon they'd started together and telling her she'd earned the right to relax. To enjoy life.

The problem was, Elizabeth wasn't convinced that she (or Henry, rather) actually *had* reached the finish line. Not being autistic was not the same as being normal. Even the words the doctor used—"speech is virtually indistinguishable from typical peers"—made that clear: Henry wasn't typical, but had learned to mimic it, like a lab-trained monkey. If he was careful, he could pass for normal, but it was a precarious kind of normal, one that teetered on the edge.

In that way, having a child recovered from autism was like having one in remission from cancer or recovered from alcoholism. Constantly being on guard for signs of anything abnormal, anything that may mean he's slipping back, while trying not to slip into paranoia. Forcing a smile when others congratulate you for beating the odds, while anxiety churns in your stomach as you wonder how long this reprieve will last.

But she couldn't say this to Kitt, to any autism mom. It would be like someone in remission crying about the possibility of eventually dying from recurrence to someone actually dying of cancer right now—not sufficiently appreciative of how lucky you have it, how your own troubles pale in comparison. So when Kitt said the bonbons thing, she didn't argue that Henry might regress. She didn't say how worried she still was—that Henry had no friends in his new class, that whenever he was sick or nervous, he reverted to his old ways of looking up and perseverating on the same phrase in a robotic monotone. No, whenever Kitt said it (which she seemed to think got funnier each time), Elizabeth just laughed along.

Except that last day. The morning of the explosion, walking to their cars, she was talking about MMS when Kitt said, "Why do you keep doing this shit? I think the protesters might have a point with you. Like I always say"—and she said her usual bonbons thing. Except this time, without laughing.

Elizabeth didn't say anything. She got Henry in the car, gave him apple slices, and waited for Kitt to settle TJ in. When Kitt closed TJ's door, Elizabeth said, "No, you wouldn't."

"I wouldn't what?"

"You wouldn't lie around and eat bonbons all day if TJ were like Henry. That's not how parenting works, and you know it. You think every mom with typical kids is going, *My kid isn't special-needs so I have nothing to do; I think I'll mail-order some bonbons from Paris*? Believe me, I'd *love* to lie around and eat bonbons all day instead of taking care of Henry—what mom wouldn't?—but there's always something to worry about, something they need you for. If it's not health, it's school or friends or *something*. It never ends. How do you not know that?"

Kitt rolled her eyes. "It's just a joke, Elizabeth. A figure of speech. I'm telling you to relax a little with this 'I can't rest until my child is absolutely perfect' bullshit."

"You have no right telling me to stop. No more than Teresa would have telling you to stop everything for TJ because he can walk."

"That's ludicrous." Kitt turned to get away.

Elizabeth stepped in front of her. "Think about it. If Rosa could wake up tomorrow and be like TJ, it'd be a miracle—that's what Teresa's doing all the therapies for. But does that mean she has the right to say you shouldn't try your hardest to get him beyond where he is now?"

Kitt shook her head. "You've *got* to lighten up. It's a frigging joke."

"No, I don't think it is. I think you're pissed. You're jealous that the boys started out the same, and Henry's improved and TJ hasn't, and you're trying to pull me down and make me feel guilty for leaving you behind. Well, guess what? I *do* feel guilty." At this admission, Elizabeth felt all the resentment gush out of her body, leaving a warm tingling, like a numb foot waking up. Here, finally, was the chance to say everything: how guilty she felt, how much she missed Kitt, how sorry she was for all her judging and nagging.

She opened her mouth to say all this, to ask for forgiveness, when Kitt slumped against the hood of her car with her hands over her face. She thought Kitt might be crying and started to go to her, when Kitt dropped her hands. No tears. Her face a mix of tired and amused, an I-can't-believe-I'm-talking-to-this-crazy-person look.

Kitt looked at her, shook her head, and said, "That is such bullshit. I tell you, you're a piece of work. Un-frigging-believable."

Elizabeth didn't say anything, couldn't.

Kitt sighed, a long, loud breath of exhaustion. "You think I'm telling you to stop because I'm hoping that, what, Henry'll become autistic again? What kind of crazy bitch do you think I am? I'm not jealous or mad at you," she said. "I mean, do I wish TJ could talk and be mainstreamed like Henry? Of course I do. I'm human. But I'm happy for you. It's just . . ." Kitt breathed again, but this time with pursed lips, like a yoga breath, an intake of nourishment to embolden her for what she was about to say. She looked at Elizabeth. "Look, no joke. I think you worked hard to get Henry where he is. It's just, you've been going for so long, you don't know how to stop. I think maybe . . ." Kitt bit her lip.

"Maybe what?"

"I think you worked hard to strip away the autism, and now you're left with Henry, the boy he was meant to be. And I think maybe you don't like that boy. He's a little weird and likes talking about rocks or whatever. He's not Mr. In-Crowd, never will be. And I think you're hoping you can change him into the kid you want instead of the kid you have. But no kid's perfect, and you can't get him to *be* perfect through more treatments. They're dangerous, and he doesn't need them. It's like continuing chemo after all the cancer's gone. Who are you doing them for—you or for him?"

Chemo after the cancer's gone. The detective last night had said this to explain the abuse complaint. Elizabeth looked at Kitt. "It was you."

"What? What was me?"

"You called CPS and said I'm a child abuser."

"What? No. I don't know what you're talking about," Kitt said, but Elizabeth could tell—the way Kitt's whole face and neck turned crimson in an instant, the jerky staccato of her words, the jumpiness of her eyes looking everywhere but Elizabeth's face—Kitt knew all about it. Betrayal, embarrassment, confusion—everything tangled around Elizabeth's throat, tight, sending spots flashing in her vision. She couldn't stand here one more second. She ran to her car. She slammed the door and got the hell out of there, sending dust swirling up like tornado funnels.

YOUNG

SHE COULDN'T FIND HER CAR. It wasn't in any of the courthouse handicapped spots or on the street in front. Pak didn't say anything, just shook his head like she was a forgetful child he was too tired to scold.

"How could you forget where it is? You just parked it a few hours ago," Mary said.

Young bit down and clenched her mouth shut. Questions and accusations were popping around her head like balls on those lottery-number pickers, and now—on a public street, with their daughter—was not the time for those words.

She found the car two blocks away, in a metered spot. As she motioned for them to come, she spotted paper under the wipers. A parking ticket? It occurred to her that she didn't remember feeding the meter. Then again, she didn't remember parking here at all. Young strode past the stench of the dumpster-filled alley, positioned her umbrella to block Pak's view of the windshield, and grabbed the ticket: $35.

In the three hours since she'd found the Seoul apartment listings—driving back to Pineburg, entering the courtroom, sitting through Detective Heights's testimony—she'd felt like she was in a dream. Not a good dream, all soft with that anything-is-possible buzz, and not a nightmare, either, but one of those dreams you'd swear was real life but with things skewed *just* enough to disorient her. *How exciting that you're moving back*, the Realtor's note had said. An international move, without a word to his wife. Had he been planning to leave her, maybe for another woman? Or was Elizabeth's lawyer right, and he'd masterminded a get-rich-quick-and-escape plan? Which was better, her husband as adulterer or murderer?

She would talk to Pak. She *needed* to talk to him, stop the scenarios from looping through her mind. During a short court recess, he'd apologized for never telling her he was fired. He said he didn't want her to know he was working two jobs, didn't want her worrying, but still, he should've told her. Pak's sincerity reminded her that he'd made mistakes, certainly, but he was a good man. She'd show him what she found—matter-of-factly, without judgment or accusation—and wait for his explanation.

Yuh-bo, she'd say, using the Korean "spouse" label like a good wife, why did you hide cigarettes in the shed?

Yuh-bo, what were you doing at Party Central on the day of the explosion?

Yuh-bo, what did you do after you left me alone in the barn?

The more she thought about it, the more she realized she was to blame for not knowing the answers. Even on the last question, the most important one—what exactly had he done before the explosion?—she'd never gotten a clear answer. She'd been too focused on what their story *should* be to press Pak for what he'd *actually* done, what exact, specific actions "standing watch" over the protesters entailed.

Young shoved the parking ticket deep down in her purse and zipped it. She helped Pak get in the car, put away the wheelchair, and started the car to go home, where tonight she'd finally ask the question she'd been too scared and stupid to voice for the last year.

Yuh-bo, did you have anything to do with the explosion?

●

IT WAS 8:00 by the time Young and Pak were finally alone. Mary usually went for a walk in the woods after dinner, but the rain didn't let up so Young gave Mary thirty dollars and said this was her last night of being seventeen and why didn't she take the family car and go meet friends? Giving her that much would mean they'd have to skimp even more for a month, but it was worth it to stop the waiting. Besides, it was a milestone, turning eighteen. They couldn't afford to go out or buy a present, and this would have to do.

When she walked in with the bag from the shed, Pak was at the table reading the newspaper he'd gotten from the courthouse recycling. Pak looked up and said, "You're wet." It must've still been raining, yet she hadn't realized, hadn't even felt the rain falling and soaking into her skin as she walked to the shed and checked the bag to make sure the apartment listings were still there, not just something she'd hallucinated in her nauseated state. It was funny how she hadn't even noticed, but once Pak said it, the wetness of her clothes agitated her to an extreme. The incriminating bag was at her feet, her accusations at her throat, and all she could focus on was the wet, coarse nylon of her blouse sticking to her skin, making her itch.

"You have something to show me?" Pak put down the paper.

Young felt confused for a moment, wondering how he knew she'd found something, but then she saw her purse, lying open, the parking ticket poking out.

She stared at her husband, looking at her like a parent at a misbehaving child. A hot flush crept up her neck, an anger that grew as she looked at him, the lack of even a hint of apology in his face for having gone through her private things.

Young strode to the table and grabbed her purse. "You went through my purse?"

"I saw you hiding it back at the car. Thirty-five dollars is a lot of money. How could you do something so stupid?" Pak's tone was gentle, but not in a kind way. No, his voice had the patronizing parental tone reserved for scolding children, coated with forced mildness to mask his anger.

And he *was* angry. She could see that now. After what happened today, her discovering his years of lies along with strangers in open court, *he* was angry at *her*. All of a sudden, this whole conversation seemed ridiculous, her anxiety over confronting him about the tin case farcical, and she didn't know whether to slap him or laugh out loud.

"What was I thinking?" she said. "Let's see, what could I possibly have been focusing on instead of parking?" As she got the bag, an overwhelming sense of power coursed through her and settled into a numbing calm. "I suppose my mind must've been on *this*." She dropped the tin case on the table. It clanged. "On all the things you've been hiding from me."

Pak stared at the case, then reached to touch it. He blinked when his index finger made contact with the edge and pulled away quickly, as if he'd touched a ghost and realized it was solid. "Where did you get this? How?"

"I found it where you hid it, in the shed."

"The shed? But I gave it to . . ." He looked at the case, then off to the side, his eyes darting back and forth as if struggling to recall something, his face scrunched in puzzlement so total that Young wondered if he really thought he'd given it to the Kangs.

Pak shook his head. "I must've forgotten to give it to them, and it ended up here. So what? We had some old cigarettes in storage, and we didn't realize it. It's no matter."

He sounded believable. But the gum, Febreze, apartment listings— those proved he had used the case as a hiding place last summer. No, Pak was lying, like he had in Abe's office. She remembered the chill she'd felt, seeing how convincing he could be, insisting on the truth of what she knew to be lies. He was continuing his same tricks and expecting her to be duped.

Pak seemed to take her silence as acquiescence. He pushed the case away and said, "Good, it's settled. We'll throw it away and forget about it." He held up the parking ticket. "Now, this—"

She snatched it from his hand and ripped it in two. "The ticket? The *ticket* is nothing. Just some money, paid and done. But this here?" She picked up the tin case and shook it, its contents rattling in clangs, then she slammed it down and opened it. "You see these cigarettes? Camels, just like the cigarette *someone* used to murder *our* patients on *our* property. And gum and Febreze, stuff people use to hide their smoking. All hidden in our shed. You think that's nothing, when you spent all day *swearing* in court that you don't smoke anymore? It's not nothing. It's evidence." She took out the Realtor's packet and slapped it on the table. "And what would that lawyer do with *this*? What would the jury say if they knew that right before the explosion, you were secretly planning to move to Seoul?"

Pak picked up the packet and stared at the cover sheet.

"I'm your wife," she said. "How could you hide that from me?"

He flipped through the packet. His eyes darted around each page as if in an effort to process it, make sense of it.

Seeing Pak's vacant look of uncertainty, Young felt her anger dissolve into worry. The doctors had warned that more symptoms might surface later. Had his injuries spread to his brain, and he'd forgotten about the listings? "Yuh-bo," she said, "what's wrong? Tell me."

Pak looked at Young's face, then her hand, appearing as if he'd forgotten she was there. He frowned, then blew out his breath in a long sigh. "I'm sorry. It was just such a stupid pipe dream. That's why I didn't tell you."

"Tell me what?" she said. A new wave of nausea cramped her stomach. She thought it'd be a relief to hear the truth, to know this wasn't all in her head, but now that he was actually confessing, looking contrite, she wished she could go back to a few seconds ago when her concerns were unconfirmed, her anger unjustified.

"I'm sorry," he said. "The cigarettes, I kept. I knew I had to quit, and I did, I never smoked, but I liked holding them. Whenever I got worried about anything, it helped, just . . . the feel, smelling them. And the smell's so strong even without smoking them, so I got the freshener and gum. I didn't want you to know because . . . because it seemed so *stupid*. So weak."

He locked his eyes, scrunched in pain and need, onto hers.

"And the apartments?" she said.

"That . . ." He scrubbed his face. "That wasn't for me. It's just . . . the business was going so well, and I thought maybe we could help my brother move to Seoul. You know how much he wants that." He shook his head. "Anyway, you saw the prices. I told him we couldn't, and that was that. I meant to throw it away, but I forgot all about it after the explosion." He sighed again. "I should've told you, but I wanted to find out the prices first. And once I did, there was nothing to tell you about."

"But the Realtor said you were moving back to Korea."

"Well, of course I told her that. If I said this was background research, what incentive would she have for helping me?"

"So you're saying you never planned to move us back to Korea?"

"Why would I do that? We've worked so hard to be here. Even now, I still want to stay and make it work. Don't you?" His face was slightly skewed to his left, his eyes wide and wondering like a puppy staring up at his master, and she felt guilty for questioning his motives.

"What about Creekside Plaza?" she said. "I *know* you didn't go to Walgreens for powder. I remember—we used cornstarch."

He put his hand on hers. "I thought about telling you, but I wanted to protect you. I didn't want you to have to tell more lies for me." He looked down and traced the green veins on her hand with his finger. "I got balloons, from Party Central. I wanted to get rid of the protesters. I thought if I could cause a power outage and blame them, the police would take them away."

The room seemed to tilt. She'd guessed this, suspected it from the moment she saw the balloons in the picture, but it shocked her to hear his confirmation. It was strange—here was her husband, admitting to concealing a crime from her, but instead of drawing her away, it made her feel better than she had all day. The fact was, he didn't *have* to confess this. She had no proof, just suspicions, and he could've easily made up a story, and yet, he chose honesty. It made her hopeful that maybe, just maybe, everything else he'd told her tonight was the truth.

She said, "Was that why you left the barn that night? Something with the balloons?"

He nodded and bit his lip. "I'm sorry. I know I shouldn't have left you alone like that. But when the police called, they said they were coming over soon to get the balloons to test them for fingerprints, so I could get proof it was the protesters and get a restraining order. And I realized—I never wiped off the balloons, and I didn't want them finding *my* prints, so I went to go get them. I thought it'd take just a minute, but I had trouble getting them down, and then I saw the protesters. I got scared about what they might try, and that's when I called you, to say I couldn't come back until after the dive was over."

"Was that why Mary was with you, to help with that? Did *she* know about all this?"

"No," he said, and Young felt something heavy lift from her chest. It was one thing to have your husband keep secrets from you, another thing entirely to have him confiding them in your daughter. Pak said, "No, I just said I needed help getting the balloons down. And she *did* help me, looking in the shed and finding sticks to try to reach them and such. I even tried boosting her up."

Young looked at their hands, now folded together on the table.

"Yuh-bo," Pak said, "I'm sorry. I should've told you all this earlier. I won't keep anything from you again."

She looked into his eyes and nodded. It made sense, everything he said, and finally, there were no lies. Yes, he'd done questionable things—lied about his job in Seoul, hidden the cigarette tin case, lied about the balloons. But those wrongdoings were small—technically wrong, but not *really* wrong. Like white lies. He really did have four years of HBOT experience in Seoul, regardless of the change in jobs, which was what mattered. And what difference did a hidden case of cigarettes make when all he did was look at them, use them as props for his thoughts? The balloons were the most troubling, because without the power outage, he would have stayed in the barn that night and turned off the oxygen and opened the hatch more quickly. But still, it was Elizabeth who caused the fire, Elizabeth who was responsible for whatever damage resulted from that action.

Young linked her fingers with Pak's, weaving them together. She told herself she was wrong to have doubted her husband. But even as she reassured him that she believed him, forgave him, trusted him, something nagged at her, something she couldn't place that told her something was wrong with his story, something tiny that kept crawling in the recesses of her mind like a weevil in a bag of rice.

It wasn't until later that night, his stories playing like a video in her mind as she lay in bed, that she realized what was wrong.

If Mary and Pak had worked together, both of them next to the utility pole for extended periods of time, why did their neighbor report seeing only one person?

MATT

THE RAIN WAS FUCKING WITH HIS MIND. It wasn't so bad earlier, when Janine was driving them home and it was storming. The violence of the noise—the rumble of thunder barely audible over the heavy raindrops pelting the car, fast and furious—had calmed him, and Matt had put his hand on the moonroof above his head, imagining the pressure of the water hitting his flesh, maybe jolting the nerves under the thick scars into feeling something. But by the time they got home, the storm had calmed, and now it was drizzling, making faint *phwat*s against his bathroom window—a muffled scratching noise that crawled through the damp air and crept through his veins, making his neck and shoulders itch.

He put his fingers under his shirt and rubbed, which was all he could do now that his fingernails were gone. It was funny, how he'd considered nails useless vestigial leftovers, but here he was, missing them intensely, needing to dig into his flesh and *scratch*. He rubbed harder, craving relief, but the slick scars on his fingers simply slid around his clammy skin, the itch intensifying all over—wriggling through his arms down to his hands, burrowing below the impenetrable layer of scar tissue. At once, the mosquito bites from the creek last night roused, the welts on his arms turning bright red like poppies in a field.

He stripped and turned on the shower, jet-massage mode. As he stepped in, the concentrated jet of cold water pierced him, obliterating the itch everywhere like a bomb. He turned the water warmer, put his head in the spray, and tried to organize his jumble of thoughts into lists. Janine liked lists, used them during fights ("discussions," she'd correct) to prove she was being logical and fair. "I'm not accusing you of anything," she'd say, "just listing facts. Here's what I know. Fact one: *blah blah*. Fact two: *blah blah*." Numbered facts were big with her, and he needed to tread lightly just now, follow her format. He closed his eyes and breathed, tried to focus on what he knew—no questions or conjecture, just concrete matters he could enumerate:

FACT #1: Before the explosion, Janine somehow found out that Mary, not a hospital intern, was the one sending him notes.

FACT #2: Janine was at Miracle Submarine thirty minutes before the explosion.

FACT #3: At that time, Janine was angry, and she confronted Mary and lied to her (saying he had complained about Mary bothering him).

FACT #4: Janine threw Camel cigarettes, 7-Eleven matches, and a balled-up H-Mart note at Mary. (RELATED FACT #4A: Elizabeth claimed she found Camel cigarettes, 7-Eleven matches, and a balled-up H-Mart note on the same night in the same woods.)

FACT #5: Janine never told him any of this at any time. She told him, the police, and Abe that she'd been home the entire night of the explosion.

It was this last fact, her secrets and lies, that got to him most. A full fucking *year*, and not a word about the cigarettes she'd taken from the safe confines of his car or pockets or wherever she'd found them and practically handed to the murderer. All that time, letting him pretend that this cigarette business was nothing to do with him, pretending that *she* didn't know he was pretending. Jesus.

Fuck the list. Fuck facts. It was time for questions. What did Janine know and not know about him and Mary? How the hell did she find out in the first place, and why didn't she come to him? Why did she go behind his back and confront a teenage girl, throw shit at her, for God's sake? And after Mary ran off, did Janine just leave the items for anyone to find? Or did she . . . could it be like Shannon said, that whoever discarded those items was the murderer, and the "whoever" was his wife? But why? To hurt him? Mary? Both?

Matt grabbed the soap scrubber. The mosquito bites were driving him crazy—the warm water must've thawed them out of dormancy—and every cell in his brain was screaming for something, anything, to rip into the itch and scratch until it bled. He scoured, rough and fast, savoring the relief of the mesh biting into his skin, the sting of the mint soap seeping in.

"Honey? You in there?" The shower door clunked open.

"I'm almost done," he said.

"It's Abe. He's here." Janine looked panicky, her forehead lined with crinkles zigzagging in different directions. "He says he needs to talk to you right now. He seems upset. I think"—she brought her hand to her mouth and gnawed at her nails—"maybe he found out."

"Found out what?" Matt said.

"You know what." Janine looked straight into his eyes. "About the cigarettes. About you and Mary."

○

JANINE WAS RIGHT. Abe was agitated. He tried to hide it, smiled and shook Matt's hand (Matt hated handshakes, hated the repulsed-yet-curious look people got before their normal hand touched his deformed one, but it was better than the awkwardness of pretending not to notice someone's hand thrust your way), but he was twitchy and ominous-sounding, saying he needed to talk to them separately, Matt first. Which probably meant Janine was right about Abe knowing about him and Mary, smoking, the whole bit. What else would've prompted Abe's looking at him that way (or *not* looking at him, rather)—like a suspect instead of his star witness?

When they were alone, Abe said, "We tracked down the rep who took the arson call."

Matt had to stop himself from letting out an audible sigh; this wasn't about Mary, after all. The intensity of his relief made Matt realize again how stupid he'd been, doing something that brought so much shame at the slightest prospect of discovery. "Okay, so who was it? Pak?"

Abe put his hands on his chin, his fingers forming a steeple, and looked at him as if deciding something. "We'll get to that, but first, I want you to look at this." He slapped down a document. "This is the bill you got cross-examined about, the one with the arson call. Look at the phone number and time of each call, and tell me if you find calls you don't recognize."

Matt looked through the list. Most were calls to his answering service, the hospital, some to his office, some to Janine's. One to the fertility clinic, which was unusual—Janine usually dealt with those—but not overly so, as he sometimes called if he was running late. "No. The only call that sticks out is the insurance one."

Abe handed him a second document: another bill, this one missing the top portion with the date and phone number. "How about this one?" Abe said. "Anything look out of place?"

This sheet, like the first, listed calls to and from his answering service, the hospital, his office, and Janine's office. "Nope. Nothing out of place," Matt said.

"Not counting the insurance call, is one of these bills more typical of the calls you usually make?"

Matt looked again. "I guess this second one because I don't normally call the fertility clinic. But why? What's this about?"

Abe touched the two sheets on the table. "These are actually from the same day. This one"—he tapped the second one—"is the record for Janine's phone, not yours."

Matt looked back and forth between the sheets. Something about the way Abe said "not yours"—mysterious, in that *gotcha!* tone he liked to use in court—told Matt this was an important point, but it was hard to think. What was he missing?

Abe said, "I understand you have the same flip phone and they got switched once, right around the day of the insurance call, isn't that right?"

Was it? That was the problem with reconstructing the past: now, August 21, 2008, was a Very Important Day, the date of The Call, but back then, it had been just another day, filled with the same errands and consultations as any other day. Who could remember if the phone switch—inconvenient, yes, but nothing you recorded for posterity—happened on this date or one of the many days just like it?

Matt shook his head. "I've no idea when that was. But why does that even . . . Wait, are you saying . . . you think *Janine* made that call?"

Abe didn't say anything, just kept staring with that stupid give-away-nothing look.

"Is that what the customer-service guy said?" Matt said. "Tell me. Right now."

Abe narrowed his eyes for a moment. "It wasn't Pak. It was someone with normal English, no accent. For some marketing study they had then, they had to make notes on anything unusual like that."

Matt shook his head. "No. There's no way it's Janine. She had no reason to call. I mean, why would she do that?"

"Well, if you're Shannon Haug, you might say she worked with Pak to get 1.3 million dollars, and she called to make sure the insurance would pay out if they went ahead with their plan to set fire to the barn and blame a third party."

Matt looked at Abe's eyes, unblinking as if Abe didn't want to miss a microsecond of Matt's reaction. "And you?" Matt said. "What would *you* say?"

Abe's lips relaxed—into a semi-smile or smirk, Matt couldn't tell. "Obviously, it depends on what you and Janine have to say. But I'd hope to be able to tell the jury that Shannon is being melodramatic as usual, and this is a simple case of spouses switching phones by mistake one day, and the wife making calls in the normal course of business, one of which just happened to be a call to check on the adequacy of insurance for a business she serves as medical advisor."

It scared Matt a little, how these lawyers could take a given set of facts and spin them in opposite directions. Not that it didn't happen in medicine—two doctors could arrive at diametrically opposed diagnoses for the same symptoms, happened all the time. But doctors were at least trying to get at the truth. Matt got the feeling that Abe cared about the truth only insofar as it was consistent with his theory of the case; otherwise, not so much. Any new evidence that didn't fit was not cause to reconsider his position, but something to explain away.

"So," Abe said, "let me ask you again. Is August 21, 2008, the day when you switched phones by accident? Let me remind you that you yourself said that Janine's records"—Abe touched the second sheet—"are more representative of the calls you normally make."

This question confirmed it. Abe was talking to him *not* to find the truth, but to coach him into corroborating the version of events that would make the Problematic New Evidence go away. It pissed him off, becoming a pawn in Abe's damage control. But not going along might mean more questions to and about Janine, which he couldn't let happen. Matt nodded. "I think August 21 is when we switched phones."

"And I would imagine that, as the advisor most fluent in English, Janine took care of many business matters, including insurance issues. Is that how you remember it?"

"Yes," Matt said. "That's exactly how I remember it."

○

HE STEPPED OUT onto the deck and watched the shadows in the curtains cast by Abe and Janine, sitting across the table like opponents in a chess match. It was raining the way he was feeling—weak and lazy, like the clouds were exhausted from all the thundering and were now slumbering, drooling warm spit once in a while. Matt hated post-storm summer drizzle like this, hated the way his skin turned puffy and sticky. But tonight, it seemed appropriate, the misery. The muggy air heavy in his lungs, weighing him down.

It had been bad enough earlier, with what he'd known then: right before the explosion, Janine had been on-site with the murder weapon, fury coursing through her. But add to that Fact #6, courtesy of Abe: she'd called Miracle Submarine's insurer to ask about arson coverage the week before its destruction by arson. Fuck!

When he saw the shadowed figures stand and leave, followed by the front door squeaking shut, he thought briefly of running away, how much easier and more pleasant the next several hours would be if he just got in his car and drove around the Beltway a few times, hard rock blaring. Instead, he went into the kitchen, not bothering to take off his shoes as Janine liked, got the Tanqueray from the freezer, and chugged. Fuck the shoes, fuck the cup.

The icy liquid went straight down, burning his throat and settling into a hot pool in his stomach. It was nearly instantaneous, the way the warmth spread outward toward his limbs, cell by cell—like dominoes, one of those long, complex designs made out of thousands of pieces, falling one by one, but so fast, the last one falling within seconds of the first.

Matt was bringing the bottle back to his mouth when Janine walked in. "I can't believe you did that," she said.

He slugged the bottle back. His tongue tingled, on the verge of going numb.

Janine snatched the bottle from him and slammed it down, the clang of glass against the granite counter making him wince. "Abe told me— you said I made that arson call. Why the fuck would you say that, to a *prosecutor*, of all people? What makes you even think that?"

Matt thought of protesting, saying he didn't say that exactly, he merely said that it was *likely*, but really, what was the point? Why pussyfoot around the periphery when he could go straight for the bull's-eye? He looked at Janine, breathed in, and said, "I know about the night of the explosion. Your meeting with Mary."

It was like flipping through the facial-emotion identification book Elizabeth used to quiz Henry with, one picture per emotion. Shock. Panic. Fear. Curiosity. Relief. All flashing across Janine's face in quick succession before finally morphing into the last emotion: resignation. She looked away.

Matt said, "Why did you never tell me? A whole *year*, and not a fucking word? What were you thinking?"

Janine's face changed then. The defensiveness zapped away, instantly replaced by a look so different, she seemed to be another person altogether. Like a bull about to charge, chin down and pupils contracted, all the pent-up indignation in her body boiled down to two pinpoints ready to fire. "*You're* lecturing *me*? Seriously? What about your cigarettes, the matches, the fucking note you wrote to a teenage *girl*? I didn't see *you* coming to me, baring your soul. Who's the one keeping incriminating secrets here?"

Janine's words were like icicles, puncturing the alcohol-infused warmth blanketing him. She was right, of course. Who was he to be self-righteous? He was the one who'd started it all—the hiding, lies, secrets. He felt every muscle deflate and slump, from his brow down to his calves. "You're right," he said. "I should've told you. Long ago."

His quasi-apology seemed to drain Janine's anger, the furrows in her brow softening at the edges. "So tell me. Everything."

It was funny, how he'd been dreading this moment when he'd have to tell her about Mary, and yet, now that it was here, he felt more relieved than anything else. He started with the truth, with being stressed about the whole fertility thing and buying cigarettes on a whim, probably as a sabotage effort. It hurt his position in the argument—in the whole marriage, really—to admit this, but that was the thing about lying: you had to throw in occasional kernels of shameful truths to serve as decoys for the things you *really* needed to hide. How easy it was, to anchor his lies with these fragments of vulnerable honesty, then twist the details to build a believable story. He said Mary found him smoking by the creek and he let her bum cigarettes even though she was too young (true), that he felt guilty (true, though not about the smoking) and resolved not to do it again (not true), but then she asked him to buy more cigarettes for her and her friends (not true), and she started sending him notes asking to meet her (true) to bring cigarettes (not true), and he ignored all her notes (not true), must have been ten at least (true), until he finally decided that all this had to end (true, although again, not because of the smoking) and sent her that final note saying it had to end and to meet him at 8:15 that night (true).

When Janine said, "So, the cigarettes I found, those are what you bought that first day?" Matt said yes, yes, of course, he bought just one pack (not true) and—the most and least truthful thing he said—"Anyway, it was just once." (True that "it" happened only once, a horrifying, humiliating once on Mary's birthday that started when she stumbled on top of him. Not true with respect to smoking.)

For a full minute after he finished his story, Janine said nothing. She sat across the table and looked at him without a word, as if trying to read something in his face. He looked back, maintaining eye contact as if daring her not to believe him. Finally, she looked away, then said, "That night before the explosion, when I found her note, why didn't you tell me then?"

"You know her. We're friends with her parents, and you might've felt obligated to tell them, and it didn't seem like that big a deal. Annoying, but . . ." He shrugged. "How'd you find out? That it wasn't an intern, I mean."

"The next day," Janine said, "I was walking by your car in the hospital lot, and I saw a note on the seat about meeting at 8:15." That was bullshit. No way he'd left that note out in the open. He'd bet anything she spent that whole morning combing through his pockets, e-mails, even trash.

"Given that HBOT ends after 8:00," she continued, "I figured there's not many people you could be meeting. Certainly not a hospital intern. So I went through the car and found another one saying something about SAT words. That made it pretty clear who it was."

He remembered that note. Mary always left her notes under the wipers, but it was raining, so she'd used the spare key in the magnetic holder under his car and taped the note to the steering wheel. She'd drawn a smiley face, and he'd laughed at her youth, the innocence.

"So why didn't you come talk to me about it?" Matt said this gently, careful to make it sound like a question of curiosity, not an accusation.

"I don't know. I guess I wasn't sure what it was all about, so I went out there to see. But the dive was delayed, and she was alone, so I just . . ."

Janine looked at her hands, using a fingertip to trace the lines on her other hand like a fortune-teller. "How did you find out?"

"I went to talk to her, last night. Abe said something about her testifying, and I hadn't talked to her in a year, so I figured I should find out what she's gonna say, you know?"

Janine nodded slowly, almost imperceptibly, and he thought he saw a sliver of relief when he said he hadn't talked to Mary all this time. "I thought she didn't remember anything," Janine said. "That's what Young said."

"Maybe not the explosion. But she definitely remembers your"—Matt searched for the right word—"visit that night. She only said something to me about it because she assumed you already told me." Matt swallowed the next words that were dying to come up his throat, the why-the-hell-didn't-you-tell-me. He'd learned early on—fights in a marriage were like seesaws. You needed to balance blame carefully. You pile too much blame on one person, let them thunk down to the ground, they're liable to stand and walk away, send you flying down on your ass.

Janine chewed the skin around her nails. After a while, she said, "I didn't see the need. In telling you, I mean. People were dead, you were burned, she was in a coma, and the notes and my talking to her, all that seemed so stupid. Petty. None of it seemed to matter anymore."

Except for the fact that you were there, at the crime scene, at the time of the crime, weapon in hand, Matt thought. The police might think that matters a lot.

As if she knew what he was thinking, how her excuse must sound, Janine said, "When the police started talking about cigarettes, I thought about saying something then, but what could I say? I drove an hour to go ask a teenage girl to stop sending notes to my husband? Oh, and yeah, by the way, before I left, I gave her cigarettes and matches, possibly the same ones that caused the explosion?"

Gave. Even as he was marveling at how she'd managed to make throwing shit at someone sound like some sort of gift, he realized the bigger significance of Janine's word choice. *Gave* implied that the recipient, Mary, took possession of the items in question. "Wait, so after you, um, gave her that stuff, did she maybe drop it and leave it behind with *you*, or did you leave *her* with it?" The alcohol was slush in his brain now, making it hard to think, but this seemed important somehow.

"What? I don't know. What difference does it make? We both left. All I know is, I told her to keep that stuff away from you and not send you more notes or anything else."

Janine said something else—something about those cigarettes being left in the woods, and it making her sick, the thought of Elizabeth, an obviously mentally ill woman, coming across those cigarettes at just the right moment and using them for murder—but Matt's mind remained fixed on the question of who last had those cigarettes. When he thought Janine had them, he'd considered the possibility of *her* having set the fire. But if Janine left first, if Mary was the one who last had them, was it possible that *she*—

"Tomorrow," Janine was saying, "Abe wants me to give a voice sample."

"What?"

"He wants me to record my voice so they can play it for the customer-service guy. It's ridiculous. It was a two-minute conversation a year ago. There's no way this guy's going to remember a voice from a year ago, right? I mean, he doesn't even know if it's a man or a woman. The only thing he knows is that the person spoke normal English with no accent, whatever that means. And think of how many people could've swiped your phone for a minute. I don't know why Abe's doing this."

Normal English with no accent. Could've swiped your phone for a minute. It occurred to him then—what he'd been overlooking because he'd never entertained the possibility, been blind to it until now.

Mary knew where he hid the spare key to his car. She could've opened his car and used his cell phone all she wanted. And she spoke perfect English. With no accent.

THE TRIAL: DAY FOUR

Thursday, August 20, 2009

JANINE

THE INTERNET ARTICLES ON POLYGRAPHS made it sound so easy: relax and control your breathing to lower your heart rate, respiratory rate, and blood pressure, and you, too, can lie with abandon! But it didn't matter how long she sat in a yoga pose, picturing ocean waves and taking cleansing breaths. Every time she even pictured Matt's phone (let alone the call), her blood went from lazy brook to Class 5 white-water rapids, as if it sensed the danger it posed and needed to escape, stat, sending her heart pumping in panic mode.

It was ironic that after all her misdeeds and lies, it was the insurance call—not even the call itself, but her switching phones with Matt on the day of the call—that was about to unravel her world. And more ironic: she hadn't needed to call. She could've easily searched online or, actually, just guessed—what fire policy didn't cover arson?—but Pak had rattled her, first with his going on about cigarettes, and then his hemming and hawing, saying maybe their whole arrangement had been a mistake, so she'd called the insurer on the spur of the moment, just as a quick check. And to have that day of all days be the one when she had Matt's phone! If he'd switched their phones on a different day or if she'd used her office phone (she'd been at her desk, right next to it!), nothing would be on that damn phone bill and everything would be fine.

She should've come forward with the truth two days ago, when Shannon first brought up the call. (Well, not the whole truth; just the part about the call.) She could've confessed to Abe and given some plausible explanation, like wanting to confirm that her parents' investment in Miracle Submarine was fully protected. They could've laughed at Shannon's overzealousness, pinning Pak as a murderer because an absent-minded husband took the wrong phone one morning. But the way that lawyer went after Pak—it made Janine panic, wonder if she'd switch her focus to Janine, investigate *her* calls, question *her* motives, pore over *her* phone records, including, possibly, her "cell tower pings." What would Shannon do if she knew that Janine had been on the premises just minutes before the explosion, that she'd had those Camels in her hands that night, that she'd lied about it for a year? Wouldn't she seize on the insurance call, use it as proof of Janine's motive for arson and maybe even murder?

It had been easy to do nothing, say nothing. And once the moment passed, she couldn't come forward later. That was the thing about lies: they demanded commitment. Once you lied, you had to stick to your story. Last night, when Abe sat her down and laid out exactly what had happened, down to the switched phone, she'd thought, *He knows. He knows everything.* And yet she couldn't admit to it, couldn't let herself give in to the intense humiliation of being caught in a lie. At that moment, he could've shown her video proof of her call, something incontrovertible, and she still would've denied it, said something ridiculous like, I'm being framed, this tape is fake! It was a type of loyalty—to her story, to herself. The more he threw at her—they found the customer-service rep, they'd find the recording soon—she became more set: it wasn't her.

Last night, after Matt's confession to her, his plea for honesty, she thought about telling him. But to explain why she'd lied about the call, she'd have to tell him everything—her deal with Pak, their decision to keep the arrangement secret, how she'd intercepted their bank statements to hide the payments she'd so carefully spread throughout multiple accounts over multiple months—and that, she wasn't sure their marriage could survive.

Still, she might've done it, confessed everything to Matt, if his own confession about Mary had been the sordid tale she'd assumed it to be. But the fact that his story was so innocuous, bereft of any wrongdoing— that had made her feel idiotic at how she'd overreacted on the day of the explosion (an understatement if there ever was one), and she couldn't.

So here she was, about to go to a prosecutor's office in a murder investigation for a voice sample. That part, she wasn't worried about. There was no way the rep would remember her voice from a two-minute call a year ago. But the lie-detector test (Abe had said it on his way out, almost casually—"If the voice sample's inconclusive, there's always a polygraph!")—what would that feel like, being behind a one-way mirror, tied to a machine, answering no to question after question, knowing that her own body—her lungs, her heart, her blood—was betraying her?

She had to beat it. That was all there was to it. Here—an article about passing polygraphs by pressing down on thumbtacks in your shoe while answering the initial "control" questions, the theory being that pain causes the same physiological symptoms as lying, so they can't differentiate between true and false answers. That made sense. It could work.

Janine closed the Web browser. She opened the Internet settings, wiped her history clean, logged off, and shut the computer down. She tiptoed into her room, careful not to wake Matt, and went into the closet to look for thumbtacks.

MATT

MARY WAS WEARING what she always wore in his dreams: the red sundress from their final meeting last summer, on her seventeenth birthday. As in all his dreams, Matt said she looked beautiful and kissed her. Soft at first, closed lips on closed lips, then harder, sucking her bottom lip, taking in the plumpness and squeezing with his own lips. He lowered the spaghetti straps and touched her breasts, feeling the softness give way to the rough hardness of the nipples. This was when the dream version of himself realized this was a dream, that only in a dream world could his fingers feel anything.

In real life, he'd pretended not to notice the dress. It was the Wednesday before the explosion, and when he went to the creek at the usual time (8:15 p.m.), she was sitting on a log, a lit cigarette in one hand and plastic cup in the other, her shoulders slumped like an old woman at the end of a long, hard day. It was infectious, her loneliness, and he wanted to take her in his arms, displace that desolation with something—anything—else. Instead, he sat down and said, "Hey there," forcing into his voice a lightness he didn't feel.

"Join me," she said, handing him another cup filled with clear liquid.

"What is it?" he said, but before he even finished the sentence, he smelled it and laughed. "Peach schnapps? You've gotta be kidding me. I haven't had that in ten years." His college girlfriend had loved the stuff. "I can't take this." He handed it back. "You're five years from drinking age."

"Four, actually. It's my birthday today." She pushed the drink back.

"Wow," he said, unsure of what to say. "Shouldn't you be celebrating with your friends?"

"I asked some people from SAT class, but they were busy." Maybe she saw the pity in his eyes, because she shrugged and said with a forced brightness, "But meanwhile, you're here, and I'm here. So come on, drink up. Just this once. You can't let me drink alone on my birthday. It's bad luck or something."

It was a stupid idea. And yet, the way she looked, her lips stretched into a smile so wide both rows of teeth showed, but eyes puffy and glassy like she'd been crying—it reminded him of one of those kids' puzzles where you're supposed to match the top half to the bottom, and the kid's screwed up, putting the sad forehead with the happy mouth. He looked at her faux smile, the mix of hope and pleading in her raised eyebrows, and tapped his cup against hers. "Happy birthday." He gulped.

They sat like that for an hour, then two, drinking and talking, talking and drinking. Mary told him how even though she always spoke English now, she still dreamed in Korean. Matt told her how this creek reminded him of his childhood dog, how he'd buried her by a creek just like this when she died. They debated whether tonight's sky was more orange-red (Mary) or purple-red (Matt), and which was better. Mary told him how she used to hate Seoul's overcrowding—classrooms, buses, streets—but now she missed it, how living here didn't make her feel peaceful but merely lonely and sometimes lost. She told him how much she dreaded starting school here, how she said hi to some teenagers her age in town and no one said hi back, just stared with these go-the-fuck-back-where-you-came-from looks, and later, she overheard them bashing her family's business as "ching-chong voodoo." Matt told her about Janine's refusal to even consider adoption, how he'd been planning his days off so they conflicted with Janine's, to avoid being alone with her in the house.

Around ten, when the vestiges of the sunset faded and darkness finally set in, Mary stood up, saying she was dizzy and needed water. He stood up, too, and was saying he should get going anyway, when she stumbled over a rock and fell against him. He tried to steady her, but he also stumbled, and they both ended up on the ground, laughing, her on top of him.

They tried to get up, but as drunk as they were, they ended up entangled, her thighs pressing and shifting against his groin, and he got hard. He tried not to, told himself he was thirty-three and she was seventeen and this was probably a felony, for God's sake. But the thing was, he didn't feel over thirty, and not just in the everyday, I-don't-feel-as-old-as-my-age way he felt around those teenage hospital volunteers, wondering how he'd gotten to be someone they called "Sir." It may have been the peach schnapps. Not the alcohol (though there was that) but the way it burned going down and settled hot in his stomach, sweet tanginess lingering in his mouth and nose. It was an instant time machine to those high school days of getting drunk with some girl and making out for hours and jerking off after, and sitting here now, drinking far too much of that shit, having one of those talk-about-everything-and-nothing conversations he hadn't had since college—he felt *young*. Besides, Mary sure as hell didn't look like an innocent girl in that dress, a trapping of seduction if he ever saw one.

So he kissed her. Or maybe she kissed him. His head was sludge; it was hard to think. Later, he'd hyperanalyze every frame of his memory of this moment for any clue that she wasn't the enthusiastic participant he'd assumed her to be—had she squirmed to get away? had she mumbled no, however faintly?—but the truth was, he'd been oblivious to everything except the parts of her body in contact with his, and her reactions, her sounds and movements—those hadn't been a factor at all. He'd closed his eyes and focused every neuron on the sensation of the kiss, the newness of her lips and tongue and teeth adding to the surreal feeling of being transported back to his teens. He didn't want this moment, the pure physicality of it, to stop, so he wrapped his arms around her, one around her head to keep her mouth against his, and the other around her hips, steering her pelvis against his like teenagers grinding. He felt a deep welling of pressure stemming from his scrotum, building and building. He needed release. Right now. Eyes still closed, he unzipped his pants, grabbed her hand, and pushed it inside his underwear. He cupped his hand over her fingers, wrapping and holding them tight around his penis, and guided them into an up-down rhythm, its masturbatory familiarity combining with the unfamiliar smoothness of her lips and palms to drive him into a fevered frenzy.

Quickly, much too quickly, he came, the throbs of the contractions so intense, they were deliciously painful, sending tingles of electricity down his legs to his toes. The loud buzz of alcohol clogged his ears and white flashes burned behind his eyelids. He felt weak, and he released his grasp on Mary's head and hand.

As he lay back, let the world go around in circles, he felt something press against his chest—but weakly, almost tentatively—and recoil. He opened his eyes. His head wobbled and the world spun, but he saw a small hand, above his chest—*her* hand, Mary's hand. Shaking. And right above it, the oval of her open mouth, and her eyes, so wide they protruded, staring at her sticky hand, then turning to look at *him*, at his still-erect penis. Fear. Shock. But most of all, confusion, as if she didn't understand any of this, didn't know what that was coating her fingers, didn't know what that *thing* was, poking out of his otherwise-on pants, like a child. A girl.

He ran away. He had no memory of how—he couldn't remember standing, let alone how he managed to drive home with that much alcohol in his system. When he woke up the next morning, his hangover mauling his body, he had a moment of desperate hope of the incident being an alcohol-induced hallucination of some sort. But the semen-stain residue on his pants, the mud caked on his shoes—those confirmed the reality of what he remembered, and shame engulfed him, bringing back the buzz in his ears, the white flashes in his eyes.

He didn't talk to Mary after that night. He tried to—to explain and apologize (and, if he was being honest, to see if she'd told anyone), but she went out of her way to avoid him. He managed to leave her a few notes—he had to go to her SAT class and find her car—but she wrote back, *I don't know why we need to discuss it. Can't we just forget it ever happened?* But he couldn't forget it, couldn't let her let him off that easy. Which was why he left her that now-famous H-Mart note, which his *wife* ended up throwing in her face, accusing *her* of stalking *him*!

It had been a year since that ordeal, but the shame and guilt and humiliation of that night—those never went away. Most of the time, they lay inert in a tightly knotted coil in his gut. But whenever he thought of Mary, and sometimes when he didn't, when he was eating or driving or watching TV, that knot of shame erupted.

That night was the last time he'd had an orgasm. It wasn't just Mary, but that plus the explosion and the amputation right after—the one-two-three punch of it—knocked out whatever sexual desire remained in him. Not that he never tried sex again. But the first time, when he started their usual foreplay—circling Janine's nipples with his thumbs—he realized: he couldn't feel anything. He had no idea if his touch was too hard or too soft, couldn't gauge her readiness by feeling her wetness. His therapists had taught him how to type, eat, even wipe his ass with what felt like baseball mitts over his hands. But there'd been no How to Get Your Wife Off session, no alternative fondling techniques. It made him want to scream, this discovery of yet another element of his life the explosion had fucked over, and he couldn't get hard.

Janine tried a blow job, and that worked for a minute, but he made the mistake of opening his eyes. The fuzzy film of moonlight made visible the long curtains of Janine's hair, swinging as her head bobbed up and down. It made him think of Mary, the way her hair had swung about her face as she pushed herself up from his body. He went soft immediately.

That had been the beginning of Matt's impotence. Janine, bless her, kept trying, resorting to things she'd once scoffed at as denigrating to women—slitted negligees, dildos, porn—but none of that compensated for his feeling clumsy and inadequate in bed, let alone his shame about Mary, and he couldn't make anything happen, even by himself. The one time he'd tried (in the bathroom after a failed Janine session, out of panic he'd lost it forever), his hand felt unfamiliar, the scars' simultaneous slickness and bumpiness enhancing every rub, not at all like masturbation. Being able to see but not feel his hand holding his penis added to the trippy feel, the sensation that it was not him touching himself, but rather a stranger, and he felt that thrill of newness. But then, the thought: Was he actually turned on by the thought of a male stranger's hand jerking him off?

A few times, he'd come close to nocturnal emissions, which Matt used to think was almost worse than none at all (with the evanescent millisecond of gratification not worth the pathetic reversion to puberty) but which he'd started praying for, if only to reassure himself that his orgasm wasn't dead, merely dormant. The problem was, Mary always invaded his dream, and some deep-seated pedophilic/rape guilt sensor woke him up. Until tonight.

Tonight, he kept going. Took off her panties. Let her take off his pants and underwear. As he got on top and spread her legs, he held up his mutilated hands and said, "You wrecked me." She said, "Because you wrecked me first," then raised her hips to push him into her, tighter, wetter, and more real-feeling than he'd felt in years, maybe ever. When he came, the dream-Mary screamed and shattered into a million glass particles, the tiny beads of glass-her exploding into him in slow motion, pushing through his skin and into his body, sending tingles of warmth and pure joy out toward his limbs.

"Honey, you up?" Janine's voice called, waking him. He clutched the blanket and turned over, pretending to still be asleep as she told him she was leaving early for the voice sample. He stayed still until she left. After he heard her car drive away, he went into the bathroom. He turned on the water and tried to scrub his underwear clean.

YOUNG

THE FIRST THING SHE NOTICED upon waking up was the sunlight. The crooked cutout that served as their window was too small to let in much light. But when the sun was in *just* the right position, like now—morning, when the sun climbed above the trees into the middle of their makeshift window, perfectly framed by the square hole— it surged in, the square beam of light so strong it looked almost solid for the first meter before diffusing into an ethereal brightness that flooded the whole shack and gave it a fairy-tale quality. Floating motes of dust glittered in the veil of sunlight. Birds chirped.

The thing about the backwoods was how dark it became on moonless nights like last night—the dark not just a lack of light, but its own presence with mass and shape. An inky blackness so absolute, it made no difference whether she opened or closed her eyes. For much of the night, she'd lain awake, listening to rain drumming the roof and breathing in dank air, and resisted the urge to shake Pak awake. She was a big believer in sleeping on problems before taking action. It was funny how American articles spouted the wisdom of resolving arguments at day's end ("Never Go to Bed Mad!"), which was the opposite of common sense. Night was the worst time for fights—its gloom intensifying insecurities and heightening suspicions—whereas if you waited, you always woke up feeling better, more reasonable and charitable, the passing time and brightness of the new day cooling emotions and deflating their power.

Well, not always. For here it was, a new day—rain stopped, clouds gone, air lightened—but instead of last night's worries seeming inconsequential, it was the opposite, as if the passage of time had cemented the reality of this changed world in which her husband was a liar and maybe even a murderer. In the surreal fuzziness of the night, there was the possibility of the new reality not being real; the morning's clarity snatched that away.

Young got up. A note on Pak's pillow read: *I went outside for fresh air. I'll be back by 8:30.* She looked at her watch. 8:04. Too early for any of her plans to investigate Pak's story—visit Mr. Spinum, their neighbor; call the Realtor who sent the Seoul listings; use the library computer to search for e-mails to/from Pak's brother—except one: ask Mary exactly what she did with Pak the night of the explosion, minute by minute.

Young stomped twice outside Mary's shower-curtained corner—their faux knock—and said, "Mary, wake up," in Korean. It was a toss-up which would annoy Mary more, her speaking English ("No one can even understand what you're saying!") or Korean ("No wonder your English is so bad—you've got to practice more!"), but she didn't want the handicap of using a foreign language for this talk. Switching from English to Korean doubled her IQ, gave her eloquence and control, and she'd need that to root out all the details. "Wake up," she said louder, stomping again. Nothing.

Suddenly, she remembered: today was Mary's birthday. In Korea, they'd made a fuss over her birthdays, decorating overnight to surprise her with signs and streamers when she awoke. Young hadn't continued this in America—her store hours left no time for anything beyond basic necessities—but still, Mary might expect something special for her eighteenth birthday, a milestone year. "Happy birthday," Young said. "I'm excited to see my eighteen-year-old daughter. Can I come in?"

There was nothing. No sheets rustling, no snores, no deep breaths of sleep. "Mary?" Young opened the curtain.

Mary wasn't there. Her sleep mat was rolled up in the corner, same as last night, and her pillow and blanket were missing. Mary hadn't slept here. But she'd returned last night. Headlights had streamed in the window about midnight, and the front door had rattled open. Had she left again, and Young hadn't heard?

She ran out. The car was there, but Mary wasn't inside. She ran to the shed. Empty. But there was nowhere else dry enough to spend the night, no place within walking distance . . .

An image came to her then. Her daughter, lying flat on her back in a dark metal tube.

She knew exactly where Mary had slept last night.

○

YOUNG DIDN'T GO IN at first. She stood at the barn's edge and opened her mouth to call for Mary, but she smelled something stale and chalky and thought of burned flesh, singed hair. She told herself it couldn't be—a year had passed since the fire—and walked in, her eyes down to avoid the indicia of fire, but that was impossible. Half the walls were gone, and mud puddles from the storm covered what remained of the floor. A swath of sunlight from a caved-in hole in the roof shone down, spotlighting the chamber like a museum display. Its thick steel frame had survived the fire intact, but its aquamarine paint was blistered and the glass portholes shattered.

Mary had slept here most of last summer. At first, they'd all slept in the shack, but Mary complained nonstop—the too-early lights-out, too-early morning alarm, Pak's snoring, and so on. When Young pointed out this was temporary, and besides, they'd all slept in one room back in Korea, per tradition, Mary said (in English), "Yeah, back when we were actually a family. Besides, if you want Korean tradition so much, why don't we just move back? I mean, how is *this*"—Mary swept her arms across the shack—"better than what we had?"

Young wanted to say she understood how hard it was to have no space of her own, to confess how hard it was for Pak and Young herself to have no privacy to even bicker, let alone other marital necessities. But the way Mary sneered and rolled her eyes—openly, defiantly, as if Young were so unworthy of respect that Mary didn't even need to *pretend* to hide her contempt—sent Young into a toxic fury, and she found herself wishing she'd never had Mary and yelling maternal clichés she'd promised herself never to say: that some children had no food or shelter, and did she realize how ungrateful and selfish she was being? (This was the quintessential skill of teenage daughters: making you think and say things you regretted even as you were thinking and saying them.)

The next day, Mary acted the way she always did during their fights: saccharine to Pak, acidic to Young. Young ignored it, but Pak (clueless as ever to filial manipulations) relished the onslaught of Mary's affection. Young had to marvel at the expert way Mary mentioned—carefully casual, with a diffident, almost apologetic tone—how badly she'd been sleeping, the way she led him to think her proposed solution, sleeping in the chamber, was actually *his* idea. Mary slept there every night until the explosion.

The night Mary came home from the hospital, she went to sleep in her corner inside their house. But when Young woke up, Mary was gone. She looked for her everywhere except the barn; it didn't even occur to her that Mary might cross the yellow tape encircling it, that she could stand to go near, much less inside, the metal tube where people were burned alive. But passing by a charred hole in the barn wall, Young glimpsed a flashlight by the chamber. She opened the hatch and found Mary inside, lying on her back. No pillow, no mat, no blanket. Her only child, motionless, eyes closed, arms straight by her side. Young thought of corpses in coffins. Crematorium ovens. She screamed.

They never talked about it afterward. Mary never explained, and Young never asked. Mary returned to her corner where she slept every night, and that was the end of it.

Until now. And here she was again, opening the hatch. The rusted hinges creaked, and pinpoint beams of sunlight pierced in. Mary wasn't there. But she had been. Her pillow and blanket were inside, and two strands of black hair—long, like Mary's—crisscrossed the pillow, forming an X. On the blanket sat a brown bag. Last night, Pak had put the bag from the shed by the door, to throw it away today. Had Mary found it when she returned home?

Young crawled in for the bag. Just as she tilted it to look in, she heard a noise. The crunch of gravel, the snapping of dead branches on the ground. Steps. Fast, like someone running toward the barn. A shout. Pak's voice. "Meh-hee-yah, stop, let me explain." More steps, a thunk—Mary falling?—then sobs close by, right outside.

Young knew she should get out and see what was happening, but something about the situation—Mary running from Pak, obviously upset, Pak following her—stopped her. Young could see inside the bag now. Tin case. Papers. She was right; Mary had found the cigarettes and Seoul listings. Had Mary confronted him, like she had?

The click-clack of Pak's wheelchair got closer. Young closed the hatch so she'd be hidden but could see out the slit opening. Maneuvering her body in the darkness, her hands touched Mary's pillow. It was damp.

The wheelchair noise stopped. "Meh-hee-yah," Pak said in Korean, his voice closer now, right outside the barn, "I can't tell you how much I regret it."

Mary's voice, shaking, her words in English separated by choked sobs: "I don't believe . . . you had anything . . . to do with it. It doesn't . . . make any . . . sense."

A pause, then Pak's voice: "I wish it wasn't true, but it is. The cigarette, the matches. It was my doing." He was talking about the tin case, had to be. Except it had no matches.

Mary's voice, in English: "But how did it end up here? I mean, out of our whole property, how did it wind up in *exactly* the most dangerous spot?" It occurred to Young then, where their voices were coming from: behind the barn, where the oxygen tanks used to be.

A sigh. Not long, but heavy—infused with dread, a desperate longing to keep silent—and Young wished the sigh could last forever, that he would not open his mouth for the next words.

"I put it here," Pak said. "I picked the spot, right under the oxygen tube. I gathered twigs and dried leaves. I put the matches in, and the cigarette."

"No," Mary said.

"Yes, it was all me," Pak said. "I did it."

○

I DID IT.

At those words, Young put her head on Mary's pillow, her cheeks against the wetness of Mary's tears. She closed her eyes and felt her body spin. Or maybe it was the chamber spinning, faster and faster, getting smaller and collapsing into a pinpoint, squashing her.

I did it. It was all me.

Incomprehensible words that meant the world was ending, so how could he say them so matter-of-factly? How could he so coldly admit to setting the fire that killed two people and remain breathing, talking?

The sound of Mary's sobs, hysterical now, broke through, and it came to Young, what she'd overlooked in her fog: Mary just discovered that her father had committed murder. Mary was suffering shock, the same shock she herself was reeling from. Young's eyes snapped open, and she ached to run out, to take Mary into her arms and cry together over the grief of learning something so horrifying about their beloved. Young heard *shh-shh*, the sound of a parent comforting a child in pain, and she wanted to yell at Pak to get away from Mary, to leave them both alone and stop tainting them with his sins, when Mary said, "But why that spot? If you'd picked anywhere else—"

"The protesters," Pak said. "Elizabeth showed me their flyer, and she kept saying they might set a fire to sabotage us, and it gave me the idea—if the police found a cigarette in the same spot as the flyer, they'd get in trouble." Of course. How convenient: set the fire, blame the protesters, collect the insurance. A classic frame-up job against the people who'd enraged him.

"But the police took them away for the balloons," Mary said. "Why did you need to do anything else?"

"The protesters called me. They said the police just gave them a warning, and there was nothing to stop them from coming back every day, until they drove all the patients away. I had to do something more drastic, to get them in real trouble and keep them away for good. I never imagined you'd go anywhere near there, let alone . . ." His voice faltered, and the image flooded her mind: Mary running to the barn and turning, then blink, her face bathed in the orange glow of the fire and her body thrown in the air, caught in the blast.

Mary also seemed haunted by that moment; she said, "I keep thinking, there was no fan sound from the HBOT. It was so quiet." Young remembered that, too—hearing the distant croaking of frogs without the usual AC fan noise masking it. The smothering purity of the silence before the boom.

"That was all my doing," Pak said. "I caused the power outage to frame the protesters. That set everything in motion—the delays, everything that went wrong that night. I never dreamed so many things could go wrong. I never dreamed anyone would get hurt."

Young wanted to scream, demand to know how he could possibly think that, setting a fire under a stream of oxygen. And yet she believed him, knew he had some plan to get everyone out in time. That was why he used a cigarette, to let it burn down slowly before the fire caught, and why he wanted to stay outside while *she* turned off the oxygen, to make sure that the flames didn't get too big before 8:20, while the oxygen was still on. He'd come up with the perfect plan to set a slow-burning fire that would scare but not hurt anyone. Problem was, the plan didn't go like it was supposed to. Plans never did.

After a long silence, in a quivering voice so quiet she strained to hear, Mary said in English, "I keep thinking of Henry and Kitt."

"It was an accident," Pak said. "You have to remember that."

"But it's my fault, all because I was selfish and I wanted to go back to Korea. You told me things would get better, but I kept being stubborn and complaining, and finally . . ." Mary broke into sobs, but Young knew: finally, Pak decided to give their daughter what she wanted and did the only thing he could think of to make that happen.

Young felt something collapse, as if someone had punched her lungs.

The thing grating at her, telling her none of this made sense, was the question of why. Yes, Pak hated the protesters. Yes, he wanted them gone. But why a fire? Their business had been thriving, and there was no reason to destroy it. Except there was. Mary had come to him, begging him to move back to Korea. Arson wasn't a spontaneous idea, born out of his anger at the protesters. He'd planned it. Everything made sense now, fit into place. The arson call, the Seoul listings—all in furtherance of his plot. And when the protesters came along, he seized on the perfect decoys.

Young felt pain in her chest, like tiny birds pecking at her heart, imagining Mary confiding in Pak last summer, crying to him about her desperation to return to their homeland. Why hadn't Mary come to *her*, her mother? In Korea, every afternoon, they'd played Korean jacks while she told her about the boys who teased her and the books she secretly read during class. Where had that closeness gone? Had it evaporated, no longer retrievable, or had it simply burrowed deep to hibernate through the teenage years? She knew Mary didn't like America and wanted to return, but only through snips and snide asides, not the soul-baring confidence Mary apparently reserved for Pak. And Pak, not coming to her, but carrying out a dangerous plan to give Mary what she wanted—making this decision by himself, with no input from her, his wife of twenty years. It felt like betrayal. Betrayal by her daughter and husband. Betrayal by the two people she loved and trusted most.

"We should tell Abe," Mary said. "Now. We need to stop torturing Elizabeth."

"I've thought about that a lot," Pak said. "But the trial is nearly over. Chances are good she won't be convicted. Once the trial ends, we can move, start fresh."

"But what if she's found guilty? She could be executed."

"If that happens, I'll confess. I'll wait for the insurance money to come through, and once you and your mother get away, somewhere safe, I'll go to Abe. I won't let her go to jail for something she didn't do. I couldn't do that." He swallowed. "I did many things wrong, but no one, *no one*, intended to hurt anyone. Remember that."

Mary said, "But she's already suffering. She's on trial for killing her son. She must be in so much pain, I can't bear to—"

"Listen to me," Pak said. "I feel horrible about what's happened. I'd give anything to change it. But I don't think Elizabeth feels the same way. She may not have set the fire, but I think she wanted Henry dead, and she's glad it happened."

"How can you say that?" Mary said. "I know they're saying she hurt him, but to say she actually wanted him dead—"

"I heard her, with my own ears, through the intercom when she thought it wasn't on," Pak said.

"Heard what?"

"She told Teresa she wanted Henry to die, that she actually fantasized about him dying."

"What? When? And why haven't you said anything? You didn't even testify about it."

"Abe said not to. He's going to ask Teresa about it on the stand, but he wants to surprise her, to get the full truth." Was that why Young had never heard about this, because Teresa was her friend and Abe was afraid she'd say something? Was there anyone who hadn't lied to her?

"The point is," Pak said, "Elizabeth wanted Henry dead. She abused him. They were going to prosecute her for that anyway, and she's already on trial. Will being on trial one more week make that much of a difference to her? And remember, if the verdict is guilty, I'll come forward. I promise you that."

Was that really true? Or was he just saying that to convince Mary to remain silent, and if the verdict was guilty, he'd come up with some other excuse and let Elizabeth die?

"Now, before we go in," Pak said, "I need you to promise me. You *will* do as I say. Not one word to anyone, including your mother. Understand?"

At this reference to her, Young's heart thumped her chest, hard and fast. Pak said, "Meh-hee-yah, answer me. Do you understand?"

"No. We should tell Um-ma," Mary said, in English as always except for "Um-ma." How long had it been since Mary called her Um-ma, what she used to call her before encasing herself in an armor of resentment? "You said she's been getting suspicious. What if she asks about that night? What am I supposed to say?"

"What you've been saying all along, that everything is fuzzy."

"No, we have to tell her." Her voice shook, sounding unsure and small like a little girl's.

"No." Pak spat this out with so much force, it rang in Young's ears, but he paused and took deep breaths, as if to calm himself. "For me, Meh-hee-yah, do this for me." Forced patience coated his words. "It's my decision, my responsibility. If your mother knew . . ." He sighed.

There was silence, and she knew that Mary must've nodded, knew he would've kept badgering her if Mary hadn't obeyed. After a minute, she heard steps and the wheelchair moving. Closer and closer, then moving past, toward the house. She thought about waiting until they were inside and running away. Or maybe going in after them, pretending not to have heard anything and seeing what they'd do. Both acts of cowardice, she knew, but she was so tired. How easy it'd be to stay here and seal the world out, lie here entombed for as long as it took for things to stop spinning, for everything to just pass and disintegrate into nothing.

No. She couldn't do nothing, couldn't let Pak just push her aside and make her any more irrelevant than he already had. She pushed the hatch, hard. It squeaked open, the dissonance of the noise piercing her ears and making her want to scream. She tried to stand. Her head banged the steel above, the thud resonating in her skull like a beaten gong.

Footsteps entered the barn, slow and cautious. Pak said it was nothing, probably an animal, but Mary said, "Mom, is that you?" Her voice was sopping with fear, but something else, too. Maybe hope.

Slowly, Young raised her body. She crawled out and stood up. She reached out to Mary in invitation to join her, to grieve together for this loss that was uniquely theirs. Mary looked at her, tears streaming down her face in rivulets, but she didn't walk toward her. Instead, she looked at Pak as if to ask permission. He held out his hand, and Mary hesitated before walking away from her and closer to Pak.

A memory: Mary as a baby between them, both Young and Pak reaching and calling for her, and their baby girl crawling to Pak, always Pak, and Young laughing and clapping, pretending not to be hurt, telling herself how wonderful it was that he was so close with their baby, unlike other men, how it was only because Meh-hee spent so much time with her—the entire day!—that she preferred the parent she hadn't seen. It had always been this way with them—an imbalance, even their positioning now, the three of them forming a skinny triangle with Young the lone castaway far from the others. Maybe all families with only children were this way, inequality in closeness and the resulting envy being inherent in all three-person groups. After all, equilateral triangles with truly equal sides existed only in theory, not in real life. She'd thought the balance would change when they were together on a different continent from Pak, but ironically, he saw Mary more than she did even then: twice a week, through Skype (which Young couldn't use, as the store had no Internet). The balance always skewed to Pak-Mary. It had in the past, and it remained so now.

Young looked at them. The man in the wheelchair, who had committed a monstrous act he'd hidden for a year and had entrusted their daughter, not her, with his secrets. And next to him, the girl with the scar, who'd already forgiven her father for the crime that gave her that scar. The girl who always chose her father, who was still siding with him now, mere minutes after this crushing revelation that should have brought her back to Young. Her husband and daughter. Her sun and moon, her bone and marrow, those without whom her life wouldn't exist, yet always out of reach and unknowable. She felt a deep pang in her chest, as if every cell in her heart were suffocating and slowly dying.

Pak looked at her. She expected penitence, for his head to droop like a dying sunflower, for him to be unable to look her in the eye, as he confessed his crime and begged forgiveness. Instead, he said, "Yuh-bo, I didn't realize you were there. What were you doing?"—not in an accusatory or nervous way, but with a tone of feigned casualness, as if testing her out, to see if he could get away with continuing to lie to her. Looking at him, at his fake smile that looked eerily genuine, she stumbled back, and suddenly, it was as if the floor had vanished and she were falling through a vacuum. She needed to get out of this space, this ruined site of death and lies. She staggered, the scorched flooring beneath her feet uneven, needing to hold out her arms for balance, like walking down a plane aisle during turbulence. She walked past Pak and Mary to the stump of a long-dead tree and wiped her tears.

"I see—you heard," Pak said. "Yuh-bo, you have to understand. I didn't want to burden you, and I thought there was a better chance of things working out in the end if—"

"Working out?" She turned and stared at him. "How could this possibly work out? A boy is dead. Five children have no mother. An innocent woman is on trial for murder. You are in a wheelchair. And Mary has to live the rest of her life knowing that her father is a murderer. There is no way anything can ever be all right." She didn't realize she was shouting until she stopped and heard her words echoing in the silence. Her throat felt raw, grated.

"Yuh-bo," Pak said. "Come inside. Let's talk about this. You'll see—everything will work out. We just have to keep going and not say anything, for now."

Young stepped back, onto a branch, the uneven footing making her wobbly, ready to fall. Mary and Pak both leaned forward and held out their hands. Young looked at the hands of her daughter and her husband, side by side, offering to steady her, support her. She looked at their faces, these beautiful people she loved, standing at the foot of the trail running along the creek, the tall trees behind them forming a canopy over their heads, sparkling strings of sunlight poking through the leaves. How beautiful it was this morning, when her life was collapsing, as if God were mocking her and confirming her irrelevance.

Mary looked at her and said, "Um-ma, please," the tender way she said "Mom" in Korean making Young want to take her daughter in her arms and wipe her tears with her thumb, the way she used to. She thought how easy it'd be to say yes, to join hands and forge this union that would forever be held tight by their secret. Then she looked up, at the blackened submarine peeking through, charred by the flames that had engulfed an eight-year-old boy and the woman trying to save him.

She shook her head no. She took a backward step, then another, and another, until she was out of their reach. "You have no right to ask me anything," she said. Then she turned from them, her husband and daughter, and walked away.

MATT

H E LOOKED FOR MARY IN COURT. He wanted to see her. Well, not wanted, exactly. More like needed. The way you don't exactly *want* a root canal, but you need to get the rot out, stop the pain. The courtroom was fuller than usual—probably the by-product of the latest news ("'Mommy Murderer' Trial: Defendant Fed Son Bleach")—but the Yoos were absent, which was strange.

Janine was already there. "I did the voice sample. They're playing it for the guy today," she whispered, and anxiety churned in his stomach, thinking about Mary's access to his car, the phone inside.

Abe turned. "Have you seen the Yoos?"

He shook his head. Janine said, "I think it's Mary's birthday. Maybe they're celebrating?"

Mary's birthday. Something felt wrong, ominous, the coming together of these unnerving things—the car-key realization, the dream, and now her birthday. Her eighteenth, legally becoming an adult. As in, able to be fully prosecuted. Shit.

Detective Heights walked up for her cross-examination. Shannon didn't waste any time with good-mornings or how-are-yous, didn't stand or wait for the whispers to die down. She just said, from her seat, "You consider Elizabeth Ward to be a child abuser, right?"

People looked around, as if to figure out where the question came from. Heights appeared taken aback, like a boxer who expects a minute of circling the ring and, instead, gets punched in the face immediately after the bell. She said, "I, um . . . I suppose that's right. Yes."

Still sitting, Shannon said, "And you told your colleagues that was critical to this case, that without the abuse claims, you had nothing on motive, correct?"

Heights frowned. "I don't recall that."

"No? You don't remember writing 'No abuse equals no motive' on the whiteboard at a meeting on this case on August 30, 2008?"

Heights swallowed. After a moment, she cleared her throat. "Yes. I do recall that, but—"

"Thank you, Detective. Now"—Shannon stood—"tell us how you handle child abuse claims in general." She walked up, her steps slow and relaxed as if she were strolling through a garden. "When you get a serious complaint, you sometimes remove children from parents' custody right away, before the investigation's even done, correct?"

"Yes, when there's a credible threat of serious harm, we try to obtain an emergency order temporarily assigning the child to a foster home pending investigation."

"*Credible threat of serious harm.*" Shannon stepped closer. "In this case, when you received the anonymous complaint about Elizabeth, you didn't remove Henry from his home, didn't even try. Isn't that correct?"

Heights looked at Shannon, mouth shut tight, eyes unblinking. After a long moment, she said, "Correct."

"Which means that you believed there was no credible risk of harm to Henry, correct?"

Heights looked over to Abe, back to Shannon, and blinked. "That was our *preliminary* assessment. Before our investigation."

"Ah, yes. You investigated for five days. At any point, if you had determined that Henry was, in fact, being abused, you could and would have removed him to protect him. That's your job, right?"

"Yes, but—"

"But you didn't do that." Shannon stepped forward like a bulldozer ramming through a barrier. "For five full days after the complaint, you left Henry at home, correct?"

Heights bit her lip. "We were obviously wrong in our assessment—"

"Detective," Shannon said, projecting her voice. "Please answer my question and my question only. I didn't ask about your job performance, although your supervisor and attorneys interested in suing on behalf of Henry's estate may be very interested to hear your admission of wrongdoing here. My question is: After five days of investigation, did you or did you not find Elizabeth to be an abuser posing a credible threat of serious harm to Henry?"

"We did not." Heights looked dejected, her words flat.

"Thank you. Now let's turn to your investigation itself." Shannon put a blank poster board on the easel. "Yesterday, you said you investigated four types of abuse here: neglect and emotional, physical, and medical abuse. Correct?"

"Yes."

Shannon wrote those categories in a column on the poster. "You interviewed Kitt Kozlowski, eight teachers, four therapists, and two doctors, as well as Henry's father, correct?"

"Yes."

Shannon wrote the interviewees on the top row:

	Father	8 Teachers	4 Therapists	2 Doctors	Kitt
Neglect					
Emotional Abuse					
Physical Abuse					
Medical Abuse					

Shannon said, "Did anyone express concerns about Elizabeth neglecting Henry?"

"No."

Shannon wrote *NO* five times across the *Neglect* row and drew a line through the whole row. "Next, anyone other than Kitt express concerns about emotional abuse or physical abuse?"

Heights said, "No."

"In fact, Henry's teacher from last year said—I'm reading from your notes—quote, 'Elizabeth is the last mother I could see traumatizing her child emotionally or physically,' right?"

Heights breathed out, almost in a sigh. "Yes."

"Thank you." Shannon wrote *NO* in both rows across all but the *Kitt* column. "Finally, medical abuse. You focused on this, so I imagine you asked detailed questions to every person you talked to." Shannon put down the marker. "So let's have it. List for us all the instances of medical abuse these fifteen other people told you about."

Heights said nothing, just stared at Shannon with a look of intense dislike.

"Detective, your answer?"

"The problem is, these people weren't aware of any of the so-called medical therapies the defendant inflicted on Henry, so—"

"Yes, we'll get to Henry's therapies in a minute. But in the meantime, it sounds to me like your answer is that these fifteen people you interviewed did not, in fact, think that Elizabeth had committed medical abuse. Is that right, Detective?"

Heights breathed, and her nostrils flared. "Yes."

"Thank you." Shannon wrote *NO* across the last row and stood back to give the jurors an unobstructed view of the easel.

	Father	8 Teachers	4 Therapists	2 Doctors	Kitt
~~Neglect~~	~~NO~~	~~NO~~	~~NO~~	~~NO~~	~~NO~~
Emotional Abuse	NO	NO	NO	NO	
Physical Abuse	NO	NO	NO	NO	
Medical Abuse	NO	NO	NO	NO	

Shannon pointed to the poster. "So the fifteen people who knew Henry best and cared for his well-being agreed that Elizabeth did not in any way abuse him. Let's talk about the one person with concerns. Did Kitt actually accuse Elizabeth of emotional abuse?"

Heights frowned. "I think it would be fair to say she questioned whether the defendant harmed Henry by saying he's annoying and everyone hates him."

"So she *questioned* emotional abuse." Shannon drew a question mark in the *Emotional Abuse/Kitt* square. "And what's your opinion on that, Detective? Is that child abuse? I have a child, a *very* teenage girl, if you know what I mean, and I admit, I catch myself telling her often that she's rude and mean and downright hateable and she's going to wind up alone with no friends, husband, or job if she doesn't change and soon." Some jurors chuckled and nodded. "Now, I know I won't win any mother-of-the-year awards, but is that the type of thing we take kids away from moms for?"

"No. Like you say, it's not ideal, but it doesn't rise to the level of abuse."

Shannon smiled and slashed a line through the *Emotional Abuse* row. "Now, physical abuse. Did Kitt actually accuse Elizabeth of that?"

"No. She merely raised the question because of the scratches on Henry's arm."

Shannon wrote a question mark on the *Physical Abuse/Kitt* square. "When you interviewed Henry, he said he got scratched by a neighbor's cat, right?"

"Yes."

"In fact, you wrote in Henry's interview notes that there is, quote, 'no evidence supporting a physical-abuse claim,' correct?"

"Correct."

Shannon drew a line through the *Physical Abuse* row. "That leaves medical abuse. That claim centers on Elizabeth's alternative therapies, specifically IV chelation and MMS, right?"

"Yes."

Shannon wrote *IV Chelation* and *MMS ("Bleach")* on the chart. "Now, forgive me. I'm not an expert on this, but it seems to me a prerequisite to medical abuse is that whatever the mother does must actually harm the child—that is, make the child sick or sicker, right?"

"That's typically the case."

"Here's what confuses me. How can Henry's treatments be abuse when he'd been getting better, healthwise?"

Heights blinked a few times. "I'm not sure that's the case."

"No?" Shannon said, and Matt caught an amused look on her face, a trace of a childlike *watch-this!* anticipation. "You're aware that a neurologist at Georgetown's autism clinic diagnosed Henry with autism when he was three?"

"Yes, that's in his medical records." Matt hadn't known that. He'd always assumed, based on Kitt's comments, that Henry's "autism" was all in Elizabeth's head.

"It was also in his medical records, was it not, that according to the same neurologist, Henry no longer had autism as of February last year?"

"Yes."

"Well, going from autism to no autism is better, not worse, right?"

"Actually, the neurologist indicated he may have been misdiagnosed—"

"Because the improvement in Henry's condition was so vast as to be unaccountable otherwise, because most kids don't improve the way Henry did, right?"

"Well, in any case, he stated that large amounts of speech and social therapy were most likely responsible for the improvement."

"The large amounts of therapy that Elizabeth insisted on, arranged for, and drove him to every day, you mean?" Shannon said, depicting Elizabeth once again as Mother of the Year. But instead of annoying Matt, it made him think: Had he been wrong? Had there been a reason for Elizabeth's obsessiveness, and had that obsessiveness caused a boy to go from autism to not-autism?

Heights's frown deepened. "I suppose so."

"Autism aside, Henry improved in other ways, too, right? He went from second percentile for weight at three, with frequent diarrhea, to an eight-year-old in the fortieth percentile, with no intestinal issues. Do you recall that from his medical records, Detective?"

Heights's face turned red. "But that's not the issue. The issue is that these so-called treatments are dangerous and unnecessary, which *does* constitute medical abuse, regardless of the actual consequences. And let's not forget: there *was* a harmful consequence for Henry, namely *death* from the well-known risk of fire from one such treatment, HBOT."

"Really? I wasn't aware that HBOT at a licensed facility constitutes medical abuse." Shannon turned to the gallery. "There must be, what, twenty, thirty families here who were Miracle Submarine clients. So I take it you investigated all these families for child abuse for undertaking such a risky treatment for their children. Is that what you're telling us, Detective?"

Out of the corners of his eyes, Matt saw many women in the gallery turn their heads nervously, looking at one another and Elizabeth as if it hadn't occurred to them that they might be considered guilty of the same things she was being condemned for. Was that why they were so eager now to believe she was an evil murderer? Because if she didn't set the fire on purpose, it might mean that their own kids were safe at home instead of in a coffin due to nothing more than chance?

Heights said, "No, of course not. You can't look at one thing in isolation. It wasn't just HBOT. She did extreme things like IV chelation and feeding Henry bleach."

"Ah, yes. Let's turn to that. IV chelation is an FDA-approved treatment, correct?"

"Yes, but for heavy-metal poisoning, which Henry did not have."

"Are you aware, Detective, of a Brown University study in which mice injected with thimerosal, a mercury preservative that used to be in many vaccines prior to 2001, became socially atypical, akin to autism, and when treated with chelation became normal again?"

Matt hadn't heard of that. Was that true?

"No, I haven't heard of that study."

"Really? The study was summarized in a *Wall Street Journal* article I found in your own files, right next to the sheet noting that Henry had seven thimerosal vaccines as a baby, back when thimerosal was still present in some vaccines."

Heights pursed her lips, as if forcing herself to say nothing.

Shannon said, "And are you aware that one of the study's researchers, a Dr. Anjeli Hall, who was an attending at Stanford Hospital and professor at Stanford Medical School, treats children with autism with, among other things, chelation?"

Matt didn't know the name, but those credentials—how could anyone dispute the legitimacy of someone like that?

"No, I don't know that doctor," Heights said, "but I *do* know that autistic children have recently died from IV chelation."

"Caused by negligence of a doctor no longer licensed to practice medicine, correct?"

"I believe so, yes."

"People die from doctors' mistakes." Shannon turned to the jury. "Just last month, I read about a child dying from a pediatrician's dosage error for Tylenol. Tell me, Detective, if I give my child Tylenol tomorrow, is that medical abuse because Tylenol is obviously a dangerous medical treatment that can kill children?"

"Chelation is not Tylenol. The defendant gave Henry DMPS, a dangerous chemical normally administered in a hospital. She got it by mail, through an out-of-state naturopath."

"Are you aware, Detective, that this out-of-state naturopath practices in Dr. Hall's office, and she was refilling a prescription Dr. Hall originally wrote for Henry?"

Heights's eyebrows raised in surprise. "No, I wasn't aware of that."

"Do you consider it medical abuse to provide medication prescribed by a neurologist who happens to teach at Stanford?"

She pursed her lips and thought for a while, and Matt wanted to say, Come on, don't be an idiot. "No," she finally said.

"Great." Shannon crossed out *IV Chelation* on her chart. "Now, that leaves the so-called bleach treatment. Detective, what's the chemical formula for bleach?"

"I don't know."

"It's in your files, but it's $NaClO$, sodium hypochlorite. What's the chemical formula for MMS, the mineral solution that Elizabeth gave to Henry, which you're *calling* bleach?"

She frowned slightly. "Chlorine dioxide."

"Yes, ClO_2. Actually, a few drops of it diluted in water. Are you aware, Detective, that companies use this to purify bottled water?" Shannon turned to the jury. "Water we buy in supermarkets contains the same chemical as the MMS formula she's been calling 'bleach.'"

Abe stood up and said, "Who's testifying here, Judge?" but Shannon kept going, her voice rising and words getting faster. "Chlorine dioxide is present in over-the-counter antifungals. Are you arresting all the parents who buy those at Walgreens?"

Abe said again, "Objection. I've been trying to be patient, but she's badgering the witness with all these questions outside the scope of her expertise, not to mention assuming facts not in evidence. Detective Heights is not a doctor, nor is she a chemist or medical expert."

Shannon's face flushed red with an indignant fervor. "That's exactly my point, Your Honor. Detective Heights is *not* an expert, doesn't know the first thing about these treatments she's labeled—based on what, I have no idea—as dangerous and unnecessary, and she hasn't bothered to learn the basics, which are all in her own files, if she'd bother to look."

The judge said, "Objection sustained. Ms. Haug, you can call your own experts, but for now, stick to what's in the record and within the scope of the detective's duties."

Shannon nodded. "Yes, Your Honor." She turned. "Detective, are you permitted to start your own investigations? In the course of one case, if you come across evidence of another parent committing abuse, for example, could you open a new case?"

"Of course. It doesn't matter how a claim comes to our attention."

"In this case," Shannon said, "you came across evidence of many other parents in your jurisdiction doing *both* IV chelation and MMS, through online discussions, correct?"

The detective's eyes flickered to the gallery before she said yes.

"How many of these parents did you investigate for medical abuse?"

Her eyes flickered to the gallery again. "None."

"And that's because you don't consider MMS and chelation to constitute child abuse, isn't that correct?" Shannon didn't say it, but Matt could almost hear the unsaid words: *Because if those treatments were abuse, half the people here should've been thrown in jail long ago.*

Heights glared, and Shannon stared right back, the staring duel lasting for many seconds, past awkward to downright painful, when Heights said, "Correct."

"Thank you," Shannon said, and slowly, deliberately, she walked to her chart and put a big, fat line through the last row, *Medical Abuse*.

Matt looked at Elizabeth, her face unchanged, still wearing the expressionless mask she'd worn all yesterday as Detective Heights portrayed her as a sadistic abuser conducting painful experiments on her child for the hell of it. Except now, she didn't look heartless but numb. Dazed from grief. And it occurred to him, what he'd known ever since he woke up: he had to tell Abe, and probably Shannon, too. Maybe not everything, but at least about Mary and the insurance call, the H-Mart note. The cigarettes, he could wait and see. But he had to go find Mary and warn her. Give her a chance to go to Abe first and confess.

He touched Janine on the shoulder. "I need to go," he mouthed, and pointed at his pager like it was some work thing. She whispered, "Okay, I'll fill you in."

He stood and walked out of the courtroom. As he was leaving, he saw Shannon gesturing to the now-decimated chart. "Detective," she said, "I'd like to clarify something we discussed earlier." Shannon wrote something on the chart and said, "This *is* what you wrote in your meeting with your colleagues, correct?"

Matt stopped at the door and looked. It wasn't until after Heights said, "Yes, that's correct," that Shannon stepped back, unblocking Matt's view of the poster. On top, above all the crossed-out categories of abuse, Shannon had written in fat letters and circled, *NO ABUSE = NO MOTIVE*.

⬭ NO ABUSE = NO MOTIVE ⬭	Father	8 Teachers	4 Therapists	2 Doctors	Kitt
Neglect	NO	NO	NO	NO	NO
Emotional Abuse	NO	NO	NO	NO	?
Physical Abuse	NO	NO	NO	NO	?
Medical Abuse	NO	NO	NO	NO	IV Chelation / MMS ("Bleach")

ELIZABETH

SHE SAW THEM DURING RECESS, outside the courtroom. A sizable contingent—twenty, maybe thirty women—from her autism moms' group. The last time she saw them was at Henry's funeral, back when she was still the tragic mother, the focal point of their sympathy and sorrow (and maybe guilt, for secretly feeling a pinch of superiority at their own children being alive). Before the arrest and news stories that stopped the visits with dropped-off casseroles. She'd expected some to attend the trial, but she hadn't seen anyone all week.

But now, here they were. Why today? Perhaps the latest news had piqued their curiosity to the pay-for-special-needs-babysitter-for-a-whole-day level. Or maybe today was the monthly meeting—yes, it was a Thursday—and they decided to take a field trip. Or . . . was it possible?

Could they have heard how her treatments for Henry—the same treatments many of them were giving their own kids—were being branded "medical abuse," and they'd come out in support?

The women were standing in a loose circle, talking and milling around like bees near a hive. As she walked toward the courtroom, getting closer to them, one woman on her phone—Elaine, the first to have tried the so-called bleach treatment, even before Elizabeth—looked up and noticed her. Elaine's eyebrows shot up and her lips spread into a smile as if she was glad to see her. Elizabeth smiled back and veered toward the group, her heart fluttering and leaping against her chest, her whole body buoyed by hope.

Elaine's smile fell, and she turned toward the group and whispered something. And now all the women were glancing at her the way they might at a rotting corpse—unable to contain their curiosity but disgusted, their eyes darting at her, then quickly away, their faces contorting as if they'd sniffed something putrid. Even as Elizabeth realized that of course Elaine's raised brow and smile were from surprise and embarrassment, the women walked inward to a huddle, their backs to her, forming a circle so tight it seemed ready to collapse onto itself.

Shannon mouthed, "Come on, let's go." Elizabeth nodded and stepped away from them, her legs feeling simultaneously hollow and heavy, making it hard to walk. For many years, this group had been the only place where she'd felt a sense of belonging as a mother, a world where she wasn't politely avoided and pitied as the (whispered, always whispered) "poor mom of that boy with"—pause—"*autism*, you know, the one who just rocks all day long." The opposite: in the group, for the first time in her life, she'd felt something akin to power. Not that she hadn't achieved before—she'd gotten honors in school, bonuses at work—but those were worker-bee types of success, the quiet kinds noticed only by one's parents. In the autism moms' world, though, Elizabeth was a rock star, a miracle worker, the leader of the in-crowd, because she was what everyone dreamed of becoming: the mother of a Recovered Child, a child who started out as a nonverbal, nonsocial, nonpresentable mess like the others, but over the years, catapulted into the realm of mainstream classes and therapy graduations. Henry had been the role model, the crystallization of the hope that one day, their own kids could undergo their own metamorphoses.

Being the object of so much envy and esteem had been intoxicating but (not being used to it) also embarrassing, and she'd tried to downplay her role in Henry's progress. "For all I know," she told the group, "Henry's gains weren't from the treatments, and the timing was coincidental. There's no control group, so we'll never really know." (Not that she actually believed this, but she thought her correlation-doesn't-equal-causation logic made her seem rational, which made nonbelievers less likely to dismiss her as one of those "antivaccine nutjobs.")

Even with Elizabeth's caveats, though, virtually everyone in the group joined the biomed stampede and rushed to get their kids on the same treatments. "Elizabeth's protocol," they called it, despite her protests that she'd merely followed others' recommendations, with only tweaks based on Henry's lab tests. When many of the other kids improved (although none as quickly or dramatically as Henry), that was when she became the true queen bee, the expert everyone turned to. Every one of the women standing outside the courtroom now had e-mailed her for advice or picked her brain over coffee, asked for help interpreting lab tests, and sent her muffins and gift cards to thank her.

And now here they were, these women who'd once been united in their admiration for her: their backs turned to her, united more tightly than ever in their condemnation of her. And here she was, the onetime near deity, shuffling away, now a pariah. And if the group's reaction was any indication, mere days away from becoming a death-row inmate.

○

SITTING IN COURT, Elizabeth looked at the chart on the easel, the ugly word *ABUSE*.

Child abuse. Was that what she'd done? After that first pinch in her neighbor's basement, she promised herself she'd never do it again—she was a proponent of positive parenting, didn't even believe in threatening or scolding—but the frustration would build over time. Weeks and months of patience, of ignoring negative behaviors and praising positive ones, then, like a riptide, fury would rush in, knocking her down and making her desperate for the sweet release that came with grabbing Henry's soft flesh and squeezing or yelling. But she never hit, never slapped, and certainly nothing to cause injuries requiring medical attention. And wasn't *that*—things that ended with blood and broken bones—child abuse, not the invisible things she did to cause a moment's pain, just enough to jolt Henry out of whatever behavior she needed him to stop? Was that any different from spanking?

She looked at the chart, all the *NOs* confirming the absence of wrongdoing, and felt anguish for Henry, the knowledge that she and those listed on the chart—the people whose job it was to protect him—had failed him. And when Shannon said, "Abe's doing a redirect on Heights, but don't worry. No one believes this abuse claim of hers," Elizabeth felt a pinch of pity for her, too, for having been so thoroughly duped.

Abe went straight to the chart. He pointed to the phrase *NO ABUSE = NO MOTIVE* and said, "Detective, when you wrote this phrase, did you mean that if the defendant didn't abuse Henry, she'd have no motive to kill him?"

Heights said, "No, of course not. There are many cases of parents harming and even killing their children without prior abuse."

"So what *did* you mean?"

Heights looked to the jury. "You have to understand the context. I'd barely begun the abuse investigation before the child and a witness were murdered. I was asking for more staff for my abuse investigation, and I was perhaps . . ." She took a deep breath, as if working up the courage to confess something embarrassing. "I wrote this as sort of a shorthand to make my point that *at that time*, which was still early in the investigation, the only motive we had was the abuse claim, so we should put more resources into that."

Abe smiled like an understanding teacher. "So you wrote that to convince your superiors to give you more power and resources. Did others agree?"

"No. In fact, Detective Pierson erased it and said I had tunnel vision, that the abuse claim was *a* proof of motive, but certainly not the *only* one.

And certainly, since then, we've uncovered a lot more proof of motive. The defendant's Internet searches, notes, fights with Kitt, so on. So it is most definitely not true that no abuse equals no motive."

Abe took a red marker and put a thick line through *NO ABUSE = NO MOTIVE* on the chart. He stepped back. "Let's explore the rest of this very organized chart from Ms. Haug. She asserts there's no abuse here because other people weren't aware of it. Detective, as a trained psychologist and detective specializing in child abuse cases, is that right?"

"No," she said. "Abusers often effectively conceal their actions and convince the child to go along with that."

"Did you find such evidence of concealment here?"

"Yes. The defendant never told Henry's pediatrician or even his father about giving him IV chelation and MMS, let alone that children have died from them. It was classic deliberate concealment, a hallmark of abuse."

Elizabeth wanted to shout out that she wasn't hiding anything, simply saving herself an exhausting argument with an old-fashioned doctor. And Victor hadn't wanted any details; he'd said he trusted her, that he didn't have time for appointments and research articles. But something about the phrase "deliberate concealment" stopped her. It had a sinister quality, the kind of guilt-wrapped feel that infused her when she told Henry before pediatrician visits, "Let's not tell him about the other doctors, because we don't want him getting jealous, do we?"

Abe stepped closer to Heights. "You mentioned this before, deliberate concealment. Why is that so important to you, as a psychologist and an investigator?"

"Because it goes to the *intent* of the action. A parent tells a child, if you do X, you'll get a spanking. The child does X, the parent spanks. It's controlled and predictable. The spouse knows about it, the child can tell their friends. Many parents do that.

"Same with medical treatments. Your child is ill, you want to try a treatment, you talk to doctors, your spouse, decide together. Fine. But you deliberately hide your actions—whether it be treatments or physical punishment—that tells me you know what you're doing is wrong."

She felt something go off inside her, like a bulb that burns too brightly and flames out, blinding and deafening her. She'd wondered what made her yelling and pinching different—and they *were* different, she knew it—from the yelling, spankings, and smacks on the head that other parents discussed, sometimes even did, in public. Was this it? That she didn't want to do it, had promised herself she wouldn't, and yet couldn't help but do it? It was the difference between a regular person having a martini before dinner and an alcoholic doing the same; the physical act was the same, but the context—the intent behind it and the aftermath—couldn't be more different. The loss of control, the unpredictability. And afterward, the cover-up.

"In your expert opinion, do these *NOs*"—Abe pointed to the chart—"indicate no abuse?"

"Absolutely not."

Abe took the red marker again and crossed out all the column headings on top. "What about the rows?" he said. "Ms. Haug separated out different types of abuse and crossed them off, one by one. Is that a valid way to analyze child abuse cases?"

"No. You can't look at each charge in isolation. One incident, by itself, may be disturbing, but not enough to constitute abuse. For example, a parent saying a child's annoying and people hate him. By itself, not abuse. Scratching a child's arm, that again may not be abuse *by itself*. And on and on, with the forced drinking of MMS and IV chelation. But when you consider everything *together*, a pattern emerges, and things that may seem innocuous in isolation may not, in fact, be so harmless."

"Is that why you couldn't remove Henry from his home immediately?"

"Yes, that's exactly why. In cases of obvious injury, like broken bones, it's easier to make that call. But in cases like this, where each incident is questionable and subtle, you have to consider multiple sources and see the whole picture, which takes time. Unfortunately, before we could do that, Henry died."

"In summary," Abe said, "does separating abuse into categories, then finding no abuse for each category—does that demonstrate there was no abuse here?"

"Absolutely not."

Abe crossed out the categories. "Now, this chart is pretty much destroyed, but before I put it away, let's focus on medical abuse. Detective, was Ms. Haug correct to list only IV chelation and MMS?"

"No. Those *were* the riskiest therapies inflicted on Henry. But again, you can't just look at the procedure in isolation." She looked at the jury. "I'll give you an example. Chemotherapy. For a child with cancer, that's obviously not medical abuse. But inflicting chemotherapy on a child without cancer would be. It's not just the riskiness at issue, but the appropriateness."

"But what about a child in remission from cancer? That's the proper analogy, isn't it, since Henry was diagnosed with autism at one time but then wasn't?"

"True. But giving chemo to a child in remission would be a classic case of Munchausen by proxy, the condition we're calling 'medical abuse.' A typical Munchausen case is when someone with a serious illness recovers. The caregiver loses the constant contact with hospitals and doctors, and tries to regain that by manufacturing symptoms to make it *appear* the child's still sick. Here, Henry was diagnosed as no longer autistic. The defendant couldn't accept that, and kept taking him to doctors and doing risky treatments he no longer needed, just so she could continue to get attention."

Elizabeth thought about the autism moms' group. Kitt used to ask, "Why do you keep doing all this shit? Why are you still coming to our meetings?" The answer came to her now: she hadn't wanted to stop because she liked being in that world—where, for the first time in her life, she'd been the best, the envy of the group. Had Henry been in HBOT last summer and been scorched alive because she'd been on an ego trip?

She felt sick. She shut her eyes and pressed her palms into her stomach to keep from throwing up, and then someone was saying something about the importance of hearing directly from the victim.

She opened her eyes. Shannon was standing, objecting, and the judge said, "Overruled. Objection is noted," and Shannon squeezed her hand and whispered, "I'm sorry I couldn't stop it. You ready?" She wanted to say no, she had no idea what was happening, she was sick and needed to get out of here, but Abe was turning on the TV next to the easel.

Heights said, "This is the video recording of Henry the day before the explosion, when we interviewed him at camp." Abe clicked the remote.

Henry's head appeared, filling the screen in a close-up shot. The screen was huge, and she gasped at the clarity of the life-size video of Henry's face, how you could see the faint freckles from the summer sun dotted across his nose and cheeks. Henry's head was down, and when the off-screen voice—Detective Heights's—said, "Hi, Henry," he kept his chin down and looked up, making his huge eyes seem bigger, like a kewpie doll's.

"Hello," Henry said in a high-pitched voice, curious but cautious. When he opened his mouth, you could see a gap in his front teeth—the shadow of the tooth he'd lost that weekend, the one she took from under his pillow and replaced with a dollar from the tooth fairy, careful not to disturb his peaceful sleeping face on the pillow.

"How old are you, Henry?" Heights's disembodied voice asked.

"I am eight years old," he said, mechanical and formal like a robot giving programmed responses. Henry didn't gaze at the camera or Detective Heights, who must have been behind or beside the camera. Instead, he looked up, his eyes wandering as if he were examining in detail a fresco on the ceiling. It occurred to her now that she couldn't remember a single conversation with him when she didn't say at least once, "Henry, don't be spacey; look at me, always look at the person you're talking to," her words spewing out like venom. Why had it mattered so much where his eyes were pointed? Why had she never just *talked* to him, asked him what he was thinking or told him he had the same color eyes as her own father's? Now, seen through the veil of her tears, Henry looked like a Renaissance painting of an angel, looking up at the Madonna. How had she never noticed the innocence, the beauty?

When Heights said, "Henry, that scratch on your arm. How did you get that?" Henry shook his head and said, "It is from a cat. My neighbor's cat scratched me."

Elizabeth shut her eyes tight. Something bitter and salty rushed down her throat as she heard her own lies emerge from those tiny lips. The fact was, the scratches on his arm were not from a cat. They were from her own nails, made on a day when they'd already been twelve minutes late to

OT which, at $120 per hour, amounted to $24 in wasted money. They were about to be late to Speech, so she told Henry to hustle to the car, but he just stood there, looking up, his eyes vacant and head rolling. She grabbed his arms and said, "Did you hear me? Get in the damn car, right now!" and when he twisted his arm away, she didn't let go. Her nails scraped his skin, a thin strip ripping away like an orange peel.

On the video, Heights asked, "A cat did that? What cat? Where?"

Henry repeated, "It is from a cat. My neighbor's cat scratched me."

"Henry, I think maybe someone told you to say that, but it's not what happened. I know it's hard, but you need to tell me the truth."

Henry looked up at the ceiling again, showing the red blood vessels across the whites of his eyes. "The scratch is from a cat," he said. "The cat is a mean cat. The cat is a black cat. The cat has white ears and long nails. The cat's name is Blackie."

The thing was, she never actually told Henry to lie. She just pretended. After the fury of the moment released and calm returned, she told Henry an alternate version. Not "I'm sorry I hurt you. Does that hurt?" or even "Why don't you listen so I don't have to punish you?" but "Oh, sweetie, look at that scratch! Have you been playing with that cat again? You need to be more careful."

The magical thing was that if she presented this reinvented version in a matter-of-fact way, she could trick him into questioning his own memory. She could see doubt in the way he looked up, his eyes darting back and forth as if alternating between two stages in the sky, trying to decide which play was the more believable. And even more magical: if she repeated it enough, consistently and without drama, it distorted his memory, created a revised version with details he added himself. This—the generic cat of her invention becoming a real one in his manipulated mind, one with a name and color and markings—convinced her, even more than the physical pain she inflicted on him: she was a gaslighting manipulator, a bad mother who broke her son.

In the video, Heights said, "Did your mom tell you to say that?"

Henry said, "My mommy loves me, but I'm annoying, and I make everything hard. My mommy's life would be better without me. My mommy and daddy would still be married and take vacations around the world. I should never have been born."

Oh God. Had he really thought that? Had *she* made him think that? She'd had moments of dark thoughts (didn't every mother?), but she'd always immediately regretted them. She'd certainly never said any of that to him. So where did he get that?

Heights said, "Did your mom tell you that, Henry? Did *she* scratch you?"

He looked straight into the camera, his eyes so wide that his irises looked like blue balls floating in a milky pool. He shook his head no. "The scratch is from a cat. My neighbor's cat scratched me. The cat is a mean cat. The cat hates me."

She wanted to grab the remote and make it stop. Unplug the TV or shove it down and break it, anything to stop the lies coming out of Henry's mouth, so much more awful and unbearable than the scratching itself. Elizabeth opened her mouth and yelled out, "Stop it. Stop," elongating the word, feeling it rebound and recoil all around the courtroom. She saw the judge's mouth open in shock at her outburst, heard the bang of the gavel as he said, "Quiet, quiet in the courtroom," but she didn't stop. She stood and shut her eyes tight and put her hands over her ears and said, "There is no cat. There is no cat," again and again, louder and louder, until the words grated against her throat and it hurt, until she could no longer hear Henry's voice.

MATT

H E SAT IN HIS CAR, trying to figure out how to get Mary alone. Young wasn't here, that much he knew; when he got here, he spied Mary helping Pak into their house, but their car was gone. He pulled over to a hidden spot, and he'd been sitting here for thirty minutes, waiting for *something* to happen—for Mary to come outside alone, for Pak to leave by himself, for some combination of courage and impatience to kick in and force his ass out of his car.

The heat was what drove him out. Not just the discomfort of marinating in sweat, but his hands. His palms didn't sweat. They turned crimson and burned, as if his scars' plastic-smooth lining were sealing in the heat, searing the underside of his skin. He told himself the pain wasn't real, those nerves were dead, but it got worse and he couldn't stand it. He got out. The backs of his thighs stuck to the leather seat, but he didn't care, just stood up fast, letting the skin rip away and sting, grateful for the relocation of pain.

He interlaced his fingers and stretched them overhead, imagining the boiling blood draining out of his hands. He stood there for another ten minutes, pacing, trying to think of something other than waiting— maybe he should throw rocks to signal Mary?—when he smelled smoke. Just his mind playing tricks again, he told himself. Being so close to the site of the fire was sending his heart quivering and blood sputtering, awakening his memory of that night's smell. He forced himself to look at the barn in the distance—the skeletal remains of its walls, the blackened submarine listing inside, bits of its previous blue peeking through the soot—and willed his brain to get it: there was no fire. No smoke.

He turned to the thick cluster of pine trees behind him and breathed in deep. Fresh and clean, green woods—that's what he expected, told his brain it should register, but the smoky smell was still there. And something else. A faint hiss in the distance. A crackle. He looked around and saw it: smoke, billowing up in a barely noticeable column before fanning out into wisps in the bright blue sky.

He felt a flicker of relief—he wasn't hallucinating, wasn't losing his mind—before panic set in. Fire. The Yoos' house? Trees were in the way, and it was hard to tell. *Turn the fuck around, run straight to the car, and drive away*, a voice in his head said. He thought of his phone in the car, how the smart thing would be to grab it and call 911.

But he didn't. He ran. Toward the smoke, through the cluster of trees. Once he got closer, the smoke seemed to be coming from the front of the house, so he ran around the side. The fire's crackle was getting louder, but there was another sound. Voices. Pak's and Mary's. Not shouting in fear or calling for help, but calmly discussing something.

Matt tried to stop running, but too late. They looked up as he rounded the corner. Pak gasped. Mary squealed and jumped back.

The fire was inside a rusted metal container in front of them. The container—a trash can?—was the same height as Pak's wheelchair, so the flames shooting out were level with Pak's face, coating it in a flickering orange glow. Pak said, "Matt, why are you here?"

He knew he should say something, but he couldn't think, couldn't move. What were they burning? Cigarettes? Were they destroying evidence? Why now?

He looked at Pak's face, eclipsed by the translucent curtain of fire, the flames appearing to lick at his chin. He thought of Henry's facefire and wanted to throw up, and it was making him wonder: How could Pak get so close to the fire—so close that the flames were reflecting off his skin, the heat penetrating into his nerves—without freaking out into a puddle of fear? Through the flames, the sharp angles of Pak's cheekbones looked eerily sinister, and Matt could picture him striking a match under the oxygen tube. It seemed real. Believable.

"Matt, why are you here?" Pak said again, and pressed his hands down on the wheelchair, as if to stand up, and he remembered Young saying the doctors couldn't figure out why Pak was still paralyzed since his nerves appeared intact. At once, he knew: Pak had faked his paralysis, and was about to get up and attack him right now.

"Matt?" Pak repeated, pressing down again. Every muscle in Matt's body tightened, and he stepped back, ready to sprint, but then Pak—still sitting—rolled his wheelchair out from behind the trash can. With Pak's body fully visible, Matt could see: Pak was pressing down to force his wheelchair through gravel.

Matt cleared his throat. "I was heading back from court, and I thought I'd check on you since you weren't there. Is everything okay?"

"Yes, we are fine." Pak's eyes flicked to the trash can, and he said, "That is for Mary's birthday. Eighteen. In Korea, it is tradition to burn childhood items. It is symbolism for becoming adult."

"Wow," Matt said. He'd never heard that, and he'd gone to a dozen Korean eighteenth-birthday parties.

As if Pak could read his thoughts, he said, "It is maybe only in my village. Young did not know this tradition. Have you heard of it?"

"No, but I like it. Janine's niece is turning eighteen soon. I'll tell her," Matt said, thinking how his in-laws did this, too—invoked some "ancient tradition" bullshit to cover a lie. He looked over Pak's shoulder at Mary. "Happy birthday."

"Thank you." She looked at the trash can, then back at him, shaking her head no. "Janine"—she paused—"is she . . . with you?" She shook her head again and frowned, her eyes widening—in a plea or threat, he couldn't tell. Either way, her message was clear: Don't tell Janine about us burning things. Whether it was a *Please* or an *Or else*, he didn't care.

"Yes, she's waiting in the car," he said, realizing even as he told this lie how nervous he was about getting out of this situation safely. "I should go, or she'll start worrying. Anyway, I'm glad you're okay. I'll see you tomorrow." He turned to go. "Happy birthday again, Mary."

He could feel their stares on his back as he walked away, but he didn't look back. He just kept walking, past the house, through the cluster of trees, past the ruins of the barn, and into the car. He locked it, cranked it on, put it in drive, pressed the accelerator, and got the hell out of there.

TERESA

SHE WAS THE ONLY PERSON in the courtroom. After the chaos of the last ten minutes—Elizabeth shouting about a cat, Shannon's minions dragging her out, the judge pounding the gavel and ordering a lunch recess, everyone rushing out, trying not to get trampled by the reporters running and talking on their phones—Teresa craved stillness. Silence. Most of all, aloneness. She didn't want to go outside and face the women who were (she was sure) flitting from café to café, scavenging for gossip. Of course, they'd be careful to coat their tattle with feigned concern to make it seem like a quest for justice for Henry ("abused for so long!") and Kitt ("five kids!—a saint, really") rather than what it actually was: the glee and excitement of being a voyeur to someone else's pain.

No, she didn't want to leave the tranquility of this empty courtroom.

Except for the temperature. When court was in session, it was hot, the old ACs too weak to fight off the steam emanating from the sweaty crowd, so she'd worn a short-sleeved dress without pantyhose. Cleared of the bodies, though, the room was downright cold. Or maybe what she felt was the chill of seeing Henry's face—his skin soft and perfect in that little-kid way, unmarred by pimples, wrinkles, and other flaws life would eventually have brought—as he said "the cat" hated him and scratched him, then witnessing Elizabeth fall apart and confess there was no cat, which meant . . . what? That *she* was "the cat"? Teresa shivered and rubbed her hands against her arms. Her hands were clammy, made her shiver more.

A wide beam of sunlight was coming through the right front window. She crossed the aisle to the sunny spot, right behind the prosecutor's table where she used to sit. She placed herself in the sun's path and sat, closed her eyes, and lifted her face into the warmth. A blinding whiteness penetrated her closed lids, sending phantom red dots flashing and whirling before her. The buzz of the AC units seemed to get louder. Like waves in a shell, the white noise swirled and bounced around her ear canals to form an ethereal whisper, an auditory ghost of Elizabeth's voice. *There is no cat. There is no cat.*

"Teresa?" a voice called from behind her. Young, peeking through a half-opened door like a child afraid of entering without permission.

"Oh, hi," Teresa said. "I didn't think you were here today."

Young didn't say anything, just bit her lower lip. She was wearing what looked like an undershirt and elastic pants, not her usual blouse and skirt. Her hair was in a bun, as always, but it was disheveled, strands falling as if she'd slept in it.

"Young, are you all right? Would you like to come in?" Teresa felt ridiculous inviting her in. Presumptuous, as if this were her home, but she had to do something to dispel Young's discomfort.

Young nodded and walked down the aisle, but tentatively, as if she were breaking some rule. Under the fluorescent lights, her skin looked sallow. The elastic around her waist drooped, and she kept tugging her pants up every few steps. When she got closer, Young glanced left, then back to her, looking confused, and Teresa realized: Young was wondering why she'd changed seats. Of course. Anyone who saw her now would assume she'd returned to the prosecutor's side to make some point. Shit. This was how rumors got started. She wouldn't be surprised if some website already had a breaking news report about it ("Mommy Murderer's Fickle Friend Switches Sides. Again.").

Teresa motioned to the window. "I moved because I was cold. The sun's warm here." She hated how defensive she sounded and, even more, felt.

Young nodded and sat, a hint of disappointment on her face. She was wearing old loafers with the backs folded under her feet, like slippers, as if she'd been too rushed to put her shoes on properly. Her lips were chapped, and crust covered the corners of her eyes.

"Young, are you okay? Where's Pak? And Mary?"

Young blinked and bit her lip. "They are sick. Their stomach."

"Oh, I'm sorry. I hope they feel better soon."

Young nodded. "I arrived late. I saw Elizabeth yelling. People there"—she motioned to the back—"they said this means Elizabeth is confessing. She scratched Henry."

Teresa swallowed. Nodded. "Yeah."

Young looked relieved. "So you think she is guilty."

"What? No. There's a huge difference between scratching and murdering someone. I mean, the scratch could've been an accident." Even as she said this, though, she knew an accident wouldn't have caused Elizabeth's breakdown. She could picture it now, Abe pointing to Elizabeth, saying to the jury, "This woman, a *violent* woman who hurt her son, an *unstable* woman on the verge of breakdown—we all saw it—on a *traumatic* day, after the police barged in with child abuse charges, after a huge fight with a friend—is it any stretch to think that *this* woman, on *this* day, would simply snap?"

Young said, "If she did child abuse but she did not start the fire, do you think she deserves punishment? Not death penalty, but prison?"

"I don't know." Teresa sighed. "She's lost her only child in a horrific way. The entire world blames her. She's lost any friend she's had. She has nothing left in her life. So if all that happened and she didn't set the fire? I'd say that's enough punishment for anything she's done."

Young's face turned red and she blinked rapidly to keep back tears that, despite her efforts, were welling in her eyes. "But she wanted Henry to die. I saw his video. What type of mother tells her son she wishes he would die?"

Teresa closed her eyes. That moment in Henry's video had disturbed her the most, and she'd been fighting not to think about it. "I don't know why Henry said that, but I can't believe she ever told him anything like that."

"But Pak said she said this same thing to you, she wants Henry dead, she has fantasies."

"Pak? But how . . ." As she said it, though, the memory she'd been pushing away came to her. *Sometimes, I wish Henry was dead. I fantasize about it.* Said in whispers in the darkened chamber, with no one nearby, except . . . "Oh my God, did Henry hear us and tell Pak? But how? He was at the other end of the chamber, watching a video."

"So this is true. Elizabeth said she wants Henry to die." It was more a statement than a question.

"No, it wasn't like that. That's not what she meant." It was hard to explain without telling the whole story of what happened that day with Mary. But how could she tell Young, of all people? "Oh my God, does Abe know about this?"

Young pressed her lips together so hard they turned white, as if she was trying to keep her mouth closed, then abruptly said, "Yes. And he is going to ask you about it. In court."

The prospect of having to explain, making people understand the context—was that possible? "It wasn't . . . it's not how it sounds. She didn't really mean it," Teresa said. "She was just trying to help me."

"How does saying she wishes her son's death help you?"

Teresa shook her head, couldn't say anything.

Young came closer. "Teresa," she said. "Tell me. I want to understand the meaning. I *need.*"

Teresa looked at her, this woman who was the last person she wanted to tell this story to. But if she was right, Abe was going to force her to tell it to everyone in court, and it would be transmitted within an hour to anyone with a computer.

Teresa nodded. Young was going to find out anyway, and she deserved to hear it directly from her. She just hoped Young wouldn't hate her once she heard the story.

○

SHE'D BEEN IN A FUNK that day. She'd left home at the usual time for their evening dive, but as sometimes happened in August, there was virtually no traffic and they got to HBOT forty-five minutes early. She needed to pee, but she didn't want to ask to use the Yoos' bathroom. Not that they'd refuse—to the contrary, they encouraged it—but it embarrassed her, the way Young kept apologizing for the boxes everywhere and repeating "temporary" and "moving soon."

She drove down the road and pulled into a secluded spot. She'd use the twenty-four-hour urine-collection container she kept in the van for times like this. It was disgusting, all right, but better than the alternative: stopping at a gas station, getting Rosa's wheelchair out of the van, finding a kind grandmother type to watch her (those bathrooms being too small for the wheelchair), which inevitably led to questions about what condition Rosa had and if there was hope and how she could be so brave, and on and on, then getting Rosa's wheelchair back and buckled in the van. It was exhausting, and it took fifteen minutes. Fifteen for a pit stop that should take two! She knew she shouldn't whine; there were so many "bigger" things to deal with. But it was these everyday indignities, these small chunks of lost minutes, that got to her most, made her think how "normal" parents had no idea how good they had it. Oh, sure—moms of infants got a taste of this, but anything was bearable when it was temporary; try doing it day after day, knowing you'd do this until you died, that you'd be fricking squatting in a van peeing into a jar when you were eighty, driving around your fifty-year-old invalid daughter to God knows what therapies they'd have by then, worrying who'd take over when you died.

She ended up going outside to pee. Rosa was asleep, and she couldn't get to the pee jar without moving her, so she got out and went to a hidden spot behind a shed, surrounded by bushes. Just as she was pulling down her pants, she heard a phone ring from inside the shed.

"Hey, hold on a sec," said a girl's voice, muffled by the wall. It sounded like the Yoos' daughter, Mary. Teresa stood still. She definitely couldn't pee. Noises—boxes being moved?—came from the shed. Then the same voice. "I'm here. Sorry about that."

A pause. "Just putting some boxes back. You know, my secret stash." A laugh.

Pause. "God, if they knew, they'd freak out. But they'll never find it. It's in a bag, in a box, under other boxes." Another laugh.

Pause. "Yeah, schnapps is great. But listen, can I pay you next week?"

Pause. "I *did* get it, but my dad found out, he went totally berserko. I apparently put it back in the wrong spot. I mean, how am I supposed to know he's totally OCD about the freaking order of the cards in his freaking wallet?" Scoff.

Pause. "No, I'll find my mom's and get the cash to pay you back. Next week, I promise."

Pause. "Okay, bye. Oh, wait. Can I ask a favor?"

Laugh. "Yeah, *another* favor." Pause. "Someone's mailing me some stuff, and I don't want my parents seeing it. Can I give your address, and you can bring it to class?"

Pause. "No, no. It's just apartment listings. I'm trying to surprise my parents." Pause. "Oh, thanks. That's really cool of you. And listen, have you checked on Wednesday yet? You know, my birthday—" Pause. "Oh, okay. Sure, I understand. For sure. Tell David I said hi."

There was the clack of a flip phone closing, then Mary impersonating her friend in an exaggerated, whiny singsong, "Oh my *God*, it's *David*, did I mention how much I love *David*? And no, I can't come to your birthday dinner because *David* might *call* me." Switch to regular voice. "Bitch." Sigh. Silence.

Teresa backed away slowly to her van. She closed the door quietly and drove away for a few minutes before stopping. She looked at Rosa, still asleep, her head flopped over like a rag doll's. Her breaths were deep and even, with a soft rasp on each exhalation—lighter than a snore, gentler than a whistle. Innocent. Sweetly beautiful, like a baby.

Rosa and Mary were the same age. If Rosa hadn't gotten the virus that ravaged her brain, was that what she'd be doing—drinking, conspiring with frenemies, stealing her money, all the things mothers prayed their kids would never do? Well, Rosa never would—prayer answered, lifetime guarantee. So why could she not stop herself from sobbing?

The thing was, it was the unexpected, unenviable things about others' lives that got to her most. People's picture-perfect portrayals of their lives in holiday cards with those braggy collages (son in soccer uniform holding trophy, daughter holding violin and medal, parents in teeth-baring smiles advertising their oh-so-happiness) and braggy letters ("Just a sampling of my amazing kids' most amazing achievements!")—those, she could dismiss as fake.

But the ordinary, even bad stuff that went uncelebrated but defined life with growing kids—the eye-rolls, the door slams, the "You're ruining my life!"—the loss of *those* things was what she grieved. She didn't expect to; when Carlos started with the teenage near-bipolar nonsense, she'd even thought, *Thank God Rosa's not like this.* But it was like multiple night feedings with newborns—yes, it was horrible, and yes, you prayed for it to stop, but not really. Because that was a sign of normalcy, and as bad as it could get, normalcy was a beautiful thing to those who lost it. So now, the fact that she'd never catch Rosa stealing a twenty from her wallet or sneaking liquor or saying "bitch" behind someone's back—it gnawed at her insides and sent cramps throbbing through her gut. She wanted all that, and she hated that the Yoos had it, and she wanted to drive away and never see them again.

But she didn't, of course. She drove back to HBOT and smiled at Young and Pak and got in the chamber. Kitt wasn't coming (TJ was sick) and neither was Matt (stuck in traffic, apparently, which was strange given her no-traffic commute), so it was just her and Elizabeth. As soon as the hatch closed, Elizabeth said to her, "Are you okay? Is anything wrong?"

Teresa said, "Sure. I mean, no, nothing's wrong. I'm just tired." She stretched her lips, willed the corners to bend upward toward her ears. It was hard to remember the muscle movements to form a natural-looking smile when you were trying not to cry, when you were swallowing and blinking and thinking, *Oh please, think about anything other than how life is shitty and this is how you might feel the rest of your life.*

"Okay," Elizabeth said. "Okay." The way she said "Okay" twice— trying not to sound hurt, like a girl being told all the lunch-table seats were taken—made Teresa want to confide in her. Or maybe it was the chamber. The empty darkness with the DVD's flickering light and the narrator's lulling voice—it felt like a confessional. Teresa stopped swallowing and blinking, scooted away from the kids, and started talking.

She told Elizabeth about her day, about the back-to-back therapy sessions and Rosa falling asleep and the pee jar. She told her about twelve years ago, how she'd said good night to a healthy five-year-old girl, gone on a two-day trip, and returned to find her in a coma. She told her how she'd blamed her (now ex-)husband for taking Rosa to the mall, not washing her hands, giving her undercooked chicken, and on and on. She told her how the doctors said Rosa would probably die, and if she didn't, there'd be brain damage, severe and irreversible.

Death versus cerebral palsy and mental retardation. *Not death, please not death, nothing else matters*, she'd prayed. But for the tiniest, most minuscule of moments, she'd thought about lifelong brain damage. Her little girl, gone, but her physical shell there as a reminder of her absence. Nursing her full-time, normal life broken like a twig. No job, no friends, no retirement.

"It's not that I wanted her dead. Of course not. Just thinking about that, I can't even . . ." Teresa shut her eyes to squeeze out the terrifying thought. "I prayed for her to live, and she did. I was so grateful—I *am*. But . . ."

"But you wonder if that was the right thing to pray for," Elizabeth said.

Teresa nodded. Rosa's death would have destroyed her, demolished her life. But she would've had the luxury of finality, of lowering the coffin and saying good-bye. And eventually, she'd have risen and rebuilt her life. This way, she was left standing, but in a purgatory state of descent, being whittled away, bit by bit, day by day. Was that better? "What mother thinks this way?" Teresa said.

"Oh, Teresa, you're a good mom. You're just having a bad day."

"No, I'm a bad person. Maybe the kids would be better off with Tomas."

"Stop, you're being ridiculous," Elizabeth said. "Look, it's hard. It's hard being a mom to kids like ours. I mean, I know Kitt says I have it easy, but it doesn't *feel* easy, you know? I worry all the time, and I drive everywhere, trying one thing after another, and this double dive . . ." She shook her head and choked out a bitter laugh. "God, I hate it. I'm exhausted. So if *I* feel like that, I can't imagine how *you* must feel, having to deal with so much more. I mean it, I don't know how you do it. I'm in awe of you, and Kitt is, too. You're an amazing mom, so patient and gentle with Rosa, the way you've sacrificed your whole life for her. That's why everyone calls you Mother Teresa."

"Well, now you know. It's just an act." Teresa blinked and felt hot tears wetting her cheeks, the familiar shame. Mother Teresa—what a joke. "God, what's wrong with me? I can't believe I told you all this. I'm sorry, I—"

"What? No. I'm glad you told me." Elizabeth touched her arm. "I wish more moms would talk like this. We need to tell each other the ugly stuff, the stuff we're ashamed of."

Teresa shook her head. "I can't imagine what my CP support group would do if they heard this. Kick me out, probably. Other moms just don't think things like this."

"Are you kidding?" Elizabeth looked at her. "Come here." She scooted all the way next to the hatch and intercom, as far away from the kids as possible. She said in a hushed voice, "Remember what Kitt said about TJ and fever?"

Teresa nodded. Kitt had been talking about the phenomenon of some kids' autism symptoms lessening with high fever, and how TJ stops head banging and even says one-syllable words when he gets sick and how heartbreaking it is when his fever breaks and he reverts. ("It's wonderful and terrible, seeing this glimpse of who he *could* be for just a day.")

Elizabeth continued. "Henry's the opposite. When he's sick, he gets completely spacey. Last time, he couldn't get his words out, even started rocking, which he hadn't done in a year. I was so scared it was permanent. I freaked out and yelled at him, thinking maybe I could snap him out of it. I even . . ." Elizabeth looked down and shook her head, as if telling herself no. "Anyway, I had this moment where I thought, why did I have him? If he hadn't been born, my life would be so much better. I'd be a partner by now, and Victor and I'd still be married, taking vacations around the world. I stopped researching regressions and started looking up islands in Fiji."

Teresa said, "That's nothing. It's like fantasizing about an actor."

Elizabeth shook her head. "Since then, when I'm really frustrated, sometimes I wish he didn't exist. I once even fantasized about him dying. In some painless way, maybe in his sleep. What would life be like? Would it really be that bad?"

"Mom," Henry called out. "The DVD's done. Can you put in another one?"

"Sure, sweetie." She buzzed Pak, asked for the next DVD, and waited for it to start before whispering to Teresa, "Anyway, my point is, we all have our moments. But they're just moments, and they pass. At the end of the day, you love Rosa, I love Henry, and we've both sacrificed everything and we'd do anything for them. So if a tiny part of us has these thoughts a tiny part of the time, thoughts we shut out as soon as they creep in, is that so bad? Isn't that just human?"

Teresa looked at Elizabeth, her kind smile that made her wonder if she'd made up the whole story to make Teresa feel better, less alone. She thought of how life might've played out: Rosa's body, long ago pillaged by maggots, now a pile of bones six feet under. She looked over at Henry and Rosa, sitting together in their fish-tank oxygen helmets, their faces bathed in the glow of the screen. She thought how Rosa would never be like Mary, who by now was probably drinking and stewing over her friend with *David* and God knows what else. Maybe it was okay that Rosa was sitting here instead, gurgling and laughing at the sounds of dinosaurs.

○

BACK ON THAT DAY, and many times since (especially right after Mary awoke from her coma with no brain damage), she'd imagined telling Young about Mary's misdeeds, the satisfaction she'd feel as Young realized that her flaunted daughter was not the flawless specimen of parental satisfaction she'd portrayed. And now, finally, was the perfect opportunity to tell her, not out of sheer pettiness, but to give context to the I-want-my-child-dead conversation. But she couldn't do it. She looked at

Young's face, so tired and confused, and she replaced Mary's name with "a teenager at McDonald's."

After Teresa's story, Young said, "Pak was right. Elizabeth said she wanted Henry to die. How can any mother say this?"

Teresa had told the whole story with no emotion, but now a lump was rising in her throat. She swallowed. "I said it, too, about Rosa. I said it first."

Young shook her head. "No, you . . . your situation is very different."

Different how? she wanted to ask. But she didn't have to. She knew. What Young thought, what everyone thought: Rosa was better off dead. Not like Henry, whose life was *valuable*, whose mother shouldn't be wishing for his death. It was what Detective Heights had said in the cafeteria. Teresa said, "It's hard when you have a disabled child, of any kind. I don't think you can understand if you've never experienced that."

"Mary was in a coma for two months. I never wished for her death. Even if she is damaged, I wanted her not to die."

Teresa wanted to yell that Mary was in the hospital, cared for by nurses. Young didn't understand that when the months became years, it changed you, that it was different when you had to do everything yourself. She wanted to hurt Young, couldn't resist the urge to strike her off the pedestal from which she could be so fricking sanctimonious. "You know, Young," Teresa said, "that girl I heard, who was breaking the rules? That was Mary."

Teresa regretted saying it before she finished, even before Young's face scrunched into wounded confusion. Young said, "Mary? You saw her in McDonald's?"

"No. It was actually here. In the shed."

"The storage shed? What was she doing?"

She felt silly now. What was she doing, getting a girl in trouble for doing stupid things all teenagers did? "Nothing. She was just moving boxes around. You know how kids are, they like having secret places to hide stuff. Carlos does the same—"

"Hide? Which box?"

"I don't know. I was outside, and I heard her tell someone on the phone she had a secret stash in some box."

"Stash? Drugs?" Young's eyes widened.

"No, nothing like that. It was probably just money. She said something about Pak catching her taking cards from his wallet, so—"

"Card from wallet? Pak catch?" Young's face blanched, like a photo transforming into sepia with the click of a button. It was obvious: Pak never told Young about Mary stealing money. Despite herself, Teresa felt a tinge of satisfaction at this additional proof of imperfection in Young's life. She felt a pinch of shame, and said, "Young, don't worry about this. Kids do this kind of thing. Carlos takes money from my wallet all the time."

Young looked dazed, too upset to say anything.

"Young, I'm sorry. I shouldn't have told you all this. It's not a big deal. Please forget about it. Mary's a good kid. I don't know if she ever told you, but last summer, she was working with a Realtor to find an apartment for you guys, as a surprise, which I think is so thoughtful and—"

Young grabbed her arm tight, nails digging in. "Apartment? In Seoul?"

"What? I mean, I don't know, but why in Seoul? I assumed it was around here."

"But you do not know this? You did not see?"

"No, she just said apartment listings, she didn't say where."

Young closed her eyes. Her grip on Teresa's arm tightened, and she seemed to sway.

"Young? Are you okay?"

"I think . . ." Young opened her eyes and blinked a few times. She tried to smile. "I think I am sick also. I must go home. Please, tell Abe we are sorry to be absent today."

"Oh, no. Do you want me to drive you? I have time."

Young shook her head. "No, Teresa. You helped me so much. You are a good friend." Young held her hand and squeezed, and Teresa felt shame spread through her body, a desperation to do whatever she could to relieve Young's pain.

When Young was halfway down the aisle, Teresa called out, "I almost forgot to tell you." Young turned. "I heard earlier, Abe said whoever used Matt's phone to make the arson call speaks English with no accent. So Pak's in the clear."

Young's mouth opened and her brow crumpled into a frown. Her eyes darted side to side and she said, "No accent?" as if she didn't know those words and she was asking the tables in front what they meant, but then her frown dissolved and eyes stilled. She closed them, and her mouth twitched as if she was about to smile or cry, Teresa couldn't tell which.

"Young? Are you all right?" Teresa stood to go to her, but Young opened her eyes and shook her head, as if pleading with her not to come. Without saying anything, Young turned her back to Teresa and walked out the door.

ELIZABETH

SHE FOUND HERSELF in an unfamiliar room, sitting on a hard chair. Where was she? She didn't think she'd been asleep or unconscious, but she couldn't remember getting here, the way you feel when you're driving home and you suddenly find yourself in your garage, unable to remember the actual drive.

She looked around. The room was tiny, its four folding chairs and TV-tray-sized table taking up half the space. Plain gray walls. Shut door. No windows, vents, or fans. Was she locked up in some holding cell? A mental-ward unit? Why was it so hot and airless? She felt dizzy, couldn't breathe. Suddenly, a memory: Henry saying, "Henry too hot. Henry can't breathe." When was that? He must've been five, when he was still mixing up pronouns and couldn't use "I." This was how it had been since he died:

everything she saw or heard, even things having nothing to do with Henry, exhumed some memory of him and sent her reeling.

She tried to push it away, but the image came anyway: Henry in his Elmo swim trunks in a portable infrared sauna. Being inside this room— its heat, smothering austerity, sealed-in cubicle feel—was reminding her of the sauna in her basement. The first time he'd gone in, that's when he'd said, "Henry too hot. Henry can't breathe." She'd tried to be patient, to explain about sweating out toxins, but when he kicked open the door— the brand-new door of the ten-thousand-dollar unit she'd spent God knows how many phone calls convincing Victor they needed—she lost it and screamed, "Goddammit! Now you've broken it," even though she knew it wasn't broken. Henry started crying, hard, and, looking at his tears mixing with snot into a mask of slime, she felt pure hatred. It was just for a moment, one she'd regret and cry over later, but right then, she hated her five-year-old son. For having autism. For making everything so hard. For making her hate him. "Stop being a crybaby. Right. Fucking. Now," she said, and slammed the sauna door. He didn't know what *fucking* meant, and she never used that word, but there was something so satisfy- ing about saying it, the aggressive percussiveness of the *f* and *k* sounds spitting from her mouth, and combined with the slam—that was enough to release her rage and calm her. She wanted to run back and say Mommy was sorry and cradle him, but how could she face him? Better to pretend it never happened, to wait for the half-hour timer to ding, then praise him for being brave, with no mention of the crying or screaming. All the ugliness vaporized away.

She always went in with Henry after that, telling jokes and singing silly songs to distract him, but he never stopped hating it. Every day, get- ting in the sauna, he said, "Henry is brave. Henry is not a crybaby," and blinked rapidly, the way he did when trying not to cry. And during the sessions, when he wiped at his tears, she swallowed and said, "Wow, you're sweating so much, it's even getting in your eyes!"

Thinking of that now, she wondered: Had Henry believed her? He sometimes said back to her, "Henry sweat so much!" and smiled. Was his smile genuine, from relief she wasn't yelling at him for crying, or fake, to pretend that his tears were sweat? Was she merely a mean mom who frightened her child, or a psychotic mom who turned him into a liar? Or both?

The door opened. As Shannon walked in with Anna, an associate, she saw the familiar hallway outside the courtroom. Of course. They were in one of the attorney conference rooms.

Shannon said, "Anna found a fan, and I got some water. You look pale still. Here, drink." She put a cup to Elizabeth's lips and tilted it, the way you would for an invalid.

Elizabeth pushed it away. "No, I'm just hot. It's hard to catch my breath in here."

"I know, I'm sorry," Shannon said. "It's a lot smaller than our usual room, but this is the only one without any windows."

Elizabeth was about to ask why no windows, but she remembered. The clicks and flashes of cameras, Shannon trying to shield her, reporters pelting nonstop questions at her: *What did you mean there's no cat? Did your neighbors have cats? Have you ever had cats? Do you like cats? Was Henry allergic to cats? Do you believe in declawing cats?*

Cat. Scratch. Henry's arm. His voice. His words—

Elizabeth felt faint, her senses draining out and the world fading to black. She needed air. She moved her face down directly in front of the small fan clipped to the table. The lawyers didn't seem to notice; they were checking voice mail and e-mails. She focused on the air, the blades whirring in a blur, and after a minute, blood returned to her head, a tingling around her scalp. "Is that a picture of Elizabeth's *nails*?" Anna said, and Shannon said, "Shit, I bet the jury's—" Elizabeth put her hands over her ears and closed her eyes, focused on the buzz of the fan that, if she concentrated hard enough, filtered out their voices and left only Henry's. *Take vacations around the world. I should never have been born. The cat hates me.*

"The cat hates me," she said, under her breath. Was he elaborating on the imaginary cat, or was he talking about her, who scratched him and became the "cat" in his story? Did he really think she hated him? And the reference to vacations—she'd said that to Teresa, once. She'd moved far from Henry, who was watching DVDs, and whispered to make sure he wouldn't hear. But he'd heard. Her whispered confession that she sometimes wished him dead—those words had bounced and echoed against the steel walls and somehow reached his ears.

She once read that sounds left permanent imprints; the tonal vibrations penetrated nearby objects and continued for infinity at the quantum level, like when you throw pebbles in the ocean and the ripples continue without end. Did her words, their ugliness, penetrate the walls' atoms—the same way Henry's pain at hearing them permeated his brain—and that last dive, when Henry was sitting in that same spot within those walls, the ugliness and the pain collided into a blast, blowing apart his neurons and torching him from the inside?

The door opened, and another associate, Andrew, walked in. "Ruth Weiss said yes!"

"Really? That's great," said Shannon.

Elizabeth looked up. "The protester?"

Shannon nodded. "I asked her to testify about Pak threatening her. It supports our—"

"But she did it. She set the fire and killed Henry. You know that," Elizabeth said.

"No, I don't know that," Shannon said. "I know you *think* that, but we've been over this. They went straight from the police station to D.C. Cell tower pings place them in D.C. proper at 9:00, so there's no way—"

"They could've planned it," Elizabeth said. "One person could've stayed behind to set the fire, but they took all the phones to establish alibis. Or they could've driven really fast, made the drive in fifty minutes, or—"

"There's no evidence of any of that, whereas there's a ton of evidence against Pak. We're in court. We need evidence, not speculation."

Elizabeth shook her head. "That's what the police did to me. It didn't matter whether I really did it, just that I'm the easiest to prosecute. You're doing the same thing. I've told you all along, you need to go after the protesters, but you're giving up on them because it's too hard to get proof."

"Damn right," Shannon said. "It's not my job to go after the real perpetrators. My job is to defend you. And I don't care how much you hate them. If they can help the jury to see Pak as a viable alternative and return a not-guilty verdict, they're your best friends right now. And you need some, because after your outburst today, you've lost any support you had. The rumor mill is that Teresa went back to Abe's side."

"It's true," Andrew said. "I saw it, passing by a little while ago. She was alone in the courtroom, and she got up and switched seats, to the prosecution's side."

Teresa, her last and only friend. The cat-scratch thing had repelled her, of course it had.

"Shit," Shannon said. "I don't know why she has to be so dramatic about it, all this walking-across-the-aisle nonsense. No wonder Abe was so smug just now."

Anna said, "We just saw him, and he said he's calling Teresa next, and he tried to rattle us. 'She's heard some *very* interesting things that will *fascinate* the jury,'" Anna said in a Southern-twang imitation. "He's such an asshole."

"I've been thinking about that," Shannon said. "He said Teresa's testifying about things she's *heard*, which means it has to be a hearsay exception, which means—"

"An admission?" Anna said.

"That's my guess." Shannon turned to Elizabeth. "Have you said anything to Teresa that could make you look bad? The way he was acting, it must be something pretty incriminating."

It could only be one thing. Their conversation in the chamber. The shameful, secret words they'd whispered to each other alone, meant to be shared with no one, never to be repeated. The words she couldn't bear to even think about, Teresa was planning to repeat in open court, and they'd soon be spread to the world through websites and newspapers.

She felt a pang of betrayal. She wanted to find Teresa and demand to know how she could turn against her when she herself said those same words, thought those same thoughts. She wanted to tell Shannon how Teresa said she wanted Rosa dead. How satisfying it would be, watching Shannon tear her apart in court. To have the all-caring Mother Teresa be cast in the role of Bad Mother for once.

But Teresa wasn't a bad mother. Teresa didn't scratch her child. Teresa didn't force her child into painful treatments that made her sob and throw up. And no matter what she may have thought or said, Teresa never made her child think she hated her. Teresa had good reason to abandon her now: she finally realized how despicable Elizabeth was, and she wanted justice for Henry against the mother who'd failed him.

"Elizabeth, can you think of anything?" Shannon repeated.

She shook her head. "No, nothing."

"Well, keep thinking. I'd like to know what's coming. Otherwise, I'll have to cross her blind." Shannon turned to her associates.

Cross. She could hear it now: "What happened right before Elizabeth said this? I mean, you weren't just saying, *Oh, I got a haircut*, and she blurted out, *I wish Henry would die*, right? I'm curious—have *you* said anything like this? Ever think it?" It nauseated her, thinking of strangers passing judgment on Teresa's most intimate thoughts, the private words she'd said only at Elizabeth's coaxing. She needed to save Teresa from having to tell that story, from the pain to her and Rosa and Carlos from the broadcasting of those words. But how?

Shannon turned to her. "Can you list everyone who spent time alone with Henry last summer? Therapists, babysitters . . . and didn't Victor come visit one weekend?"

"Why?"

"Well, it's just, you can interpret what you said in different ways, and we're brainstorming what 'There is no cat,' could mean, why a person might say that."

"*A* person?" Elizabeth said. "*I'm* the person. I'm the one who said it, and I'm right here. Why don't you just ask me?"

No one said anything. They didn't have to. They didn't ask her because they didn't need to. It was obvious, they knew the answer, but they didn't want to be constrained by the truth in their "brainstorming" on how to spin this.

"I see," Elizabeth said. "Well, I'll tell you anyway. What I meant by—"

Shannon put up her hand. "Stop. You don't need to . . ." She sighed. "Look, it doesn't matter what you meant. What you said is not evidence. The judge told the jurors to disregard it, and in a perfect world, that would be the end of it. But this is real life. They're human, and there's no way it won't affect them. So I need to neutralize it by giving them alternatives to you being a child abuser."

Elizabeth swallowed. "But how . . . What's the alternative?"

"Someone else could've hurt him," Shannon said. "Someone Henry wanted to protect, someone you maybe had suspicions about, and it upset you so much hearing Henry covering up for that person, you had a breakdown in court."

"What? You want to take some innocent person and accuse them of child abuse? A teacher or therapist or Victor? Victor's wife? My God, Shannon!" Elizabeth said.

"Not accuse," Shannon said. "Merely hypothesize. Distract the jury from stuff they're thinking about you, which they're not supposed to be thinking in the first place. All we'll do is point out some theoretical reasons why you *could* have said that."

"No. That's crazy. You know that's not true. You think *I* scratched him. I know you do."

"It doesn't matter what I think. It matters what evidence I can present and what arguments I can make. And I'm not going to back away from something just because it's not very nice. You understand?"

"No." Elizabeth stood up. Blood rushed out of her head and the room seemed to shrink. "You can't do that. You need to stick to just saying this has nothing to do with who set the fire. You can convince the jury of that."

"No, I can't," Shannon said, her words finally losing that veneer of forced calmness. "I can argue it till I'm blue in the face, but if the jury thinks you hurt Henry, they won't want to side with you, no matter who they think really set the fire. They'll want to punish you."

"Then let them. I deserve it, anyway. I won't let you bring innocent people into this."

"But they—"

"Stop," Elizabeth said. "I want this over. I want to plead guilty."

"What? What are you talking about?"

"I'm sorry, I really am, but I can't do this anymore. I can't go back in there for one more second."

"All right, all right," Shannon said. "Let's calm down here. If it bothers you that much, we won't do it. I'll just focus on the point that the scratch is not relevant to the ultimate—"

"It doesn't matter," Elizabeth said. "It's not just this. It's everything.

The scratch, Pak, the protesters, Teresa, the video, I need it all to stop. I want to plead guilty. Today."

Shannon didn't say anything, just took deep breaths through her nose, mouth clamped shut, as if trying hard not to lose it. When she finally spoke, her words were overly slow, like those of a mother reasoning with a tan-truming toddler. "A lot's happened today. I think you need a break, we all do. I'll ask the judge to adjourn for the day, and we can all sleep on it."

"That won't change anything."

"Fine. If you still feel like this tomorrow, we can go to the judge. But you need to really think this through. You owe me that much."

Elizabeth nodded and said, "Okay. Tomorrow," even though she knew she wouldn't change her mind. They could throw her in prison and melt the key into a metallic puddle and she wouldn't care. Thinking this, knowing everything would end soon, Elizabeth felt her panic of the past moments lift, restoring her senses. It was like when your foot falls asleep, the numbness turning to tingling, itching, then pain as it awakens, except it was happening to her whole body. Suddenly, she was aware of her sweat, the stickiness around her hairline, the wetness under her arms. "I'm going to the bathroom. I need some water on my face." She left without waiting for a response.

She saw Young almost immediately, in a phone booth a few steps away. From her angle, she could see the side of Young's face, sallow and pasty, the way her shoulders drooped like a marionette with cut strings. She thought of Young pushing Pak's wheelchair into court, the man who became paralyzed because he tried to help Henry and Kitt. And now her own lawyer was vilifying him, all to divert blame away from her.

Elizabeth stopped and waited for Young. After a few minutes, Young hung up and came out. The moment their eyes met, Young gasped, her eyes widening in surprise. No. It was more than surprise. It was fear. And something else she couldn't quite make out—lips quivering, knitted brow, eyes drooping at the outer edges. It looked like sorrow and repen-tance, but that didn't make sense. She must be misreading it, like when you stare at a word too long, and even a simple word like *are* looks foreign and you no longer know how to pronounce it. The expression on Young's face had to be pure hostility for putting her family through misery.

Elizabeth stepped toward her. "Young, I want you to know how sorry I am. I didn't know that my lawyer was going to blame Pak. Please tell him how sorry I am. I wish this week had never happened. I promise this'll be over soon."

"Elizabeth, I am . . ." Young bit her lip and looked away, as if unsure what to say. "I hope this will end very soon," Young finally said before walking away.

Tomorrow, Elizabeth wanted to call out. *I'm pleading guilty tomorrow.* The words were bursting out of her. "I'm pleading guilty tomorrow," she said, softly, but aloud. It was ridiculous. She was getting sent to death row, not getting married. Still, now that she'd decided, her relief was ballooning into excitement, making her wish she had a friend to share it with. Plus, apologizing to Young had siphoned out some of her guilt. This confirmed it. She was right to want to end everything as soon as possible.

She went into the bathroom, took some toilet paper, and wiped the sweat off her face. On her way out, she ran into Shannon and Andrew, who were going to meet with the judge. Anna was still in the room, on the phone. When she walked in, Anna closed her laptop and mouthed, "One minute—I'll be right outside," and left.

Elizabeth sat at the table and put her hands by the fan to cool off. Anna's laptop was sitting on some papers, and she was tempted to read it. No. None of it mattered. Their strategies, arguments, witnesses— irrelevant. She looked around and saw her purse next to Shannon's purse and briefcase in the corner. She'd been wondering where she left that. As she went to get it, she saw a legal notepad in Shannon's briefcase pocket. It was crooked, and a partial phrase peeked out. *GUILTY PLEA CH—*

Guilty plea change? Guilty plea chance? Guilty plea chat?

Elizabeth moved the notepad with one finger, just enough to make out the phrase. In Shannon's neat handwriting, on the top left corner, read *GUILTY PLEA CHALLENGE?* She lifted the notepad out. It was a bullet-point list in Shannon's handwriting:

- VA guilty plea req.—"knowing, voluntary & intelligent" met if mentally incompetent? (Anna)

- Precedent for challenging own client's guilty plea on competence grounds (Andrew) (Pull cases re: guilty plea as "fraud on the court")
- Conflict of interest, need to withdraw first?—ethical rules (Anna)
- Mental competence evaluation—mtng Dr. C <u>tonight!</u> (Shannon)

Guilty plea. Mental competence. Challenging own client's guilty plea. Her throat tightened, the collar of her blouse pressing into her neck, making her gag. She undid the top button and breathed in deeply to take oxygen into her lungs.

Let's sleep on it, just to make sure, Shannon had said. If you still want to, we'll go see the judge tomorrow, she'd said. But she wasn't planning to let Elizabeth plead guilty. Not tomorrow. Not ever. Shannon was launching an offensive against her own client. She was planning to say Elizabeth was crazy, she was defrauding the court—anything she needed to keep the trial going. She was going to drag Elizabeth back and make her watch the rest of Henry's video. She was going to force Teresa to testify about the shameful thoughts they'd shared in secret. She was going to lie about Victor or whoever was convenient and accuse them of abuse. She was going to blame Pak and drag him through the mud, and worse, she was going to use the protesters to do it.

The protesters. Ruth Weiss. ProudAutismMom. Thinking of that woman, she felt the familiar punch of hatred so strong that she got dizzy, had to touch the wall for balance. That woman had burned Elizabeth's little boy, all because she wanted to make a point, to proselytize her "autism theory" (nothing more than a justification for her own parenting style, in reality). And it was Elizabeth's own fault for not stopping her. That woman had stalked her on autism chat boards, threatening and bad-mouthing her, even going to CPS, and Elizabeth had ignored the escalation and let it get out of control, enabling that woman to take extreme action without fear of consequence. And now, because of her own inaction and cowardice, Ruth Weiss had gotten away with murder and was poised to bring more pain to another of her victims, Pak.

No. She couldn't let that happen.

She stood up and paced. She needed to get out, but there was no window to climb out, and Anna was right outside the door. Even if she could somehow get out of the building, what could she do? She didn't have a car, and it wasn't like taxis were roaming the streets. She could call one, but it might not get here before people realized she was gone. Still, she had to try.

She went to get her purse. As she reached, Shannon's purse next to it moved and its contents shifted. It was as if the jangling inside loosened some deep-seated image in Elizabeth's mind. An image of herself doing something she should've done long ago.

She gripped Shannon's purse and stood up. She knew exactly where she needed to go and what she needed to do. She just had to do it. Quickly, before anyone caught her. Before she could change her mind.

MATT

MATT AND JANINE WAITED FOR ABE outside the judge's chambers standing side by side. Another couple stood nearby, younger, and from their frequent kissing and joint admiring of her ring, he guessed they were waiting to be married. They probably thought he and Janine were getting divorced—Janine's face was all frown, and she kept whisper-yelling, "Tell me *right now*. What the fuck are we doing here?" while he stayed silent, shaking his head.

It wasn't that he didn't want to tell her. The problem was, he knew Janine. Knew she'd argue for not telling Abe the *full* truth—her being there that night, for example, or his smoking with Mary. Knew she'd tell him to plan and practice his exact wording. And the thing was, he was sick of it, the hiding, scheming, enumerating facts, and on and on. He needed to face Abe and spew it all out, fuck the consequences.

Abe and Shannon walked out, each with an underling. "Abe, I need to talk to you, right now," Matt said.

"Sure, we're adjourned for the day. We can use this room." Abe opened the door to a conference room across the hall.

Shannon raised an eyebrow, and it occurred to Matt: she needed to know, too, even more than Abe. But how much of his confession would survive Abe's legal-technicalities filter and actually reach her? And wasn't that why he hadn't told Janine first, to bypass any conspiratorial she-nanigans? He said, "Ms. Haug, you, too. I need to talk to you both, together."

Abe shook his head. "That's not a good idea. Let's first—"

"No," Matt said, sure more than ever that Shannon needed to hear this. "I won't say anything unless we're all in the same room. And trust me, you want to hear this." He walked into the room, pulling Janine along, and Shannon followed. Abe stood in the doorway, glaring and fuming.

Shannon positioned her legal pad and said, "Shall we get started?" She said to Abe, "If you're leaving, would you close the door behind you?"

Abe's eyes scrunched into an I'd-like-nothing-better-than-to-kill-you-right-now look before he stepped in and sat across from Matt. He didn't take out a pad or pen, just leaned back, crossed his arms, and said to Matt, "All right, let's have it."

Matt reached for Janine's hand under the table. She snatched it away, pursing her lips like she tasted something bitter and was trying not to spit it out. Matt took in a deep breath. "The insurance call. You know, the one about arson."

Abe uncrossed his arms and leaned forward.

"I remembered something. Mary had access to my car. She knew where I kept a spare key." He looked at Abe. "English with no accent."

"Wait," Shannon said. "Are you saying—"

"Also," Matt said, afraid he wouldn't be able to continue if he stopped, "Mary smoked cigarettes last summer. Camels."

Abe said, "And you know this because . . ."

"We did it together. Smoking, I mean." Matt felt heat burst in his cheeks, and he willed his capillaries to constrict and stop the blood from rushing to his skin's surface. "I'm not a smoker, but one day, on a whim, I got cigarettes and I was smoking before a dive and Mary happened to show up and I gave her one."

"So just once, then," Abe said, more a statement than a question.

Matt looked at Janine, her face infused with dread and hope, and he thought about last night, his telling her it was just that once. "No. I got in the habit of smoking by the creek, and she was out there sometimes, so I'd see her. Maybe a dozen times the whole summer."

Janine's mouth opened in an O at her realization that he'd lied last night. Again.

"And you both smoked, every time?" Shannon said.

Matt nodded.

"Camels?" Shannon said.

Matt nodded. "And yes, I bought them at a 7-Eleven."

"Jesus," Abe said, shaking his head and looking down like he wanted to punch the table.

Shannon said, "So the Camels and matches Elizabeth found—"

"*Allegedly* found," Abe said.

Shannon swatted the air like Abe was a gnat, keeping her focus on Matt. "What do you know about those, Dr. Thompson?"

Matt felt a surge of gratitude toward Shannon for not asking the questions he was dreading, about what else happened during these "meetings" (sure to be said with tonal quotes) and exactly how old Mary was. He looked Shannon straight in the eye and said, "The cigarettes and matches were mine, what I bought."

"And the H-Mart note about meeting at 8:15?" Shannon said.

"Mine. I left that for Mary. I wanted to stop. Quit, I mean. The smoking. And I figured I should let her know, and apologize, you know, for getting her into a bad habit, so I sent her that note, and she wrote 'Yes' and left it for me the morning of the explosion."

"Jesus frigging Christ," Abe said, looking at a blank spot on the wall and shaking his head. "All those times I brought up the H-Mart note, and you . . ." Abe shut his lips.

"So how did they get out into the woods where Elizabeth found them?" Shannon said.

This was where he had to tread lightly. It was one thing to purge yourself of your own story, damn the consequences, but this next part was Janine's story, not his. He glanced at Janine. She was staring blankly at the table, her face drained of color like a refrigerated cadaver. "I'm not sure why that's relevant," Matt said. "She found them where she found them. Why does it matter how they got there?"

"It matters because the prosecution here"—Shannon glared at Abe—"has said repeatedly that the cigarettes and matches Elizabeth had were used to set the fire. So we need to know who else had them and could've used them before discarding the rest for her to find."

Matt said, "Well, I was sealed up in HBOT, so I couldn't—"

"I took them. I gave them to Mary," Janine said. Matt didn't look at her, didn't want to see her eyes welling with fury at him for putting her in this situation.

"What? When?" Shannon said.

"Around eight, before the explosion." Janine's voice had a slight shake to it, like she was cold and shivering, and Matt wanted to take her in his arms and transfer his warmth. "I suspected there was something . . . someone Matt . . . Anyway, that day, I went through Matt's car—glove box, trash on the floor, trunk, everything—and I found them."

Matt reached for her hand and squeezed it. She could've just said she found the note, but she didn't. It felt like forgiveness, her admitting to snooping through his stuff, giving details. Like she was saying it wasn't all his fault; they both did stupid things.

"Are you saying you went to Miracle Creek that night?" Shannon said.

Janine nodded. "I didn't tell Matt. I just wanted to see what this meeting was. Anyway, the dive was running late—Matt called to let me know—and I saw Mary, so I stopped her and gave her everything and told her she was a bad influence and to leave him alone, and I left."

"Let me get this straight," Shannon said. "Less than thirty minutes before the explosion, Mary Yoo was by herself, close to the barn, in possession of Camel cigarettes and 7-Eleven matches. That's what you're telling me?"

Janine looked down and nodded.

Shannon turned to Abe. "Are you dropping the charges? Because if not, I'm moving for a mistrial."

"What?" Abe stood, the color that had drained from his face returning. "Don't be melodramatic. Just because there was some hanky-panky going on here doesn't mean your client's innocent. Far from it."

"There was deliberate obstruction of justice, not to mention perjury. On the stands. By your star witness."

"No, no, no. Whose cigarette it was, whose note—these are fun little side mysteries. Your client wanted to get rid of her son, and she was alone with the weapons in hand at the time the fire was set, and nothing that's been said here changes any of that."

Shannon said, "Except that Mary Yoo is now—"

"Mary Yoo is a kid who almost died in the explosion." Abe pounded his fist on the table, sending Shannon's pen rolling. "She had no motive whatsoev—"

"No motive? Hello? Have you heard anything they've said? A teenager, having an affair with a married man. Gets jilted, confronted by the wife. Totally humiliated, furious, wants to just *kill* the guy who, oh, by the way, happens to be inside the thing she sets an explosion to. Are you kidding me? It's classic murder-mystery stuff, not to mention the nice little side benefit of 1.3 million dollars from the insurance she herself called to verify."

"We didn't have an affair," Matt managed to say, though not loudly, and Shannon whipped her head his way. "What?"

He started to repeat himself, but Janine cut in, said something, but quietly, looking down, almost murmuring, something about the call.

Abe seemed to have heard. He stared at her, said, "What did you say?" Shock flowed through his words, his face.

Janine closed her eyes, let out a deep breath, and opened them again. She looked at Abe. "I made the call. It wasn't Mary. You were right; Matt and I switched phones that day."

Abe's mouth opened, in slow motion, then froze, no words coming out.

Janine turned to Matt. "I invested a hundred thousand dollars in Pak's business."

Invested $100,000? Janine calling about arson? These were so far afield from anything he'd expected that his brain couldn't make sense of them, couldn't process how they fitted into any of this. Matt stared at his wife's lips through which those words had come, the dilated black pupils covering almost the entirety of her irises, the earlobes that dangled bright red from her cheeks, all the elements of her face tilting in different directions like one of those Cubist portraits.

Janine continued. "I thought it was a good investment. He had patients lined up, and they'd all signed contracts and paid deposits, and—"

Matt blinked. "You took our money? Is that what you're saying? Without telling me?"

"We'd been fighting a lot and I didn't want another fight. You were so against HBOT, you were irrational about it. I thought you'd say no, but it seemed like such a no-brainer. Pak was going to pay us back first, so we'd have all our money back in four months, before you even missed it, and then we'd get a share of the profits going forward. We had all that money just sitting in our accounts, and it wasn't like we needed it."

Shannon cleared her throat. "Look, I can give you the name of a good marriage counselor to work this out, but let's get back to the arson call. What does all this have to do with that call?" she said, and Matt felt another wave of gratitude to her. For forcing his attention away from the fact that his wife had lied yet again, all because she didn't want the bother of a potential fight. Was that better or worse than why *he'd* lied—because he didn't want to stop meeting a girl?

Janine said, "A few weeks after the dives started, Pak said he found a pile of cigarette butts and matches in the woods. He figured it was just teenagers, but he was worried about them smoking near the barn, and he wanted my advice about whether to put up warnings about oxygen and smoking being forbidden. We discussed it and decided against it, but it made me nervous about our money. In the beginning, Pak didn't want to get insurance, and I had to tell him I wouldn't invest unless he did. And it occurred to me—what if he got some bare-bones policy to appease me, and it didn't cover random kids setting fire to the barn for the hell of it? So I called, and the guy assured me arson coverage is included in all their policies, and that was that."

No one spoke for a minute, and Matt felt the fog around his brain dissipate, the world righting itself, just a little. Yes, she'd lied. But so had he. And somehow, finding out about Janine's wrongdoing came as a relief; it eased his guilt about his own sins, the two deceptions canceling each other out.

Abe said, "So that means—"

Just then, someone knocked and opened the door. One of Abe's assistants. "I'm sorry to interrupt, but Detective Pierson's been trying to reach you. He says someone called claiming to have spotted Elizabeth Ward outside, by herself."

"What do you mean? She's here, with my team," Shannon said.

"No," the guy said. "Pierson just talked to them, and they said she left. Something about you giving her money?"

"What? Why would I give her money?" Shannon said as she and Abe ran out. Behind them, the door creaked closed before clicking shut.

○

JANINE PLACED HER ELBOWS on the table like tripod stands and covered her face with her hands. "Oh my God."

Matt opened his mouth to say something, but he didn't know what. He looked down at his hands and realized: he'd been clutching them together, the scars on his palms sliding and pressing against each other. He thought of the fire, Henry's head, Elizabeth on death row.

"You should know," Janine said, "Pak already paid back twenty thousand dollars before the explosion, and he promised he'll pay the eighty thousand back as soon as insurance comes through. And if that doesn't happen, I'll pay you back from my retirement fund."

Eighty thousand dollars. He looked at his wife's face, the earnestness in her eyes and deep furrows between her brows, and he wanted to laugh. All this fucking drama over eighty fucking thousand dollars, which (she was right) he'd never even noticed was gone, in the aftermath of the explosion. Instead, he nodded, said, "All this is making me rethink everything. I didn't get a chance to tell Abe, but I saw Pak and Mary burning something today. I think maybe cigarettes. You know, in that metal trash can they have?"

Janine looked at him. "You went over there today? When? When you said you were going to the hospital?"

Matt nodded. "This morning, I realized I needed to tell Abe everything, and I figured Mary deserved a warning. But I got there, and they were burning stuff, and it made me wonder if maybe . . ." He shook his head. "Anyway, I came straight here, grabbed you, and—"

"And fucking ambushed me. With no warning."

"I'm sorry. I really am. I just needed to come clean, and I was afraid I'd lose my nerve if I didn't do it right away."

Janine didn't say anything. She just frowned at him, like he was a stranger and she was trying to figure out why he looked familiar.

"Say something," he finally said.

"I don't think," she said—slowly, word by word, with each syllable separated—"that it's a sign of a good marriage that we've both been hiding stuff from each other for a year."

"But we talked about this, last night—"

"And I really don't think it's a good sign that even after we said we'd tell each other everything last night, we still didn't."

Matt took a deep breath. She was right. He knew that. "I'm sorry."

"Me, too." She swallowed and covered her face again and scrubbed hard, like she was rubbing off dried-in grime. Something vibrated in her purse, and she reached in for her phone. She looked at the screen and smiled, a crooked, tiny smile of sadness and fatigue.

"What is it?"

"Fertility clinic. Probably confirming our appointment." He'd forgotten; they were supposed to go after court today, to start in vitro fertilization.

She stood and walked to the corner, facing it, like a kid in time-out. "I don't think we should go."

Matt nodded. "You want to reschedule? Tomorrow?"

She leaned against the wall, her head on it as if she was too weak to hold herself up. "No. I don't know. I just . . . I don't think I can do this anymore."

He went to her and wrapped his arms around her. He'd braced himself for her pushing him away, but she didn't, just leaned back into him, letting him spoon her. They stood like this for a while, his heart thudding her back, and he felt something tingly—sadness, but peace, too, and relief—spread through his chest and permeate through to her skin. They had a lot more talking to do—to each other, the police, Abe, maybe a judge. There would be many more questions to ask and answer, of each other and of themselves. And there would be no fertility clinic—not tomorrow, not next week. He knew that, could tell in the way their embrace felt like good-bye. But in the meantime, for the present, he savored this: the two of them together, alone, not saying anything, not thinking, not planning. Just being.

The door opened behind them, and footsteps rushed in. Janine jerked, like someone drifting to sleep being startled awake. Matt turned. Abe was grabbing his briefcase and running out.

"Abe? What's wrong? What's happening?" Matt said.

"It's Elizabeth," Abe said. "We can't find her anywhere. She's gone."

ELIZABETH

A CAR WAS FOLLOWING HER. A boxy silver sedan, the nondescript type she imagined undercover cops drove. It had been behind her in Pineburg, and she'd told herself to relax, it was just some-one leaving town after lunch, but when she turned onto a random road, it also turned. The car kept its distance, so she couldn't see who was in it. She tried slowing down, speeding up, then slowing again, but the car maintained the same distance, which seemed like something, again, that undercover cops would do. There was a clearing ahead. She pulled off and stopped. If she was caught, so be it, but she couldn't keep this up. Her nerves were frayed and fried.

The car slowed but kept coming. She thought for sure it'd stop and the window would slide down to reveal guys in sunglasses holding up badges, *Men in Black*–style, but it rolled by. It was a young couple, the guy driving and the woman studying a map. They turned off onto a large driveway marked by a grape sign.

Tourists. Of course. In a rental car, following the Virginia winery-trail signs. She slumped back and took deep, slow breaths to get her heart to stop fluttering against her rib cage the way it had ever since she decided to steal Shannon's car. It was a minor miracle she'd made it this far, past all the near misses along the way. In the room, while she was transferring Shannon's keys to her own purse, Anna had walked in and she'd had to tell a quick lie about needing tampons and Shannon having said to get change from her wallet. Thankfully, Anna didn't insist on accompanying her to the bathroom, but two guards were manning the courthouse doors, so she had to wait for a big group to arrive and slip out while they were checking bags. Finding Shannon's car was easy, but there was an attendant at the booth. She'd forgotten she'd have to pay—did she have cash?—and what if he recognized her and knew she wasn't allowed to drive? She put on Shannon's sunglasses and hat from the glove box, pulled the visor down, and looked away as she paid, but she definitely heard "Sorry, ma'am, but are you—" as she drove away.

Driving through town had been the worst part. She'd planned to take the back streets, but she saw a gaggle of autism moms, so she turned the other way, which led to the crowded Main Street. She pulled the hat down her forehead and drove at a Goldilocks speed—fast enough to blur by and escape notice, but not so fast as to draw it. She had to stop twice for pedestrians, and the second time, she saw a man carrying a big bag—a photographer?—squint in her direction, as if trying to make out her face, and she wanted to take off, but a mom was sauntering across the crosswalk holding a toddler and pushing a stroller, stopping every two feet to correct the stroller from veering. Just as the man started walking her way, the crosswalk cleared and she took off, praying he wouldn't alert anyone.

And now here she was. Out of Pineburg, with no cars around. She had no idea where she was, but neither would anyone else. She looked at her watch. It was 12:46. Twenty minutes since she left. Long enough for someone to have noticed her absence.

She set Shannon's navigation system for Creek Trail, the road between

I-66 and Miracle Creek she'd driven back and forth all last summer. It was somewhat out of the way, but it was important to get on a road she knew. Plus, no one would search for her there; even if the police guessed she was headed to Miracle Creek, they'd figure she'd take the direct route.

Creek Trail was a winding country road—barely two lanes of pot-holed asphalt lined by trees so thick they formed a protective covering high above, the trees reaching sixty, seventy feet. A tree-tunnel roller coaster, Henry had called it. It was strange, being on this road. The last time she'd driven here was, of course, on the day of the explosion, a day just like today—a sunny day following torrential rain, with swaths of sunlight slashing through the slits in the canopy of leaves overhead and pools of mud splashing up into tear-shaped stains on the car windows. Which meant that the last time she'd made that turn, Henry had been alive. This thought—Henry sitting and talking behind her, their breaths commingling, her lungs taking in the air expelled from Henry's—made her grip the steering wheel harder, sending her knuckles spiking up.

A bright yellow sign with a U-shaped arrow came into view, warning cars of the hairpin turn—Henry's favorite—ahead. On the morning of the explosion, suffering from a throbbing headache (she couldn't sleep after the CPS visit the previous night), she'd said right at this spot how much she hated this road, how these curves made her nauseated. He'd laughed and said, "But it's fun—it's a tree-tunnel roller coaster!" The high pitch of his laughter had pierced her temples, and she'd wanted to smack him. She'd said in a frosty tone how insensitive he was being, and he should practice saying out loud, "I'm sorry you're feeling sick—can I do anything to help?" He'd said, "I'm sorry, Mommy. Can I help?" and she'd said, "No. It's 'I'm sorry *you're feeling sick*—can I *do anything* to help?' Try again." She'd made him repeat her exact wording twenty times in a row, starting over whenever he got even one word wrong, his voice quivering more and more each time she made him try again.

The thing was, there was nothing magical about her wording, no functional difference between his words and hers. She'd only wanted to torture him, bit by bit, as payback for her frustration. But why? That day, she'd been convinced he was still (after four years of social-skills therapy!)

not reading social cues. But here, away from the moment, away from *him*, it occurred to her how she could as easily have interpreted his laughter as him trying to lift her spirits or just being playful, like any normal eight-year-old boy dealing with his crabby mom. In fact, his labeling the road a "tree-tunnel roller coaster" had been downright creative—why hadn't she seen that? Was it possible that everything she'd regarded as a remnant of autism was nothing more than the immaturity inherent in kids, the kind that mothers could find either annoying or adorable depending on their mood, except that Elizabeth—because of Henry's history, because she was so damned tired all the time—found everything he did irritating?

A squirrel ran out, and she veered, easily avoiding it. She was used to critters here—she'd seen at least one a day last summer. In fact, a deer around this spot was what had prompted her decision to quit HBOT only hours before the explosion. She'd been driving home after the morning dive, distracted with thoughts about the protesters' threats and her fight with Kitt, and she saw the deer too late and braked off the road into a rock, messing up the car's alignment. Her car felt wobbly, and after she dropped off Henry at camp, she tried to figure out when she had time to take the car in, especially since she'd spent two hours researching HBOT fires from the protesters' flyer before concluding that Pak's rules (all-cotton clothing, no paper, no metals) were sufficient to prevent similar accidents. She had looked up at her schedule on the wall for that day:

7:30	Leave for HBOT (H breakfast in car)
9–10:15	HBOT
11–3	Camp (get groceries, make dinner for H)
3:15–4:15	Speech
4:30–5	Eye-tracking exercises
5–5:30	Emotion ID homework
5:30	Leave for HBOT (H dinner in car)
6:45–8:15	HBOT
9–9:45	Home, sauna, shower

Looking for a break in the schedule, it occurred to her for the first time how exhausting this must be for Henry, even more than for her. She couldn't remember the last time he'd actually eaten at a table, not in the car on the way to or from one therapy or another. Everything from speech and OT to interactive metronome and neurofeedback: every waking hour packed with practicing speech fluency, handwriting, sustained eye contact—nonstop work on things that were hard for him. Henry never complained, though. Just did what he was told, making progress day by day. And she'd never seen how amazing that was for a kid because she'd been too busy seething with self-pity and resentment at him for not being the child she'd wanted: an easygoing kid who loved cuddling, with good grades and friends constantly calling for playdates. She'd blamed Henry for having autism, for the crying and researching and driving that came with it. And the hurting.

She looked up again and imagined tomorrow's schedule with nothing but *9:30–3:30 Camp* on it. A day with no rushing, no running late, no yelling at Henry to please, for the love of God, stop being spacey and move faster. A day when she could do nothing for an hour, maybe nap or watch TV, and more important, when Henry could play games or ride a bike. Wasn't that what the protesters and Kitt were saying he needed? She wrote on her notepad *NO MORE HBOT!* and underlined it so hard the pen broke through the paper. Circling those words, she felt every organ in her body become buoyed, suspended in a glorious weightless state, and she knew: she needed to stop. Stop the therapies, the treatments, all the running around. Stop the hating, the blaming, the hurting.

The rest of the afternoon, she spent in giddiness. She called Henry's speech therapist and canceled that day's session (and a bonus: she'd called in time to avoid the two-hour-notice penalty fee). She picked up Henry at the regular camp dismissal time with the other kids for maybe the third time ever. They came straight home, and instead of coaching him through vision-therapy and social-skills homework, she let him plop down on the sofa with a bowl of organic coconut-milk ice cream and watch whatever show he wanted (within reason: Discovery and National Geographic channels only) while she looked up cancellation policies on the websites of all the therapists he went to—there were so many!—and sent e-mail after e-mail giving the required notice.

Miracle Submarine was the only problem. She'd gotten a discount for prepaying for forty dives upfront, and Pak's "Regulations and Policies" document said nothing about refunds. What's more, there was a full penalty for same-day cancellations. A hundred bucks, down the drain. She hated that (wasting money was her pet peeve). It wasn't enough to change her mind, but it rankled her, deflated her bubble of excitement about her stop-everything decision, which was what led to Mistake #1, the first in the series of her decisions and actions that led to Henry's death: calling Pak (instead of e-mailing) to try to work out a deal, maybe by finding someone to take over their contract for at least a partial refund. Strangely, though, when she called the barn phone, no one answered and the usual answering machine didn't pick up. She hung up and was about to try Pak's cell when her phone rang.

If she'd looked at caller ID, she wouldn't have answered. But she didn't (Mistake #2). She assumed it was Pak returning her missed call and answered, "Hey, Pak, I'm so glad I caught you. I'm—" at which point Kitt interrupted and said, "Elizabeth, it's me. Listen—" at which point *she* said, "Kitt, I really can't talk right now," and went to hang up but Kitt said, "Wait, please. I know you're mad, but it wasn't me. I didn't call CPS. I know you don't believe me, so I spent all day online and calling people, and I found out. I know who it is."

Elizabeth thought about pretending not to have heard and hanging up, but her curiosity got the better of her, so—Mistake #3—she stayed on the line and listened to Kitt go on and on about how she cross-referenced every autism chat board and managed to find a protester who disapproved of the group's growing militancy and how she got her password to their message board and, voilà, there it was, a treasure trove of threads by ProudAutismMom complaining about Elizabeth's dangerous "so-called treatments," planning protests at Miracle Submarine and, finally, the smoking gun, bragging about her call to CPS last week.

Elizabeth listened to it all, didn't say a word, and when Kitt finished, curtly thanked her, hung up, and went back to the special treat she'd been making for dinner, Henry's favorite—"pizza" with fake "cheese" (grated cauliflower) on homemade coconut-flour crust. But putting a slice on the fancy china she'd laid out for their sit-down dinner, her hands shook with anger, with hatred. She knew that woman hated her. But an entire group talking about her behind her back and planning to bring her down—it burned her. Humiliated her. She pictured that silver-haired woman spewing venom, reporting her "abuse" to CPS, not caring how that might ruin her life or Henry's, gloating that she'd stop Elizabeth no matter what. What would that woman think when Elizabeth didn't show up tonight? Would she bring out the champagne? Pop the cork and toast to the group's success in slaying an evil child abuser?

No. She couldn't not show up tonight. She couldn't let that hateful, smug, so-called ProudAutismMom think that she'd won. She couldn't give that bully the satisfaction of thinking she'd been shamed into hiding. And it was more than that. Now that the call with Kitt had popped her bubble of impulsivity for good and she was no longer giddy, she could see: her canceling everything left and right on a moment's whim, without consulting any of Henry's teachers—it was rash, irresponsible, downright cocky. And canceling HBOT tonight, with no way of getting any money back—what sense did that make? It wasn't as if HBOT was harmful. Since she'd already paid the hundred bucks, why not do one more dive? Finish out the day, endure the driving one more time, which, knowing it was her last, might heighten her anticipation and bring closure. She could even sit out the dive, ask the others to supervise—Kitt had done that once when she was sick—and go to the creek to really mull things over in total peace and make sure she was making the right decision. And best of all, she'd pass by that silver-haired woman. She'd tell her she knew all about her plans, the CPS call, and if she didn't stop, *she'd* file a complaint against *her* for harassment.

Elizabeth looked at the place setting for two already on the table, the crystal glass next to the chilled wine, and slid the serving spatula under the pizza slice on Henry's plate. For the next year, every night when she lay down for sleep or sometimes when she woke up in the morning, she'd close her eyes and visualize a parallel-world version of herself doing what she should've done in this moment: shake her head, scold herself not to let this stupid woman she'd never see again affect her so much, leave the pizza on the plate, and call Henry to dinner. In this alternate universe, after dinner and wine at home, she'd be curling up with Henry on the sofa marathon-watching *Planet Earth* when Teresa would call about the fire, and she'd cry for her friends and kiss Henry's head and thank God she'd decided to stop—and just today!—and months later, driving back from Ruth Weiss's murder trial, she'd shudder to think how she almost went to that last dive just to spite that woman.

But in this reality, the one she was stuck in, she didn't leave the pizza on the plate. She kept it on the spatula and—Mistake #4, the Biggest Mistake, the irrevocable act that sealed Henry's fate, which she'd regret and relive every day of her life, every hour of every day, every minute of every hour, over and over for as long as she lived—she lifted the pizza off the fancy plate and moved it to a paper plate for the car and called out, "Henry, put your shoes on. We're going for one last submarine ride." Throwing everything in the car, she felt a pang, thinking of the beautiful table settings, the lights sparkling off the crystals, and she was tempted to turn around right there and go inside, but that woman's smug smile and stupid silver bob popped up in her mind, taunting her, and she didn't. She swallowed, told Henry to hurry, and tried to think of tomorrow. Tomorrow, everything would change.

In the meantime, though, she tried to make up for it. She brought wine and chocolates to have by the creek—she'd be too exhausted by 9:30 when she got home for her planned celebratory drink, and she'd be damned if she let those despicable protesters ruin everything. She usually didn't let Henry watch *Barney*—"junk food for your brain," she said, and always had him sit away from the DVD-screen porthole—but as a treat, she arranged for Henry to sit by TJ and watch it. She asked Matt to help Henry, but Matt seemed annoyed and she didn't want to impose too much, so she crawled in and set everything up, hooking up his oxygen hose to the spigot and putting on his helmet. She told Henry to be good, and she wanted to kiss his cheek and tousle his hair, but his helmet was already on, so she crawled out and walked away. That was the last time she saw Henry alive.

Ten minutes later, sitting by the creek and finally sipping wine, she thought of Henry's reaction when she said she was sitting out this dive. He was in the helmet he hated—he gagged and said the ring around his neck choked him—and yet his whole face relaxed. He was happy. Relieved. To be free for an hour from her, the mother who was never satisfied, the mother who constantly nagged. She gulped more wine, felt the cool acidity sting then soothe her roughened throat, and she thought how she wanted to rip that helmet off as soon as he came out, how she'd wrap her arms around him and tell him she loved him and she missed him, and she'd laugh and say yes, she knew it was silly to miss him when they were apart for just an hour, but she still did.

Alcohol gushed through her arteries, infusing her pores with warmth, her fingers tingling as if thawing from the inside, and she looked up at the sky, darkening into a dusky violet. Her eyes focused on a puffy cottonball of a cloud, a perfect white like whipped frosting, and she thought how tomorrow, she could bake cupcakes for breakfast. When Henry asked what that was for, she'd laugh and say they were celebrating. She'd say she knew she didn't show it often, maybe ever, but she treasured him, adored him, and it was that love and the accompanying worry that made her so crazy, and they'd have a new life with much less craziness. Not a perfect life, because nothing and nobody could be perfect, but that was okay because she had him and he had her. And maybe she'd take frosting in her finger and dab it on his nose to be silly, and he'd smile—that huge, little-kid smile of his with the gap in his top teeth, just a sliver of white where the new tooth was growing in—and she'd kiss his cheek, not just peck but really squish her lips into his puffy cheek and squeeze him in her arms and savor the deliciousness for as long as he'd let her.

○

NONE OF THAT happened, of course. No cupcake, no kisses, no new tooth. Instead, she identified her son's corpse, picked out a coffin and gravestone, was arrested for his murder, read op-eds debating whether she belonged in a nuthouse or on death row, and now she was driving a stolen car toward the town where he'd been burned alive because of her.

That was the crazy thing, that it was *she*—with her pride and hatred and indecision and miserliness—who'd caused Henry's death. Had she really thought she could claim victory over the protesters by returning for one more dive? And the no-refund hundred dollars she'd prepaid—had her son really died over a hundred bucks? And when she got there and found out the protesters weren't there anymore, and what's more, the sessions were delayed *and* there was no AC, why hadn't she left right then? And later still, when she found the cigarettes and matches—Smoking! Near pure oxygen!—she should've immediately thought of fire. Was it the alcohol she'd already had, or the giddiness of triumph in discovering that the protesters were locked up? She'd warned Pak earlier how dangerous those women were, so why did she assume the most they'd do was start a fire when everyone was gone? Why did she underestimate the lengths to which they might go for their cause?

Elizabeth pulled over and stopped. None of it mattered. There was no parallel universe to teleport to, no time machine to take her back. All this week, when things got too bleak and she wanted everything to end, she'd tried to keep herself going with thoughts of vengeance for Henry, with the anticipation of seeing Shannon take down that vile woman, Ruth Weiss. Now that Shannon was refusing to go after the protesters, what was left to hope for?

She pressed the button that put the top down on Shannon's car. It was funny—back in the courthouse, she'd wished she had her own car, but now she realized how much better a convertible would be. Less risk of anything going wrong. She thought it'd be cooler here, in the higher elevation of the hills that divided Miracle Creek from Pineburg, but the humidity overtook her quickly with the top down. She unlatched her seat belt and debated whether to move her seat forward or back; on the one hand, moving too close to the airbag was dangerous, but on the other hand, sitting too far back heightened the chance of falling out in a crash. She decided to keep her seat where it was and pulled the seat belt back on—she hated the dinging noise cars made when seat belts were off.

It was all done, it was time to go, but she hesitated. There were so many things she hadn't considered. What if this didn't work? Or what if it did, and Shannon kept on trying to clear her name and brought up that horrible insinuation about Victor and the scratches? What if Abe decided to go after Pak in her absence? Should she—

Elizabeth shut her eyes tight and shook her head. She needed to stop this nonsense and effing *act* already. The fact was, she was a coward. She was an inhibited ball of indecision who didn't trust her instincts and hid her cowardice under a guise of deliberation. This was the real reason Henry was dead: she knew she should stop HBOT but she was afraid to, and she waited as always to make sure she didn't forget anything, make her stupid pro/con list, think of every contingency. She hurt her own son, abused him and made him believe she hated him, and forced him into a chamber to burn while she sipped wine and popped bonbons in her mouth. It was time to unpause her plan and do what she knew she had to do, what she'd known for the last *year* she had to do, with no pros or cons, no analysis, no hesitation.

Elizabeth clutched the steering wheel and started driving. Her fingers pulsed against the leather as she turned to keep the car from veering into the guardrail and trees lining the road. The bright yellow CAUTION sign came into view, which meant the spot was just up ahead. The first time she drove by it, she'd felt that strange pull, like when you stand near a cliff's edge and have the urge to jump. She'd seen the curve, the sudden clearing of trees, the guardrail crumpled and bent down, almost like a ramp into empty space, and she'd thought how easy it'd be to let go, just go straight and fly into the sky.

She slowed down to turn with the road, and saw it straight ahead. She was afraid they'd have fixed it by now, but it was still there. The bent spot in the guardrail. The gray metal crushed flat like a ramp. A bright beam of sun hit it like a spotlight, as if summoning her, wooing her. She pressed the button to unbuckle her seat belt, and she felt her heart pounding in her wrists, on the undersides of her knees, against her skull. She pushed the accelerator, all the way down. She saw it then. Beyond the curve, a round fluffy cloud with a dark spot in the middle, like the one she'd pointed out to Henry last summer and he'd laughed and said, "It looks like my mouth, with my missing tooth!" and she'd laughed back, amazed—he was right, it *did* look like his mouth—and lifted him up in the air, hugging him tight and kissing the dimple on his cheek.

In front of the cloud, the heat and sunlight created undulating waves in the air. Like an invisible curtain in the sky—inviting her, welcoming her, to flight, to fire. She leaned forward, and as the tires thunked onto the flattened guardrail, she saw the bright, beautiful valley below, shimmering in the sunlight, like a mirage.

PAK

H E HATED WAITING. Whether for the water to boil or a meeting to start, waiting meant being dependent on something outside his control, and rarely had that been as true as today, being stuck at home with no car, no phone, and no idea where Young was. After he and Mary finished burning everything, there was nothing to do, so they'd sat, waiting and drinking barley tea. Or rather, he had. Mary had poured herself some, too, but she hadn't drunk any. She stared at the mug as if at a TV screen, blowing once in a while, making ripples in the amber liquid, and he thought about saying it wasn't hot, hadn't been for an hour, but he said nothing. He understood her need to break the oppressiveness of waiting, just waiting, and he wished he could pace. That was the thing—one of the many things—about being paralyzed: you couldn't exactly wheel yourself back and forth to satisfy the achy craving for motion you got during stifling periods of stillness like this.

When Young finally walked in at 2:30, a surge of relief engulfed him. Relief that she'd returned, and alone, not with the police. (He'd told Mary not to be afraid, Young would never report them, but at the sight of her, he realized he hadn't been quite sure of that.) "Yuh-bo, where have you been?" he said.

She didn't answer him, didn't even look at him, just sat with a cold steadiness that sent panic tingling in his chest.

"Yuh-bo," he said, "we've been worried. Did you see anyone? Talk to anyone?"

She looked at him then. If she'd looked hurt or scared, he could've dealt with that. If she'd yelled, furious and hysterical—that, he'd prepared for. But this woman with a blank face like a mannequin—her features austere, her mouth unmoving—was not his wife of twenty years. It scared him, seeing this face he knew so well and yet didn't recognize.

"Tell me everything," she said, her voice like her face: flat, with none of the singsong up-and-down of emotion that, now it was gone, he realized formed its essence.

He swallowed and forced composure into his voice. "You already know everything. You overheard me telling Mary before you ran off. Where did you go?"

Young didn't answer, didn't seem to even hear his question. She fixed her eyes on his, and he felt heat, like a laser beam cutting into his eyes, his brain. "You need to look me in the eye and tell me everything. The truth this time."

He was hoping she'd talk first, that she'd unload her anger by saying exactly what she'd heard, so he could tailor his story. But it was clear. She wasn't going to talk. He nodded and put his hands on the table—the same spot where, just last night, she'd thrown the bag from the shed and he'd been forced to create plausible-sounding stories on the spot. After this morning, she had to be thinking those were all lies. He had to start there.

"I lied last night," he said. "The Seoul listings weren't for my brother. It was for us, to move to after the fire. I'm sorry I lied. I wanted to protect you."

He expected her to soften at this show of vulnerability and atonement. But if anything, her eyes hardened, her pupils contracting into pinpoints of pure black, making him feel like a criminal. He reminded himself that this was his goal, for her to believe he was the villain, and continued with the mix of truth and lies he'd decided on. He said he called a Realtor and realized they couldn't afford to move back. He said he decided on arson to get the needed money and called (on someone else's phone, in case of an investigation) to verify the arson provision.

The part about the protesters was easier—truth always was—and he told her about that day: his frustration with the police for doing nothing, leading to his balloon power-outage plan; his temporary relief after its success, but that woman calling and threatening to return and cause more trouble; his decision to plant a cigarette exactly where their flyer said, to frame them and get them into real trouble so they'd stay away for good.

A few times, he tried to catch Mary's eyes to warn her not to contradict him, but her gaze was still fixed on the full tea mug. When he was done talking, there was a long silence before Young said, "There's nothing you left out? That's really the whole truth?" Her face was composed, but there was pleading in her voice, a core of sadness wrapped by desperate hope, and he wished he could say of course not, she knew him, knew he wasn't a man who'd endanger people's lives for money.

But he didn't. Some things were more important than honesty, even with your wife. He said, "Yes, it's the whole truth," and told himself it was for her own good. If she knew the real truth, the entire truth, that would devastate her. He had to protect her. That was his job, his highest duty, as head of the family: protect his family, no matter what. Even if that meant having the woman he loved consider him a callous criminal. Besides, he *was* responsible. He'd created the plan to frame the protesters for attempted arson. That day, as he lit the cigarette, watching the smoke swirl up from the red tip, his heart had thudded wildly, nervously, picturing pure oxygen flowing mere centimeters away, but he'd still gone ahead, sure he'd thought of everything and nothing would go wrong. Hubris. The worst sin.

Young blinked—rapidly, as if trying not to cry—and said, "So it was all you? You did everything with no help, no involvement from anyone else?"

He forced himself to keep his eyes focused on Young. "Yes. No one else knew. I knew what I was doing was dangerous, and I didn't want anyone involved. Everything, I did alone."

"You took Matt's phone and called the insurance company?"

"Yes," he said.

"You called the Realtor about Seoul?"

"Yes."

"You hid the listings in the shed?"

He nodded.

"You bought Camels and hid them in the tin case?"

Pak nodded, kept nodding as the questions kept coming with shorter pauses between, feeling like one of those bobblehead dolls. It made him nervous, her asking only about the things he'd lied about. And asking leading questions, like Shannon in court—was she goading him into a trap?

"And you meant for the cigarette to actually start a fire? You were really trying to get insurance, not just get the protesters in trouble?"

He felt dizzy, like he'd fallen underwater and he couldn't figure out which way was up. "Yes," he managed to say. Softly. Barely audible, even to him.

Young closed her eyes, her face pale and still, and he thought of a corpse. Without opening her eyes, she said, "I came back just now, thinking maybe, just maybe, you'd be honest with me. That's why I didn't tell you what I found out. I wanted to give you a chance to tell me yourself. I don't know whether to be impressed or upset that you've put so much effort into making up such a complicated story to deceive me."

All the air seemed to go out of the room. He breathed in and tried to think. What did she find out? What could she know? She was bluffing, had to be. She had suspicions, that was all, and he needed to maintain his stance. Silence and denial. "I don't know what you're talking about. I've confessed everything. What more do you want from me?"

She opened her eyes. Slowly, as if they were heavy curtains being raised one millimeter at a time for dramatic effect. She looked at him. "The truth," she said. "I want the truth."

"I've given you the truth." He tried to sound indignant, but his words sounded weak and distant, as if someone said them far away, and what came through his lips was an echo.

Young narrowed her eyes, as if trying to decide something. Finally, she said, "Abe found the person who took the insurance call."

Pak felt burning in his eyes, and he fought his need to blink, to look away.

"The caller spoke perfect English, no accent. It couldn't have been you."

Thoughts whirred in panicky speed, but he forced himself to stay calm. Denial. He had to stick to that. "Obviously, this person's wrong. You can't expect someone on hundreds of calls a day to remember all the voices a year later."

Young put something on the table. "I went to see the Realtor, from the Seoul listings. She remembered them very well. She said it's unusual for people to move back to Korea, and even more unusual for a young girl to be calling."

Pak forced himself to keep his eyes on Young, to intensify the indignation in his voice. "That's why you think I'm lying? A few strangers misremembering voices from a year ago?"

Young didn't answer, didn't raise her voice to match his. In that same gratingly calm tone, she said, "Last night, when I showed you the listings, you looked so surprised. I thought you were surprised I'd found your hiding place, but that wasn't it. You'd never seen those listings before." Pak shook his head, but she kept talking. "And the tin case, too."

"Now, you know that was mine. You handed it to me yourself in Baltimore, and I—"

"And you put it with the rest of the pile for the Kangs and gave it to Mary to deliver." Pak felt fear in his bowels, crawling and gnawing. He'd never told her that. How did she know?

As if in answer, she said, "I called them today. Mr. Kang remembered Mary dropping everything off and said how fortunate we are to have such a helpful daughter." Young glanced at Mary. "Of course, they didn't know she kept the tin case with the cigarettes for herself. No one did. Until last night, you thought that case was in Baltimore."

Bitter saliva slithered up his throat, and he swallowed. "I *did* give Mary the pile for the Kangs, that's true. But I took out the case first. I'm the one who put it in the shed."

"That's not true," Young said with an absolute certainty that churned his stomach. If she was bluffing, she was giving the performance of her life. But how could she *know*, with no doubts? He said, "You don't know that. You're guessing, and you're wrong."

Young turned to Mary. "Teresa heard you talking on the phone in the shed." Mary kept staring at the tea, gripping the mug so tightly he thought it might break. "I know you sent the listings to a friend's house. I know you used your father's ATM card. I know you hid everything in the bottom box in the shed." Young shifted her gaze to Pak. "I know," she said.

He wanted to keep denying, but too many specifics were piling up. He had to admit some things, maintain credibility. "All right, the listings were hers. She wanted to move back to Seoul, and she got them to show me. So now she's feeling guilty, like that caused everything, when *I'm* the one who came up with the arson plan. So I wanted to take the blame for everything, try to remove her from this completely. Can you understand that?"

"I understand wanting to take all the blame, but you can't. I know you. You'd never start a fire around your patients, no matter how small or contained. You're too careful."

He had to keep talking to keep her from saying the words he was terrified she'd say. "I wish you were right, but I *did* do it. You have to accept that. I don't know what you think *really* happened, but you seem to think Mary was involved somehow. But you heard me confessing to her this morning, how shocked she was. We didn't know you were there. We weren't staging our conversation."

"No, I don't think you were. I believe you were telling her the truth."

"So you know I did everything. The cigarette, matches, I mean, what more—"

"I thought about it. A lot," Young said. "Everything you said you did, over and over. Picking the spot, gathering sticks, building the mound, putting the matches in, the cigarette on top—so much detail about every aspect of setting the fire. Except one thing."

He didn't say anything, couldn't. Couldn't breathe.

"The most important thing. And I kept thinking, why would he leave that out?"

He shook his head. "I don't know what you're talking about."

"I'm talking about actually starting the fire."

"Of course I did. I lit the cigarette," he said, but the familiar memory rushed to him. His panic that night when the protesters called, taunting him that they'd be back and they wouldn't stop. Seeing their flyer and getting the idea to make it look like they tried to burn down his business. Remembering that hollow tree stump in the woods he'd come across, the used cigarettes and matches he'd seen there. Running to it, retrieving the fullest matchbook and longest cigarette among the discarded bunch. Building the mound. Lighting the cigarette, letting it burn for a minute. Then putting his gloved finger on the tip, putting it out.

As if she could see into his mind, Young said, "You lit it but you put it out. You wanted the police to find it just like that—make it look like the protesters *tried* to start a fire but the cigarette went out too early and it failed. You didn't start the fire. You never intended to."

He felt fear—so hot it felt cold—unfurl across his body in strands, overtaking it. "That makes no sense. Why would I confess to doing something I didn't do?"

"As a decoy," she said. "To keep my focus away from where you're afraid it might go if I keep digging."

He breathed. Swallowed.

"I know the truth," she said. So quietly he strained to hear. "Have the decency to be honest with me. Don't make me say it."

"What do you know?" he said. "What do you *think* you know?"

Young blinked and turned toward Mary. Her composure broke then, her face grimaced in pain. He hadn't been sure until that moment. But the way she looked at their daughter—so tenderly, with all the sadness of the world—he knew. She'd figured everything out.

Before he could do anything, before he could tell her to stop, don't say anything, don't say those devastating words and make them real, Young reached out to Mary's face and brushed away her tears. Gently, delicately, like she was ironing silk.

"I know it was you," his wife said to their daughter. "I know you set the fire."

MARY

A T 8:07 P.M. ON AUGUST 26, 2008, eighteen minutes before the explosion, Mary was leaning against a weeping willow after having run for a minute straight through the woods. After Janine threw cigarettes, matches, and a crumpled note at her, Mary had said in the calmest tone she could manage, "I don't know what you're talking about," pivoted away from her, and walked in the opposite direction. One foot, then the other, focusing on keeping her pace steady, fighting her instinct to run and scream—forcing her nails into her palms and pressing her tongue between her teeth, applying more and more pressure until *just* to that point of breaking through and drawing blood. After fifty steps (she'd counted), she could no longer stand it and started running, the fastest she could—muscles burning in her calves, tears blurring her vision—until she felt dizzy and her legs went rubbery, and she crumpled against the tree and cried.

Whore, Janine had called her. Stalking slut. "You can bat your eyes and twirl your hair and act like some innocent girl, but let's be honest, we both know what you were doing," she'd said. Sitting here, away from Janine—the role model her father had invoked as who she should aspire to be, why he'd wanted her educated in America—it was so easy to think of everything she could, *should*, have said. It was Matt who brought cigarettes and got them smoking. Matt who started writing notes to meet up. And yes, she'd been lonely here and grateful for his company, but seduce? *Steal?* This man who'd pretended to be a caring friend before exposing his true motives, who held her down and pushed his tongue into her mouth as she tried to scream out, who got on top of her and forced her hand inside his pants, wrapping it around himself so hard it hurt, using it like an object to pump up and down, up and down?

But she didn't say anything. Just stood there, listening to Janine's ugly words, letting them penetrate her skin and burrow into her brain, spreading their tendrils and taking root. And now, even as she told herself that Janine was wrong, that Matt was the one at fault here and she the victim, a voice inside her whispered, hadn't she liked the attention? Hadn't she noticed him staring from time to time and felt the satisfaction of knowing she was desirable, perhaps even more so than Janine? And on her birthday, hadn't she worn a sexy outfit, asked him to drink with her, and when he started kissing her—softly, romantically, exactly how she'd imagined her first real kiss should be—hadn't she kissed him back, and for a moment, before the night's dark turn, hadn't she imagined a fairy-tale ending with flashes of *I love you*, peering into eyes, and other cringe-inducing clichés she couldn't bear to think about now?

She'd thought the humiliation of her birthday night had killed that pathetically naïve hope, but Matt's weeklong campaign of writing multiple daily notes and following her to SAT class had somehow revived it. She'd agreed to meet him, and after sneaking in chugs of her father's rice grain alcohol for courage and walking to the creek, there had been a microsecond when a part of her—the tiniest speck in a nauseatingly

Disney-fied subsection of her brain—had pictured Matt standing by the creek, waiting to declare love, to confess his desperate inability to live without her, to explain his behavior on her birthday night as a never-to-be-repeated moment of insanity driven by inebriation mixed with passion. Right then, with the soju sloshing in her stomach, her heart thumping in anticipation—that's when she'd seen Janine. The shock of that moment, the mortifying realization that everything had been a setup for his *wife* to tell her off for him! Thinking about it now, pressing her forehead against the willow tree bark to stop the pain behind her eyes from spreading, shame frothed through her, filling and threatening to burst every organ, and she wished she could disappear, just run away and never face Matt or Janine again.

She heard a noise then. A distant knocking noise from the direction of her house. Janine. It had to be Janine knocking for her parents, to complain about their slutty daughter seducing and stalking her virtuous husband. She imagined them at the door, horror overtaking their faces as Janine showed them her notes and the cigarettes, depicting her as a pathetic girl sexually obsessed with her husband. Shame and fear flashed through her again at this thought, but something else, too. Anger. Anger at Matt, the man who'd taken her loneliness and twisted it into something sick, then lied to his wife about it. Anger at Janine, the woman who'd been so quick to assume her husband's innocence without even stopping for Mary's side of the story. Anger at her parents, who'd ripped her away from her home, her friends, and put her in this situation. Most of all, anger at herself that she'd let all this happen without fighting back. No. No more. She stood and marched toward her house. She would not let them judge her without hearing everything Matt had done.

It was then—walking to her house, her anger at her own past impotence mixing with her shame, the combination of that and her headache overpowering her—that she saw it: a small white stick by the back of the barn. A cigarette. Positioned perfectly to start a fire that would burn down the barn and destroy Miracle Submarine. A fire like the one she'd dreamed of just a week ago.

• • •

THE IDEA HAD COME on her seventeenth birthday. Right after Matt ran off after their night of drinking ended with The Thing (she couldn't bear to label it), she'd retreated to her safe place amid the weeping willows, half sitting, half lying against a rock, chain-smoking cigarettes, trying to keep from crying or throwing up.

After she finished her third or fourth cigarette, she dropped it and reached for another. She was focusing on lighting the next one as quickly as possible—she needed the smoke to neutralize the smell lingering in her nostrils, a combination of the sickly sweetness of peach schnapps and the pungent fishiness of semen—while simultaneously keeping her head and torso absolutely still to keep the world from spinning and the alcoholic sludge in her stomach from lurching. But her fingers were still shaking and it was hard to see without moving her head, and as she lit the match, she dropped it.

The fire didn't catch—it landed close to the water and fizzed out right away—but moving her eyes down to the ground, Mary noticed flames a few feet away; apparently, a cigarette she'd dropped earlier had landed on a pile of leaves. She knew she should stomp it out right away, but something stopped her. She crouched before the fire and watched it—orange, blue, and black waves whirling and growing—and remembered Matt's teeth shoving against her lips, and his tongue, jabbing her lips open, forcing her *No* down her throat. She remembered him crushing her fingers onto his penis, using her hand like an object to pump and squeeze, up and down, each pump accompanied by a grunt that stank of fermented peach and made her cough into his tongue, and the lukewarm, viscous spurt of semen that clung even after she scrubbed her hand in the creek until it turned bright red, the scratch mark from his zipper a white line across her hand. She remembered how stupid she'd been with her SAT classmates earlier. After they all said they couldn't make her birthday dinner, she said it was no problem, and actually, she was meeting up with a guy later anyway, a *doctor*, and when they teased her, said he sounded like an old perv who was just after sex, she said he was a gentleman, a friend who cared and listened to her problems and was going through a hard time himself. They'd laughed, called her naïve, and they'd been right.

She poured the rest of the schnapps onto the fire. Right when it hit, the flames whooshed, and she felt wild happiness that the flames would reach her, consume her, and destroy everything. Matt, her friends, her parents, her life. Gone.

The fire died out almost immediately, its pre-death expansion lasting a second, and she made sure it was completely out before leaving. But later that night, sleeping in the chamber, she'd dreamed of the fire, the flames from the willow grove spreading and engulfing the barn to destroy the business that kept them tied to this town she hated, to the man she wished would disappear. She didn't think about it again after she woke up—she'd tried to wipe her mind clear of that night, had tried to keep busy with SAT studies and research into college and housing options in Seoul—but now, almost a week later, here it was, right next to the barn: a cigarette sticking out of a pyre of twigs and dried leaves, positioned precisely in the middle of an open book of matches. It felt like a gift to her, an offering. As if fate were calling to her, inviting her to light the cigarette, telling her to come on, go ahead, this was exactly what she needed right now, mere minutes after the humiliation of Matt's wife screaming that she was a stalker and a whore, as shame and anger were searing her insides. Just burn it down and destroy it.

She walked toward it. Slowly, cautiously, as if toward a mirage that might disappear. She crouched in front of the mound and reached her shaking hand to pick up the cigarette. Somewhere in the back of her mind, it occurred to her that it was charred, as if someone had lit it but it had gone out before the pyre caught on fire, but the question of who and why wouldn't come until later. After waking up in the hospital and for the next year of her life, she'd be consumed with it. But for now, she didn't care. It didn't matter. It only mattered that this cigarette was *meant* to be lit and the pyre meant to be in flames. She thought of the swoosh of the flames by the creek when the schnapps hit it, the warm comfort of the fire, and she wanted it again. Needed it.

She picked up the matchbook, tore a matchstick, and struck it. It lit, and she quickly placed the matchbook and cigarette in the middle of the mound. The matchbook caught fire in its entirety, and the cigarette burned, its tip a bright red. She felt a warmth deep in her chest, that same comfort, and she blew on the fire, gently, feeding the flames, encouraging the mound to catch, sending bits of ash from dried leaves floating lazily up the smoke. Her face grew hot, and she stayed until the entire mound was on fire, then she stood and backed away, step by step, watching the flames, willing them to get bigger, higher, hotter, to destroy this decrepit building and everything inside.

When she turned away to walk to her house, the magic of the moment, the surreal feeling of this not quite being real, zapped away. It was past 8:15, so the patients were all gone—and yes, the patient parking lot was empty, she checked, and besides, Janine had said the dive ended earlier—but what if her father was still in the barn, cleaning up? No, the barn was obviously empty as well; he always turned off the AC *after* cleaning, and the AC was off now, its loud fan silent, and the lights were off. Still, her heart thumped as she thought of what she'd done—arson, a crime, the police, jail, her parents—and she stopped, thought about going back and stomping out the fire before it got out of control.

"Meh-hee-yah. Meh-hee-yah!" Her mother's yell came from inside the house, obviously annoyed she couldn't find her. It felt like rocks hitting her in her chest, those caustic six syllables wrapped tight around a core of her mother's disapproval, and just like that, Mary was furious again, the calm that came from lighting the fire and walking away gone. She turned and ran.

She was almost to the shed—she desperately needed a smoke, right now—when she saw her father outside, dialing his phone. He looked up and said, "Oh, good, I was about to call you. I need your help." He put the phone to his ear and motioned for her to come. After a few seconds, he said into the phone, "You always think the worst of her, but she's here, helping me. And the batteries are under the house kitchen sink, but don't leave the patients. I'll send Mary to grab them." He turned and said to her, "Mary, go, right now. Take four D batteries to the barn," then said back into the phone, "I'll come in one minute and let the patients out. Remember not to say . . . Yuh-bo? Hello? Are you there? Yuh-bo!"

Patients. Let them out. Barn.

Those words whirled around her head like a cyclone, sending her spinning. She turned. Ran, as fast as her legs would move. Please, God, please let the fire have gone out. Let it have been a dream, a nightmare. Let her have misunderstood her father's words. How could there be patients in the barn? The last dive was over long ago, Janine confirmed it. The AC was off. The lights were off. The cars were gone. What was happening?

She couldn't breathe, she couldn't run anymore, the rice alcohol was creeping up and burning her throat and the ground was moving up and down like waves and she was going to fall and somewhere in the distance her mother was calling out her name, but she kept running. Approaching the barn, she saw: the lights were out. Parking lot, empty. AC, off. It was quiet, so quiet, she couldn't hear anything, except . . . oh God, there was noise coming from inside the barn, a faint sound like someone hammering, and from behind the barn, the crackle of flames, eating away at the wood. Smoke was rising from behind the barn, and when she turned the corner to face the back wall, she felt the fire, hot on her face, so hot she couldn't get closer even though her brain was screaming at her to get right up next to it, to throw herself on the wall and use her body to put out the fire.

She heard her mother's voice, calling her, saying "Meh-hee-yah." Quietly. Gently. She turned and saw her mother gaze at her, her unblinking eyes drinking her in as if she hadn't seen her in years. Just before the boom, before she felt herself lift up in the air, she saw her mother walking to her, her arms wide open. She wanted to run to her. To hug her and ask her to hold her tight and make everything okay again. The way she used to when she was a little girl, when her mother was her Um-ma.

YOUNG

A S SOON AS YOUNG SAID THE WORDS accusing her daughter of murder, Mary looked up and met her eyes, the scrunched wrinkles on her face relaxing into the smoothness of relief. Finally, the truth.

Pak broke the silence. "That's crazy."

Young didn't look at him, couldn't stop looking into her daughter's eyes and drinking in what she saw there: a need for her, a longing to connect, to confide. How long had it been since they'd had real intimacy, contact beyond the fleeting glances they exchanged while discussing the logistics of everyday life? It was strange, almost magical, how this connection changed everything. Even the difference in their language—Young and Pak speaking in Korean, with Mary responding in English, as always—which had felt awkward in the past, now added to their inti-macy, as if they'd created their own private language.

Pak said, "What exactly are you saying? You think we conspired? I set everything up and asked Mary to do the most dangerous part?"

"No," Young said. "I considered that, but the more I thought about it, the more I realized—you'd never start a fire with people inside. I know you. You could never be that callous with people's lives."

"But Mary could?"

"No. I *know* she'd never risk people's lives." She stroked Mary's face, just the gentlest touch to let her know she understood. "But if she thought the barn was empty, if she thought the dives were done and no one was inside . . ."

The creases remaining on Mary's face vanished altogether, and tears pooled in her eyes. Gratefulness that her mother knew and, more than that, understood. Forgave.

Young reached to wipe away Mary's tears. "That's why you kept say-ing how quiet it was. You kept repeating it after you woke up, and the doctors thought you were reliving the explosion, but that wasn't it at all. You were wondering how people could've been inside and the oxygen on when everything was off. You didn't know about the power outage."

"I'd been away all day," Mary said, her voice sounding crusty as if she hadn't spoken in days. "By the time I got back, the parking lot was empty. I was sure the dives were over. I thought the oxygen was off and the building was empty."

"Of course you did," Young said. "The earlier dive was delayed, so the lot was full and the last group had to park down the road. When the ear-lier patients left, the lot became empty. How could you have known?"

"I should've checked the other lot. I knew they parked there that morning, but . . ." Mary shook her head. "None of that matters. I set the fire. It wasn't an accident. I did it. I meant to do it. It's all my fault."

"Meh-hee-yah," Pak said. "Don't say that. It's not your fault—"

"Of course it's her fault," Young said. Pak looked at her, his mouth open in shock as if to say, How dare you say that? She said to Mary, "I'm not saying you intended for people to die, or even that you could've foreseen it. But your actions have consequences, and you're responsible for them. I know you know that. I've seen you, how tortured you've been, all your tears. It's been killing you, going to court, seeing how your choices have destroyed so many lives."

Mary nodded, a fresh wave of relief flooding her face at this acknowledgment of her culpability. Young understood—sometimes, when you were guilty of something, others' pretense that you weren't responsible was the unbearable part. It was infantilizing, demeaning.

"When I first woke up in the hospital," Mary said, "I thought maybe I imagined the whole thing. It wasn't that I didn't remember. I had a clear memory of that night—something happened earlier and I was really upset, more than I've ever been, and I was walking by the barn, and a cigarette and matches were right there. I didn't plan to do anything, but when I saw that, it was like . . . like fate, like that was exactly what I wanted to do right then, just burn it down and destroy it, and it felt so good when I started the fire. I stayed there watching it and feeding the flames and making sure the barn caught on fire." Mary looked at her. "But I was so confused because I didn't think the oxygen tank would explode when it's shut off, so I kept thinking, it must have been a dream, like the coma messed with my memory. And that made sense, because why would a cigarette have been right there?"

"So that's why you never came forward? You really didn't know?" Young said, careful to keep doubt out of her voice. She could see how much Mary wanted to believe this, that she'd honestly dismissed her memory as fake until Pak confirmed today that the cigarette was real and told her how it came to be there.

Mary looked away, toward a square of bright blue out their faux window. She breathed in deeply and looked at Pak, then Young, and smiled a sad little smile. "No, I knew that was"—she shook her head—"just me being stupid. I knew it really happened."

"So why did you not come forward?" Young said. "Why did you not tell me or your father right away?"

She bit her lip. "I was going to. The day after I woke up, when Abe came to visit. But before I could, you told me about Elizabeth, how they had all this proof she planned to kill Henry, and I thought, she must be the one. She built the mound of twigs. She put the cigarette and matches there. I figured she ran away after she lit it, so she wouldn't be nearby when the tank blew up, but the cigarette went out by accident before I found it, maybe a strong gust of wind. And it made me feel so much better, like I didn't *really* start the fire. Elizabeth did, *she's* the one to blame, and my relighting the cigarette was more a technicality, just allowing it to continue doing what Elizabeth meant for it to do."

Young said, "So that's how you made peace with her being on trial?"

Mary nodded. "I told myself she was guilty. She deserved it because she meant to do it and *would* have if the cigarette hadn't happened to go out. I figured, she probably didn't even realize anyone intervened at all. For all she knew, her plan worked, and everything that happened was what she planned. It made me feel less guilty, but then . . ." Mary closed her eyes and sighed.

"But then you saw her this week."

Mary nodded and opened her eyes. "It wasn't like what Abe said at all. There were so many questions at trial, and it occurred to me for the first time: What if she's not the one? What if someone else set everything up, and she had nothing to do with the fire?"

"So you didn't realize she might be innocent until this week?" This was what Young had guessed, hoped, but it was important to verify this, that her daughter hadn't hurt an innocent woman on purpose.

"No. Just yesterday, I started thinking it might be"—Mary bit her lip, shook her head—"some other person, but I still thought Elizabeth was the most likely one. But then this morning, Ap-bah told me it was him. That was the first time I knew it wasn't her."

"And you?" Young turned to Pak. "When did you realize it was Mary? How long have you been covering for her?"

"Yuh-bo, I thought it was Elizabeth. All this time, I was convinced she came across my setup and started the fire. But last night, when you showed me the stuff from the shed, I got so confused. I started getting suspicious, but I couldn't figure out how Mary could possibly fit into all this. It scared me, just thinking about it, so I covered for her. She saw the bag from the shed when she came in, and she told me everything this morning. That's when I told her that I left the cigarette, not Elizabeth. That's when you heard us."

Everything made sense now. All the pieces fit so elegantly. But what was the picture they formed? What was the solution?

As if in answer, Mary said, "I know I need to tell Abe everything. I almost did it earlier this week, in his office, but I kept thinking about the death penalty, and I was so scared, and I . . ." Mary's face contorted into a mass of shame and regret. Fear.

"Nothing will happen to you," Pak said. "I'll come forward if she's found guilty."

"No," Young said. "Mary needs to confess. Now. Elizabeth is innocent. She lost her child, and she's on trial for killing him. No one deserves that kind of pain."

Pak shook his head. "We're not talking about some innocent mother who's done no wrong. You don't know what I know about her. She may not have set the fire, but she—"

"I know what you're going to say. I know you overheard her saying she wants Henry to die, but I talked to Teresa, and she explained it. She didn't really mean that. They were just talking about feelings every mother has, feelings *I've* had—"

"That you want your child to die?"

Young sighed. "We all have thoughts that shame us." She took Mary's hand and knitted their fingers together. "I love you, and in the hospital, I ached, seeing you in pain. I would've changed places with you if I could. But in a way, I loved that time. For the first time in so long, you needed me and let me care for you and hold you without pushing me away, and I . . ." Young bit her lip. "I secretly wished you wouldn't get better and we could stay a little longer."

Mary closed her eyes, and pooled tears slid down her cheeks. Young grasped her hand tighter and continued. "And I don't know how many times we argued and, just for a minute, I wished you'd disappear from my life, and I'm sure you've thought the same about me. But if that were to actually happen, that'd be unbearable. And if someone were to discover those worst moments and blame me for my child's death . . . I don't know how I could live with myself." She looked at Pak. "That's what we're putting Elizabeth through. We have to end it. Now."

Pak wheeled away to the window. The cutout was above his head, so he couldn't look outside, but he sat there, facing the wall. After a minute, he said, "If we do this, we need to say I started the fire, alone. Mary wouldn't have done anything if I hadn't put the cigarette there. It's only right that I take the blame."

"No," Young said. "Abe will connect Mary to the cigarettes, the Seoul apartments—everything will come out. It's better to come clean now. It was an accident. He'll see that."

"You keep saying it was an accident," Mary said, "but it wasn't. I set the fire on purpose."

Young shook her head. "You didn't mean to hurt or kill anyone. You didn't plan anything. You started the fire on impulse, in the heat of the moment. I don't know if that matters in American law, but it does to me. It sounds human. Understanda—"

"Shhhh," Pak said. "Someone's here. I heard a car door."

Young rushed to peer out over Pak's head. "It's Abe."

"Remember, keep quiet for now. No one is to say anything," Pak said, but Young ignored him and opened the door. "Abe," she called out.

Abe didn't say anything, just kept walking until he was inside. His face was flushed, the tight coils of his hair beaded with sweat. He looked at each of them in turn.

"What is wrong?" Young said.

"It's Elizabeth," he said. "She's dead."

○

ELIZABETH. DEAD. But she just saw her, talked to her. How could she be dead? When? Where? Why? But she couldn't say anything, couldn't move.

"What happened?" Pak asked. His voice was shaky, sounded distant.

"A car accident. A few miles away. There's a curve with a broken guardrail, and the car went off the road. She was by herself. We think . . ." Abe paused. "It's early yet, but there are reasons to suspect suicide."

It was strange, how she could hear her own gasp and feel her knees buckle and know she was surprised, shocked even, and yet she wasn't. It was suicide, of course it was. The look on Elizabeth's face, the way her voice sounded—full of regret, yet resolute. In hindsight—and if she was being honest, even at the time—it was obvious.

"I saw her," Young said. "She said she was sorry. She asked me"—she peered at Pak—"please apologize to Pak." A look of shame coated his ashen face.

"What? When was this? Where?" Abe said.

"In the courthouse. Maybe 12:30."

"That's right around when she left. And if she apologized . . . that makes sense." Abe shook his head. "She had sort of a breakdown in court today, and, well, she apparently wanted to plead guilty. My guess is she felt too guilty to continue with the trial. And given that Pak was who her lawyers were blaming, it fits that she would've felt especially guilty toward him."

Elizabeth, guilty toward Pak. Dead because of that guilt.

"So this means the case ended?" Pak said.

"The trial's obviously over," Abe said, "and we're searching for a note or something more by way of a definitive confession. Her apology to you, Young, would certainly weigh in on that. But . . ." Abe glanced at Mary.

"But what?" Pak said.

Abe blinked a few times, then said, "We have to follow up on some things before the case is officially closed."

"What things?" Pak said.

"Loose ends, some new information Matt and Janine just gave us." His tone was casual, like this wasn't serious, but it made Young nervous, the way he focused on Mary, as if to gauge her reaction. And the way he emphasized "Matt and Janine"—there was subtext there. A secret message that, based on the way she blushed, Mary understood.

"Anyway," Abe said, "I'll arrange to have you all come in for some questions. In the meantime, I know this is shocking and a lot to absorb. But hopefully, you and all the other victims can find some peace and move forward."

Victims. The word grated at Young, and she forced herself not to wince. Her legs felt weak. Achy, like she'd been standing for hours.

Once Abe left, Young leaned against the door, her forehead on the rough, unfinished wood. She closed her eyes and remembered meeting Elizabeth in the courthouse, just a few hours ago. She'd figured out by then that it was Mary, had known that Elizabeth was innocent. She could see that Elizabeth was feeling ashamed and alone, and she let her *apologize* to her and said nothing. For all her talk of how they should confess immediately and save Elizabeth from one more moment's torture, when given the opportunity to take action, to tell Elizabeth the truth, Young didn't. She ran away. And Elizabeth died.

Behind her, Pak sighed, long and heavy, again and again, as if he was having trouble drawing oxygen into his lungs. After a minute, Pak started speaking, back in Korean again. "None of us could've known . . ." His voice broke. After another minute, he cleared his throat. "Maybe we should talk to Matt and Janine, find out what Abe was talking about. If we can get through this one last thing, maybe . . ."

Young felt a tickle in her throat. Soft at first, then building as Pak continued talking about what they needed to say to Abe, and she couldn't stand it anymore, she needed to laugh or sob or both. She clenched her hands into fists, shut her eyes tight, and screamed like Elizabeth had in court—was that just this morning?—until her throat hurt and she ran out of breath. She opened her eyes and turned. She looked at Pak, this man who hadn't taken even five minutes to mourn Elizabeth's death before planning the logistics of their cover-up, and said, back in Korean, "We did this. We killed Elizabeth, we pushed her to kill herself. Do you even care?"

Pak looked away, his face crumpled up in so much shame that it pained her to look at him. Beside him, Mary was crying. She said, "Don't blame Ap-bah. It was my fault. I set the fire and killed people. I should have come forward right away, but I kept saying nothing. And now, Elizabeth is dead, too. I did this."

"No," Pak said to Mary, "you kept silent because you thought Elizabeth set up the fire to kill Henry. This morning, as soon as you found out she didn't, you wanted to go to Abe. If I hadn't stopped you . . ." Pak's voice trailed off. He shut his eyes tight and clenched his teeth, as if it took all his effort to keep his face from crumbling.

"We can all make excuses," Young said. "Until this morning, you both thought Elizabeth was guilty in her own way and deserved to be punished. And maybe, given the way everything unfolded, that's even understandable. But that doesn't change the fact that we all lied—to each other and to Abe. We've been lying about so many things for a year, deciding for ourselves what's just or not, what's relevant or not. We're all to blame."

Pak said, "What happened is tragic, and I'd give anything to change the past. But we can't. The only thing we can do is to move forward. In a strange way, this is a gift to our family."

"A gift?" Young said. "An innocent woman's torture and death is a *gift*?"

"You're right. That's not the right word. I only meant there's no reason to come forward anymore. Elizabeth is gone. We can't change that. So—"

"So we might as well take advantage of it, consider ourselves *lucky* that she killed herself?"

"No, but what would be the point of confessing now? Maybe if she had family, someone who's affected, but there's no one."

Young felt blood drain from her limbs, her muscles lose their strength. Something seemed stuck in her throat, like an invisible hand choking her. "So say nothing and pretend Elizabeth set the fire? The blame will die with her, and we'll get insurance money and move to L.A. and Mary will go to college? That's your new plan?"

"There's no chance of anyone being hurt by this. This will all end," he said.

"I know you believe that, but you believed that about your first plan, too. You thought putting a cigarette by the oxygen wouldn't hurt anyone, but two people ended up dead. Your second plan, letting Elizabeth go through the trial—another death. And now you have a third plan, another plan where you *know*, you're *sure*, everything will be okay? How many more dead bodies will it take before you learn? You can't guarantee results. This started as an accident, but covering everything up has turned all of us into murderers." Her throat hurt, and she realized she was shouting and Mary sobbing. For the first time she could remember, the sight of Mary's tears didn't make her want to ease her daughter's pain. She wanted Mary to hurt, to think of what she'd done and feel an unbearable shame, because the alternative would mean the unthinkable, that she was a monster.

Mary put her elbows on the table and covered her face with her hands. Young pulled Mary's hands away from her face. "Look at me," she said to Mary. "You've been trying to just wish this away, like a little kid with a monster in a nightmare. But you can't escape this." She looked at Pak. "You think staying silent won't harm anyone? Look at our daughter. This is killing her. She needs to face what she's done, not run away. You think if she gets off, she'll have a moment's peace? That you or I will? This will stay with her and destroy her."

"Yuh-bo, please." Pak wheeled to her and grabbed both her hands. "This is our daughter. Her life is just beginning. We can't let her go to prison and ruin her life. If being silent tortures us, then we should be tortured. That's our duty as parents, the duty we assumed when we brought a life into this world, to protect our child, to sacrifice whatever we need to. We can't turn our own child in. I'd rather say that I did everything. I'm willing to make that sacrifice."

"Don't you think I'd give my life a hundred times over to save hers?" Young said. "Don't you think I know how painful it'll be to see her in prison, how much I'd rather suffer myself? But we have to do the hard thing. We have to teach *her* how to do the hard thing."

"This isn't one of your philosophy debates!" Pak slammed his hand on the table, his words spitting out in frustration. He closed his eyes for a moment, breathed in deeply, and said slowly, with forced calmness, "This is our child. We can't send her to jail. I'm the head of this family, and I'm responsible for us. It's my decision, and I say we say nothing."

"No," Young said. She turned to Mary and gripped her hands. "You're an adult now. Not because you had a birthday and you're eighteen, but because of what you've gone through. This is your decision, not mine, not your father's. I won't make it easy for you; I won't threaten to go to Abe if you don't. You need to make the hard choice. Go to Abe or not, it's up to you. Your responsibility, your truth to tell."

"So if she says nothing, you'll do nothing? You'll let Abe close the case?"

"Yes," Young said. "But if you say nothing, I won't stay. I want nothing to do with the money. And I won't lie. If Abe asks, I won't say what you did, but I *will* say that I know with absolute certainty that Elizabeth didn't set the fire and clear her name. She deserves that much."

"But he'll ask who did. He'll ask how you know that," Pak said.

"I'll say I can't say. I'll refuse to answer."

"He'll force you. He'll throw you in jail."

"Then I'll go to jail."

Pak sighed, a heavy breath of exasperation. "There's no need for that. If you'd—"

"Stop," Young said. "I'm done playing tug-of-war." She turned to Mary. "Meh-hee-yah, this isn't your father versus me. You're not choosing sides. This is your own battle, and you need to think for yourself what is right and make your own choice. You taught me that. You remember? In Korea, you were twelve, just a child, and you said you knew I didn't want to move to America and you asked how I could blindly follow someone else's decision about my life. I scolded you and told you to just obey your father, but I was ashamed. And so proud of you. I've been thinking a lot about that lately. If only I'd spoken up back then . . ." Young looked down and shook her head.

She raked Mary's hair with her fingers, letting it drape across her face. "I have faith in you. You know what it's like to live in silence. You know the relief you felt when you finally told us the truth. A few days ago, when I was talking about insurance money and moving away for college, you asked me how I could think about that when Henry and Kitt were dead. Think about that. Think about Elizabeth. Draw strength from that."

Pak said, "Nothing we do can bring them back. You're asking Mary to destroy her life for nothing."

"Not nothing. Doing the right thing is not nothing." Young stood up and turned away from them, her husband and daughter, and she stepped toward the door. One foot, then the other, waiting for Mary to stop her, for her to yell out, Wait, I'm coming with you. But no one said anything, did anything.

It was bright outside, the sun hitting her eyes so fiercely she had to squint. The air was dense and humid, the way it always got in late afternoons in August. The sky was clear, with no sign yet of the thunderstorm that would hit in a few hours. The pressure and heat from the full sun, building and building until the sky cracked into a ten-minute storm, enough to relieve the pressure and start the night's cooldown. Then tomorrow, the cycle would begin again.

Inside, she could hear muffled voices. She walked away, not wanting to hear what Pak must be saying, his ordering Mary to be patient and wait for Young to come to her senses. She walked to a nearby tree, a giant oak with gnarled knots all over its trunk, like scar tissue covering old wounds.

Behind her, the door creaked open and footsteps approached, but she kept facing the tree, afraid of what she'd see on her daughter's face. The footsteps stopped. A hand pressed on her shoulder, a gentle pressure. "I'm scared," Mary said.

Tears stung Young's eyes, and she turned. "I am, too."

Mary nodded and bit her lip. "Ap-bah said if I confess, he'll say he did everything on purpose, for the money, and my story's a lie I made up to make it seem more like an accident. He said if he tells Abe that, he'll probably end up getting the death penalty."

Young closed her eyes. Pak was clever. Threatening their daughter with yet another death, his own. She opened her eyes and grabbed Mary's hands. "We won't let that happen. We'll tell Abe everything, including your father's threat. He'll believe you. He'll have to."

Mary blinked, and Young expected her to cry, but instead, she stretched her lips into a pained smile. Suddenly, a memory: Mary throwing a tantrum as a little girl, maybe five or six, and after Young gently said she was disappointed in her behavior, Mary getting a handkerchief from their dresser, wiping away her tears, stretching her lips into a smile, and saying, "Look, Um-ma, I'm not crying anymore," looking dignified, just as she was now. Young hugged her daughter tight.

After a moment, her head still on Young's shoulder, Mary spoke, in Korean for the first time all day. "Will you come with me? You don't have to say anything, but will you just stand with me?"

Tears blocked Young's words, and she couldn't do anything but keep holding her daughter close, stroking her hair and nodding over and over again. Soon, she would gently push her daughter away, just a little, help her stand upright on her own, and say she loved her and she'd be proud to come and stand with her as she told the truth, however painful it was. She would say she was sorry for having failed her, for leaving her alone all those years in Baltimore and not standing up for her, and if she could, she'd never leave her again. She would ask the questions that remained and tell the stories still untold. She would do all this, eventually—in a minute, or an hour, or a day. But standing still right here, feeling the weight of her daughter's body leaning against hers, her warm breath on her neck—for now, that was all she needed.

AFTER

November 2009

YOUNG

SHE SAT ON A TREE STUMP outside the barn. Rather, where the barn used to be until yesterday, when the new owners demolished its remains and took them away, piece by piece. All that was left was the submarine, lying on the dirt, waiting to be taken to a junkyard somewhere, the juxtaposition of its steel and wires against the grass and trees looking like a tableau out of some science-fiction film.

This was Young's favorite part of the day. Early in the morning, so early that night blended with day. Moonlight shone, but not a full moon. Just a sliver, casting the faintest light on the submarine. She couldn't see it, exactly, not the charring or the paint blisters or the jagged teeth of the portholes' broken glass. She could see only its outline, and in this light (or rather, lack of light), it looked the same as last year when it was freshly painted and gleaming.

At 6:35, the chamber was still a shadowy black oval, but in the distance, the sky was brightening. She looked up at the clouds, the hint of peach in the grayness, and remembered the disorientation she'd felt looking at the clouds on the Seoul–New York flight, her first time on an airplane. She'd gazed out the porthole to watch her homeland fade away as the plane ascended into a thick layer of clouds. When they emerged above, she marveled at the beauty of the clouds' constancy—the uniformity of their variations, the patterns in their randomness—as they stretched to the horizon. She looked at the metal-smooth wing, fluttering slightly as it grazed the clouds' diffuse edges before slicing the cottony blooms in perfect precision, and she had a flickering sense of wrongness, that she didn't belong in the sky. It felt like hubris. Rejecting your natural place in the world and using an alien machine to defy gravity and dislocate yourself to another continent.

At 6:44, the sky turned a soft mauve, the black of the night fighting against the sun and losing. The chamber's charred spots were becoming visible, but still, it was dark enough that they looked like shadows, or maybe moss growing over the metal and making the machine a part of the landscape.

At 6:52, the sky was a delicate blue, the color of newborn nurseries. The submarine's aquamarine paint, once so glossy it looked wet, now looked pockmarked.

At 6:59, bright beams of sunlight penetrated the thick foliage and hit the submarine at once, as if all the stage lights had switched on to spotlight the show's star. For a second, the light was so bright that a halo encircled the submarine, hiding its imperfections. But Young stared straight on, forcing her pupils to adjust and constrict, and she saw the proof of the crime: black charring everywhere; the porthole glass melted as if the submarine were crying; the whole tank tilted like an old man with a cane.

She closed her eyes and breathed. In, out. Though it had been over a year, the smell of ash and burned flesh still clung to the tank's carcass, mixing with the morning dew to form a charcoal stench. Or maybe that was her imagination. Her conscience, telling her tiny particles were infiltrating her lungs and she might, at this moment, be breathing in the cells of the people incinerated in that chamber.

She looked toward the creek. She couldn't see the water, hidden behind the thicket of leaves stained in bright yellows and reds, no pattern to the colors as if toddlers had run around with paint cans, spraying trees at random. She imagined Mary sitting behind those trees, her feet centimeters from the water, smoking and laughing with Matt Thompson and, one night, being held down by him, assaulted; then, on a different night, being screamed at by his wife, told she was a stalker. A whore.

It was funny, how before Mary's full confession—rather, confessions, as she'd had to repeat it multiple times, to Abe, the public defender, and the sentencing judge in the course of pleading guilty to felony murder and arson—she'd believed that Mary needed to accept whatever punishment she received. But now that Mary and Pak were in prison, she wondered if it was truly fair that Mary faced years in prison—ten minimum—when many others who'd contributed to the causal chain that night got nothing. Yes, Mary set the fire. But she wouldn't have if Janine hadn't lied that the dive was over and Matt had left. She *couldn't* have if Pak hadn't left the cigarette and matches where he had. And Matt—he was the causal root of everything: without him, without his actions and lies to Mary and Janine, they wouldn't have done what they'd done the night of the explosion. Even the cigarette Pak placed under the oxygen tube was Matt's, from his trash pile in the hollow tree stump. And yet, the law considered Janine a mere bystander, assigning no blame to her. And Pak and Matt got nothing for their roles in causing the fire itself; Pak received fourteen months in jail and Matt a suspended sentence with probation, but both for perjury and obstruction of justice. She heard that Matt and Janine were getting a divorce, which comforted her somewhat; as much as she tried, Matt's treatment of her daughter was the one unpunished act in all this that she could not forgive.

And herself, most of all. So many things she should and could have done differently at so many points along the way. If she'd stayed in the barn and turned off the oxygen in time. If she hadn't lied to Abe for a year. But more than anything, if only she'd confessed everything to Elizabeth that last day. She'd told all this to Abe and pleaded that she, too, needed jail, but he'd called everything she'd done "tangential" and refused to file charges.

At 7:00, her watch beeped. Time to go in and pack the rest of her things. It had been just about this time when the protesters arrived that morning, starting the entire chain of events. She didn't blame them, exactly. But if they hadn't come, Henry, Kitt, and Elizabeth would all be alive now. Pak wouldn't have caused the power outage, the dives wouldn't have been delayed, and the oxygen would've been off and everyone gone by the time Mary set the fire, which she wouldn't have done anyway because Pak wouldn't have left any cigarette anywhere.

That was both the best and worst part, that all that happened was the unintended consequence of a good person's mistakes. Teresa once said that what really got her, what kept her up at night and drove her to keep looking for a cure, was that Rosa wasn't supposed to be this way. If she'd been born with a genetic defect, Teresa could live with that. But she'd been healthy, and she had gotten this way because of something that shouldn't have happened—an illness not treated in time. It was unnatural, avoidable. In the same way, Young almost wished Mary had done this intentionally. Not really, because of course she didn't want Mary to be evil, but in a way, it was worse knowing that her daughter was a good person who made one mistake. It was almost as if the fates conspired to manipulate that day's events in *just* such a way as to lead Mary to light that match. So many pieces had to fit: the power outage, the dive delays, Matt's note, Janine's confrontation, Pak's cigarette. If just one of those things hadn't happened, at this moment, Elizabeth and Kitt would be driving Henry and TJ to school. Mary would be in college. Miracle Submarine would still be running, and she and Pak would be getting ready for a full day of dives ahead.

But that was the way life worked. Every human being was the result of a million different factors mixing together—one of a million sperm arriving at the egg at exactly a certain time; even a millisecond off, and another entirely different person would result. Good things and bad—every friendship and romance formed, every accident, every illness—resulted from the conspiracy of hundreds of little things, in and of themselves inconsequential.

Young walked to a tree with red leaves and picked up the three brightest leaves she could find on the ground. Red for luck. She wondered how these woods would look in ten years, when Mary was out of prison. She'd be in her late twenties. She could still go to college, fall in love, have children. That was something to hope for. In the meantime, Young would continue to visit her every week—if any good came out of the last months, it had to be the revival and deepening of her relationship with her daughter. She brought Mary her favorite philosophy college texts, and they discussed them during their visits, like a two-person book club, with Young speaking in Korean and Mary in English, eliciting puzzled looks from the other inmates.

It had been harder with Pak, especially at first, when she'd been so angry with his stubbornness, but Young forced herself to visit regularly, and with each visit, she felt a thawing from him, a deepening repentance and acceptance of responsibility not only for the fire and Elizabeth's death, but for his attempt to control them into silence. Maybe, over time, it would get easier to see him, talk to him. Forgive him.

Teresa arrived and parked by the construction equipment—a loader crane, the workers said. She was alone. "Is Rosa with your church friends?" Young said as they hugged hello.

Teresa nodded. "Yup. We have a *lot* to do today," she said, which was true. They'd already moved most of Young's things into Teresa's guest room ("Stop calling it a guest room; it's *your* room now," Teresa kept saying), but they still had a dozen errands on Shannon's checklist for the building-dedication ceremony at noon. Since the *Washington Post* article last week, the number of attendees had tripled, and now included the D.C.-area autism moms' group, many former Miracle Submarine families, Abe and his staff, all the detectives and *their* staff, and—a last-minute surprise—Victor. Of course, Victor was the one who'd made the entire endeavor possible, when he (in a bizarre twist) inherited Elizabeth's money and told Shannon he didn't want it, that he thought Elizabeth would want it used for something good, maybe autism-related, and would Shannon take care of that? Shannon had consulted Teresa, and together, with Young's help, they were creating Henry's House, a nonresidential "home base" for special-needs children providing on-site therapy as well as day care and weekend camps.

"I got something." Teresa handed Young a bag.

It held three portraits in matching wooden frames, plain but stained a deep, rich brown. Elizabeth, Henry, and Kitt, with their names and dates of birth and death inscribed on the bottom. "I thought we could put them in the lobby, under the dedication plaque," Teresa said.

A lump formed in Young's throat. "It is beautiful. Very appropriate."

In front of them, the men were getting ready to take the chamber away. Watching them fasten a cable around it, she remembered last year, when other men had delivered it to this spot and untied the binding. Pak had planned to call the business "Miracle Creek Wellness Center," but seeing the chamber, the way it resembled a miniature submarine, she'd said, "Miracle Submarine." She'd turned to Pak and said it again. "Miracle Submarine—that's what we should call it." He'd smiled and said that was a good name, a better name, and she'd felt a thrill, thinking of children climbing inside and breathing in pure oxygen, their bodies healing.

The crane beeped and lifted the chamber before pivoting to place it over a truck. The arm lowered, and as the chamber's steel met the steel of the truck bed, a booming thud sounded, and Young flinched. Looking at the barren ground, she felt an ache start from the center of her chest and radiate. All their hopes and plans, gone.

As the men secured the chamber to the truck, Young looked down at the portraits in the bag and thought of Henry's House. The lives lost, the pain at its foundation—she and her family could never repay that. But she would see TJ every day; she'd drive him to and from Henry's House, take care of him between therapies, and provide respite to his father and sisters, ease their lives just a little bit. She'd work alongside Teresa and help her take care of Rosa and other children like her, TJ, and Henry.

Teresa reached out and clasped her hand. She closed her eyes and felt her friend's warm, soft hand in her left and the silky handle of the bag in her right. The truck rumbled and beeped again, and she opened her eyes. In the distance, beyond the stretch of burned, dead dirt, beyond the carcass of the submarine now slowly moving away, a patch of wildflowers in yellow and blue stood, and looking at it, she felt her despair displaced by something simultaneously heavier and lighter. *Han.* There was no English equivalent, no translation. It was an overwhelming sorrow and regret, a grief and yearning so deep it pervades your soul—but with a sprinkling of resilience, of hope.

She tightened her grip on Teresa's hand and felt her squeeze back. They stood together, hand in hand, and watched Miracle Submarine fade into the distance.

ACKNOWLEDGMENTS

A first book owes many debts, and my biggest is to my husband, Jim Draughn, who served countless roles throughout every stage of my writing process: reader, listener, editor, counselor, courtroom-scene consultant, family chef and chauffeur, and maker and bringer to my writing nook of coffee, omelets, martinis, and whatever else I needed to finish the next chapter. What would I have done without you? I wouldn't have written this book, that's for sure. I wouldn't have written anything at all; it was you who first told me, years ago, that I was a writer. Thank you for making me believe it and giving me the tools and space to try.

To Susan Golomb, my superstar agent extraordinaire, thank you for picking a no-name newbie out of the slush pile, for believing in this book and being its impassioned advocate. You, along with Maja Nikolec,

Mariah Stovall, Daniel Berkowitz, and Sadie Resnick at Writers House, supported and guided me every step of the way.

To Sarah Crichton, the smartest editor and publisher anyone could ask for. You *got* this book—the tingles I got the first time we talked!—and you knew exactly what we needed to do to bring it to the next level, and to the next, and to the next. Thank you for pushing me. And to the amazing, first-rate team at FSG, especially Na Kim, Debra Helfand, Richard Oriolo, Rebecca Caine, Kate Sanford, Benjamin Rosenstock, Peter Richardson, John McGhee, Chandra Wohleber, and Elizabeth Schraft: thank you for turning my words into a beautiful book I'll always be proud of.

To FSG's sales director, Spenser Lee, I'm grateful to you for so wholly embracing and championing this book. And to my publicists, Kimberly Burns and Lottchen Shivers, our work together has just begun, but I'm so lucky to be in your expert hands, guiding me through the whole process. Thank you to Veronica Ingal, Daniel Del Valle, and the entire sales, marketing, and publicity team for working so hard to bring this book to the world.

To my writing group—Beth Thompson Stafford, Fernando Manibog, Carolyn Sherman, Dennis Desmond, John Benner, and honorary long-distance member Amin Ahmad—thank you for sticking with me through multiple drafts and revisions, from nonsensical first draft to galley proofs. And for the prosecco. We can't forget the prosecco.

To Marie Myung-Ok Lee, whose generosity knows no bounds, who introduced me to every writer, editor, and agent within her considerable sphere of friends. And to dear friends Marla Grossman, Susan Rothwell, Susan Kurtz, and Mary Beth Pfister, who were my earliest readers and biggest cheerleaders, who answered countless panicked calls and requests for help on everything from brainstorming titles to selecting author photos. You are the sisters I chose for myself, and the best friends anyone could ask for.

Many many others helped to make this book what it is today. Nicole Lee Idar, Maria Acebal, Catherine Grossman, Barbara Esstman, Sally Rainey, Rick Abraham, Mary Ann McLaurin, Carl Nichols, Faith Dornbrand, and Jonathan Kurtz provided early and honest feedback.

John Gilstrap and Mark Bergin patiently answered my questions about explosions and fingerprints. (Any remaining errors are definitely mine.) Annie Philbrick, Susan Cain, Julie Lythcott-Haims, Aaron Martin, Lynda Loigman, and Courtney Sender helped me navigate the mysterious world of literary agents and publishers. And Missy Perkins, Kara Kim, and Julie Reiss plied me with wine repeatedly and often. Along with my No Pressure No Guilt book club and my Fair Weather Hiking Mamas group, you all provided much-needed support and kept me sane.

And finally, those dearest to my heart. To my parents, Anna and John Kim, my um-ma and ap-bah, thank you for sacrificing your lives in Korea to bring our family to this foreign land, all for my future. Your selflessness and love astound and inspire me. My ee-mo and ee-mo-boo, Helen and Philip Cho, who gave us a home in America—I wouldn't be here without you, literally. And to my three boys: thank you for putting up with the chaos and craziness of my writing life, day in and day out, for giving me hugs and kisses (sometimes even voluntarily!), and for fueling my writing by taking me through the entire range of human emotion—from blinding worry and furious frustration to out-of-my-mind, can't-stand-it love and protectiveness—on a daily, often hourly, basis. I'm proud of you, every day. I love you. You are my miracles.

And now, we come full circle, back to Jim, my first and last reader, my love, my partner in life. I know I said it already. But it bears repeating. It's nothing without you. Thank you, love. Always.

A NOTE ABOUT THE AUTHOR

Angie Kim moved as a preteen from Seoul, South Korea, to the suburbs of Baltimore. She attended Stanford University and Harvard Law School, where she was an editor of the *Harvard Law Review*, then practiced as a trial lawyer at Williams & Connolly. Her stories have won the *Glamour* Essay Contest and the Wabash Prize in Fiction, and have appeared in numerous publications, including *Vogue*, *The New York Times*, *Salon*, *Slate*, *The Southern Review*, *Sycamore Review*, *The Asian American Literary Review*, and *PANK*. She lives in northern Virginia with her husband and three sons.